THE DELIVERANCE OF EVIL

THE DELIVERANCE OF EVIL

Roberto Costantini

Translated from the Italian by N. S. Thompson

Quercus

Quercus

New York • London

ISBN 978-1-62365-002-5

Library of Congress Control Number: 2013937742

Distributed in the United States and Canada by
Random House Publisher Services
c/o Random House, 1745 Broadway
New York, NY 10019

Manufactured in the United States

2 4 6 8 10 9 7 5 3 1

www.quercus.com

For Lorenzo

For the People of Libya

It is only light and evidence that can work a change in men's opinions; which light can in no manner proceed from corporal sufferings, or any other outward penalties.

—John Locke

JULY 9, 2006: THE INVISIBLE MAN

IF THINGS HAD GONE *differently that first time, perhaps I wouldn't have killed all the others. I often wondered about this at the beginning. After all these years I don't even know how many I killed anymore, and now the question has changed: Would I be a better person if I had killed only her in a single moment of madness? Today I no longer hate the women I kill—after all these years they're just rag dolls. What I hate are the men full of wisdom, the men who pontificate. Any one of them could have found himself in my position that first time. And it is to these men, who live without remorse or honor, that I intend to dedicate myself. And to one in particular.*

JULY 9, 2006: THE MOTHER

WHILE THE LEFT BACK *of Italy's national soccer team was taking a run-up to deliver the decisive penalty in the 2006 World Cup, Giovanna Sordi got up from the worn sofa in the small apartment where she had lived for fifty years. She had no one to say good-bye to; her husband Amedeo had joined Elisa ten years earlier. From that day on and every day since, she had left flowers on their graves. And although she had never received any justice in all those years, she would find the truth now. Slowly she crossed the living room of the small apartment. She passed by the closed door of the room where her dream was born and vanished. She went out onto the balcony, taking no notice of the jubilant cries of the people around and the crowds in the street: she knew exactly what to do.*

She landed on the pavement sixty feet below at the very moment all of Italy exploded into unrestrained joy.

PART 1

JANUARY 1982

"PLACE YOUR BETS" WERE the first words I heard Angelo Dioguardi say.

I'd entered the smoke-filled room where they were playing poker only because the bar cart was in there, and it held a bottle of Lagavulin.

I knew three of the four players by sight, but not the tall young man with long ruffled blond hair, sideburns, and blue eyes, in front of whom almost all of the chips were piled.

"Holy shit, Angelo, that's more than a month's earnings," grumbled the young lawyer with whom he was battling for the pot. I could see this meant the lawyer earned ten times my own salary.

The young man gave a contrite smile. He looked almost apologetic. He was the only one who wasn't smoking, and the only one without a glass of whiskey in front of him. I glanced at the table as I poured myself some of the Lagavulin. They were playing a round of Teresina poker. Based on the cards that were shown, the lawyer looked to be the winner. But there was only one card face down that, if it was the fair-haired guy's, would give him a lead the lawyer couldn't beat.

I shot him a brief glance, and he sent me back a friendly smile. I left the room without waiting for the lawyer's decision.

Camilla was waiting for me outside the room. She was the reason I was there that evening. Our host was Paola. I'd met her when she came to the local police station to report the presumed theft of her schnauzer, which had gone missing while it was running around the park. Paola was very pretty, if a little too refined for my taste. I had found her dog for her, which had only been lost and not stolen after all, and then I asked her out for a pizza. Nine times out of ten my rough-edged charm, combined with the badge of rank, did the trick in these situations. But Paola just laughed heartily and added, "I have a very good boyfriend, and I'm very faithful. But I might have a close friend I could introduce you to; she likes men like you, a bit surly and macho. Perhaps you'd like to come over tomorrow evening . . ."

She lived in a luxury apartment in Vigna Clara, one of Rome's best neighborhoods. The apartment was on the third floor and overlooked a quiet little piazza: open, tree-lined, no noise. It was paid for by her parents in Palermo so she could study in Rome. Her friend Camilla wasn't bad, except she was a bit of a snob. But during the previous dozen years I'd decided, given I'd lost the one woman who had meant something to me, I'd make do with the sum of the particulars of others. At thirty-two I could manage to think of at least one positive particular in every pretty woman who happened to come within reach. Naturally I'd discovered a long time ago that "the particulars" of a woman are only discovered during sex, when the gestures, the looks, the words, and the sighs manage to be almost truthful.

That wasn't happening on that particular evening, though. Paola's friend was spending the night at Paola's place, so I wasn't going to get her into bed. Toward midnight I got ready to say good night. As a young police captain, I had to get up at half past six the next morning. I was getting ready to leave when the poker players came back into the living room: three beaten dogs and the fair-haired one with his blue eyes lit up.

"Paola, your boyfriend must have made a pact with the devil," said the lawyer as he waved good-bye with the others to the evening's hostess.

The blond guy slumped into the armchair across from mine. Now that he had finished taking them to the cleaners, he was ready to enjoy the bottle of Lagavulin. He poured himself a generous measure and, seeing my glass was empty, filled it without even asking. He raised his glass in a toast. His clothes, his wild hair and five o'clock shadow—everything about him made him seem out of place in that house and with those people. Which meant he was more or less like me, except I was a master in the art of hypocrisy, a true chameleon of the secret intelligence service who had learned how to conceal his contempt, while he was just a kid from the outlying suburbs and the one who was genuinely out of place.

"To this magnificent whiskey and those who appreciate it," he toasted, displaying the working-class *romanesco* accent of the outer suburbs.

He offered me a cigarette. He smoked those awful Gitanes without a filter that left tobacco on your tongue and a foul smell everywhere.

"But they taste great," he said. "And I count them out carefully, no more than ten a day."

No one in Rome's elite smoked those cigarettes. Marijuana was in, but plain cigarettes smacked of the slums. Of course, it was clear the fair-haired guy didn't belong to the elite. I thought that if Paola had chosen him and was so faithful to him, then the guy had to have hidden qualities. And the only ones that I could think of were those you demonstrated in bed.

"So, you're the big winner?" I asked him. He nodded, but showed no interest in pursuing the subject.

"Then you really are lucky. There was only one king left that could have given you a straight. Out of ten possibilities, at least."

He didn't say a word. (Only after a good deal of whiskey could I get him to confess that he'd held nothing more than two nines.) "Professional secret," he said, making it clear he was letting me in on a very special confidence. By then the lawyer was already downstairs and on his way out.

While Paola and Camilla were chatting in the kitchen, Angelo asked what I did for a living.

"*Bravo*, Michele. At least you've got something to get up for every day."

I shook my head. "In reality, it's all routine. In a district like this, about the biggest case I'm going to crack is your girlfriend's missing schnauzer."

"Oh, you're the one who found the dog? He smiled and nodded in the direction of the kitchen.

"Camilla's cute," I said. "Too bad she's sleeping here tonight."

He thought about this for a moment. Then I saw him get up and stagger into the bathroom without even closing the door, followed by the sound of retching and moaning. The girls rushed in, as I did too. He was lying on the bathroom floor, looking pale, having thrown up in the sink.

"Should I call a doctor?" asked Paola, panic in her voice.

"No, no," he groaned. "Girls, go make some coffee, would you? Michele, stay here a minute."

Ejected from the bathroom, Paola and Camilla went back to the kitchen, and Angelo winked at me.

"I'm totally fine, but let's scare them a little more."

He stuck two fingers down his throat. More retching, and the girls raced back into the bathroom.

"I'm calling a doctor," said Paola, more concerned than ever.

"No, it's okay. The worst is over. I'll take care of him." I spoke in the same authoritative voice I'd used when she'd come to report her missing schnauzer. Decisive, calm, reassuring. I knew what I was doing.

Angelo went on a good while longer, with more well-feigned sounds of retching and groaning. Then I took him on my shoulders to carry him to Paola's double bed.

"Christ, you're heavy," I said as I put him down.

"You have to suffer at least a little in order to get it . . ." He winked at me again and started to moan softly.

The girls came in with black coffee. Angelo tried it with groans of disgust.

"What should we do?" The girls were hanging around for instructions, subdued now by my air of calm in the face of Angelo's collapse.

"Let him stay the night," he said, taking Paola's hand. "If I feel bad again, at least he'll be here to help."

I bravely offered to sleep in the living room with the schnauzer, seeing that Camilla was in the guest room. My gesture was greatly appreciated. Then, later that night, it occurred to Camilla that the dog's snoring might be bothering me, and so she had me move into her bed.

And that's how I came to know Angelo Dioguardi.

. . . .

The police station in Vigna Clara was about exciting as a nursing home. In that well-off residential district of Rome, a policeman lived the life of a retiree. Well-ordered streets, beautiful homes, greenery everywhere, its inhabitants all formally educated and having achieved economic success by any means, legal or otherwise: tax evasion, bribery and corruption, carefully controlled contracts. All these were means that the Italians, especially in Rome, had employed since the end of the war as they sought the good life, whatever the cost.

I'd been stationed there for almost two years, thanks to my brother Alberto and his contacts in the Christian Democrats.

"Think of it as time to recuperate, Mike," he said when I started there. "Take a couple of years to get yourself back together, and then decide what to do with yourself. Time to straighten up."

As if his younger brother's previous turbulent thirty-two years could be wiped away. But then Alberto had always been like that. He was an optimist, highly intelligent, forceful—qualities he shared with our father, who left Palermo for Tripoli after World War II.

A Sicilian from the lower middle class, Papa studied engineering in Rome and became a wealthy businessman in Libya, one of the few who was able to steer through the murky waters of Italian politics, granting it the absolute minimum attention possible and using it only when necessary. And in order to marry the daughter of Libya's biggest Italian landowner, Papa was willing to become the most dedicated of Catholics from conviction and for convenience in order to get into the right circles, and he was willing to do business with Jews on the one hand, Arabs on the other, and Westerners with both hands together.

Alberto shared some of my father's skills, but he was a better person by far: sensitive, well-adjusted, generous, and even-handed. A model son. In complete contrast, I was the one who, right from the beginning, hated my school run by the Christian Brothers, and spent all my time with a Diana 50 air rifle, shooting turtledoves from a three hundred feet away. I was the one who only passed his exams each year because *Commendatore* Balistreri was a big shot in Libya.

My troubled childhood was spent serving as an altar boy with a priest who couldn't keep his hands to himself and fighting with the Arab and Italian boys my age. I grew into a lonely, turbulent, and angry adolescent. I devoured Homer, Nietzsche, and the early works of Mussolini. No calculated decisions or compromises: only honor, action, courage. My path was clearly marked: at seventeen, I left behind me the first dead in a Cairo shaken by the Six Days War; at eighteen, I killed my first lion in Tanzania. At nineteen, I was plotting against Gaddafi, who had just taken power. At twenty, I claimed the right to decide on the death penalty for those who were traitors.

Then Rome and college. By 1970, I'd even managed to pass a few classes. Over time I made the natural progression from the *Movimento Sociale Italiano* to the ultra-right extra-parliamentary *Ordine Nuovo*, with its two-bladed Fascist ax and SS motto "My honor is loyalty." Three years spent clashing with the Reds—posting manifestos by night, days spent attending fiery meetings. Then, at the end of 1973, a Christian Democrat minister ordered the *Ordine Nuovo* to disband and had its leaders arrested. An act of madness that let loose dozens of youths, some too young and naive to see the distinction between conflict and the abyss. While many of my friends chose armed conflict, killing enemies, I paused to reflect. I understood they were moving toward bombing ordinary people, collaborating with common thugs, betraying our ideals, and so I agreed to help the secret intelligence service stop them. After four years of being a chameleon, working undercover for the security forces, it was still plausible that I was on the side of the good people who were preventing massacres of the innocent. Then, in 1978, the Red Brigades seized Aldo Moro and right-wing criminality joined forces with left-wing terrorism. Intelligence was ignored. Aldo Moro was assassinated. I protested, and my cover was blown. At that point I could have continued and ended up in a block of cement at the bottom of the sea, or else I could renounce changing the world and ask my brother for help.

It was my brother, *Ingegnere* Alberto Balistreri, who brought me back from the edge of the precipice. The Minister of the Interior owed him a favor. So I managed to obtain a philosophy degree, using my credits from the early 1970s and taking some more classes. Then they let me join the police, and I passed the exam to become police captain. In 1980 I received my first posting in Vigna Clara, one of Rome's quietest neighborhoods.

But at night I wanted to get away from that false Rome and keep my distance from the rich and their neighborhoods and the historic center, where the city's chaos and decadence were on display. I rented a studio in Garbatella, a working-class quarter built by Mussolini, where apartments cost very little in those days and true Romans took the cool spring air sitting outside the cheap bistros that served the best food and wine in the city.

In fact, I dedicated myself to the only real passion I had left: women. Any woman, of whatever kind, race, or age, so long as she was good-looking and didn't waste my time with the usual runaround. I was voracious; I wasn't looking for friendship, intrigue, or protection. They lasted so little time that I didn't take the trouble to learn their names. I only needed to know them in the most thorough way possible, something not too difficult for a young good-looking police officer of a certain rank. *Hic et nunc* was the way for Michele Balistreri; nothing of sin, confession, regret. I was one of the elite—those the world doesn't understand, those who don't give a damn what the world thinks of them. Nor what God thinks, either.

As Alberto used to say to me, and I used to echo, this was only a moment to reflect, a little bit of rest, sailing slowly along a quiet river, carried along by a gentle current. After the turbulent years I'd experienced, this was exactly what I needed: solitude, a cushy day job, eating well, screwing a lot, playing poker, thinking about nothing at all. It was a delicate balance between pleasure and boredom. No emotional ties. Love was a country where it had rained salt, and it had turned into a desert.

But I told myself over and over I would leave as soon as I could. I'd never become a senile old cop, stuck at a desk and serving a cowardly and corrupt state. I'd go back to Africa to hunt lions and leopards, far from false and sanctimonious Italy. Far from everything I detested. Far from the battles I had lost.

. . . .

A few days after our first encounter, Dioguardi readily agreed to play poker with me and two of my friends in the police. This was odd, because we'd only just met and I myself would never have risked putting my money on the table with three strangers who knew each other well. But, as I came to find out, Dioguardi was the opposite of me in many ways—and one was being able to trust his neighbor.

We played until two in the morning in the back room of a piano bar near Piazza di Spagna. In less than half an hour, I realized he was a world-class player. He had technique, imagination and daring. After two hours he'd won a pile of money. Then, in the following hour, he lost more than half of what he'd won.

"You lost on purpose," I said, after the other two had left.

He shook his head, embarrassed.

"I was doing a few experiments, things I could use to improve. I do it when I'm winning comfortably."

"As in a preseason friendly game against a bunch of amateurs."

He smiled. He admitted that he played rarely, and only then with wealthy old boys. He won a lot of money, but he was a little ashamed of it and never boasted. I discovered later that he donated all his winnings to charity. His fabulous bluffs in the game were little sins for him, something that—along with his Catholic ethics—was nothing to be proud of.

We went into the crowded bar. A group of young men were singing to the piano music, led by a beautiful black woman.

As soon as she spotted him, she called out, "Angelo, Angelo, come over here!"

He tried to wave her away, but she kept calling him. In the end he went over and the girl pressed his lips to hers. I saw him blush and step back. Then she raised his arm, as if declaring him the winner, and turned to the crowd.

"This is my friend Angelo, the best undiscovered vocalist in Rome, who will now sing for us."

In the field of singing, too, he was in a class by himself. He performed every song the crowd requested and ended with a rendition of

"My Way" almost worthy of Sinatra himself. After his performance, he introduced me to the woman, then left us alone just long enough for me to get her phone number. He'd figured me out.

It was after three when we left.

"Michele, let's go to Ostia."

"Ostia? It's January. What would we do at the beach?"

"There's a little bakery there. At six they bring out the best pastries anywhere near Rome."

He wanted to talk. Me too. This was really strange because, over the years, my desire to socialize with other men had worn off. We went in his beat-up Fiat 500, and half an hour later we were parked on the promenade. The stars were out. It was cold, but there was no wind. We opened the windows to smoke. The sea was a millpond; we could smell the sea air and hear the waves lapping a few yards away from us. There was nobody around.

Unlike me, Angelo was always willing to talk about himself. He was born poor in a Rome where everyone except his parents was getting rich, some legally and some less so. He'd grown up in the poorest area of Rome. He was the son of a small-time singer and a fortune-teller, two starving wannabe artists who later moved to the country; two failures, at least by societal standards, both dead from cirrhosis of the liver when Angelo was still a teenager. But he said they had both given him a great deal. His vocalist father had given him his singing voice, and from his fortunetelling mother he learned to bluff and think on his feet.

In time he had gained two things: a well-off girlfriend, Paola, who worshipped him and would marry him within the year, and a small real estate business, thanks to her uncle, Cardinal Alessandrini. The cardinal was just over fifty and was responsible for arranging housing for the thousands of priests and nuns who came to Rome to study or else a few days of pilgrimage and sightseeing. The Vatican owned hundreds of convents, hostels, and apartments and their running had been entrusted to Angelo Dioguardi who, although he'd given up on his education, was a good Catholic and was obviously to be the husband of the Cardinal's niece. Although Angelo was manifestly unsuited to an office job, he applied himself with dedication and energy—exactly the opposite of how I handled my employment. And he was the opposite of me when it came to women, too. He knew a lot of them, but he never took advantage because of his unshakeable loyalty to Paola. In love, he was an idealist in search of the single perfect relationship. This would turn out to be the ideal situation for someone like me, who was always on the prowl: Angelo drew them in, and I closed the deal.

"Are you really completely faithful to Paola?" I asked. I was expecting him to give a speech on love in reply, but Angelo surprised me.

"She's beautiful, kind, smart, rich, and the niece of a cardinal who gave me a job, and I'm a poverty-stricken nobody who didn't finish school. I can only be thankful; I've no right even to desire anyone else."

We were still there at dawn. We got out to stretch our legs. The bakery was closed, but the lights were on and it was emanating a yeasty smell. I took a cigarette from my second pack. I offered him one, seeing as he'd finished all his.

"No thanks, Michele. A pack of Gitanes every two days and no more."

"You're too strict with yourself, Angelo. You should let yourself go once in a while."

He ran a hand through his wavy blond hair, then pointed to the water.

"How about a dip?"

"Are you crazy? It's January and dawn."

"You won't feel cold once you're in. And it'll give you a perfect appetite."

That's exactly what he said—a perfect appetite. He switched on the Fiat's headlights and directed them toward the few yards of sand that separated us from the water. A minute later he was stripped down to his briefs.

"Come on, let yourself go, Michele," he said.

Then he ran to the water and dove in. I saw him swimming furiously in the beam of the headlights. I don't know what came over me—something I hadn't felt for many years. A minute later I was in the water, too. The cold took my breath away, but the more I swam to warm myself up, the more I felt a joy I'd forgotten, brazen, irresistible, that took over my whole body.

As promised, the pastries, still warm from the oven, were perfect.

. . . .

So I began to get to know Angelo better. Underneath that affectionate, sunny, and angelic face lay a heart left on its own too soon and seeking a safe and permanent harbor. Love and work were a refuge for him. No strange ambitions, no adventures: a more or less regular life. No more than ten Gitanes a day, no more than a couple of glasses of whiskey. That way he stayed clear-headed when he played poker. Every time we went into one of Rome's piano bars—something we did often in the following months—the same thing happened. The singer knew Angelo and called him on stage. The female singers always tried to take him home, but he was incorruptible. In this he was truly my opposite, or perhaps he was what I could have been. Angelo was unassailable.

He laid down strict rules for us when it came to poker. Spots were limited to a certain number, and at the end of the evening the jackpot was divided according to the number of chips we had. He almost always won, and the few times he lost I was sure he'd lost on purpose, just as he'd done during our first game. In the beginning we played with my brother, Alberto, and another engineer, a colleague of his. They tried to persuade Angelo to use their high salaries and stocks and shares to bankrupt a casino but, ever in line with his Catholic morality, Angelo wouldn't do it.

We saw each other almost every evening. The standard routine was pizza for four: myself, Angelo, Paola, and my girlfriend of the moment. Then came a short stroll through Trastevere. We'd stop for a smoke, and drink one last beer in the splendid piazza by the church of Santa Maria. At that point, there was a choice: either I went off with my girlfriend or, with Paola's blessing, Angelo and I would say good-bye to the two of them and ride around Rome in my Duetto or his Fiat 500. (This usually happened when I was no longer interested in sex with that night's companion.) We would stay in the car and talk. Unending icy winter nights with the windows down to let out the smoke. Warm spring nights when we squashed the first mosquitoes. Our conversations ranged from chat about sports and politics to deeper existential problems. Despite not having finished school, Angelo was a great debater and could defend his Christian vision of the world divided between good and evil.

We were inseparable on those magical metaphysical nights that filled our lives for no apparent reason whatsoever.

MAY 1982

ANGELO'S OFFICE WAS LOCATED in the residential complex where Cardinal Alessandrini lived. There were low-rise buildings, each three stories high, surrounded by a park, on Via della Camilluccia in one of Rome's greenest residential areas. Alessandrini lived on the top floor in one of the buildings and had given the other floors over to Dioguardi for his offices. The third floor was used for administration; the second floor was open to the public—that is, priests and nuns looking for accommodations.

On one of my days off, a Saturday at the beginning of May, I went to meet him there. It was a glorious morning—the skies clear, the sun already warm. In my old Alfa Romeo Duetto, I crossed the historic city center crowded with tourists. Every so often I slowed to admire a young female visitor. Near the Colosseum I saw a German blonde with huge tits and the words *Über alles* printed on her T-shirt. In Piazza di Spagna, American girls in shorts were sitting on the Spanish Steps, and in Piazza del Popolo, where the bars were already full, two gorgeous Japanese girls were taking turns photographing each other. Eventually I drove up the winding slopes of Monte Mario and came to Via della Camilluccia. A huge green gate barred the entrance to the park where the two low-rise blocks were situated, separated by a huge fountain, a tennis court, and a swimming pool. It was a little corner of paradise allowing some privileged people to live a separate life, far above that wonderfully chaotic city crawling with people and traffic.

I drove the car up to the gate. A severe-looking woman in her sixties came out of the gatehouse. She looked me up and down skeptically, unable to decide whether I was an encyclopedia salesman or some lackey of one of the rich people around there. I stared back at her with one of my own surly looks, a gift that came naturally to me.

"Can I help you?" she asked with a Southern accent.

"I'm a friend of Angelo Dioguardi's."

"You'll have to park outside. Only the residents can park inside."

She saw me surveying the handful of vehicles parked on the enormous grounds. Among them was a stupendous Aston Martin, Angelo's Fiat 500 and, gleaming in the sunshine, a Harley-Davidson Panhead.

"The Count doesn't want nonresidents' cars past the gate. And if it was up to him, you know, nonresidents wouldn't even be allowed in on foot," the concierge added with a note of disapproval, whether for the nonresidents or the count I couldn't decide.

Fortunately, parking on that quiet green road was no problem. The residents all had garages, and there were no stores or restaurants around, only trees, well-tended flowerbeds and Filipino au pairs pushing strollers carrying the children of the wealthy. Their parents were off having coffee in Piazza Navona or out on the golf course.

"You have to walk to the far end of the grounds. Go around behind the pool and the tennis court, and you'll get to Building B. You can see the balcony from here; you can't miss it," she explained, as though talking to a small child.

As I passed Building A, the one nearer to the gate, I felt I was being watched. I turned upward and caught sight of a reflection on the third-floor balcony. Someone was spying on visitors through a pair of binoculars. I stopped to admire the Aston Martin parked in front of the entrance to the building. The Harley stood beside it. I went around the large fountain and onto the pathways between the tennis court and the swimming pool; tall trees prevented me from making out Building B.

I came across a lanky and energetic young man. Thick red curls, blue eyes, freckles, probably not more than twenty. He was wearing a priest's cassock.

"Are you lost?" he asked in a thick American accent.

"I'm not sure. I'm looking for Angelo Dioguardi in Building B."

"You're not a priest," he said, smiling as though he'd said something witty. He explained, "Only priests and nuns come to see Angelo. I'm Father Paul, assistant to Cardinal Alessandrini."

He accompanied me to Building B's front door.

"Angelo is on the third floor. Call me if you decide you'd like to become a priest. Maybe I can help."

He really was a bit too much of a joker for a first encounter. I recognized it instantly as a way of covering up his insecurity—and Father Paul's insecurity exuded from every pore.

I went up on foot. As I was going past the first floor, a girl with the features of a young goddess came out of a door. She was wearing a long white nurse's coat, and I would have considered feigning illness on the spot. That kind of a uniform tends to disguise the figure, but no kind of dress could have hidden that curvaceous outline.

She stopped dead, her eyes lowered. "Please, go ahead," she said, pausing to let me pass. Her voice was soft and childlike, a little dreamy, like her smile. Her arms were full of ring binders.

"Can I help you?" I offered. She kept avoiding my eyes and shook her head, distracted. A ring binder fell to the tiled floor. While I was bending down to pick it up, I caught the scent of her soap. "I'm really sorry," she said, absurdly overapologetic.

I couldn't persuade her to give me any ring binders, and we went up to the second floor in silence. She ushered me through a small door into a long corridor with several doors leading off it.

"Mr. Dioguardi's office is at the end," she said. She hadn't once met my eyes, and she quickly disappeared into the first room on the right.

I found Angelo behind a desk, buried under papers, ring binders, and folders of every kind. Behind him hung a huge photo of the Pope.

I almost laughed at the sight of him in that setting. In the workplace, his complete inability to keep things neat was striking.

"I know, Michele—your brother looks the part behind a desk, but I look silly. Worse, here I am making a mess in a job that demands organizational skills."

"At least you've got some good-looking coworkers," I said, gesturing toward the corridor.

"I guess you saw Elisa," he replied, laughing.

"If that's the kind of young goddess you have carrying your bits of paper . . ."

He explained that Elisa Sordi had been there for two months as a weekend assistant; she was in college, studying to become an accountant, and would be taking exams in June. She was only eighteen.

"And from whence does this manna from heaven descend on you?"

"Paola's uncle, Cardinal Alessandrini. Our illustrious neighbor the senator, Count Tommaso dei Banchi di Aglieno, introduced him to Elisa. The cardinal and the count do favors for each other, even though their morals and their politics are polar opposites: the cardinal's a Catholic democrat, and the Count's an anti-Church monarchist despot."

"I think they've done you a favor this time, Angelo. Sure, she's a bit young, but you know I don't hang about . . ."

He shook his head with a smile.

"She's not your type, Michele."

"And why not?"

"She's awkward, incredibly shy, and a very devout Catholic—someone like me, who really believes."

"Is that what you think of me, Angelo Dioguardi? That I'm only a collector of fucks from cheap sluts?" I asked in a tone of obviously feined disdain.

I expected him to laugh but instead he made a face. It was the noise of ring binders falling to the floor behind me that made me realize what was happening. Blushing, Angelo rose to help the girl gather them up. I turned round with my most innocent smile. Elisa was standing there with a stunned expression on her face, a look of shock in her eyes. Not having the gift of invisibility at my command,

I excused myself and went to the men's room, where I remained for a long time, cursing myself. The face I saw in the mirror was that of a vulgar idiot who had just made a complete fool of himself.

I went back into Angelo's office only when I was sure Elisa would no longer be there. He gave me a sardonic grin that made me furious.

"Asshole! What's so funny? You could have warned me, couldn't you?"

"I tried to, Mike. Anyway, Elisa certainly knows what you're about now. But if she has a sudden stroke and loses her memory, I'd say you've got a chance . . ."

We ended up shutting the door and settling down for a chat over a beer. There was no ashtray, because Angelo didn't smoke in his office, so I used the wastepaper basket. Angelo explained his work to me. The Vatican sent him the scheduled arrivals, and his three regular staff allocated the available housing to the priests and nuns—in separate quarters, naturally—while his responsibility was to take care of hostels and convents for any upcoming conventions. As for emergencies, such as unexpected arrivals, he was always on call, no matter the time of day. That was why he needed extra help on Saturdays and sometimes Sundays too. This extra help came in the shape of that young goddess Elisa Sordi, the girl about to take her exams in accountancy.

"So, on Saturdays you're here alone with her. How do you resist?"

"There's nothing to resist. I've already told you, Elisa's off limits. Go on, admit it: the truth is that my being faithful to Paola upsets you, and you'd feel better if I stepped over the line once in a while."

That wasn't true. I wasn't jealous of the self-control he applied to this renunciation. I'd had to work on self-control a good deal myself and was still alive because I'd learned it the hard way before anyone had had a chance to kill me. But I really didn't understand self-control applied to sex—it was like sucking mints to hide bad breath. And I wanted my friend to see it as I did: self-imposed faithfulness was like renouncing life itself. And that really was a deadly sin.

At half past one, Elisa knocked and put her head around the door, avoiding my gaze.

"May I go out for something to eat?" she asked.

It seemed an old-fashioned request, like asking for permission to go to the bathroom. I went to the window to watch her leave. A young man was waiting for her outside Building B's main door.

"You said she was a little saint," I said to Angelo.

"Shit, Mike, you're still planning on trying to get into her pants? That's Valerio Bona, an old friend of hers. Anyway, it's no business of ours."

The goddess was going off with a guy her own age who was short and skinny and wore glasses. It was absolutely ridiculous—such a waste. He looked like a loser. She'd taken off her white coat. She was dressed simply and modestly in loose-fitting pants. A sweatshirt tied around her waist camouflaged her splendid behind.

I could have some fun with a girl like that.

I intended to do everything I could to cancel out my tactless behavior. After all, it was only the first time we'd met.

. . . .

Angelo had to discuss a couple of matters with the cardinal before we could go for some lunch.

"Come with me, Michele. He'll be happy to meet you. It's always useful to know a policeman," he said with a grin.

The cardinal's penthouse was enormous: a spacious living room, several bedrooms and bathrooms, together with a large balcony overlooking the grounds, with a view all the way to the entrance on Via della Camilluccia, where the gatehouse was located. The living room was full of young African priests and nuns speaking French. It was like a deluxe Catholic youth hostel.

"These are the people we have to find places for. They should have left this morning but there's a coup d'état going on in their country, and they've closed the airport," Angelo explained.

The only white face apart from ours was that of Alessandrini, who was mingling with the young clergy in his everyday clothes. He poured lemonade into their glasses from a large carafe. A short, middle-aged man who radiated great energy, his lively, intelligent black eyes stood out against his cropped gray hair.

He came up to me with a smile and an outstretched hand. "You must be Michele Balistreri," he said. Then, turning to Angelo, he added, "Help yourselves to lemonade. I'll be back in a minute."

He picked up the telephone and spoke in perfect English.

"You can tell His Holiness that, with all due humility, I do not agree. There's no violence. It's a bloodless coup. The fact that they're not Catholics is another matter, but we can find a way to have a dialogue."

He came back, pushing his glasses higher on the bridge of his hooked nose.

"The current Vatican hierarchy has no love for communists, exactly the same as you."

I looked at Angelo, who shook his head. No, he definitely wasn't the type to gossip about me with the cardinal. Either the cardinal could read in my face what I was thinking or he had looked into my background because I hung out with his niece's future husband. I didn't care.

"I don't agree with the Vatican on any subject. Not even on communists."

The Cardinal ignored my comment and led us to the only corner of the living room not taken over by noisy young Africans.

"Your Eminence, we have some problems," Angelo said. "We can't manage to find places for all of them in our housing and the hotels are booked with tourists. We're looking for about twenty beds."

This was a different Angelo Dioguardi than the one I knew. He was awkward and insecure. The cardinal was too important for him.

Alessandrini laughed. "My poor Angelo, I see you can't multiply beds like Our Lord did with the fishes! But it's no problem. The priests will stay with me. Naturally, you'll have to accommodate all the sisters. You can never be sure . . ."

"Your Eminence, this is a big apartment, but there aren't enough beds. We're talking about twenty priests. Where will you put them all?"

The cardinal pointed to the terrace. "I slept out there last night to keep cool. It'll be no problem for them—they're used to it in Africa. I've already sent Paul to get some sleeping bags from San Valente."

Angelo relaxed and the cardinal turned to me. "So, you're a policeman?" I had heard the word spoken with a thousand different shades of meaning: often ironic, sometimes even offensive. But Alessandrini said it with pure curiosity. At the same time, he was telling me that he knew all about me. In that residential complex, you entered only on foot and after all your details had been checked.

"I wanted to be a policeman when I grew up, but the Lord had plans for me to serve a different kind of justice," he said.

I had my own opinions about the conflict between earthly and divine justice, but I figured it wasn't the right time to discuss Nietzsche and the Gospels. This powerful and friendly man may have been admirable, but I didn't find him likable. He was a priest and, after years of religious schooling, I knew that a pleasant manner could merely be ash over hot coals. I had learned to be wary even as a young child, from the moment in the fifth year of primary school when a soft hand infiltrated my shorts while I was being told about the goodness of Our Lord.

He read my thoughts. "Yes, I know, you're very much the layperson and opposed to the Church, or perhaps even opposed to religion. Look, I respect justice on earth, but I also recognize its tragic errors. In this world, justice is often in the wrong hands."

I was losing patience. "If we waited for the next life, we'd be living in tears, tormenting ourselves with our sins. When remorse turns to penitence and absolution, it's only a way of avoiding life."

Seeing Angelo's look of alarm, I stopped, but the Cardinal wasn't the type to be offended by an insignificant nonbeliever like me.

"Mr. Balistreri, I realize that the only sin you recognize is what we call crime. And punishment is meted out on earth, possibly in prison. But it was the justice of the Enlightenment, not faith, that instigated the guillotine of the revolutionaries, and they didn't only decapitate the guilty."

"While no mistakes were made under the Inquisition, is that it?"

"The Inquisition is one of the Church's many embarrassments. And really it was earthly justice."

Cardinal Alessandrini had very clear ideas and was willing to promote them even if they went against Vatican dogma.

I would have preferred to wait in Angelo's office for Elisa to come back, but I realized after opening my big mouth about easy lays and sluts it was better to allow things to settle. And so I let myself be

persuaded to accompany Angelo to the church of San Valente to help
Father Paul.

While we were walking back over the grounds toward the exit, I
glanced up at the third-floor windows. Elisa's office window was the
only one wide open. I lit a cigarette and again saw the sun's reflection
from Building A's penthouse balcony.

"There's someone up there who likes playing around with
binoculars."

Angelo nodded. "Manfredi, Count Tommaso's son. He's a bit
strange, but if I were him I'd have problems too."

It seemed impossible to have problems in this branch of paradise.
But I'd learned that family wealth doesn't immunize people against
the world, especially when they're young.

"What kind of problems does he have, apart from a problem with
spying on passersby?"

"Manfredi's problem is his father. The count's a very powerful politician, the leader of a party that wants to bring the monarchy back to
Italy. He's got vast economic resources, thanks to his family's invest-
ments in Africa. Timber, minerals, livestock."

I'd also had an important man for a father. I could guess what
Manfredi's problems might be. But there was far worse, as I soon
learned from Angelo.

"The count married a very young woman named Ulla from an
aristocratic family in the north of Europe. She was only seventeen at
the time. She got pregnant right away. She continued to go riding
and the fetus suffered. Manfredi was born with a severe birthmark
and a harelip—you can barely look at him. Apart from that he's a
healthy kid and highly intelligent, but a difficult character. I feel
really sorry for him; I don't know what I'd do in his place."

The little freak with the binoculars got no sympathy from me.

"There are worse things in life, Angelo. There are people who live
quietly with much worse disabilities. Anyway, why don't they operate
on him?"

"They've consulted plastic surgeons all over the world. The birthmark is too big to be removed—the technology just isn't there yet.
Maybe someday."

A blue car entered the grounds and parked next to the Aston Martin. A member of the entourage got out and quickly opened the rear door. The man who emerged immediately commanded respect. He was about forty-five, dressed in an impeccable blue pinstripe suit despite the heat. Tall and ramrod straight, he wore his black hair combed back from his wide forehead. He had a long aquiline nose, a thin mustache and a well-trimmed goatee. He didn't so much as glance at us. He whispered in his bodyguard's ear, then slipped through the front door of Building A.

"Real friendly," I observed.

Angelo smiled. "The Count doesn't much like human contact, especially with those who are not his peers."

The bodyguard came up and, pointing to me, addressed Angelo. "Is the gentleman with you?"

"Yes, he is," Angelo replied, cowed.

"Then please inform your guest that these grounds are private property and smoking is strictly forbidden," he said sharply. He turned and walked away.

I'd never heard of a residential complex that banned not only parking, but smoking, too. A place where they spied on you from the balcony and knew all your details. I could see why young Manfredi's life might have been difficult. I was careful not to stub out my cigarette on the ground for fear I'd be set upon by a pack of Dobermans or transferred to some forgotten police station up on a mountaintop.

Angelo explained that the count occupied all of Building A and owned the entire residential complex. The Vatican only rented Building B. As we were passing through the gate, he introduced me to Gina Giansanti, the concierge.

"Next time, finish smoking before you come in," she said. I wasn't sure whether that was a rebuke or a gesture of solidarity.

At the gate, I turned around and gave a little wave to the binoculars reflected on the balcony. *Bye-bye, Manfredi.*

. . . .

The church of San Valente was fifteen minutes from the complex along the Via Aurelia Antica. The Saturday traffic was calm. Many stores were closed, and Romans were having lunch at home or picnicking in one of the parks. We drove down a small lane and I parked on a patch of unkempt grass between overgrown shrubs and hedges. Everything was tumbledown, left to its own devices. The church was small, very simple. Its walls were peeling from decades of exposure to the sun. On the opposite side of the grass stood a small white house. Next to it was a single tree that had been planted recently.

A dozen children between ten and thirteen were playing soccer and a blond girl of about twenty was acting as referee. Another girl was clearing a long table set outside, directly under the tree.

We went around to the house. Disorder ruled everywhere; the place needed a great deal of work. The lanky Father Paul, sweating copiously in his cassock, was loading sleeping bags into an old Volkswagen Beetle.

"Angelo!" he called. "And Angelo's friend, the soon-to-be priest."

This time I smiled at him—his desire to reach out was almost painful. We helped him to load the car.

"Eat with *noi*?" said Paul finally, in his mixture of English and Italian, as we washed our hands in a simple bathroom with a chipped basin.

"Would you like to eat something?" Paul asked.

We sat outside, and the blond woman brought us plastic cutlery and some lukewarm soup. Then she said she was going to wash the dishes.

"Don't the children help?" asked Angelo. I knew that as a child he'd cooked, cleared the table, and washed his own dishes.

"*Difficile*, only at start," explained Paul. "Would you like to speak to a *bambino*?"

"Thanks, maybe next time," I said. "I have to be back at the station. I've only got time for a cigarette, assuming we can smoke here."

Paul burst out laughing. "I don't smoke myself, but I'm not crazy about it like the count. You're free to kill yourself."

I opened my second pack of the day and went to light a cigarette. Angelo signaled to me not to.

"Long time in Rome?" I asked Paul. I was consciously omitting verbs, as if this would help him understand better.

"Almost one year. I'm taking some classes and working with Cardinal Alessandrini. When I'm finished I'm going to open an orphanage like this in Africa. If you hurry and become a priest, you can come with me."

Then Paul grew serious.

"How old were you when you knew police work was your vocation?" That's the word he used: vocation.

"I don't know whether it's my vocation, but I became a policeman two years ago."

I saw him make a quick calculation about my age. He came to the conclusion that he still had some years to go in order to be certain of his own vocation. I imagined that, in the years to come, several of his firmest convictions would be strenuously put to the test.

SUNDAY, JULY 11, 1982

I HADN'T SHUT MY EYES for almost two weeks. The World Cup coming to an end in Spain had disrupted Italian life. After an uncertain start, Italy had beaten Argentina, Brazil, and Poland. Those were evenings of unforgettable excitement that segued into poker with Angelo, Alberto, and other friends and, for me, often ended in bed, each time with a different woman.

On the day of the final against Germany, Rome was in the grip of a creeping sense of triumph that was ready to explode into ecstasy. Shops selling national flags had sold out. Those unable to buy one in time had hung out three colored towels to simulate the national tricolor. Then even the towels sold out and desperate latecomers were forced to put out painted sheets.

No one doubted Italy would win the World Cup that evening. Rome woke more peacefully than usual under a clear blue sky: it was as if the entire population wanted to conserve its energy to play the final against Germany. Even the usual Sunday exodus to the beaches was largely reduced for fear of getting stuck in traffic coming back and not being in front of the television set at half past eight.

I took the opportunity to stay inside the police station in peace and quiet and sign some papers. Not that there was much to do, but I wanted to be sure I'd have no problems that evening. Angelo called a little before lunch, having just come back from Mass with Paola.

"Wait until you see what I've got planned for tonight, Balistreri."

"After seeing how you organize the folders in your office, I have my doubts about your planning skills. What's up?"

"We're all going to Paola's for the final; your brother's bringing his German girlfriend, so we can tease her a bit. We'll eat and have a drink during the match. When it's over, Paola and the others are going to raise hell out on the streets—"

"Excuse me, Angelo, but what if we lose?"

I already knew the answer. "It's not going to happen, Michele. That's not part of the plan."

"Okay, so we win. What happens next?"

"Next we stay in the apartment—you, me, Alberto, and a colleague of his—and play a little poker. When the others come back from celebrating, you can go off with one of the women. They'll all want to keep partying."

"Okay, Angelo. But I'm not letting the Duetto out on the road today with all this traffic. Can you come and pick me up here at the station in that old wreck of yours? I knock off at five o'clock sharp."

"I don't know if I can. Father Paul called and there's a bit of problem. I have to drop by the office about five thirty."

"Shit, on a Sunday? Have you got to find a little bachelor pad for our jumped-up Yankee priest?"

"Don't be crude, Michele. I have to drop in on Cardinal Alessandrini—there have been some unexpected arrivals. I had to call Elisa and ask her to come in, too."

Suddenly my hostility toward the idea transformed into enthusiasm. I hadn't seen the young goddess again, but I remembered her very well.

"Why don't I come with you? That way I can apologize."

Was I joking or was I serious? I didn't really know myself.

"No, we're not going to see Elisa. We'd only be in her way. I have to check in with the cardinal about assigning the housing, that's all."

"Okay, Angelo, I'll go up and say hello to Elisa on my own. Pick me up at five."

This promised to be an interesting evening. At Paola's there were always good-looking young women from the upper crust of Rome, and they were my ideal targets. Euphoria in the case of victory, plus my dark attractiveness, meant one more victory guaranteed.

I went down to the bar opposite the office in the piazza. The roads were totally deserted. Inside, in the cool of the air-conditioning, a crowd with nothing better to do was mouthing off loudly about the coming game. I ordered a sandwich and a beer and listened to the cross-currents of several voices. There was no doubt we would beat the Germans. We always did.

"Even in war we showed the Nazis!" yelled a long-haired freak with a hammer and sickle tattooed on the back of his dirty hand. He and his buddies were passing around two cigarettes with an unmistakable smell.

I looked at my watch—I still had some time, and I had the inclination. I was in civilian clothes, so I took out my badge. I waited for the joint to make its way to the tattooed guy, and then I went up to him.

I showed him my badge and took the joint from his fingers. "You're under arrest for the use of a narcotic substance," I announced.

He looked at me in shock. "What the fuck?"

"And also for insulting a public official. Would you be so kind as to accompany me to the police station?"

I was using bureaucratic police language on purpose, knowing how much they hated it. The long-haired freak placed a grubby hand on my shoulder. As expected, the owner of the bar went out to call the men on guard outside the police station to come over and help. There wasn't much time.

"Remove your hand immediately or I'll add assaulting a police officer to the charges against you," I commanded, trying not to laugh.

The tone and the terminology finally produced what I wanted: he gave me a shove and I fell to the ground like a leaf.

This was the scene my colleagues encountered when they entered. The long-haired freak wouldn't be watching the game that evening, not even inside Regina Coeli prison. I would have him slammed in a cell where he would spend a very uncomfortable night.

· · · ·

I gave instructions to the men as soon as I was back in the office. They could watch the game on the set they'd brought in. They were grateful. But I made it clear that in exchange they were not to contact me—no interruptions for any reason—after eight o'clock. I repeated myself. For any reason whatsoever.

"What if someone gets up on the opposite roof and wants to jump off?" one of the men joked.

"You tell him to jump off tomorrow," I responded, and I made it clear I wasn't joking in return.

By four I'd finished the pointless paperwork and started thinking about Elisa Sordi all alone in her office on a Sunday afternoon in a completely deserted city. I was tempted not to wait for Angelo and go to Via della Camilluccia by myself, but Elisa probably had a lot to do, and after that first unfortunate meeting with her advised prudence.

My twisted mind hit on an indirect solution. At ten to five I called Angelo's office.

The shy voice I knew very well answered after two rings.

"This is Michele Balistreri. I believe we've met."

She was silent. I went on.

"I'm waiting for Mr. Dioguardi, who's about to come and pick me up at the police station. Is he there in the office with you?"

"No, he hasn't been here all day. He's supposed to come by later. Should I give him a message, sir?"

That "sir" reassured me that despite the fact that I'd made an ass of myself, she still had some respect for me. Either that or she was afraid of me, which would be even better.

"No thanks. Perhaps I'll drop by with Mr. Dioguardi later."

She said nothing, and I put the phone down without saying good-bye.

I felt a little embarrassed about the phone call. I dialed Paola's number. She picked up the phone.

"I'll put him on, Michele. We've just had a nap and he's coming out to pick you up."

"Okay, see you later," I said.

"Michele, what's wrong?" said Angelo, sounding worried.

"Nothing. I just wanted to be sure you wouldn't forget to come and get me. I called the office thinking you were there and got Elisa."

He was silent for a moment. "Are you sure that was accidental? Anyway, I'll be out of here in five minutes and with you in another five."

He arrived ten minutes later, just after five o'clock. It was stiflingly hot, so he had opened the roof of the old Fiat, which still stank of sweat, beer and Gitanes. We pulled up on Via della Camilluccia a few minutes later; there was hardly anyone on the roads. The street was calm, silent, shaded by its magnificent trees.

"I'm going to have one before going in," said Angelo. We approached the green gate with our cigarettes lit. The concierge scowled at us, but we stopped outside to smoke.

"What are you doing here, Gina? Today's Sunday," Angelo asked her.

"Getting my bags ready. I'm leaving tonight."

"Without seeing the game?"

"Couldn't care less. I'm going to India tonight."

"India? What are you going to do there?" I asked, surprised.

Gina looked at me with disapproval.

"I go every year to volunteer for two weeks. Cardinal Alessandrini arranges everything for me, so I can report on how things are going over there."

"Have you seen Elisa?" Angelo asked her, to stop me from saying anything inappropriate.

"Elisa's been up in the office slaving away since this morning, poor girl. She did go out for lunch. I saw her when she came back with Valerio. She rang on the intercom half an hour ago and I went up to get some papers to take to Cardinal Alessandrini."

Angelo said, "We're going to see the Cardinal, so Elisa can go home."

I said. "I'll wait for you here."

He shot me a warning look.

"Remember, I can see you from the cardinal's balcony, so no fucking around."

Although it was some distance away, Building B's balcony was well in sight of the gate, and vice versa. Something of a letdown.

"I won't move, I swear," I said with my fingers crossed.

Angelo went off and I was left on my own with Gina. I stood on one side of the gate, having a smoke; she was on the other, polishing the gatehouse windows so she could leave them gleaming. She began to warm up to me a bit.

"I'm sorry about the smoking, but the count's nuts about it, and his son's even worse."

Certainly Count Tommaso dei Banchi di Aglieno didn't enjoy the sympathy of the severe concierge. And even less, that young idiot with the binoculars.

I looked up toward Building A's balcony. A fleeting reflection, then nothing. Manfredi was feeling shy.

Angelo came out onto Building B's balcony with Alessandrini. They gestured to me and disappeared inside. The concierge's intercom buzzed. "The cardinal's asking for you to go up," said Gina. "I'll say good-bye now. I have to go to mass before I leave."

Fucking cardinal—as if I was interested in his chitchat. I was thinking about trying my luck with Elisa when a blue car rolled up to the gate. The driver rushed to help out Count Tommaso dei Banchi di Aglieno, while Gina opened the gate for him. I found him right in front me, impeccably dressed and looking cool and collected despite the heat.

"You're Dioguardi's friend the police captain, correct? Are you here on official business?"

I took it as a given that he was joking and gave a stupid little laugh. The count looked at me as if I were an idiot. Without another word he turned and walked toward the entrance of his block. I stayed there, watching him go, angry with myself for having felt uneasy—an unpleasant sensation to which I was not at all accustomed.

Then I set off toward Building B, not sure what to do. I risked getting lost again between the tennis court and the swimming pool, and again I encountered Father Paul, just as I had the first time.

"The cardinal is expecting you."

This time he was serious—not a trace of his usual smile. He seemed tense: his blue eyes troubled in his freckled face, his red hair in disarray. He'd even enunciated carefully to make himself understood.

"Will you be watching the final tonight, Paul?"

I asked him in order to stall for time more than anything else, since I was fighting a little internal battle with myself.

"Yes, in San Valente, with the children. Now if you'll excuse me, I'm running late." And off he went without saying good-bye.

I stopped to look up at Elisa's window. Again it was the only one open, and this time there was a flower on the windowsill. She must have put it out there when the sun wasn't beating down on that spot, as it was now. I still didn't know what to do, so I stood there for a couple of minutes, thinking about her, undecided.

Then I went to the elevator and pressed the button for the top floor.

I found Angelo on the cardinal's landing. We crossed the huge deserted living room in silence and went into the private study. Cardinal Alessandrini was there, dressed in his red robes. He was sitting behind his imposing desk and leafing through some papers, probably the work from Elisa that Gina had brought him. In those vestments and in that room he looked different. He looked like an energetic and intelligent priest, but he also looked like a man who had some power and would always want more. Angelo seemed worried; there must be a problem, some work that was unsatisfactory.

"Captain Balistreri, were you going to leave without coming up for a visit?" asked the cardinal. His tone was cordial enough, but there was an edge to it. Something was not quite right.

Angelo went out onto the terrace; I saw him smoking while he leafed nervously through some files.

"I didn't want to impose. I know that you and Angelo have urgent business. Is something wrong?"

Alessandrini pointed to the chair opposite him. "Nothing that will force you to miss the game, but your friend needs to get to the bottom of the matter. Can I offer you a lemonade?"

Obviously it was some problem with accommodation that Angelo and Elisa hadn't resolved. That friendly man in red must also have been a very hard man when he wanted to be.

The cardinal opened a small fridge and filled a glass with cold lemonade.

"You're young, Balistreri, but I know you've accomplished a lot."

This was exactly what he said, confirmation that he had a real and proper dossier on me.

"I've accomplished some good things and some bad things, like everyone."

"The important thing is to learn from one's mistakes. Even your dear Nietzsche's Übermensch will one day have to stand before God."

Well, I'd committed a grave error twelve years ago. A mortal sin, from which only a priest could absolve me. But I had no desire to talk about it with the cardinal.

I tried to change the subject. "I see that at least here we can smoke," I said, pointing to the terrace.

"Naturally, the Vatican falls outside the count's 'jurisdiction,' so do join Angelo if you wish," he joked. He was affable, playful. But he was a little distracted, as if pursuing some thought of his own.

I went outside and, while Angelo was working, smoked a couple of cigarettes.

Then the telephone rang in the study, and while the Cardinal answered it I asked Angelo how much he still had to do. "Almost done," he grumbled. He was serious, deep in thought. I cursed Alessandrini and his power over my friend. I didn't like to see him under the thumb of his priestly boss.

The cardinal's call was brief. He said, "We'll meet there at a quarter to seven." Then he hung up the phone.

Angelo went back inside and handed the papers to the Cardinal.

"Everything's in order, Your Eminence. I'll leave the arrangements on your desk so that tomorrow morning you can confirm everything before the guests arrive. I'll see what I can do about the other thing."

"I'm sure you will. Well now, I suggest we go down. It's ten past six and I have to be at the Vatican. And I believe you have plans this evening?"

"Won't you be watching the final, Your Eminence?" I asked.

"I too am flesh and blood, Balistreri. I shall try to be back by eight thirty."

We went down in the elevator. I gave a last glance at the open window on the second floor. I had to stop thinking about her.

Gina wasn't at the gate; she must have gone to Mass. The cardinal said good bye in a hurry and got into a taxi that was waiting by the gate.

We were getting into the old Fiat when the count came out of Building A along with a much younger woman and a tall young man with muscles rippling beneath his red T-shirt. He wore a full-face motorcycle helmet. As usual, the Harley was parked next to the Aston Martin. The count placed a hand on the young man's shoulder and opened the gate with his remote control. Then they all left, the count and the women I assumed was his wife in the James Bond car, the kid on his *Easy Rider* bike.

. . . .

When we got to Paola's there were already a number of people there. Angelo went straight to the kitchen, being one of the cooks, while I offered to set the large table in front of the TV. Then I helped Paola to welcome the other guests while Angelo was busy cooking. This way I could get a good preview of the female talent coming in. My brother Alberto came along with the elegant German girl who would later become his wife. Every so often I went into the kitchen and found Angelo sweating more than ever over the gas stove and glasses of wine. He was completely consumed with preparing the *penne all'arrabbiata* together with Cristiana, a petite girl with long red hair, large tits, and a pair of jeans that perfectly framed her notable bottom. From that moment my visits to the kitchen increased, ending with me hanging around to chat with her.

By eight o'clock, about fifty people were squeezed into every nook and cranny. The heat of that stifling afternoon was still entering the open windows. The neighboring housing blocks gave off the laughter of groups of friends gathered for the event. I glanced down at the street. Absolutely deserted.

The atmosphere in the house was festive. After several glasses of white wine, I got into a discussion with Cristiana about whether it would be better to get it on after a victory or after a defeat.

"You're nice enough, Michele, but I know better than to trust you. Paola warned me about you."

In reality, Paola was a good friend. She knew very well that that type of advice attracted the girls like flies to honey.

"Watch it. I could arrest you for insulting a public official."

"And would you have to handcuff me, Captain?" she laughed.

"First, I'd handcuff you. Then I'd interrogate you, and I'm tough. If you offered any resistance . . ."

"Oh, you'd have to punish me to get me to talk. You might have to get out a whip."

I glanced pointedly at her butt.

"That doesn't work on women who like it."

She blushed, but laughed. The part of the evening after the game and the poker was in the bag. Not much of an effort that evening. Besides, with all the cigarettes and alcohol, it was better like that. I peeped into the kitchen. Sweating like a pig and now almost drunk, Angelo was putting the finishing touches on a magnificent rice salad in the colors of the Italian flag.

Then the game started. I sat on the floor and leaned against Cristiana's legs. I was drinking, smoking, and praying for Paolo Rossi.

. . . .

The first half was scoreless. Strung out from the tension and the heat, Italians flooded the streets, balconies and terraces to cool down and get some fresh air. Paola's phone rang.

"It's my uncle. He wants to speak to you," she said to Angelo, looking puzzled.

I saw a line deepen on Angelo's forehead as he listened to the cardinal.

"I'll come right away," he mumbled, and he put the receiver down. His voice was thick with drink.

I was concerned. "Same problems you were dealing with this afternoon?"

He looked at me vacantly. "They can't find Elisa."

"Who can't find Elisa?"

"Her parents. They're really worried. They say she was supposed to come home to watch the game with them and she never showed up. They contacted the cardinal."

I laughed. "They contacted the cardinal? She's out with some friends watching the game. Typical overprotective Italian parents."

Angelo shook his head. "Elisa would have told them if she'd changed her plans."

I was irritated. "Really? This has to happen tonight? Okay, let's go. We'll reassure her parents and be back in time for the second half."

I was really annoyed at this bother, but it wouldn't take long with the lack of traffic and I couldn't let him go alone in that state.

We were both drunk. I drove Angelo's car, and we were on Via della Camilluccia within five minutes. The Aston Martin was parked next to the Harley-Davidson. From the illuminated terrace of Building A came the sounds of a party. The count had guests for the game.

The cardinal and Elisa's parents were waiting for us beside the large fountain. Amedeo and Giovanna Sordi were a little over fifty. Elisa's father was a tall, gaunt man. His hair was already white. Elisa, their only child, they told me, had gotten her height and bearing from him. From her mother she'd gotten those deep-set eyes. Those eyes were looking at us worriedly.

"We're so sorry, Mr. Dioguardi, sir, tonight of all nights," Elisa's mother said. Her father stood off to the side. Mr. Dioguardi. The poor are too respectful of those in power, which is why they stay poor.

The cardinal turned to Angelo. "Did you see or hear Elisa after we said good-bye this afternoon?"

Angelo staggered a little, his cheeks flushed. He managed to mumble, "No. I told her that if I hadn't come back by six thirty it meant that everything was fine and she could leave."

"I spoke to her several times today," said the mother. "I also called her in the office just after five. She told me that Mr. Dioguardi was leaving, and that if everything went smoothly she'd be home by seven thirty. When she wasn't home by then, I just assumed something had come up. I didn't want to call and bother her."

Her husband gazed at her protectively. "Amedeo wanted to drive over and pick her up, but Elisa never wanted to inconvenience him. At eight I began to worry. I called the office, but no one answered. Now we don't know what to think."

I stepped forward. "I'm a friend of Dioguardi's and a police captain," I said, trying not to slur my words. "Perhaps Elisa simply changed her mind and went to watch the game with some friends."

Giovanna Sordi stared at me. I can't have looked very good, but I guess the fact that I was a policeman reassured her..

"She would have called us, Captain," she said respectfully.

Parents fool themselves into thinking they know everything. That thought came to me together with the fact that the second half of the game was about to begin. I assumed an exceptionally professional manner.

"Maybe there's no phone where she is. Procedure would dictate that we wait and see what happens when the game is over," I said firmly.

I noticed a shade of annoyance on the cardinal's face, but unlike the two parents he made no objections.

"Let's do that," said the cardinal. "Mr. Sordi, head on home now while there's no traffic. If Elisa calls or comes home, let us know. Your wife can stay here with me until the game ends. If Elisa hasn't called by then, Captain Balistreri will tell us what to do."

I was getting worked up, not about Elisa Sordi but about the Italian national team. And I was also drunk. I drove as fast as I could to Paola's, while Angelo sat beside me with his eyes shut tight.

. . . .

The second half had just started.

"What's wrong?" Alberto asked when we entered the crowded living room. As usual, he was the only one to show concern.

"Nothing serious. A woman who works with Angelo didn't go home. I'm sure she's out with friends watching the game, but her parents are worried."

Alberto shot me a disapproving glance, just as Cardinal Alessandrini had, but he didn't say anything.

I snuggled between Cristiana's legs with my wine and cigarettes. Italy's three goals gave rise to an equal number of roars across the country. Come the third, people left the television to fly down to the streets, or out onto balconies and terraces. The noise of car horns and air horns added to the thunderclap of fireworks.

On the referee's final whistle, tens of thousands were already in the streets. In a few minutes the traffic was jammed solid, people sitting on car roofs shouting with joy, waving flags, sounding air horns, and beating drums. Columns of red, white, and green smoke were everywhere; the night was painted with the national colors.

Amid this deafening racket, the telephone rang. While Angelo went to answer it, I had an uncomfortable feeling in my stomach. Alberto looked at me.

"If she hasn't showed up, you'd better get over there right away."

His tone was calm, but forceful, leaving no room for argument. It was the same tone my father used when I was little. *You must learn to be more responsible, Michele.*

"The cardinal says we have to get back there with the office keys."

Angelo was less drunk now, and more worried.

It was no longer possible to go in the car with the uproar unleashed on the streets, but the complex was fairly close by, so we walked through the celebrating crowds, pushed and shoved by everyone and pushing and shoving everyone back in turn. It was a ridiculous situation: in the middle of the most unbridled joy, there we were like two drunken branches battered left and right in the wind.

It took us twenty minutes. I was in a state of near delirium about the glorious victory and the probable hook-up with Cristiana. The thought of Elisa only crept in every once in a while.

Cardinal Alessandrini and Elisa's mother were waiting for us. She looked hopeful. We went straight to Building B. Elisa's window was closed, though the flower still sat on the windowsill. Alessandrini was very tense; Angelo was white as a sheet. The office door was double-locked, as it was supposed to be. Angelo's hand trembled from tension and alcohol as he opened it. I told everyone to stay out, but the cardinal objected.

"You're a civilian, Your Eminence. I'm a policeman. Wait here."

But he ignored me and turned to Angelo.

"Stay here with Elisa's mother, Angelo."

He went in without even looking at me. I didn't care. I wanted to get away as soon as I could—to play poker, and then take Cristiana to bed.

We switched on the lights. Everything was in perfect order. Folders in storage boxes, windows closed. There was no sign of Elisa Sordi. We looked through the papers on her desk in the unlikely event she'd written down some kind of appointment. Nothing. We found her time card in its place in the rack where the staff's cards were kept. She had been the only one in that day. Her departure was properly stamped at six thirty.

Angelo locked the office, and Alessandrini stepped to one side and spoke quietly to me.

"You and Angelo are extremely drunk," he said, not beating around the bush. "Go home. I'll go to the police with Elisa's mother and file a report."

I thought this was an excellent idea and only made a feeble protest that the Cardinal didn't even hear. So off we went. As well as our smelling of alcohol and smoke, I'd even let a burp escape my lips.

When we got back my brother had left. No poker. But Cristiana soon returned with Paola. I carried her to the guest room and shut the door.

She stood by the door, her cheeks flushed.

"Michele, I'm engaged to a man who works in Milan. We're getting married soon."

I'd heard that story before. Michele Balistreri was every woman's dark little secret, that borderland that girls know, that they fear and dream about without daring to get too close. They soon understood that if they strayed over the line of good behavior with Michele Balistreri, they could always go back to being cosseted by reassuring guys like Angelo Dioguardi, the ideal boyfriend and companion for life. It was much more enjoyable like this; I enjoyed corrupting their good principles to the point where they not only slipped out of their clothes but also the protective layers built up from years of education and self-control. Along with their panties they handed over that part of themselves they knew existed but were ashamed of, the part that no fiancé had ever seen before and no husband after. They never truly fell in love with me out of an instinct for self-preservation, but when I disappeared they couldn't forgive me. I took away with me the most secret side of their face, even if I was perhaps the only man who had never tried to deceive them.

I unbuckled the belt around her jeans.

"I don't have my handcuffs, so I'll have use this."

She unfastened my leather belt.

"And if I refuse to cooperate with the police, you can use this to punish me."

It was going to be a hell of a night. I forgot all about Elisa Sordi.

MONDAY, JULY 12, 1982

SPENDING THE NIGHT AT Paola's also gave me a huge logistical gain. I was only two strides from the Vigna Clara police station and could therefore sleep in longer. And that morning I needed it. I ignored the alarm completely, having told the station I'd be late. Cristiana was sleeping at my side and from the bedroom next door there was no noise. In the end, what forced me to get up around eleven was hunger.

I didn't wash my face or brush my teeth. I just quietly slipped on jeans and a T-shirt and went down to the café in the piazza. A crowd was discussing the previous night's win. The sidewalks were packed with people who should have been at work, just like me. In the general throng, I put myself right with a tall coffee and a pastry.

"On the house," declared the man behind the bar, obviously a soccer fan. "Only Germans pay today."

I bought the *Corriere dello Sport* and went back to Paola's apartment. I wanted to read all the details of the big win in peace and quiet. I stretched out on the sofa in the living room with the paper and my cigarettes to enjoy reports on the game.

After a while, I heard Cristiana and Paola talking in the kitchen and smelled coffee. They came in with a steaming cup for me, as well as some toast and jam. They were in slippers and robes, their eyes still puffy.

"There you are, fit for a king," Cristiana said. She leaned down and I gave her a quick kiss.

"Paola," I said, "Angelo won't be happy if he wakes up and knows I've seen you in this state . . ."

"Angelo went out at seven thirty. The big jerk woke me up."

I was a little surprised, but then I remembered that he had problems to sort out with the priests and nuns. I dove into my second breakfast, then went back to reading the paper. My head hurt, but my spirits were sky high.

Angelo called a little after noon. Paola handed me the phone.

"The police are here, Michele. From your precinct." He sounded scared.

"Who's there?"

"Your deputy, Capuzzo. Elisa's mother reported her disappearance at midnight, and this area is in your precinct. I told Capuzzo I know you, but I didn't say you were at Paola's. They were looking for you at your house. They don't know where you are."

Good man, Angelo, but this was still a real hassle. "I'll be right over."

I phoned the office, pretending to know nothing. They said Capuzzo was looking for me and gave me a number where I could reach him—the number for Dioguardi's office. I called and a secretary put me through to Capuzzo.

"What's up?"

"Captain, a young woman is missing. She works for your friend Dioguardi."

"Who reported it?"

"The mother. She came to the station at midnight. She was with some priest. I told him the procedure for filing a missing persons report about an adult is complicated, that we have to wait twenty-four hours."

"Listen, between you and me, Capuzzo, the young woman in question is a hot ticket. Chances are she's off celebrating the big game with some lucky son-of-a-bitch."

"The priest is really leaning on us. He must have clout because halfway through the morning the rapid response team was ordered to go and check out the situation."

I took some time to make myself presentable. Sure, dressed in jeans and T-shirt I hardly looked professional, but there was no time to go home and change. I made my way on foot through the many knots of idlers discussing Italy's triumph. All the balconies were displaying the national flag. It must have been the first time since Mussolini's era. Perhaps since the day they hanged him upside down in Piazzale Loreto. *A country without honor.* I squashed the thought that had followed me throughout adolescence; this wasn't the right moment.

The regular concierge wasn't at the gate; she was probably already on her way to India. In her place was a polite young woman who resembled her—her daughter, I assumed. I was smoking when I got to the green gate. I showed her my police badge and entered with the cigarette still in my mouth. I wasn't Angelo Dioguardi's friend this time; I was the police. Just let Count Tommaso dei Banchi di Aglieno try to impose his medieval rules and regulations on me.

The reflection from Building A told me that Manfredi was on the lookout. I was in such a bad mood that I almost pointed in his direction to threaten him. Instead, I waved my cigarette in greeting. I hoped he would tell his arrogant shithead of a father. I knew all this aggression was motivated by feeling liked I'd come off looking stupid during my single brief encounter with the count. Knowing that only made me angrier.

Capuzzo was waiting for me in Angelo's office. My friend looked as if he'd slept little and badly—dark circles under his bloodshot blue eyes. He was unshaven, and his hair stuck out all over.

It was really too much. I took him to one side.

"What the hell's gotten into you, Angelo?"

He shook his head.

"We're assholes, Michele. Such assholes."

"Why, because we didn't do anything last night? Elisa's out with some guy, I'm sure."

"You really are an asshole," he said to me.

He'd never insulted me like that before. I decided to let it go. He was sensitive, that was all.

"So, Capuzzo, who saw the girl last?"

"We don't know, Captain."

"What do you mean you don't know?"

"Her time card was stamped six-thirty, but Signor Dioguardi told us that he went away at six-fifteen with you and the cardinal, and the only people who live in the other building left at the same time. The young priest, Father Paul, had already left when you arrived, and the concierge went to mass at six, then took a bus to the airport. She was seen in church, but the village where she's staying in India has no telephone, so—"

I interrupted him.

"Okay, Elisa left a little after we did, two hours before the final, planning to go home and join her parents. Then she probably ran into someone she knew. He whisked her away to watch the game at his beach house, and she's still there with him recuperating after a long night."

"No," Angelo said, giving me a dark look.

"No? How do you know?"

"I already told you, Elisa's not that type."

I grabbed him by the arm and dragged him to one side. "Listen, you might fall for that shit, but I know a lot more about women than you do. Elisa the saint spent Sunday night fucking some lucky bastard. And tonight she'll come home all apologetic."

Angelo turned his back on me and left the room.

"Go fuck yourself, Angelo Dioguardi!" I shouted after him.

Capuzzo looked on, appalled.

"She's an adult, Capuzzo, and the law is clear. We can't do anything until there's an official report. Yesterday the concierge told us she saw Elisa after five, just before Angelo and I arrived. Even if she punched out at six thirty, let's say she disappeared at five. Get a photo from her mother. It should be easy to find a good one. Just don't get a photo of Elisa in a bathing suit or we'll have thousands of reports from perverts. Her face is unforgettable all by itself."

I carefully avoided mentioning that I'd spoken to her on the phone myself around five o'clock, a few minutes before Angelo came to pick me up at the station.

Capuzzo took notes. "Captain, what should I tell her parents and that priest?"

"Tell them that these are the procedures and it's a free country and not a Church state. And tell them to get off my back."

I left without saying good-bye. I was angry with Angelo and irritated with Cardinal Alessandrini.

Next to the fountain was the skinny kid with the glasses I'd seen with Elisa from Angelo's office window. He looked lost.

"Where are you going?" I barked.

He gave a half jump from fear and I saw the small gold crucifix swaying around his neck.

"Who are you?" he asked nervously, adjusting the glasses on his nose.

Of course, the right and proper thing. I showed him my badge and he became even more nervous.

"Where are you going?" I asked.

"To see a friend of mine, but I'm not sure if she's there."

"What's your friend's name?"

"Elisa Sordi. She works in the office on the third floor of Building B."

"Did she watch the game with you last night?"

He turned pale.

"With me? No, I was at home with my parents."

"You didn't see Elisa yesterday?"

He thought for a minute.

"Yes, just for a moment right after lunch. Why are you asking me all these questions?"

"Because Elisa never went home after work yesterday."

"Oh my God," he muttered.

"Was that unusual for her?"

He hesitated. Finally, he spoke.

"Yes, it is unusual, because—"

"Because she's not like that, I know. Is she your girlfriend?"

He stepped back and blushed, running a hand through his smooth, fair hair, and adjusted the glasses again.

"No, no. We're friends, close friends, but—"

"And what's your name?"

"Valerio. Valerio Bona."

"All right, Mr. Bona. Elisa's not here. Go home. I'm sure you'll see her tomorrow."

I was angry, but I didn't want the whole day to be ruined. On the way back to Paola's I bought a copy of the *Gazzetta dello Sport*. I wanted to read another take on our triumph. When I got back I was covered in sweat from walking in the sun. In the apartment the air conditioning was on and Cristiana was waiting for me on the bed, wearing only her underwear. She was on the phone.

There was little else to discover about her after that night, and I wanted to read the paper. But I noticed she was on the phone with her fiancé in Milan.

I pulled off her underwear while she was promising caresses to her fancy man.

. . . .

Cristiana woke me later in the afternoon.

"There's someone called Capuzzo on the phone for you."

What a pain in the ass work is.

"Capuzzo, what the hell do you want?"

"Sorry, Captain. I took the liberty of calling you there."

"It's all right, Capuzzo. What's up?"

"She hasn't come home."

I checked the time. A quarter to six.

"Okay, let's put out a bulletin."

"Already done, Captain. That priest—the cardinal—came by at five. He made some phone calls, and Chief Teodori is here."

"Who the hell is that?"

"Rapid response team, section three," Capuzzo said in a funereal voice. "He told me to track you down right away."

Section three. The homicide squad. This was all about Cardinal Alessandrini and the power of the Vatican. So much for it being a free country. The Pope chose the head of the government; the cardinals chose who was to investigate the presumed disappearance of an adult girl.

I drank some whiskey to calm myself and smoked yet another cigarette. Then I took a taxi to Via della Camilluccia. Waiting for me in

Elisa's office were Capuzzo, Cardinal Alessandrini and an obese man with his tie loose and his thin white hair disheveled who introduced himself as Chief Superintendent Teodori. They were sitting around the desk. I had the impression that Alessandrini recognized the crumpled T-shirt and jeans he'd seen me in twenty-four hours earlier, but he made no comment.

"Good afternoon, Balistreri," Teodori said by way of greeting. He didn't shake my hand or indicate that I should sit. His tone wasn't exactly cordial.

Well, I wasn't going to be intimidated by a priest and a fat bureaucrat with a desk job. I didn't say hello to anyone, just took a seat.

"You know the story, Balistreri," Teodori said.

Old policemen irritated me in general; they were out of place. It was a profession to have from age thirty to fifty, then retirement. That is, for the unsuccessful, obviously.

Better to starve to death than find yourself at fifty still in the service of this fucking country.

Besides, as my high school teachers said, Michele Balistreri didn't recognize authority either by age or profession. "Severe problem with ignoring authority, linked to childhood traumas in his relationship with his father" as the psychologist diagnosed years later when he examined me for recruitment into the Secret Service.

"I've already arranged for a bulletin to be issued, Teodori," I said. I used just his last name, no title, exactly as he'd addressed me. Then I looked at Cardinal Alessandrini. "But I see that divine justice considers this insufficient."

Teodori's face got red, but Alessandrini smiled.

Real power wears a mask of cheerfulness.

"Don't take this the wrong way and please excuse me, Captain Balistreri," he said, emphasizing the title for Teodori's benefit, "but there are precise rules to follow in these situations, and you have followed them. In my opinion, however, this is not a normal situation."

And obviously between my judgment and his, it was his that counted for more. I didn't refer to this in any way—there was no need. Besides, the presence of Teodori bore ample witness to it.

"The cardinal knows Elisa Sordi and her family well, and he says it is highly unlikely that she has stayed away for so long," Teodori explained, as if I were a stupid child.

I decided not to help extricate Teodori from the difficult situation by telling him what he should do.

He turned to the cardinal, a little embarrassed.

"Naturally, Your Eminence," he said, "Captain Balistreri has followed the proper procedures."

I noticed the slight trembling of his sweaty hands. The room was stiflingly hot, despite the fact that the window was open. Elisa's flower was still sitting on the windowsill.

"The rapid response team will handle this case from now on. The local precinct will continue its investigations, but they're going to be stepped up," Teodori continued, addressing the cardinal.

I looked at Capuzzo, who was staring at the floor. It wasn't true; there was nothing to step up. Teodori was telling the cardinal a lie.

The cardinal read my thoughts.

"In what way will they be stepped up, Chief Superintendent Teodori?"

I saw the fat man turn pale and look at me uncertainly. But I was damned if I was going to help him out—the semiretired bureaucrat could sink in his own shit.

"We'll send a description to the border patrol and Interpol," he said at last.

He was lying, and knew he was lying. Perhaps he could push procedures forward by alerting colleagues on the Italian borders, but being a pain in the ass to Interpol over grown woman who had disappeared a little over twenty-four hours ago, without any sign of kidnapping or act of violence . . .

Alessandrini decided to take pity on him and rose from his seat.

"Very well, Chief Superintendent Teodori. Please thank the head of the rapid response team for assisting us."

Us. Who was this *us*? Himself and Elisa's parents? Or the Vatican higher-up who had called the Minister of the Interior? Perhaps the pontiff himself?

There was a knock on the door. Father Paul appeared, looking younger and more lost than usual.

"Your Eminence, I going San Valente if no more use to you."

The American priest's Italian was really improving.

"Wait for me downstairs, Father Paul," Alessandrini told him sternly.

I had the feeling that what happened next wouldn't be pleasant for Father Paul, whose eyes wandered around the room and came to rest on Elisa's desk, where they remained for a second. Then he went out, followed by the Cardinal.

. . . .

"This is serious, Balistreri," Teodori said. He was sweating like a pig while he tried to fill his pipe, and he was spilling tobacco all over Elisa Sordi's desk. I realized that the meeting and the impromptu search of the evening before had compromised anything Forensics might find in the room.

Capuzzo looked at me in alarm. He knew what I thought about detectives who smoked a pipe: low-grade imitators of Maigret. But I didn't say anything. My absence from the office could cause me some difficulties, but fortunately I had Angelo and the faithful Capuzzo to cover for me.

"Serious? Why is that, Teodori?"

"Because this isn't just any old residential complex."

He was irritated, as if it were the most natural thing in the world that investigative efforts should vary according to what was being investigated. He had the yellowish eyes of someone who suffered from liver problems and had blotchy skin that also suggested heart troubles. He made me feel sick, him and what he represented.

"Because of Cardinal Alessandrini?" I asked ingenuously.

Teodori swept his heavy, sweaty hand over Elisa's desk, disturbing several papers.

"Not just that. Someone far more important than the cardinal lives in the other building: Count Tommaso dei Banchi di Aglieno, senator and president of the Italian neo-monarchist party."

"I saw him yesterday afternoon. Then I saw him again when he was leaving at about a quarter past six," I offered innocently.

"I know, and do you know where he was going? To a meeting with the Minister of the Interior," Teodori said. He shook his head with concern. He was conveying what kind of person would have a meeting with a powerful Christian Democrat minister on a Sunday afternoon. The kind of person the count was.

"But he was with his wife," I said.

"He must have dropped her off somewhere on his way to see the Minister. Don't you get what we're dealing with here?"

I had understood, but Teodori felt obliged to inform me in detail. This was a great family with castles, estates, and its roots in medieval Italian history. The count's father's brother had fought on Franco's side with the Fascists and after the war had run off to Africa, where he'd accumulated great wealth and property. Count Tommaso's father had fought with the 10th MTB squadron and, when the association between the House of Savoy and Mussolini was broken off, had remained on the King's side. After the war he presided over the pro-monarchy committee that lost the referendum in 1946 and following this dishonor had shot himself in the head. Count Tommaso was fourteen years old and had assumed the burden of bringing the monarchy back to Italy.

Elisa Sordi, on the other hand, was a beautiful young woman from a working-class neighborhood who stumbled into a luxurious residential complex where she was surrounded by powerful men.

"Capuzzo, naturally you checked if there were—"

"Everything, Captain Balistreri, everything. Despite the crazy celebrations, no deaths reported. Just some injuries from fireworks and a few kids who fell off car roofs—nothing serious."

"All we can do is wait," said Teodori.

"Well, apart from alerting our colleagues on the borders and Interpol," I added sarcastically.

Teodori turned his yellow eyes on me. He wondered if I was more ignorant or arrogant.

"Naturally," he said. "But let's hope this beautiful young lady is recovering somewhere from a long night of celebrating."

Clerics and aristocrats. Mussolini had always distrusted both their tribes. He'd flattered them to keep them happy in order to hide the basic distrust he felt. And I felt the same way too. But I wouldn't have allowed myself to be fucked over as he had.

We agreed to touch base with Teodori the next morning. Then I tried to find Angelo, but he'd already left. I called Paola's apartment. Cristiana replied.

"They're not here. Paola had tickets for *Aida* at the Caracalla Baths. Can you come and pick me up, Michele?"

I made an excuse. I'd gotten all I'd wanted from her, and I didn't want to risk her leaving her fiancé. I wanted to spend the evening drinking and trying to score in some bar, far away from the luxe life, illustrious people, and Elisa Sordi.

FRIDAY, JULY 16, 1982

FOR SEVERAL DAYS THERE was neither sight nor sound of her. Teodori, whom I spoke to every day on the telephone, maintained that the girl's disappearance could be an "elopement," possibly even abroad. She had done it secretly, perhaps, because she was lacking the courage to be open about it.

I tried not to think about it, squashing the thought like an annoying insect. I hadn't seen or heard from Angelo and had shut myself away between the office and the studio apartment in Garbatella, rotating the casual female company picked up in Trastevere's bars and dives. I was smoking more than usual, drinking more than usual, and screwing more than usual. More than anything else, I didn't want to be alone. As if those things could keep away the gnawing pangs I felt over Elisa Sordi.

Teodori called me on the Friday. A homeless man sleeping on the banks of the Tiber just past Ponte Milvio had found a woman's body. I raced over there with Capuzzo, as if by going fast we could make up for the time I'd wasted back when it counted.

On the dry riverbank, exposed by the summer drought, a group of policemen stood around a dead body. The corpse, which was naked, had been attacked by insects and was in an advanced state of decomposition. It was covered with injuries from rats and shrubs along the river, along with obvious knife wounds and cigarette burns. Although heavy blows had devastated the face, I could see it was that of Elisa Sordi. There was no mistaking that incredibly beautiful hair, the figure, the color of her skin. I had seen other corpses, but this death was new to me; it went way beyond the usual violence.

Teodori was standing in front of the body, white as a sheet. His hands were trembling, and he was sweating feverishly in his absurd suit and loosened tie. Capuzzo was holding on to his stomach and trying to breathe deeply, his mouth gaping wide. I had to take control of the situation. I sent Capuzzo away before he threw up. A forensic pathologist was bent over the girl's corpse.

I approached Teodori. "We should clear everyone away so that Forensics can—"

"Of course, of course!" he said. He gave orders, and then we were alone with the pathologist.

"Is it Elisa Sordi?" Teodori asked me. It was as if she were a relative and I was there to identify her.

I nodded yes, then walked away to have a cigarette. At the top of the hill, a line of the usual curiosity seekers had formed along the road. They were lazily licking away at ice cream cones, craning their necks in order to better enjoy the spectacle. I called Capuzzo and two officers and told them to break up the crowd. When I had finished my cigarette, I went back to Teodori, who was talking to the medical examiner.

"She's been dead for days. There are signs of violence. It was a slow and painful death. Unless she was dead before she was beaten and burned—we'll know after we do an autopsy."

Teodori looked lost in thought.

"What was the cause of death?" he asked.

The medical examiner shook his head. "I don't think she drowned. She must have been dead already when she was dumped in the river. Cardiac arrest or suffocation. She's been dead for several days, maybe even since Sunday."

I saw that young, devastated body with different eyes. I thought of that summer twelve years ago, in 1970, when I was escaping over the sea from what I had left in the sea, and from the mistakes I never wanted to call sins, as Christians do. That cycle of feelings that leads to a kind of paralysis: guilt, remorse, repentance. The lifeblood of the soul. Wounds that never heal.

. . . .

Elisa's parents were sitting on a bench in the police station. A friend had told them after hearing news of the discovery on the radio. It was the wonderful new world of news in real time with a plethora of private radio stations hunting for the sensation that only bad news could guarantee. No one was taking any notice of the two poor things. Police officers and members of the public walked past them, going about their everyday business. From an open office door you could hear the laughter of those making plans for the weekend.

When they saw me coming, they rose to their feet like two well-disciplined schoolchildren and immediately I realized I couldn't look them in the face. Mr. Sordi put an arm around the shoulders of his Giovanna, who was crying silently. In the summer half-light of that squalid office, my eyes went from Amedeo Sordi's gray jacket, which was too large for him, to the furrow in his brow now deeper than the lines scored from cheek to mouth in his pale complexion, to the single tear running from Giovanna Sordi's eyes, to the beam of July sunlight that came in through a window and reflected on the glossy photo of her daughter she held in her hands. They spoke not a word and asked me nothing.

The last thing these parents needed were the condolences of a young policeman frustrated with his own failure. In the end, I managed a rote "I'm sorry for your loss." Then I shut myself in my office. What was I sorry about? The destruction of a young life? Two parents who might as well have lost their own lives? That weekend I might not go dancing and get drunk in one of the clubs by the beach. I might not fuck anyone that weekend. That would go on for several days, a week perhaps. Then I'd start my routine again: office, poker, whiskey, women, sleep.

But those two parents would never sleep easily again. Every night they would look into their only daughter's bedroom, as empty as the rest of their lives. And they'd think of me, blind drunk, saying "Perhaps Elisa's gone to watch the game with some friends."

I squashed the thought angrily. What was done was done. Only the future counted.

I downed a bottle of whiskey and reflected on the fact that this wasn't the kind of childish melodrama that usually nourished my baser instincts. I was no longer the "Michelino" who watched Westerns, the fearless cowboy who killed all the bad guys. I was a man of thirty-two who didn't give a shit about anyone, not even himself. I knew the reasons well enough—they were all very clear.

So, what the fuck was I looking for? Did I want to seek absolution? Did I want to escape eternal regret by tracking down the evildoers? And what was evil?

It changed little; fate was not in agreement with me anyway.

SATURDAY, JULY 17, 1982

THE HEAD OF HOMICIDE handed the investigation over to Teodori. At first I wondered why they'd chosen someone of retirement age who was past his prime. I still didn't understand all the subtleties of politics, in particular the politics of the Christian Democrats.

What I did know was that there were powerful forces surrounding Elisa Sordi's death. A luxury residential complex, a cardinal, an aristocratic senator who wanted to bring back the king to rule Italy: spiritual power on the one hand, temporal power on the other. On the other side, two parents from the working class and some girl of theirs from the outskirts. In all probability she'd asked for it, mixing with bad company or some random meathead attracted by her exceptional beauty.

I was assigned to be Teodori's deputy in the investigation because I was the precinct captain and was familiar with the residential complex, its inhabitants, and the victim. I'd even been on Via della Camilluccia that day, just before Elisa Sordi went out for her last walk before the World Cup final. I'd spoken with her that afternoon, as the phone records showed. That was an accident, of course. I'd been looking for Dioguardi. In any case, I was Teodori's ideal stooge.

It was another indication of the superficiality of the Italian police's bureaucracy that no one in the Flying Squad went to check the personal details in my file. If they had, they'd have kept me a thousand miles away from the paradise of Via della Camilluccia and that inquiry.

Reconstructing the facts was the easy part. After lunch, Elisa worked in her office. Her mother spoke to her just after 6:00, immediately after my call. Before 6:30 the concierge had gone to her office to pick up a file to take to Cardinal Alessandrini. But no one saw Elisa Sordi when she left at 6:30. By that time, the complex was deserted. I had seen Paul leave, and then all the others afterward. The priest from the neighboring parish confirmed that he had seen the concierge, now in a village in India, in the front pew at Mass that evening.

When I went to Teodori's office for the first time, his young secretary, Vanessa, caught my eye right away. She was tall and wore her black hair in a pageboy. She was narrow through the hips and chest, but she had great legs.

Teodori had a small office, a clear sign he wasn't held in much esteem. The posters on the walls were of Italian seaside resorts in the middle of winter. Pretty depressing. He was slumped behind a desk that was in chaos, pipe tobacco all over the place, no air-conditioning, and a ceiling fan that made his papers fly around, adding to the general disorder.

"The problem is that we don't know whether the girl was taken away before, during, or after the match. The first results of the autopsy indicate that she was already dead on Sunday, but it's impossible to give a precise time with the body in the condition it's in." Teodori's tone was grave.

"We don't know whether she was taken forcibly or went with someone of her own free will," I objected.

Teodori gave me a funny look. "Balistreri, don't let your imagination run wild. The violence lasted for a long time. A psycho did this. An animal who gets pleasure from making people suffer."

"Okay, but maybe she knew this animal."

"Sure—one of her friends from her neighborhood," Teodori agreed. The Sordis' working-class neighborhood was certainly a long way from Vigna Clara and Via della Camilluccia, but it was hardly a notorious breeding-ground for maniacs.

I tried to object. "Elisa's parents say she didn't have a boyfriend. She was always in the office or at home studying. She never went out at night. Every so often, on a Saturday or a Sunday afternoon she saw Valerio Bona."

"We have to know where Bona was on Sunday from 6:30 on."

Of course, Bona was from a less well-off neighborhood, too, a member of the violent working class. A perfect suspect.

"We really should find out about everybody else, too," I put in.

Teodori looked surprised. "Everybody else? Who else?"

"Everybody who lives on Via della Camilluccia, where she worked. She was extraordinarily beautiful—she could have turned anybody's head."

Teodori's eyes were more yellow than usual. This line of reasoning didn't agree with his liver. "If you're referring to the senator, I've already checked the register at the ministry of the interior. Just for the record, obviously. The senator arrived at 6:50 p.m. and was with the minister from 7:00 to 7:30. From there he went straight home, where he entertained guests, and he didn't go out again."

"Who told you he didn't go out again?"

Teodori shot me a look. "All the general staff of his party were guests at his home, to see the match. Don't you think that's enough?"

"There were a lot of people, and maybe in the heat of the excitement," I said, to provoke him more than anything else.

He ignored me and continued talking.

"His son and his wife came home around 8:00. They watched the game, too, and then celebrated on the terrace."

How Teodori had come to know these details was a mystery.

"But before that? I saw them going out with the count around twenty past six. What did they do between that time and eight o'clock?"

"I don't know, and I see no reason to ask them."

Now Teodori was acting decidedly testy, banging the stem of his pipe forcefully on his desk, staring at a spot on the floor toward which he was directing his thoughts.

"Look, Teodori, I don't want to be a pain, but I find it hard to believe that there was a forcible kidnapping in the middle of a Roman street, even on a Sunday evening without many people around. She would have reacted. Someone would have heard her screaming."

"Young man, no one would authorize you to question these highly respectable people just because you find something hard to believe."

"There's also the distance," I added, putting a cigarette in my mouth.

"Please don't smoke in here. What about the distance?"

I still didn't know if he was really like this or just trying it on.

"The Tiber runs through all of Rome. The spot where her body was found is close to Via della Camilluccia."

"Exactly. The girl leaves her office. Someone attacks her and takes her down to the river."

"But how? By car? In broad daylight at six thirty in the evening? Rome was nearly deserted, but no one heard or saw anything?"

The phone rang and Teodori picked it up.

"No, no, I can't come right now. Tell the medical examiner I'll be there later."

His whole face was yellow. We were wasting time.

"You were saying, Balistreri?"

He stroked his sparse tufts of white hair with his sweaty hands.

"My thought is the murder occurred in a different way. Someone she knew gave her a lift, and they went down there together in agreement onto the riverbank. Perhaps Elisa thought they were only going to talk. And only then, among that foliage, the fury of the assassin was revealed. We need to get authorization to question Valerio Bona and all those in Via della Camilluccia."

Naturally Teodori decided to start with the working-class kid in the glasses.

. . . .

We tried to find Valerio Bona at his parents. They told us he'd gone to Mass, as he did every weekend, and then he had plans to go to Ostia, where he was participating in a regatta. We could try to speak to him at the sailing club at the end of the race.

It was already lunchtime, and Teodori decided he couldn't possibly go all that way to Ostia, where he might end up stuck in a traffic jam. When I offered to go alone, he appeared relieved.

"Naturally this would be informal, without a lawyer. He could refuse to speak to us," I explained.

"We're investigating a murder, not a bag-snatching. If Bona makes trouble we can interrupt his weekend, and tomorrow morning he can come in for an official interrogation."

Our wonderful justice system at work: it was already mapped out.

I called Angelo. We hadn't seen each other since our argument in the Camilluccia complex.

"Want to grab some dinner?"

"I'm not really in the mood, Michele."

It was time to make a move before the rift between us became permanent. I didn't want to lose this friendship because of my stubborn pride.

"I was wrong, Angelo, and you were right."

The only reply was silence. After a while I heard his voice, and it was more friendly.

"It's not your fault. Even if you'd started looking for her right away . . ."

He was generously coming to my assistance. As always.

"We don't know, Angelo. Maybe when they called us at the end of the first half Elisa was still alive. Maybe she was even alive after the game."

He sighed. I felt his suffering over the telephone line.

I changed the subject.

"I have to go to Ostia to question Valerio Bona. We want to know where he was when Elisa left the office."

"Michele, he's a good kid."

"Sometimes even good kids fuck up."

Silence. It was his way of showing disapproval. Maybe he was thinking that I was just going after the weakest link in the chain. We said good-bye.

I could easily have taken the train to Ostia, but I didn't feel like mingling with tourists and beachgoers. I hated public transportation.

Although there was no hurry, I put the siren on the roof of my Duetto and got there in half an hour. There was a huge crowd. Cars were parked everywhere. The beach was overflowing with people, and the glistening sea was full of swimmers and boats.

If she weren't dead, perhaps Elisa would have been there among the those who were eating ice cream, sunbathing, and swimming. Instead, her wounded body was lying in cold storage in the mortuary and her parents were looking at her empty room in a house in the suburbs.

I found the sailing club easily. The regatta was under way. I sat at a table under an umbrella on the terrace and relaxed with coffee and a cigarette. The two-man boats were Flying Dutchman class. Valerio Bona was in one of them. I deduced from this that Elisa's death hadn't shaken him up too much. Inexplicably, the kid had irritated me since the first time I'd laid eyes on him. And that gold crucifix round his neck. Elisa was out of his league. He was puny, and he had a small personality, too. That's what I thought as I sat in the sun and smoked. From there the boats were white dots moving along between buoys on the blue of the sea. I asked the people at a neighboring table, who were using binoculars to watch the regatta, if they knew who Valerio was.

"Of course. He's been sailing here since he was a child. He's in the second position in number twenty-two."

They lent me their binoculars. It took a while to find number twenty-two and get it into focus. What I saw was a surprise. Valerio Bona, wearing a sailing cap and sunglasses, was at the helm, his crucifix gleaming in the sun. His bearing and his every gesture suggested absolute calm and command of the situation. And yet they were at the end of a close-hauling maneuver with over twenty knots of wind. I watched his features closely. Only his lips were moving as he spoke to his partner at the jib. In the stretch before the wind, number twenty-two jib bed over and over, forcing the leading boat to do the same, and in the end Bona succeeded in passing it and crossed the finish line first. Through the binoculars I saw him take off his cap and sunglasses. There was no smile on the little bastard's face. He appeared to thank his fellow crewman.

I kept watching him as the crews came back to the marina to moor the boats. Valerio Bona was receiving compliments from all the contestants, thanking them in a serious and polite manner as he shook their calloused hands. He was confident, relaxed. Then his gaze met mine and he recognized me. I waved a hand to greet him. His face changed rapidly, and I saw once again what I had seen on the other occasions. He was ill at ease, anxious, insecure. Out of his boat, Valerio was without the shell that protected him from the world around him.

He came toward me, putting on sunglasses to cover his worried look. It would have been too easy to scare him.

"We've met before, Mr. Bona. I'm Captain Michele Balistreri and I'm investigating the murder of Elisa Sordi."

I showed him my badge, but he had already stopped a few feet from my table. "What do you want?" he asked hesitantly. I decided to play bad cop.

"You should get yourself a lawyer. You need to come to the police station for formal questioning."

His hands were trembling slightly. While he was standing there staring at me, some more sailors came by and congratulated him.

"Way to go, Valerio!" they said, clapping him on the back.

But he was no longer on the waves, he was back on land—a land that he felt was hostile and difficult. Here not even his faith was enough to calm him down and protect him from far worse weather.

"Please sit down. I'd like to ask you some questions. If you don't feel like answering them, we can always go to the Homicide offices back in Rome."

My authoritative tone convinced him. He sat facing the sun, staring at the sea, probably wishing he were still out there on a boat.

"When we met on Monday you said that you were a friend of Elisa Sordi's. Were you her boyfriend?"

I deliberately chose a yes-or-no question so he'd have to answer. He shook his head.

"No, we were just good friends."

The emphasis on *just* betrayed his disappointment. At the same time, having seen Elisa Sordi myself, I realized it couldn't have been easy for a guy to be just friends with her.

"How long had you known her?"

He pointed to the sea. "We met right here, last summer. She came to see a regatta with a group of friends, and a friend of hers introduced us to each other."

"Were you interested in her?"

I could sense the hostility behind the dark lenses. "Elisa was a lot like me. We came from similar families and we were both religious. We lived in the same neighborhood; we were practically neighbors. Most Sundays we went to Mass together."

I'd never had any sympathy for little couples who go to Mass together, especially since adolescence. Did they go there to pray or to be seen together?

"And did you speak only of God and works of charity, or did you do other things together, Mr. Bona?"

He ignored my tone. "Elisa was curious about everything; she wanted to know all about boats, about the wind and sails. I took her out and we talked a great deal. Or rather, I talked. She asked questions and listened."

I could just see it: he carefree and assured at the helm, she reassured by his shyness on land. Valerio Bona was the only male friend possible for a girl like Elisa Sordi. A faithful little altar boy. But perhaps she hadn't taken into account how, in the end, a friendship like that was impossible for an eighteen-year-old. However shy or awkward he was, he was still a young man with raging hormones.

"Did you see her often after that?"

"That summer we used to come to the beach on my moped and go out in the boat almost every day. Then we'd go for a walk, and at eight I'd take her home. Elisa's parents wanted her home for dinner. They're old-fashioned."

"So there was nothing between you?"

"I already told you, we were good friends. Is that really nothing?" Now his hostility was stronger than his insecurity. I could make use of that.

"A close friendship with a beautiful young woman your age. Was that enough for you, Mr. Bona?"

He twisted the cap in his hands and skirted that direct question.

"Elisa wanted to earn a little money to help out her parents, so I gave her a hand."

"Really? How?"

"I work for Count Tommaso dei Banchi di Aglieno. I mentioned her to him, and he mentioned her to Cardinal Alessandrini, who sent her to Dioguardi."

Quite a paper trail. "And what do you do for the count?"

"I do some filing and I type his correspondence on his computer."

I could hear in his tone that he didn't like the count much. It was probably the only thing we had in common. I decided this was the moment to change the subject.

"Were you here for a regatta last weekend?"

He nodded to show he was.

"But Elisa Sordi wasn't with you, was she? She had work to do."

He nodded again.

"While waiting I checked the regatta calendar. I saw that you won, but the Sunday regatta was in the morning."

"Yes, there are three heats: two on Saturday and the third on Sunday morning. Last Sunday I went to early Mass on my own, because Elisa had to work. Then I came here."

"What did you do after the regatta?"

"I went straight back to Rome. The game was that evening. I didn't want to get stuck in traffic coming back from the beach. I'm a big soccer fan."

"Did you go to see Elisa Sordi?" I already knew part of his reply, because I knew what Gina had said.

He was hesitant.

"I called her at work from a pay phone at about half past one, as soon as I got to Rome. I wanted to have lunch with her, but she wasn't there. She'd already left. So I hung around Via della Camilluccia and waited until she came back."

"Did you look for her in the cafés in the area?"

"I just waited on the corner and watched for her to come through the green gate. I didn't want that weird guy with the binoculars or Gina to see me. When I spotted Elisa I went up to her."

"Did you arrange a meeting for later?"

"No, Elisa said she wouldn't be done until six at the earliest. Then she had to go home to watch the game with her parents. They didn't want her to be late."

"But you could have waited for her and taken her home on your moped, seeing as you were neighbors."

It was difficult to decide how much his unease was habitual and how much was due to the question.

"No, Elisa didn't want me to wait for her." He was now somewhere between scared and aggressive.

"Was she upset? Did you argue?"

"I couldn't understand why she didn't want to—"

It was time to go in for the kill.

"Maybe she was meeting someone else."

He turned pale. I sensed his eyes were troubled behind the dark glasses, even though I couldn't see them.

"She hadn't arranged to meet anyone else," he answered stubbornly, his hands now worrying the gold crucifix, as if God could help him.

"How can you be sure? Couldn't she have been screwing around with someone without you knowing about it?"

This was too much even for someone as timid as Valerio Bona. "How can you talk like that about someone who's just been killed?" he said, standing up.

I stood up as well, and I towered over him. "You're right. I meant to say she could have been having sex with someone without you knowing about it. Is that better?"

He was both indignant and scared. "Elisa wasn't that kind of girl—"

"Give me a break," I said, interrupting him. "Do you know how many times I've heard that about girls who then turn out to be total sluts?"

I hated myself a little for being so rough, but I wanted to see whether Valerio Bona was capable of attacking someone and striking them. He tried to land a punch, but I was too strong for him, and too quick. I grabbed his wrist with an iron grip.

"Don't be stupid. I could arrest you for assaulting a public official."

A good many people had stopped to look at us. Several sailors came menacingly close. I waved my badge.

"Keep your distance and mind your own business," I ordered.

I was making him look bad on his home turf. I was doing it on purpose, because he was hiding something from me. I didn't give a damn about the consequences for him—a pious little neurotic fixated on God, sailing and his computer, who locked himself in the bathroom to masturbate after talking to Elisa Sordi.

I let go of his wrist. "Now, tell me what you did last Sunday."

Valerio Bona was shaking. "In the afternoon I went to the park in Villa Pamphili. I had an exam two days later; I had to study."

"And you were there all afternoon?"

"Until seven forty five. The sun was going down, so I rode my moped home to watch the game with my parents and some relatives."

"You didn't see anyone all afternoon?"

"There weren't many people in the park. I was completely alone with my books under a big tree."

"And you got home just in time for the start of the game?"

"Just before. My cousins were already there."

"And after the match you went out to celebrate?"

His face grew dark again. "They did, but I didn't. I was worried about the exam. I wanted to get some sleep."

"You stayed home alone? You, the big soccer fan?"

"Yes. I watched a few commentators talking about the game, and then I went to bed."

I decided to leave it at that, even though his story was hard to believe.

"You mentioned a weird guy with binoculars. Who did you mean?"

"The count's son. He spies on everyone from his balcony."

"Do you know Manfredi?"

Valerio made a face.

"He usually keeps his helmet on so people can't see his face. But three Saturdays ago I paid Elisa a surprise visit and found him there chatting with her. As soon as I got there, he found an excuse to leave. He didn't say one word to me."

"Did Elisa say what he wanted?"

"She met him outside in the courtyard a few months ago, one morning when it was raining. He had an umbrella, so he walked her from the gate over to Building B. Then he called her on the intercom around the time when she usually went and got a cappuccino in the bar. It was still raining, and he offered to walk her over again. I think he kept tabs on her with the binoculars and knew her schedule."

"Could be. Did you say anything to Elisa?"

"Yes, but she didn't think anything of it. She said he was always very polite and kind and every so often he came to the office to talk. She felt sorry for him."

"Elisa never said whether he hit on her?"

"She was positive he'd never do anything like that, but I'm not so sure. A guy like that . . ."

Elisa Sordi had been either a naive, kind-hearted soul or a tease. If I hadn't seen how embarrassed she'd been that day in Angelo's office, I would have assumed the latter.

"Did you ever see Manfredi again?"

"Just once, in the courtyard. He was wearing his helmet. I was waiting for Elisa next to the fountain. I was smoking a cigarette. He came up and told me to go outside the gate if I wanted to smoke. He stood there next to his Harley-Davidson and waited for me to go outside. Then he left."

"Did you see him on the balcony last Sunday when you were talking to Elisa?"

"I saw the reflection of his binoculars. He was spying on us."

"How did your exam go, Mr. Bona?"

He grimaced.

"Elisa's disappearance ruined my concentration. I withdrew."

I nodded over to boat number twenty-two.

"But her death hasn't affected your sailing abilities."

He looked at me seriously.

"You don't understand. The only time I stop thinking about it is when I'm on the boat."

"And when you do think about it, what do you think?"

"That Manfredi's dangerous," he said, immediately regretting his words. "Well, I think . . . maybe . . . I mean, I don't know."

I left feeling strangely satisfied.

. . . .

I arrived at the rapid response team headquarters after three hours stuck in traffic. Teodori had told me to wait for him. Vanessa wasn't there, so I went straight into his office.

On the desk sat a framed photograph of a teenage girl who was pretty enough, if a little chunky. She was wearing a lot of makeup. I knew that Teodori was separated from his wife and that he had an eighteen-year-old daughter named Claudia. A detective who had a daughter the same age as the murder victim. That might have helped Teodori understand the victim's state of mind, but he was too afraid that he might disturb the illustrious guests on Via della Camilluccia to act on it. And Claudia Teodori was certainly very different from Elisa Sordi—you only had to look at the photo to see that.

The light on the phone blinked to indicate two messages. Years working for the secret intelligence service had taught me that any source was legitimate and every opportunity should be taken. The first message was from a woman.

"Good afternoon, Mr. Teodori, this is the Via Alba clinic. We would like you to come by as soon as you can to see your daughter and talk to the doctors. Good-bye."

The second message was from a man.

"Teodori, Coccoluto here. I wanted to tell you not to worry. I've spoken to the public prosecutor and the judge. If we can find out who slipped her the pills she can plead a lesser charge."

Coccoluto worked in juvenile crime involving drugs and alcohol. Now I knew why they'd chosen Teodori for this investigation. He could be blackmailed. His daughter must have gotten into big trouble. It would be hard to convince him to disturb the tranquility of Via della Camilluccia. However, there was one pathway open, even if it was a very narrow one. I left him a message saying I'd call him later in the office.

. . . .

I parked the Duetto and went up to Gina's gatehouse, now occupied by her young daughter.

Five minutes later I was at the door of Building B penthouse. Father Paul, worried and much less his usual sparkling self, came to open the door.

Alessandrini sat at the same desk where I'd seen him the previous Sunday. He didn't get up to shake my hand.

"Any news, Captain Balistreri?"

"Not at the moment. I'm here to ask for a helping hand."

"Earthly justice isn't my field, Captain."

I decided that getting straight to the point was the best way with this man.

"You can help by allowing me to investigate this little corner of paradise."

I caught Paul's glance at the Cardinal. Alessandrini gave me a serious stare.

"And you think you need my permission? It appears to me that you're doing a fine job upholding the Italian state's freedom from the Vatican's shackles all on your own. However, you can ask me anything."

"There's also Building A," I said.

Alessandrini took off his glasses and massaged his temples, smiling.

"I imagine Chief Superintendent Teodori wouldn't approve of this conversation."

"If you want Elisa Sordi and her parents to get justice, you have to help me investigate. The girl worked for the Vatican. You have every right—"

The cardinal interrupted me with a gesture. "As you've seen, I have no problem getting the police involved. But that isn't the point. Elisa's body was found by the river. She'd left the office."

"She likely knew the killer. The river's too far to walk from here. Elisa must have gone there in a car or on a motorcycle. No one saw or heard a thing. Surely if she'd been kidnapped by a stranger she would have screamed."

"Even so, she had friends in her neighborhood, school friends—there are thousands of possible suspects," objected Alessandrini.

"I agree. But that would require her running into one of them. Dioguardi told Elisa only the night before that she'd have to work on Sunday, and until he and I came to your apartment, no one knew when she'd be able to leave."

Alessandrini was silent for a moment. "Very well. I'll see to it that you can question everyone so that you can clear away even the slightest suspicion. But the count won't be happy. You'll see."

"Thank you. We need to question everyone who lives or works here, including you, Your Eminence."

Alessandrini was silent for a while. Then he spoke.

"You want to know my whereabouts on Sunday after we left here with you and Angelo? As you'll recall, I took a taxi at six twenty. I entered the Vatican at six thirty. I went to pray in a chapel below the offices, where I remained for about an hour."

"Were you alone?" I asked. For some reason this powerful man didn't unnerve me. The difficult question came out lightly, easily.

"There are no witnesses who can confirm I was there. I came out of the Vatican toward eight, and that is recorded. I was here at home by about ten past eight, in time to see the game. Count Tommaso was parking his car precisely as I was exiting the taxi. We waved to each other from a distance. He was in a hurry, presumably because he had guests."

"Was his wife with him?"

The cardinal thought for a moment. "No, I don't think so. Before the game started I walked out onto the terrace. Rome was deserted by then. I saw Manfredi arrive on his motorcycle at eight fifteen."

"Was Manfredi alone?"

"Yes, he was wearing his helmet, as usual. He got off very quickly. He probably didn't want to miss the start of the game. He went right into Building A."

I wasn't satisfied, but there was little else I could ask. I turned to Father Paul.

"We met downstairs on Sunday about five thirty. I was coming up to see the cardinal, you were in a hurry—you were going to San Valente."

He looked at the cardinal and received a small nod. Permission to speak. "I went straight to San Valente. There was another volunteer there, Antonio. He drove the children to the parish youth club in our bus. They were there until eight."

"And what did you do for those two hours?"

"I cooked. At eight, when Antonio returned with the children, everything was ready. We ate in front of television."

"And after the game?"

"Antonio and I put the children to bed. Then we also went to sleep."

"Did you know Elisa Sordi, Father Paul?"

There was a shade of apprehension in those blue eyes that darted to Cardinal Alessandrini for a moment and then turned back to me.

"Of course."

"Did you ever talk to her?"

I felt Alessandrini's eyes on me, but I kept my gaze on Paul. Beneath those freckles something was stirring. He ran a nervous hand through his red curls.

"Every so often Elisa brought some papers here. Two, maybe three times."

"What did you talk about?"

It appeared to be painful for him to remember.

"About my vocation," he replied in a whisper.

I had to keep myself from laughing. Valerio Bona went to Mass with Elisa. Father Paul talked about his vocation with her. Manfredi escorted her courteously to a nearby café. Then someone dragged her under a bridge, violently murdered her, mutilated her body, and tossed it in the river like a piece of garbage. Perhaps after making the sign of the cross.

"Was Elisa planning to become a nun?" I spat out sarcastically.

Paul answered seriously.

"Perhaps. She asked many questions about the religious life."

I turned to Alessandrini.

"Do you know anything about this, Your Eminence?"

"I never exchanged more than a few words with the young woman when she delivered some documents. We spoke only about work."

The cardinal was deep in thought. It must have been a disturbing thought, because his usually affable features had hardened in a stern expression.

I turned to Paul. "Did you ever visit her in her office on the third floor?"

Now the flush and embarrassment were clear. "On Saturday she called me on the intercom."

"You mean the day before she disappeared?"

"Yes, about five o'clock. She asked if I would take some books up to the cardinal. We spoke for a few minutes."

"And what did you speak about?"

"About her work, that she was there on a Sunday, but that was okay. She said something strange: that she wanted me to hear her confession. I told her I wasn't a priest yet."

"And then she left?"

He hesitated, then continued. "I waved good-bye from the terrace. She was standing by the fountain with Gina. They both saw me and waved."

There was the motive for this little confession. There was a witness, the concierge, who would be coming back from India and perhaps would remember that they had exchanged good-byes.

"Then another thing happened," added Father Paul, looking worried.

My instinct told me what that was, before he could say it. "She waved good-bye to someone on the terrace of Building A?" I asked.

I could read the stunned look on Paul's face, and for the first time a mixture of respect and fear on the face of Cardinal Alessandrini.

"You knew already?" murmured Paul, confused.

"I don't know anything, except that I'm more convinced than ever that evil lurked in this little earthly paradise."

Father Paul nodded. "The boy with the binoculars is strange. He—"

Alessandrini decided it was time to put an end to this conversation.

"This isn't paradise, Captain Balistreri, but neither is it hell. You won't find any evil here. However, I will take what action I can, as I promised, so that the count will be obliged to cooperate with the police. As for Father Paul and myself, I think we have told you every-thing we know."

I had one more question for Paul, but I couldn't ask it then. *Did you see Elisa Sordi the Sunday she died?*

. . . .

I left as July's unrelenting sun was finally setting on the horizon. I looked up at the third-floor window, the office where Elisa Sordi used to work. The flower that had sat on the windowsill since before her death was now drooping and shriveled. I caught the usual reflection from Building A's penthouse. From there Manfredi could keep an eye on everything and everyone. He could see without being seen, the ideal condition for him. He could see Elisa Sordi's window. And in that moment, he could see me. I couldn't resist the temptation. I lit a cigarette and, blowing smoke through my nose, waved good-bye to him.

I walked across the magnificent grounds, enjoying my cigarette and the singing of the birds. I was in Rome, but it felt like the countryside. I glanced at the swimming pool. A woman in a bathing suit was lying on the grass, tanning in the sun's last rays. I'd already caught a glimpse of her while she was getting in the car with the count the previous Sunday. She could have been my age, although her physique was that of a twenty-year-old, lean and slender. I saw her face sideways on, extremely delicate features and tiny crows' feet in the corners of her eyes. She turned to look at me, her eyes a greenish-blue.

"Strictly speaking, smoking isn't permitted on the grounds," she said politely. It was a warning more than anything else. I looked instinctively toward Building A's terrace, but it was hidden by the trees.

I should have said that I had lit it on purpose to provoke that overbearing husband of hers and her nosy young son. In that way we could have spoken. Instead, I did something very unlike me, meaning I did the diplomatic thing. I mumbled a few words of apology, stubbed the cigarette out on the ground and then picked up the stub and put it in my pocket. I cursed myself; the count was making me feel uncomfortable in a way I never had. I'd met men who were just as powerful and dangerous, but the difference was that I appreciated some things about Count Tommaso dei Banchi di Aglieno. Or at least I would have appreciated those things at one time, in my bad years: uncompromising belief in an idea, whatever the cost. There were other things I detested in him, such as fidelity to a king who had rejected Fascism and favored a medieval aristocratic system that left power over land and people in the hands of a few.

Whatever it was, I'd had a bellyful of that unease and wanted to get away from there as soon as possible. I crossed the city in my Duetto with the top down in the first cool of sunset. Thanks to a special permit I was allowed to enter the historic center, which was closed to traffic. I parked nonchalantly next to a squad car below the Spanish Steps, showing my badge to the men in uniform. I bought a large cone of pistachio and chocolate ice cream and leaned against the Duetto looking around, shamelessly eyeing up the beautiful female tourists. And between the fountain and the steps there were plenty of them, some already looking curiously at the red Spider and the dark sun-tanned young man not giving a shit about the cops while peacefully enjoying his ice cream. A platinum blonde, suntanned and elegant in high heels, was coming out of Via Condotti with a Gucci shoulder bag and wearing a short Valentino dress. She was about ten years older than I was.

It took me only a moment to see the moped coming and the two kids without helmets. The one behind stretched out his arm to grab hold of the bag and wrench it from the blonde in one swift move. In an instant and with a loud slap, my pistachio and chocolate cone was plastered over the eyes of the one in front. The moped wobbled off course, hit the edge of the fountain, and overturned, taking the two kids with it as it fell.

The patrolmen ran over. I again showed my badge and recovered the lady's Gucci bag, leaving my colleagues to deal with the two little would-be thieves.

"They're juveniles, Captain. We'll take their names and let them go if they don't have records," one of the officers said.

I shot a glance at the two kids. They were from the suburbs for sure. One was wearing an earring; the other had a Che Guevara tattoo on his muscular biceps. "No. Lock them up. A night in jail will be good for them."

The woman was waiting for me off to the side. She held her shoes in one hand.

"Broken heel," she explained with a smile.

She was as tall as I was, even without her shoes. Then I noticed the wedding band and diamond ring on her left hand.

"You can't walk around barefoot. Let me give you a ride," I offered, pointing to my car. She smiled.

"I haven't ridden in one of those in ages, but I remember it was fun."

The patrolmen were watching me, and I could imagine what they were saying to each other.

"Where do you live?"

"In London, with my husband and two children," she replied.

"Well, I can hardly take you all the way there. Where are you staying in Rome?"

She pointed to the Spanish Steps leading up to Santa Trinità dei Monti.

"I'm at the Hotel Hassler up there. But if you're not in a hurry, I'd love a tour. This car is bound to make me feel like a kid again, and I see you can drive through the zones forbidden to common mortals."

In the Duetto with the top down, we crossed the city. The golden domes of Rome's many churches were lit by the setting sun. I drove slowly into the pedestrian area. Mine was the only vehicle. All around us were Romans and tourists heading out on a Saturday night. She asked me to show her Piazza Navona and do a loop around the Fountain of the Four Rivers, and I obliged her, to the surprise of the tourists.

"This is the car from *The Graduate*, isn't it?" she asked me, while we were driving up toward Santa Trinità dei Monti.

"Yeah, the one Dustin Hoffman drives."

"It suits you. You're as good-looking as he is, but taller."

It was dark by the time we got to her hotel.

"Thanks for rescuing my bag. And thanks for the tour," she said, turning toward me.

I couldn't tell whether she was teasing me or being serious.

"And I'm sorry about your gelato," she continued. "If it weren't impossible to park here in front I'd ask you to come in with me—the gelato at this hotel is exceptional."

I put the top up and left the car directly under a sign that said no parking. all vehicles will be towed. On the windshield I left my own sign, one that clearly said, police. on duty.

The vanilla gelato came with strawberries and whipped cream, and champagne was delivered as she was taking a shower. She stepped out of the bathroom in her robe, and I opened the bottle.

"You won't believe it, Michele, but this is the first time I've strayed in seven years of marriage. I'm a little nervous."

"Let me take care of it. Just sit back and relax."

She laughed as I slipped the robe off of her and lowered her naked body onto the bed. She laughed as I tied her wrists together with the belt from the robe. She laughed while I placed the sleep mask thoughtfully provided by the hotel over her eyes. She laughed some more as I spread the vanilla gelato, the whipped cream, and the strawberries on the most sensitive parts of her body.

Then I began to eat my dessert.

SUNDAY, JULY 18, 1982

I DIDN'T GO BACK TO see Teodori. I didn't even phone him. After my ice cream treat, I dozed off between the hotel's elegant sheets and slept like a baby.

I left early in the morning. The elegant lady was going off to Florence where she was to meet her husband, who was arriving from London. I had the impression she'd perhaps enjoyed things too much and gave her a wrong number so I wouldn't have her in my hair again, then went back to my apartment in Garbatella where I went back to sleep.

The telephone woke me toward midday. I thought it would be Teodori and answered rudely in a sleepy voice. I'd taken a day off and didn't want anyone being a pain in the ass.

"Michele, you sound awful. Rough night?"

It was my brother, Alberto. I'd completely forgotten about his invitation for lunch and an afternoon of cards. His girlfriend was back home in Germany visiting her parents, and he didn't have one of his usual working weekends. He'd invited Angelo and me for lunch, and then a colleague of his was to join us for some poker.

My exemplary brother was excellent at everything, even cooking. A cum laude degree in engineering, a job as an executive for a multinational, good contacts in all the political parties, with the exception of the extreme far right, a beautiful apartment with a terrace, and a girlfriend who would be the perfect mother to his future children. I should have hated him, but I admired him instead. Not only had he gotten me out of trouble, but he'd never made a big deal out of it, and because his manner wasn't my father's utilitarian moderation, which was the acceptable side of arrogance. No, Alberto was a moderate in his soul; he believed compromise was the source of well-being and happiness for everyone.

Angelo was already there when I arrived; he and Alberto enjoyed cooking together, and their styles complemented each other. Alberto was a sophisticated chef, Angelo a down-to-earth cook. My job was to set the table, clear the table, and put the dishes in the dishwasher.

We ate pasta salad and Caprese salad and sipped white wine. It was extremely hot, but the terrace had a little pergola roof.

"You look tired. Aren't you sleeping well?"

There was no irony in my brother's question. As usual, he was simply worried about me.

"It's so hot and noisy at night. Thank God it's Sunday and everybody's at the beach. Last Sunday everyone stayed in town to see the game."

"Italy's win was so good for the country, though. Sales taxes alone were far above average."

"A country whose citizens pay taxes on the basis of soccer results isn't exactly a great civilization."

Such a country deserves a police captain who drives around pedestrian zones in his Duetto to pick up female tourists.

We talked politics so that we could talk about ourselves without making personal judgments, because we are the way we see the world. And the way I saw it was still quite brutal. On the one hand there were the honest and innocent, usually the impoverished. On the other there were the criminals and cheats, including the many in suit and tie who sat on boards of directors, in government, in public administration, and in the Vatican.

In my younger years I had dreamed that this system would explode and drag the wheeler-dealers who infested Italy into the mud, shamed and ruined. But the only ruin was mine. I cooperated with the secret intelligence service as soon as I realized that my neo-fascist friends had become murderers, manipulated by special interests and attacking entire groups of innocent and defenseless people. They had dishonored our ideals. But the intelligence service was linked to those same special interests, as I came to understand during the kidnapping of Aldo Moro in 1978. At that point, serving the state in an official capacity became the only way for me to avoid spiraling out of control.

"I'll never let myself be caught up in that dirt, Alberto. I think I'll relax for another couple of years and then go back to Africa and hunt lions and take idiot tourists on vacations."

Alberto shook his head, somewhere between amusement and concern.

"Italy was a poor country ruined by the war. Now it's risen up again. These politicians, Catholics and Communists, industrialists and the Church, also did a few good things, don't you think?" my brother said.

"They're the ones who advised Mussolini to go to war and then abandoned him. They were all over industry and in the Vatican. Then, suddenly, at the end of the war they all were anti-Fascists."

"That's just not true. It was Mussolini who declared war and decreed the racial laws. Anti-Fascists were persecuted and killed by Fascists, just like the Italian military killed members of the Libyan resistance."

Only Alberto could risk making a comment like that in front of me and not suffer any consequences.

My high school history teacher in Libya was a skinny guy with a beard who wore a parka, jeans, and gym shoes. A young left-wing teacher who had accepted that poverty-stricken position in Tripoli in order to have a permanent job. He never missed an opportunity to tell us what he thought of our colonialist grandfathers and fathers. One day, an hour before recess, he was talking about Italo Balbo, Marshal Graziani, and the criminal clique that deported and massacred the Libyan resistance. I knew this to be true, but this guy had no right to talk about it and link our colonialist families with actions like those.

Together with two kids who thought as I did, I went up to him in the courtyard during break.

"My grandfather came to Libya in 1911. He organized the olive-oil industry. He and other Italian colonists built roads where there had been only sand, made the water drinkable, and set up the vocational schools for young Arabs. Is he a criminal?"

The teacher was smoking, and that also irritated me, given that it was forbidden for the students. He gave us an icy look.

"We'll discuss it in class, Balistreri."

I was beside myself. The advice my father and my brother Alberto gave me frequently, *Always count to ten*, vanished. It was as if I'd finally discovered who I was and was fed up with having to hide it. As I gave the teacher a shove and he fell to the courtyard cobbles, I knew that my life had reached a turning point. I'd read somewhere that very few of our adolescent actions have a determining effect on our adult lives. Well, that was one of the few.

While the teacher was shouting and all our classmates watched us with their mouths open, the three of us grabbed hold of him. I would have preferred to do it on my own, but it would have been impossible. I took his legs and the other two an arm each. We carried him to the goldfish pond like that and chucked him into it, along with our fears and school careers.

I smiled at my brother again. He knew what I was thinking.

"Thank you for reminding me. But this decadent and corrupt democracy will hand the country over to the Communist party or, worse still, into the hands of the Red Brigades." I was fully convinced of this, while Alberto was very relaxed about it.

"It'll never happen, Michele. You underestimate the Catholics' pragmatism and you overestimate Communism. It doesn't make sense anymore—it's over."

Naturally, as ever, he was right and I was wrong. It was a debate that had been going on all our lives, with variants cropping up according to the circumstances. It was a kind of mantra on our disagreements.

Angelo listened with interest, but in silence, to these discussions of ours, but never offered an opinion. It was one of his ways of getting to know us. While Alberto went to make the coffee, I was left alone with him. We sat there with a last glass of wine and a cigarette watching the slow Sunday traffic crawling alongside the Tiber five hundred feet below.

"Whoever did it knew her," I said, without looking at him.

"I don't want to talk about it, Michele, not as a friend. As a witness and even as a suspect, no problem. But only with Superintendent Teodori in an official capacity."

Angelo was sad, and sadness was so out of place in him I was put off from continuing.

"Just one thing, Angelo. Did you see or hear Elisa on Sunday morning?"

"I've already told you. I was with Paola the whole time until I came to pick you up at five. I called Elisa from Paola's at about two thirty. She reassured me that Gina would deliver the papers to the Cardinal at five o'clock. There was no need for me to come by. I never heard from her again. Maybe Teodori hasn't told you, but he's already questioned Paola about my whereabouts, and about yours, too, Michele."

So these were the investigations Teodori felt he was allowed to conduct. Valerio Bona, Angelo Dioguardi, and even Captain Michele Balistreri. The nobodies, leaving the untouchable ones in peace. Well, now it was time to shift gears.

I left Alberto's in the late afternoon, and it was evening by the time I arrived at the Villa Alba clinic. A nice quiet place, green and discreet. Visiting hours were long over. The reception area was deserted, except for one old nurse. I quickly showed her my police badge so she wouldn't be able to remember my name.

"I'm here to see Claudia Teodori," I said firmly.

"Visiting hours are over," she said stiffly, but not unkindly.

"I understand, and I wouldn't normally ask you to make an exception, but we're seeking confirmation of the toxicology report, and need it now."

"But we sent it right after the accident, when she was admitted."

"The copy you sent wasn't legible. The prosecutor's office wants me to take a look at the original."

"Why is it so urgent?" asked the nurse, perplexed.

"There's a meeting going on right now. The prosecutor wants to determine whether it was involuntary or premeditated. And the toxicology report is crucial to that."

"Premeditated? She was driving under the influence of drugs and alcohol. Do you think she hit the tree to kill her friend on purpose?"

In the end I got a look at the clinical file. When she arrived there with some abrasions, Claudia Teodori was out of her mind on amphetamines. Driving in that state was equivalent to firing both barrels of a loaded shotgun in the middle of a crowd. So much for premeditation. Unless the girl knew she'd taken them, which was all still to be proven.

MONDAY, JULY 19, 1982

PRESENTED MYSELF PUNCTUALLY AT eight in the morning at the Homicide office, ready to put up with Teodori's displeasure. Vanessa shot me a smile while she finished applying black polish to a long fingernail. It was the first time I'd seen her in a miniskirt.

I gave her an admiring glance. "You're looking pretty this morning."

"I've got an appointment with my landlord. I'm behind on my rent." She said it seriously, without looking at me, as she finished off her nails.

Teodori was in his office with a cappuccino and a brioche. His watery eyes were more yellow than usual and his cheeks were pale. But he was cheerful, even smarmy. He wanted something.

"Come in, Captain Balistreri. Do take a seat. Would you like my secretary to get you a coffee?"

I declined; his sudden kindness made me suspicious.

"There's been some progress," he began, dunking the pastry in the cappuccino so that some of the coffee overflowed onto his desk. "We have the autopsy results. Death definitely occurred on Sunday, a few hours after the game at the latest. The pathologist can't pinpoint the time exactly, but based on the state of decomposition and taking the Tiber's water temperature into account, he's sure it wasn't any later than that."

He paused for effect. "So, the murder took place between six thirty, when Elisa Sordi left Via della Camilluccia, and midnight."

I understood very well why this was good news for Teodori. All the illustrious suspects had an alibi, while Valerio Bona did not. I decided Teodori's good humor was such that I could risk smoking in his office, and I lit a cigarette. He didn't even notice.

"The victim has multiple lesions, hematomas from heavy blows, stab wounds, cigarette burns, and bites. It was long and painful. At least half an hour. She suffocated after a cloth or a cushion was placed over her mouth."

"Were the wounds inflicted before she died?" I asked.

"The hematomas, yes, including the one that fractured her cheekbone and her right eye socket. As for the bites, the cuts and the burns, it's hard to know given the state of the body. Also, some of the cuts and bites may have been caused by branches or by rats. There's one other important point, however: there was no sexual violation."

I took in the information with some surprise.

"No penetration in any orifice?" I asked, incredulous.

I hadn't realized Vanessa had come in to take away the cappuccino cup. She stood there, a mocking smile on her face, waiting for Teodori's answer. It was the second time something like this had happened to me, but Teodori's secretary was a very different person from Elisa Sordi. She was merely amused by the question's obscene nature and by our embarrassment.

"Would you like anything, Captain?" she asked as she picked up Teodori's empty cup.

I gave an explicit glance at her long legs in order to make my response crystal clear.

"Not for the moment, thanks, Vanessa. Perhaps something a little later, though."

The young woman went out and Teodori, a little unsettled, continued speaking.

"It's a good thing you were with Dioguardi the whole time; otherwise I'd be forced to consider you a suspect, especially given your history with women."

His tone was jocular, but not entirely. And I didn't like that kind of joke, even less coming from someone like Teodori

"Chief Superintendent Teodori, I've never hit a woman in my life, let along cut one or suffocated one. And unlike the man we're looking for, I enjoy good old-fashioned penetration."

Teodori handed me the pathologist's report.

"Not so fast, Balistreri. One more thing has come to light. Read it for yourself."

Signs of pregnancy terminated in the previous fifteen days.

No different from the rest, neither more nor less. This was my first thought, transgressive and cruel, accompanied by a small sense of relief, which was shameful. Elisa, like all the rest, was no saint. And in part she was asking for it.

"We need to interview all her male friends. At school, in her neighborhood, Valerio Bona," said Teodori.

"And those living on Via della Camilluccia, of course."

Strangely, Teodori smiled.

"Certainly, Via della Camilluccia as well, but let me handle that." He put on a bold and courageous face.

Now I understood all his tiptoeing. Cardinal Alessandrini must have kept his promise. But the pressure from the Vatican's high spheres was suppressed, and it all came down to Teodori's courageous and independent decision. Nevertheless, he didn't want me under his feet with my doubts about those illustrious citizens.

"How's your daughter, Claudia, feeling?" I asked him point-blank.

He jumped. He couldn't meet my eyes.

"I don't follow. What's my daughter got to do with anything?" he asked.

"Nothing. Just asking. Any good news from the medics? Or from Coccoluto or the judge?"

I wanted to make it very clear to him that I wouldn't accept any obstacles tumbling down from on high that he was obliged to submit to because of his family troubles. I didn't give a shit about his concerns.

There was a long silence, and then Teodori looked at me. "Captain Balistreri, my daughter's eighteen. She lost her mother six years ago to cancer. I've never had enough time to spend with her, and she's had trouble both in school and otherwise. This year she failed her exams. Ten days ago she also failed her driving test, but that evening she snuck off with my car and went to a club by the beach with a friend. They were dancing and drinking all night, and they took some pills. On the way home the car slammed into a tree. My daughter suffered minor injuries, but her friend died. They're saying my daughter had the pills before they went out, but she insists someone drugged her drink in the club. As you know, there's a difference."

He was hoping to attract my sympathy, him and his stupid spoiled daughter, but I'd seen far worse in Africa. Children of three years old wandering the gutters under the open sky, stomachs swollen with hunger, flies clustered around their eyes. I'd never had even a crumb of compassion for the debauched Italian bourgeoisie.

Teodori was forced to accept my presence on the job. The senator had already invited us over and was expecting us at ten o'clock sharp in his private offices on Via della Camilluccia. Teodori made me promise not to ask any indiscreet questions. As if there were discreet questions in a murder investigation.

As I was leaving, Vanessa handed me a business card. "In case you have an urgent need, Captain Balistreri."

On it was her telephone number.

. . . .

The private offices occupied the first and second floors of Building A, underneath the count's penthouse. We took a car, and we were at the gate within ten minutes. Teodori parked outside, the first sign that he intended to respect the powers-that-be. Gina's daughter opened the gate and said that the count's personal secretary was expecting us on the second floor. I looked toward the terrace and saw the usual reflection. I immediately lit a cigarette and made the usual sign of greeting mixed with disrespect.

"Who are you waving to?" Teodori asked with alarm.

"The count's son, Manfredi."

He looked startled. "You know Manfredi?"

"We've seen each other a few times from a distance."

Teodori's uncertain look betrayed all his tension. He was being forced to take me there against his will and now things were coming out that he didn't understand.

The Count's personal secretary was what you would have imagined: an elderly man with gray hair, impeccably dressed with the monarchist party's badge in his buttonhole. He led us into a drawing room, which was furnished with a few items of antique furniture that were clearly valuable. On the walls hung paintings of great land and sea battles. Heavy curtains blotted out the sunlight. A wealth that was very different from the Roman bourgeoisie; this was aristocratic opulence, dark and serious, and in some ways menacing.

We waited standing, looking at the paintings. Teodori seemed intimidated, as if those painted battles were there to warn him about what was in store for him. The wait was only brief, however; one of the count's many fixations was punctuality.

I had already met him, but this time the effect was more striking. His cold black eyes sat above an imposing hooked nose, below which was drawn the subtle lines of his lips, mustache, and a well-groomed goatee. He was half a head taller than I was and towered over someone the size of Teodori. While he was shaking his hand I noticed his restrained repugnance over the head of the investigation's careless appearance.

When it was my turn the grip was stronger than before. He stared briefly into my eyes. "If you wish to proceed with this case you will have to do so in a dignified manner. At least in this residential complex."

So the little monster with the binoculars had tipped him off about my excesses. Besides, it was his way of giving us confirmation that at any moment he could have chucked us out and blocked the case. I held my tongue.

A waiter brought coffee and bottled water for the count, who turned to Teodori.

"I'm somewhat perplexed by this visit. I agreed to meet with you because the minister of the interior explained to me that there's been pressure from the other side of the Tiber to clear up any possible implications in this sad business of the girl."

He said "the other side of the Tiber" with a look of disgust. The minister of the interior had asked the count for a favor. Small favors between the powerful. All for the sake of that girl. In those few words and the way he pronounced them was revealed the count's vision of the world. A no-account plebeian, probably of loose morals, as those people always were, had gotten herself killed, most certainly by another plebeian, and it had all happened far away from the residential complex on Via della Camilluccia.

"Thank you," Teodori said. "We'll be quick."

"I can give you the next half-hour, then I'm off to Parliament for a vote."

"Then I'll get right to it. Did you know the young woman in question, Elisa Sordi?" Teodori began.

"One of my employees, Valerio Bona, gave me her résumé. I recommended her to the cardinal, but I hadn't met her. I don't normally have any contact with these people."

He said it exactly like that, *these people.*

"You didn't even know her by sight? She worked here for a pretty long time," I put in.

"I may have crossed paths with her in the courtyard, but honestly, I take very little notice of the other building. The two buildings are quite separate, as you can surely see."

"Turning to Sunday, July 11," Teodori said haltingly.

"Please proceed." The count knew perfectly well what this was about, but he wanted to make him feel even more ill at ease.

"We're trying to reconstruct the movements of all the people present in the residential complex on that day," Teodori explained.

"And can I ask what this has to do with a crime that was committed some ways away by people who have nothing to do with us?"

Teodori explained apologetically, "Well, it would be extremely useful to be able to reconstruct the victim's whereabouts that day. If anyone saw her—"

"What time did she arrive on Sunday?" asked the count, cutting him off.

He wasn't rude, but emphasized with every gesture that we were wasting his time without any reason and that he would decide when the conversation was over.

"Her card was punched at 11:00. Before that she went to Mass with her parents. Then she took public transportation to the office."

"I had already left. My parliamentary group was meeting at the Hotel Camilluccia, five minutes from here. I got there at half past ten. I returned home a little after five in the afternoon. I encountered Captain Balistreri below. He was chatting with the concierge. I took a shower, got dressed, and went out again with my wife and son at about a quarter past six. At the time, Captain Balistreri, you were leaving with Cardinal Alessandrini and Mr. Dioguardi."

I nodded in agreement and the count continued.

"I went to the minister of the interior's office for a short meeting we had scheduled some time ago. I came back here a little before the start of the game—I had invited several party members over for dinner. Coming back, I crossed paths with Cardinal Alessandrini, who was also coming home. My guests had already arrived. We watched the game and later celebrated quietly on the terrace with a toast."

Teodori watched me uneasily. He had no idea how to proceed, and if it had been up to him we would have left there and then.

I spoke as gently as I could. "Did your wife and son come with you to the minister of the interior's office?"

The question signaled a new turn in the conversation. The count shot me a quick glance and then turned to Teodori.

"I understood that you wanted to know whether any of us had seen the girl here."

"Or anywhere," I said, without allowing Teodori to respond.

This time the count's eyes met mine and remained there, but I read no embarrassment or fear in them, just a brief glimmer of respect.

"Do you think a member of my family could have had anything to do with that girl?"

He was alluding to the vast social gulf between the Banchi di Aglieno family and someone like Elisa Sordi.

"Perhaps a chance encounter? Assuming they weren't with you at the minister's."

The count smiled. "No, no matter how often the Minister's my guest here, this was a brief meeting to discuss some work. I dropped my wife, Ulla, in the city center, near the ministry. The shops were open in the area and she wanted to take a walk. She came home alone by taxi."

"And your son?"

"Manfredi left at the same time we did, on his motorcycle. He went to do a little weight training at his gym, one of the few in Rome that's open on Sunday afternoon. He came home a few minutes after I did, just before the game started."

We had reached a critical moment. "We also need to speak to your wife and your son," I said.

There was a long moment of silence. I had the impression that the count was weighing the pros and cons. To prohibit an interview with his family would create embarrassment, with the Minister being leaned on by the Vatican, and this would mean in some way contracting an awkward political debt for him. He decided it wasn't worth the trouble.

"Of course, but I must warn you that Ulla is very upset about what happened and my son, Manfredi, as perhaps you know, has issues and must be treated carefully."

"Perfectly clear, Count," said a thankful Teodori. "We'll be as brief with them as we were with you."

"Then I will escort you upstairs—they are both at home."

The penthouse was as large as it was gloomy. Dark parquet floors, heavy curtains, antique furniture. A long hallway led to two drawing rooms in succession. The first was covered in tapestries depicting battles in the Italian colonies and big game trophies from Africa and South America. The second was a museum of eighteenth and nineteenth-century furniture interspersed with modern black leather sofas. I was struck by the total absence of mirrors or any reflective surfaces. The count sat us down in another room while his personal secretary went to get the wife.

Ulla arrived immediately, as if she'd been forewarned. She was wearing a fancy sweatsuit, the expensive kind that's not made for sweating. Her hair was gathered in a short ponytail, which made her look younger, but the tiny lines etched around her mouth and her stunning blue-green eyes showed that she was over thirty, and that her life wasn't without stress. She didn't mention our brief encounter beside the pool, and we introduced ourselves.

She had little to add. On Sunday morning she left the apartment early to go to Mass. I caught a flash of disapproval on the count's face.

She returned at eleven and noticed Elisa, a beautiful young women she'd seen before, talking to Gina Giansanti..

"I didn't leave the house for the rest of the day. I slept a lot, because I was exhausted and guests were coming over to watch the game. When my husband returned at about five thirty, I gave final instructions to the cook and then went out with him to take a walk. He dropped me off on Via del Corso. It would have been six thirty, or maybe a little later."

"Did you by any chance see Elisa while you were walking downtown?" asked Teodori.

"No, absolutely not."

"Did you buy anything?" I asked.

She looked at me a little surprised, as if she was making an effort to remember.

"No, nothing. I hailed a taxi in Piazza Venezia and got here about a quarter past eight, a few minutes after my husband."

"Was Manfredi already home?" I asked.

"Manfredi got here soon after, about eight twenty. He always stays at the gym for at least an hour."

I understood why Manfredi didn't like the company of strangers and mirrors as soon as I saw him enter the room. Apart from that face, he was a normal kid: he was muscular, with powerful but not excessive pectorals and biceps, and almost as tall as me. But from the neck up he was a disaster area, a terrible trick of destiny. A harelip and mauvish birthmark as large as an apricot disfigured his face up to the swollen eyelid of his left eye. He had smooth black hair down to his shoulders and kept it over his face to cover the disfigured part. The only visible eye was very striking, having the same sea-green color as his mother's.

"The cop who makes funny faces," he said. He had the guttural voice of a young man who hadn't yet learned to control his hormones. He hadn't yet learned his father's art of self-control, but certainly displayed a good amount of aggression.

"Superintendent Teodori and Captain Balistreri want to ask you a few questions, Manfredi," said the count.

The young guy said nothing, but waited for us. In the air I picked up on something I knew very well: the apparent calmness of someone who's making an effort to contain his anger, an exercise in which I was highly specialized.

I observed this muscular young man with the disfigured face and wondered what thoughts passed through his head every day. It wasn't enough to get rid of mirrors to accept himself—perhaps he had to eliminate the negative reactions of others. Who could tell? A glance too many, a girl's giggle. An opinion was forming inside me. For just a second I wondered if it was an opinion or a prejudice. But I was used to trusting my instincts.

"It would be of great help to us if you could tell us whether you saw Elisa Sordi on Sunday," Teodori said. I wasn't happy with this opening shot, but I refrained from making a comment.

"I saw her from the terrace through my binoculars," Manfredi replied without a moment's hesitation.

"Binoculars?" exclaimed Teodori, taken somewhat by surprise.

"They were a gift from my father. The same ones the Italian Royal Navy used."

"And on Sunday you saw Elisa Sordi from the terrace through your binoculars?"

"Yes, three times. I saw her arrive around eleven. She spoke briefly with Gina and waved to my mother. Then I saw her leave about one, and she came back around two."

"Was she alone?"

"She went out alone. She came back with the guy who works on my father's computer."

"Were they arguing?" Teodori asked hopefully.

For a moment Manfredi brushed aside the lock of hair from the left side of his face. I believed it was so he could better observe the idiot in front of him.

"I could see, but I couldn't hear anything. The kid was waving his hands, but I don't know if they were arguing."

"What was she wearing?" I asked all of a sudden.

I saw a shadow cross the count's face, but he couldn't veto that kind of a question.

Manfredi didn't even glance my way.

"Blue jeans, a white sleeveless blouse, and low-heeled casual shoes."

"Was she wearing a bra?"

There was no need to look at the count to feel his hostility. I saw the embarrassed look Ulla gave her son. Manfredi didn't blink an eye.

"Yes, I remember seeing a strap fall down her arm."

As I had presumed, he was very observant.

"I truly do not understand what this type of question has to do with the matter," said the count.

"We didn't find the girl's clothes at the crime scene. Every detail is important, including whether she was wearing underwear."

Manfredi gave me a challenging look.

"Obviously, I couldn't say whether she was wearing panties or not."

There was no trace of irony in his voice; he wanted to get back at me for the way I'd acted in the courtyard.

"Manfredi!" Ulla said.

"Manfredi," the count repeated, "this is no time for jokes."

"I'm sorry," he said evenly. "I only wanted to help the police."

"Think back to Sunday," Teodori said. "Did you ever see Elisa close up?"

"No. Right after lunch I went to my room to rest. The air condition-ing was on. I was tired and I fell asleep. I only woke up when my father got home, just before six. Then we went out together about half past."

"And you went to the gym, and obviously you didn't see her there," Teodori suggested helpfully.

"I didn't see her. I came home in time for the game, which I watched in my room."

"Alone?" Teodori asked.

"I don't like crowds. The living room was full of people."

"And did you go out after the game to celebrate?" continued Teodori.

"I just said that I don't like crowds," the kid replied testily.

"Was there anyone in the gym with you?" I asked. Teodori looked nervous, but the count was calm.

"Just my personal trainer."

"Did you have a session scheduled with him?"

"We always see each other on Sunday afternoon from six forty five to seven forty five, when the gym's deserted."

"Of course, you don't like crowds," I said, knowing the remark was cruel.

The kid said nothing. He stared at me with his tough-guy attitude, rendered grotesque by his deformed lip and the mauve birthmark on the left side of his face covered by his long hair. The moment had arrived. I could feel Teodori champing at the bit, wanting to get away. As far as he was concerned, there was nothing more to ask.

I turned to the count.

"I know that your son spoke with Elisa Sordi before Sunday, July 11, and I'd like to ask him some questions that would aid us in our investigation. But these are sensitive matters. I think it would be better if we spoke to Manfredi alone, without his parents present."

Teodori turned pale and desperate, as if we were on one of the sinking ships in the pictures on the wall.

"These are routine questions," I explained. "But we have to ask them, especially since we believe that your son spoke to the victim alone at least once in her office."

The count looked at Manfredi, surprised. His tone was icy.

"In her office?" he asked his son.

More than any fear in his tone, it was surprise and disdain that his son, the future Conte dei Banchi di Aglieno, should be gossiping with a little slut from the suburbs. He would have found it more dignified if I'd said Manfredi had taken her to the banks of the Tiber, hit her, knocked her around, suffocated her, and thrown her in the river, rather than wasting time chatting with the worthless girl.

Manfredi looked at his father, then at his mother. Finally, he stood.

"Let's go to my room," he ordered, never letting down his guard. Teodori, clearly upset followed us hesitatingly down the length of the half-shadowed hall.

Manfredi's room was at the end of the hall. It wasn't particularly large. The ceiling was midnight blue and the walls were completely covered with posters, many of them for heavy-metal bands: Iron Maiden, Judas Priest, Motörhead, and Venom. The figures in the posters did not show their faces. They wore masks or had their backs turned. Unexpectedly, there was a photograph of his school class on the wall and I could understand why immediately. Manfredi was half hidden behind the teacher; you could see only his muscular body and the unblemished side of his face. There were no reflective surfaces in the room—the glass in the windows was nonreflective. There was a door to his private bathroom. The light outside entered weakly through the single window covered by a thick curtain.

There were a good many books, a lot for a young kid, and evidently all read. Among works of history, philosophy, and art, and collections of prints of ancient Rome, I recognized *Mein Kampf* and Nietzsche, *Beyond Good and Evil.* The last time I had seen those works I was in my own bedroom in Tripoli. On the wall, scrawled in black felt-tip in an angry adolescent's hand, was the aphorism I remembered well: *The great epochs of our life come when we gain the courage to rechristen our evil as what is the best in us.*

Manfredi leaned against a wall, as far away from us as possible. Then he turned directly to me.

"So, what else do you want to know?" he asked me.

"Just if and when you spoke to Elisa Sordi before Sunday, July 11," Teodori said meekly.

"Of course I spoke to her. So did everybody around here, everybody our age, at least. Even the young priest with the red hair spoke to her. Or do you think I've got less right than a priest to talk to a pretty girl?"

Terrified, Teodori mumbled something incomprehensible. Now he really was in a painting on the living room wall, aboard a sinking ship.

"You had as much right as any of us," I said, looking him straight in the eye. "As for hoping it would go beyond talking, well, that's another story."

His biceps flexed and his pectorals swelled. I watched the open palms of his hands. There were posters of martial arts movies on the walls, too, and I had no doubt the kid had more than a passing knowledge of the subject.

He told us calmly how he had first met Elisa Sordi. He knew what time she arrived in the morning. On that particular morning it had been raining, and through his binoculars he saw that she didn't have an umbrella. His account matched the story Elisa had told Valerio Bona.

"What did you talk about?"

"She asked me what I was studying. I told her I was doing classical studies at a private school. We just talked for a minute. She had work to do."

"Four Saturdays ago you went to see her in her office."

"She told me I could come by anytime."

He spoke as if this was the most normal thing in the world. As if a monster like that could hold any interest for a young goddess like Elisa Sordi. Perhaps the boy thought his family status gave him a special right over any peasant woman admitted into that paradise. A kind of modern *ius primae noctis*.

"Are you saying Elisa Sordi wanted your company?"

I put all the irony and incredulity I could into the question. He looked at me a long time while the only sound in the room was Teodori's labored breathing. This kid was going to hate me forever, whether he was guilty or not.

"I'm telling you what happened. If you don't believe me, that's your problem."

"All right. And what did you talk about?"

His smile made his face look even more grotesque.

"About true and false emotions. About love."

The little monster was trying to palm me off as if I was a child.

"You talked about love? Could you be more specific, please? It's important. Who said what?"

"There was something preying on Elisa's mind; she was upset. I think there were problems with that guy who followed her around."

"Did she say so?" Teodori asked hopefully.

"Not really. She did say that anyone who kept seeking the impossible in love would only end up unhappy."

My thoughts went back to the autopsy results. *Signs of termination of pregnancy carried out in the previous fifteen days.* A relationship that had been going on for some time—her period was late, a pregnancy test, then abortion. The conversation with Manfredi probably happened when the pregnancy was already discovered, several days before the abortion.

"Did you have sexual relations with Elisa Sordi?" I asked him point-blank.

Strangely, he had to stop and think. "I assume you've already considered that and determined it was impossible," he replied sarcastically.

"You could always have raped her," I said brutally.

"Captain Balistreri, that's enough! I don't approve of these tactics," Teodori said. Then he turned to Manfredi in an attempt to seem impartial.

"Ignore that comment, please. But you do need to answer Captain Balistreri's question."

"No," said Manfredi, "I don't need to do anything. I'm not answering anymore questions. I didn't kill Elisa Sordi. Whoever did was luckier than I am."

What on earth did that mean? Was he just referring to his face? There was no way of knowing. We took our leave with many apologies on Teodori's part. The count and Ulla were nowhere to be seen. The count's personal secretary saw us out, like a bouncer hustling a drunk customer out of a bar.

. . . .

We went back to Homicide in the car, myself at the wheel. Neither of us said a word. Then I saw the tears flowing silently from under Teodori's dark glasses.

"What's wrong?" I asked him. I was used to women's tears, and no longer gave them any thought, but coming from a grown man they got on my nerves.

"I've been on the force more than thirty years, Balistreri. And now, at the age of sixty, I find myself in this terrible situation: my hands are tied, and a young guy like you treats me like a fucking piece of shit."

His words contained both rage and humiliation. In a flash I realized that this was the pain of an ordinary, decent man reduced by circumstances.

"Don't worry, I won't say a word to anyone and Coccoluto will help your daughter out."

"Right, Coccoluto will help her out—if I look the other way in this investigation," he said bitterly.

So doubt had crept into his mind as well, after seeing Manfredi—his face, those muscles, that room with its violent posters, *Mein Kampf*—and hearing about his sweet little talks with Elisa.

"That's the price your conscience has to pay if you want Coccoluto to invent an imaginary dealer to save your daughter from the charge of murder."

"But he really exists, damn it!" he exploded in rage. "Claudia told me his name, but I swore not to tell anyone because she's afraid of what this animal will do. He hangs out with a dangerous crowd."

I looked at him in silence. Yellow tears. We only suffer like this for our children. I thought back to my father and what he went through because of me. And what I went through because of him. And Elisa Sordi's parents expecting justice. I was an insensitive shit, but I could sort this problem out. I didn't give a damn about any dangerous drug dealer, having seen far worse. And all of a sudden I felt sorry for Teodori and his yellow eyes.

I rested a hand on his shoulder.

"Teodori, why don't you pretend I'm *not* the police and tell me the name of this dealer?"

. . . .

After talking to Teodori, I found out more from a former colleague in the secret intelligence service. Claudia Teodori's dealer was a small fry by the name of Marco Fratini. He came from a good family. A drop-out from a private religious university, he was a handsome guy from one of Rome's wealthy neighborhoods and fond of the club scene. Except that one day, after skipping yet another exam, the father hits the roof and cuts him off completely. The good little bourgeois kid isn't studious but he's clever, so he immediately comes up with an alternative source of income. Given his clean appearance and excellent social contacts, he becomes the perfect pusher of amphetamines in the most fashionable clubs. He then discovers that some of those pills, dissolved in beer on the sly, make the girls easier to bend to his desires.

I could easily have picked him up and beaten the truth out of him. The only real danger was the gang that supplied him with the merchandise. To have them lose an important sales channel purely on account of saving Claudia Teodori could have led to even more serious consequences for the girl. I needed a plan.

．．．．

"Once you're in the car, don't take more than a minute, Vanessa. I don't want you putting yourself into any danger."

She laughed. "He'll be the one in danger. But please explain, Captain—what can I do in a minute?"

I told her, running my fingernails from her knee up her thigh: "Anything to get it over with in a minute."

She gave me a malicious look. "Captain, for years I had a boring boyfriend, especially in bed. So I learned a couple of tricks to speed things up. Should I describe them, so you can choose exactly what I should do to this little prick?"

"Theoretical discussions of sex aren't my thing. Just be careful."

The Striscia di Mare club in Ostia was packed with the youth of Rome and the surrounding area, all of them there to dance on the sand to Olivia Newton John. I arrived around midnight with three trusted colleagues, chosen for their impressive builds and beat-up faces. We made our way through the sea of mopeds parked outside the entrance. The bouncer had been notified beforehand and let us jump the line to a chorus of muttering and curses.

The dance floor on the sandy beach held an ocean of writhing figures. The guys were stripped to the waist, the girls mainly in shorts and tank tops or bikini tops. Many were stunning, but Vanessa naturally stood out, her magnificent legs shooting out from a pair of black leather shorts. She was the only one wearing ankle boots on the sand, and the tightly clinging top advertised her toned and muscular shoulders and arms. Her hands were decked with rings and ended with very long, black-polished nails. It was a costume I had suggested myself.

Fratini spotted Vanessa as soon as she hit the dance floor. He watched her dance alone, drinking beer from a bottle. She looked promising to him, I could tell. Of course, the extra handful of pills the guy from Marseilles gave him as a tip for his services as a dealer would come in handy for softening up this unbelievably hot girl.

He moved in with his gleaming smile as Vanessa was getting another beer from the bar by the dance floor.

"I'd pay anything for a private dance with you," he said, leaning close to her at the bar. Vanessa looked at him and gave a laugh.

"Maybe, but first let's see how you do in public."

They danced for nearly half an hour before he succeeded in dropping two yellow tablets in her beer. I was at the other end of the bar and gave her the sign that everything was going according to plan.

Vanessa began to behave exactly as Fratini expected her to. She was uninhibited, wild. When he invited her to go for a walk, she accepted readily.

They went out into the dark parking lot, where a cool breeze was coming in from the sea. Fratini was ecstatic. No little yellow pills for him, of course—that stuff made you lose control, like that idiot Claudia Teodori who had crashed her car.

As usual, he'd parked a little way off. He opened the back door of his BMW to reveal its white leather seats.

"Get in," he ordered.

Vanessa was laughing giddily.

"Get in yourself," she said teasingly. Then she pushed him down onto the seat and crouched between his knees.

Fratini laughed and tried to undo her shorts, but she brushed her long black fingernails from his knees up to his crotch.

"Ladies first," she said in a promising tone.

She pulled his jeans and his underwear down to his knees and began to stroke his penis. Her ten black painted nails were pin points of pleasure. Then she took him into her mouth.

"Damn, you're driving me crazy," Marco Fratini groaned.

He came in less than half a minute. Immediately after he did, Vanessa herself began to moan, but in a different way. Then she threw up in his lap. Fratini drew back, looking, horrified, at his penis—covered in a mixture of vomit and sperm, which was now dripping all over the BMW's white leather seats. Vanessa collapsed in a heap, heaving, froth bubbling from the side of her mouth. A moment later the other rear door of the car opened and two strong hands grabbed him by the armpits and lifted him from the car. A shove made him trip over the jeans that were still around his ankles. He fell half-naked to the ground.

Terrified, he found himself facing me and my three accomplices, who looked more like ex-cons than policemen. Trembling, he tried to stand and pull up his jeans, but another, more forceful shove was enough to send him back to the ground.

I bent over Vanessa, who gave me a wink.

"It's bad," I said to my accomplices seriously, "but no ambulances. If the boss finds out, we're fucked. Take her to the car. Her stomach needs to be pumped."

"She'll tell her father," one of my three guys said, playing his part.

"No, I'll talk to her later. She'll keep her mouth shut. If she doesn't, her father will have her hide and then ours. He'll rip the balls off this fucker here and feed them to him."

Lying half-naked on his back on the cobblestones, scared shitless, Fratini began to sob. One of my guys carried Vanessa to another car and took her away.

"Who are you?" Fratini mumbled, trembling all over.

I gave him a pitying look. "You just drugged and raped the only daughter, the underage daughter, of a capo in the Magliana gang. We were supposed to keep an eye on her, but the little bitch gave us the slip and hooked up with you, dickhead."

Marco Fratini saw that he was already dead. He'd always been unlucky; now he'd drugged the underage daughter of a dangerous criminal. Him, a former university student from a good family! They'd tear him to pieces.

"But I didn't did do anything to her," he whimpered.

I ripped the jeans brutally from his ankles and pulled out the yellow tablets. His sobs turned desperate.

"You're in the deepest shit possible. Even if we do everything we can to keep that spoiled little slut's mouth shut, she's used to doing just whatever the fuck she wants. And if there's a guy who turns her on she keeps coming back for more."

"But I'll disappear. I'll leave, I swear!"

He was on his knees, pulling up his briefs.

"Like we're going to fucking run that risk," I said to the two gorillas on either side of me.

"If we beat him to death here in the parking lot, they'll think it was just a fight outside a club," one of them observed.

"That way he'd be out of our hair forever," added another, totally calm.

"I'm sorry," I said, shaking the blackjack I'd taken from my pocket, "but we don't have much choice. To be on the safe side, we either put you six feet under or in prison. But we can't send you to prison, so that only leaves one choice."

Fratini had pissed himself and was trembling like a leaf. He raised his hand like a kindergartener. "But maybe I can send myself to prison," he said.

In great detail he told us about how he'd drugged Claudia Teodori and the accident that followed. A girl had died. If he confessed to having put pills in her glass without her knowing, then they'd give him a good few years in jail. He wouldn't ask for any extenuating circumstances.

After consulting briefly with my two accomplices, I advised him that we also had important friends in the police, that we would check his story and if he was lying we'd be back to rip his balls off ourselves.

When we deposited him in front of the police station in Ostia, he thanked us with tears in his eyes.

A short time later, while Fratini was making a full confession about the pills he'd secretly put in Claudia Teodori's beer, Vanessa and I were alone on a boat moored in Ostia's harbor. It belonged to a wealthy uncle of hers.

The sea breeze provided a bit of relief from the suffocating heat. We sat on the deck drinking ice-cold beer.

"What was the most difficult part?" I asked her.

She laughed, now a little drunk.

"Having to swallow that pill you gave me to make me throw up. Shit, Michele, it made me really sick."

"Without my little pill you'd have had to swallow something a lot worse."

She picked up a rope and held it out to me. "Do you know how to tie knots? It's important on a boat."

She wrapped the rope around my wrists, rapidly tied it into a double knot to secure me, and then knotted the rope tightly to the rudder.

"Good," she said, sitting back down. "Now you won't fall into the sea."

She took off one ankle boot. Her toenails were painted black to match her fingernails. She stretched out her leg and began to run her foot up my thigh.

TUESDAY, JULY 20, 1982

TEODORI LOOKED LESS PALE and less swollen, and his eyes were a little less yellow. He had shaved and his jacket, tie, and shirt matched. He was bursting with energy and optimism. His office was covered with photos of Elisa Sordi, the autopsy report, and, the biggest surprise of all, the possible alibis of not only Valerio Bona but also the inhabitants of Via della Camilluccia.

"We checked," he said, beaming. "Valerio Bona is the only one who isn't covered for the whole afternoon; then, after eight, he's got witnesses who say he was at home, although with all the chaos after the game we can't be sure."

"Father Paul?"

"The other volunteer, Antonio Orlandi, has confirmed his whole story."

"And Manfredi?"

"Same thing. His personal trainer at the Top Top is a Polish guy named Jan Deniak. He says Manfredi was with him for at least an hour, from a 6:45 to 8:00, doing weight training in the gym."

The rejuvenated Teodori had even very discreetly verified the count's movements: first at his party's meeting, then at the minister of the interior's. Everything had been confirmed, except there were no witnesses to Ulla's shopping expedition. Then from eight fifteen onward they were all at home with friends. And there was no doubt about Manfredi. Teodori had even double-checked when Cardinal Alessandrini arrived at and left the Vatican.

Almost apologetically, he continued, "We also ascertained that Dioguardi was with his girlfriend all day. Then he came to get you at five, and then the two of you were together after leaving Via della Camilluccia."

So you even checked my alibi.

"And the telephone records for the Sordi house?"

"The girl had nothing arranged for Sunday, so she didn't tell anyone she was going into the office. She was supposed to spend the day with her parents, going to mass, and then come home before the game."

"Did she make any calls from the office on Saturday or Sunday?"

"Only on Saturday, to tell her mother and Valerio Bona that she'd be working the next day. No outgoing calls on Sunday, only incoming calls from Angelo Dioguardi and her mother—and you, of course, Captain, when you were looking for Dioguardi."

There was no sarcasm in his "of course." If Teodori were harboring any doubts about my call, he'd let them go after Fratini's arrest.

When it came time to go Teodori took my hand in his. "I'm eternally grateful to you, Balistreri. I don't even want to know how you did it."

I didn't dare tell him for fear of his having a heart attack. The victim of the crime was back after a busy night, right there typing away at her desk, dressed soberly to cover the marks left from the night before.

FRIDAY, JULY 23, 1982

F OR THREE DAYS NOTHING new developed. We had tracked down all of Elisa Sordi's friends in her neighborhood and at school, questioned them, gotten their alibis, and checked telephone records. Result: zero point zero. No one regularly saw Elisa Sordi except Valerio Bona. No one knew she was at work that day except Valerio Bona, Dioguardi, and the inhabitants of the residential complex on Via della Camilluccia.

The last person to see Elisa Sordi alive, just after five o'clock, was the concierge, Gina Giansanti, who was in India and couldn't be reached. But the fact had been reported by her directly to me and confirmed by Cardinal Alessandrini, to whom she had delivered Elisa's work.

It was impossible to find out anything about Elisa's abortion. After abortions had narrowly escaped becoming illegal again in the previous year's referendum, the few clinics that performed them had thrown up a wall of secrecy; then there were the countless doctors and clinics that performed them on the sly. Abortion might have technically been legal in Italy, but it still felt clandestine.

Thankfully, my contacts in the secret intelligence service had made good use of those seventy-two hours. The information on Antonio Orlandi and Gianni, aka Jan Deniak, was interesting. When you dig for information, you find things. Always.

Besides volunteering for Alessandrini, Antonio Orlandi was a gym teacher in a private middle school. I went to see him in San Valente around seven in the evening, when he'd just begun his shift, taking advantage of Father Paul's absence. The kids were playing soccer, boys against girls, with Orlandi in goal.

It was still hot: you could hear the cicadas, and the cool of sunset was still a few hours off. The grass was overgrown, the white house where the kids lived was flaking, the single tree was pathetic. And yet there was a happy, positive atmosphere. Orlandi joined me under the tree. He was just over thirty with a clean and tidy air about him, though he came across as being perhaps a little too tidy.

"Your colleagues have already questioned me, several times," he said. He was turned away from me, watching the kids' game as intently as any World Cup final.

"Children are wonderful, aren't they?" I said casually.

"Sure," he replied. "All children are angels."

An answer straight out of the catechism. "Which do you like better, little boys or little girls?"

He looked at me, alarmed. "Aren't you supposed to be asking me about Father Paul's whereabouts on the day of the match?"

"No, my colleagues have already taken care of that. Father Paul got here before six. You took the kids off on a treasure hunt, and when you came back around eight Father Paul was here and supper was ready. Then you watched the game, put the kids to bed and about midnight you went to sleep yourselves. Is that right?"

"Yes, that's right," he said, now more at ease.

"How did you get your teaching job, Mr. Orlandi?"

Orlandi lit a cigarette and I did the same. He took his time answering.

"Cardinal Alessandrini told me the position was open," he said. I knew this already; I was only interested in the difficulty he had in spitting it out.

"Had you taught before?"

"I'd been a fitness instructor in a gym, but I had a physical education teaching degree."

"Did you apply for any public school jobs?"

"No," he said.

"Why not? Everyone else does."

He said nothing. I was torturing him.

A boy and a girl started to squabble. Orlandi got to his feet.

"Sit back down and answer my questions," I ordered. "Those kids you have no business teaching can work things out by themselves."

He looked at me, stunned. "What do you mean? Those children—"

I interrupted him as sharply as I knew how.

"At the age of seventeen you went to a parish on the city outskirts. You were charged with acts of obscenity in a public place in the presence of a twelve-year-old girl. What's a person with your record doing working here?"

I saw him stagger. He sat down heavily on the seat, his face in his hands.

"I didn't do anything," he murmured.

"Bullshit. The police report says you had your pants down."

"It was a public park. I was taking a leak behind a tree, the girl wandered away from her aunt, and she saw me."

"I don't think so. You were given a six-month suspended sentence. You avoided the charge of soliciting a minor because you were a minor, too, and because your lawyer was very good. He was paid for by the Vatican Curia."

"I never touched her, and it's never happened again," he said, terrified.

"You were given a pardon by Cardinal Alessandrini. If it weren't for him you wouldn't be teaching and you certainly wouldn't be here."

"That's true," he mumbled, "but what's this got to do with Father Paul?"

It was a stupid question. Orlandi was a pervert. Not to mention an idiot. If he was lying about Father Paul's alibi, he had good reason to do so.

. . . .

Jan Deniak worked in the evening as a bartender in a club in Trastevere. I called Angelo to come with me, as we'd seen very little of each
other and I was missing his company. He agreed to come, but I could
sense the split between us hadn't completely healed.

We drove up in the Duetto with the top down around ten. Piazza
Trilussa was crowded with drunk people. We couldn't get anywhere
with the car. The kids didn't give a damn about the cars wanting to
get through; they continued to down their beers in the middle of the
road and didn't even turn round.

"Let's leave it, Michele. We can park along the river, and it's only a
couple of steps to the club."

I honked the horn at a little group blocking the way. A girl
squealed and dropped her bottle of beer. The big guy she was with
turned around.

"Hey, shitheads, stuff that horn up your ass."

I was already out of the car, but the group continued to hurl insults.
I turned to the tall guy. "What did you say?"

Something in my tone or my look warned him off. "Well, is that
any way to behave?" he said, while the others got quiet.

I took the bottle of beer from his hand and spilled the contents on
the ground.

"Get out of the way right now," I ordered.

It was over the top. As with Valerio Bona, I was able to lead him
where I wanted. I saw him let fly, and I ducked. Then I let fly back
with an uppercut. The blow hit him right in the solar plexus and he
doubled over, gasping desperately for breath. I was waiting for him to
react again; I really wanted to hurt him. I felt a rage inside me, strong
and powerful. The guy had nothing to do with it, but I was careful not
to finish him off, so I could continue hitting him. At a certain point,
Angelo put a hand on my arm.

"Michele, please."

His look of suffering got to me. He knew where all the anger came
from. I went back to the car and without looking around, I put it
in reverse while the guy, still on the ground, was trying to catch his
breath. The road along the Tiber was packed with cars, so I parked on
a zebra crossing; seeing as I wasn't going to pay any fines, and given I

was on duty—not out on a bender like those degenerate young thugs. They were Italy's nouvelle riche, the Italy of the 1980s: easy money, tanning salons, fancy gyms, night clubs, weed for the poor, coke for the rich.

The club was impassable, the crowd spilling over outside. Beer, laughter, mopeds passing by, the smell of marijuana. The bartender all muscle in the black T-shirt was our Jan Deniak. One of those Poles who, thanks to the pope, had said good-bye to Communism's crap. A well-built athletic bartender. I wanted to observe him a little before I acted.

"Paola and I broke up," Angelo said out of the blue.

So that was why he'd agreed to come with me. Was he trying to make me feel guilty? No, Angelo Dioguardi was anything but mean. Something unbearable must have happened; unbearable, that is, for my sensitive friend, not for a cynic like me. Our very behavior on that awful night had been unbearable, so unbearable as to wreck Angelo and Paola's relationship.

"What does that mean for your job?" I asked, though I could guess the answer.

"I've given notice to the cardinal to find someone to take my place. I don't want to work there anymore."

"Bullshit, Angelo. You're not responsible for what happened."

I said it in a rage; if there was any responsibility it was mine. I was the policeman, not him. He shook his head, but said nothing. I could hardly recognize him. I tried to make him laugh.

"You could always make money from singing. With your voice you could fill any piano bar in Trastevere."

"No, I'm going to make money playing poker. Gambling's my real talent. And with the proceeds I'm going to make charitable donations, if I'm successful."

"So you're going to go pro?"

I had no doubt about his exceptional ability, but it was a tough world. For a nice guy like him it didn't look too promising.

"They won't eat me alive, Michele. I can look after myself, you'll see."

"Shame. I was counting on your presence in the piano bars to help me pick up women. Now that you're a free man we can team up."

I was trying to make him laugh, but the joke fell flat.

It must have been nearly impossible for Angelo Dioguardi to live with the guilt. He was a Catholic who believed in the last judgment, while I was a cynic who didn't believe in anything.

. . . .

Jan Deniak wasn't happy to see my badge. No one, guilty or innocent, was ever really happy to see a policeman's badge, but especially not a young immigrant in his place of work. He told the other bartender he was going to step out for five minutes, and then he led me through the fire door to a deserted backyard behind the bar that was filthy, strewn with garbage bags. I could still hear the laughter and the mopeds outside, but we were alone.

"I've got five minutes," he announced, flexing the overdeveloped, veiny muscles in his arms and shoulders.

I laughed. "Would you talk that way to the police in your wonderful communist homeland?"

He gave me a surly look. "I know my rights. I can turn around and go back to the bar whenever I like."

"And I can ask you to come down to the police station and hold you there for twenty-four hours. Have you learned the word *homicide* since you arrived in Italy?"

"What are you talking about?" he said, cutting me off. The bastard had balls, I had to give him that. I had to soften him up a bit before we got to the point.

"Anabolic steroids and other substances used to juice the muscles."

There was a moment of hesitation. "I don't know what you're talking about."

It was satisfying still having friends in the secret intelligence service. The lives of ministers, entrepreneurs, ordinary citizens, and criminal suspects were an open book. Jan Deniak was unlucky. Normally, no one would have been interested in him. But he was the personal trainer to a famous surgeon for whom he also did special sexual favors, and in exchange he received illegal drugs that he then sold at exorbitant prices to wealthy clients in the gym. Unfortunately for him the famous surgeon happened to be the brother of a minister under surveillance by my former colleagues.

"So, let's talk about Sunday, July 11. Do you remember that day?"

"Of course—you won the World Cup." He was relieved by the change of subject. Poor deluded fool.

"And you did weight training with Manfredi that evening from seven to eight, half an hour before the start of the match. There can't have been many people in the gym."

"Only Manfredi and me. I already said that down at the station."

"Bullshit. Time to start telling he truth."

He sneered and flexed.

"Oh, you're a tough guy, is that it?"

He hadn't noticed the rubber nightstick I slipped from my left sleeve. The blow to his right elbow paralyzed his arm and put him in obvious agony. I gave him a second blow to the kneecap before he could utter a sound.

The rubber nightstick is a wonderful tool, because it leaves no visible marks.

Jan fell to his knees, screaming in pain. "I'm going to fucking kill you, you bastard."

I gave him a slap on his forehead with my open hand so that he rolled over in the middle of the garbage. While he was trying to get up again, moaning in pain, I showed him the first photograph.

"You must be really good at giving blow jobs, Jan—the surgeon looks very pleased here."

He opened his eyes wide. He was still gasping for breath. I kicked him in the balls, but not too hard.

"Look, your Polish friend in the Vatican doesn't approve of swearing. And neither do I."

I waited while he tried to get up. After several attempts, he leaned heavily against the backyard wall so that he wouldn't fall over. I showed him other photographs. These depicted his friend handing him boxes of drugs. His eyes flickered from the photos to my face and back.

Leaving nothing to chance, I added, "The friends of mine who took these photos get really mad if anyone files a complaint. And if they get really mad they don't make a report—they just do away with people."

"What do you want from me?" he asked, now with a good deal of humility.

"I told you before: I want the truth. Manfredi was in the gym with you from seven and eight. Right?"

His hesitation was enough to give me the reply I wanted, but not enough to resolve the question for Teodori, the prosecutor, and the chief of police. Jan Deniak was between a rock and a hard place, and he was paralyzed. I had to help him choose.

"You're in big trouble, Jan. You won't go to prison for giving blow jobs to the surgeon, but you will go to prison for trafficking in anabolic steroids."

He looked at me. "Manfredi and I were there, I swear. We had an intense session, and it was a very hot day."

The phrase was left dangling. I took a little while to understand. He was sharper than he looked.

"Doesn't the gym have air-conditioning?" I asked.

Jan even managed a quiet laugh. "Sure. It's a luxury gym. No one could train in this heat."

That was that. Jan Deniak preferred being charged with giving false evidence to any possible trouble for Manfredi and the count. I had a full house with aces.

SATURDAY, JULY 24, 1982

E VEN THOUGH IT WAS Saturday, the electric company supplied the records of the gym's energy consumption by the end of the morning. Between seven and eight there was no noticeable increase in electricity. When the last members left at lunchtime on Sunday, the air-conditioning had been turned off, and it hadn't been turned back on the entire afternoon.

Jan Deniak was brought into the police station for questioning, and his lawyer advised him to tell the truth.

"I must have confused the days," Jan said. "Manfredi probably came at that time the day after."

"But his personal schedule is filled in between seven and eight on Sunday," countered Teodori, still hoping to find another explanation.

"I don't fill that in. The client does it."

There was still one question that remained to be asked, but neither Teodori nor the prosecutor wanted to address it. So I did.

"So, you were confused about the days, Mr. Deniak. Did anyone contribute to your confusion?"

He gave me a hateful look. I stared at him with half a smile and a finger in my mouth. I wanted to give him a good reminder of the photo with the surgeon before replying.

Jan capitulated. "Two or three days after, Manfredi reminded me that during the training we did together on Sunday afternoon I'd promised to let him try the new machine for the dorsal muscles. I told him that it hadn't been Sunday but Monday, but he insisted it had been Sunday. In the end, he convinced me I had been mistaken."

The rest of the afternoon was long and extremely busy. Teodori and the public prosecutor spoke on the telephone to the chief of police, who called them to a meeting in his office. Teodori ordered me to go home, and I had the feeling he wanted to take the credit for it all, but I didn't give a damn. I was preoccupied with the thought of having a threesome with Vanessa and Cristiana.

Teodori kept me informed by phone. The ministry of justice and the rapid response team must have regretted getting both of us involved. Since Teodori's personal issue had been resolved, he was a different man. The order for Manfredi dei Banchi di Aglieno's arrest was signed just as the fiery red sun was slipping out of sight.

Teodori called me back shortly after Manfredi arrived at the police station.

"He's not giving an inch, Balistreri, insisting he was at the gym and they didn't turn the air-conditioning on."

"Bullshit. He did it. We all know it—me, you, the chief of police, and the minister. Even that prick of a father of his, the king's best friend. Now he'll have something else to occupy his thoughts beyond bringing the cowardly royals back to Italy."

I was over the moon, but feeling wicked. I only wanted to slam that little monster in the cells and get my friendship with Angelo Dioguardi back on the rails. I wasn't thinking of Elisa Sordi, or her parents. Only of myself . . .

"The count's here at the rapid response team office. He brought his wife and the best criminal lawyers in Italy."

"Are you concerned, Superintendent Teodori?"

He laughed under his breath. Then his voice softened.

"The charges against Claudia have been dropped. And Manfredi is going to jail this evening, mark my words."

I wasn't invited to watch, nor was I invited to Manfredi's questioning. I couldn't have cared less. It was Saturday night. The case was over, and I was satisfied. There was nothing else I could do. I couldn't give the girl back to her parents, and I couldn't give life back to her.

What's done is done.

I wanted a good dinner, whiskey, and cigarettes in the company of Vanessa and Cristiana. They were made for each other—a sadist and a masochist, respectively. There was no reason to argue over me, there was enough of me to go around.

SUNDAY, JULY 25, 1982

THE PHONE WAS DRILLING into my brain. I felt the weight of Vanessa's head on my thigh and caught the damp smell of sex from Cristiana where my cheek was resting. My eyelids were heavy blinds shut down on my apartment's stale smoke. My tongue was stuck fast to my teeth, palate, and gums. It had been one of those magical nights when my wildest fantasies had finally come true.

I didn't want to answer the phone; I just wanted to sleep. But the ringing wouldn't stop. I managed to open one eye. The digital clock said seven twenty.

"Oh, fuck off, will you?" I groaned.

Several minutes passed. The phone continued to ring. It was like drops of water eroding my brain, going ever deeper, up to the point where I began to wonder what was reality and what was dream.

Teodori sounded upset.

"Get down to Via della Camilluccia right away."

"Jesus, what happened?" I asked, suddenly awake.

"Manfredi's mother threw herself off the balcony at dawn."

. . . .

It was raining in Rome. A summer storm. The drops beat on the Duetto's roof while I was parking in front of that violated paradise. I'd never liked rain. In Africa the sun was always out, but in Italy it rained even in summer. I couldn't bear the sense of sadness that rain gave me. It was as if something were coming between life and me and slowing it down.

There were screens all around Building A. Behind them were Teodori, the forensic guys, the forensic pathologist, and Cardinal Alessandrini in a sweater and dark trousers. Parked in a corner were the count's Aston Martin and Manfredi's Harley Davidson. Ulla's body was covered with a sheet from which a stream of blood was mingling with the rain. I felt a desperate need to smoke, but it was neither the time nor the place.

Teodori was shattered. He put a hand on my shoulder and pointed to the sheet.

"The body's about to be taken away."

I gently lifted one corner of the sheet. Ulla was fully dressed. Maybe she'd had a sleepless night; her delicate features had been crushed when she hit the pavement.

"Any witnesses?" I asked Teodori without much hope.

Teodori pointed to Gina Giansanti's young daughter, who was slumped in a chair next to the gatehouse.

"She starts work at six o'clock. Through the gatehouse window she saw the countess come out onto the terrace, climb onto the railing, make the sign of the cross, and throw herself off. It was five past six."

"So she waited for a witness," I muttered.

"I don't understand, Balistreri. Why would she want a witness?"

"To be certain that no one could accuse her husband of throwing her off."

Teodori looked at me, shocked.

"Enough with the accusations, Balistreri. Manfredi's in prison and rightly so. But this family has suffered enough, and that includes the count."

However, I still wasn't convinced. Something had come out in the talk with Ulla—some detail, a fear. Now I was certain something was missing. All of a sudden I felt a little twinge of anxiety.

You did what you could. And that monster's guilty.

We were interrupted by the chief of police and the undersecretary to the minister of the interior. They approached Teodori and Cardinal Alessandrini, pointedly ignoring me.

"We're really in the shit . . . Oh, I'm sorry, Cardinal!" groaned the undersecretary, looking at the sheet. Typical example of Christian Democrat piety, I thought.

The chief of police whispered to Teodori. "You're certain about the arrest last night? I mean, one hundred percent certain?"

I caught Teodori's worried look and nodded yes.

"I'm absolutely certain this young man killed Elisa Sordi," Teodori said.

Cardinal Alessandrini turned around and stared at me. There was no need to speak. He wasn't so certain. We were ordinary mortals, and therefore fallible.

I felt a sudden chill. It was the unseasonably cold dawn at the end of July, the rain sticking my shirt to my skin, or else it was the fear of having gotten it all wrong. Irritated, I went over to the young concierge.

I had her repeat in detail what she had seen. Between her tears, she confirmed everything, with no room for the slightest doubt. The countess was alone on the balcony; she climbed onto the railing of her own accord, then made the sign of the cross and leaped into the air.

"Your mother's coming back from India today, correct?"

"She flew into London from Bombay yesterday, and she landed in Rome an hour ago. She called me to say she was taking a taxi. I didn't have the heart to tell her."

"She doesn't know Elisa Sordi is dead?"

"I don't think so. She was in an out-of-the-way village with no telephone."

At that moment Building A's main door opened. Count Tommaso dei Banchi di Aglieno was dressed in his usual impeccable manner. His haughty face was set in a fixed, inexpressive mask.

The Christian Democrat undersecretary came forward. "Excellency, may I extend to you my most heartfelt condolences and those of the minister of the interior."

The count glared. The undersecretary, unnerved, took two steps back, sending him straight into the approaching chief of police. The rain was coming down harder. It would take a lot of rain to wash away Ulla dei Banchi di Aglieno's blood from that pavement. Rivulets of water, mud and blood were coursing over the ground. When the count went over to the sheet and lifted it, a clap of thunder exploded overhead, making us all jump. All except him. He calmly let the sheet fall. He looked at the undersecretary and the chief of police, who averted their eyes.

"Please thank the minister on my behalf," he said coldly. Then he turned on his heel and went back inside.

Ulla's body was loaded onto an ambulance and taken to the morgue. I was the first one to see the taxi arriving at the green gate; the young concierge rushed to open it, and the cardinal turned to follow her.

"Stop," I said firmly. I put myself between him and the gate.

"Why are you stopping me?"

"Gina is a witness and must be questioned by the police before anyone tells her what's happened."

"I thought you had already solved the case, Captain Balistreri," Alessandrini said.

I ignored his comment. "We're not in the Vatican here. I expressly forbid you to speak to Gina Giansanti before we do." I was beside myself, numb with anger and cold.

Alessandrini turned around and saw the two women hugging. Mother and daughter held each other tightly. The young woman choked out words mixed with sobs, while Gina listened. I moved toward them, but before I could stop her, Gina ran toward us and kissed the cardinal's ring, tears streaming from her eyes.

"Eminence, help me. I can't believe it. First Elisa, and now the countess."

Teodori approached a little uncertainly; he hadn't met Gina Giansanti before. The cardinal grasped both the woman's hands without saying a word. She stared at him, begging him for comfort. I stepped between them.

"Ms. Giansanti, we need to speak to you right away."

The concierge looked at me, bewildered.

"What do you want with me?"

Teodori introduced himself in a manner more reassuring than mine. We went into the small house where Gina Giansanti lived. Her daughter made coffee, and we sat around the kitchen table. The house smelled strongly of floor wax and soap. She'd cleaned everything to a shine for her mother's return.

"Ms. Giansanti," Teodori began, "are you aware that on the day you left for India another terribly unfortunate event occurred?"

The woman lifted red-rimmed eyes red. "My daughter just told me about Elisa Sordi."

I had the impression that her look went beyond the window behind me toward an indistinct point in the open square. Teodori shook his head in annoyance, watching the daughter pour out the coffee. "What have you said to your mother, young lady?"

The girl was trembling. "Only that Elisa Sordi was killed and the countess committed suicide."

"Did Manfredi kill Elisa?" Gina Giansanti asked. The harsh mask of her face had become fossilized in pain.

Teodori looked at her in amazement.

"How did you know?" he asked her.

"Because that boy's a monster, and his father's worse than he is. The poor countess, on the other hand, was an angel, like Elisa."

I decided to get the point, before the blanket of impressions and emotions veiled Gina Giansanti's recollections like a mist.

"Do you remember the Sunday afternoon of the final? I came here with Angelo Dioguardi toward half past five; you'd already packed your bags to leave."

"I remember perfectly. I'd gone up to Elisa's office a little before that, and she'd given me some papers to take to the cardinal. Then you arrived with Dioguardi. He went up to see the cardinal while you finished a cigarette. When Dioguardi called you she'd already joined them."

"When Dioguardi, the cardinal, and I left at about ten past six, you weren't there anymore."

"No. I went to Mass and I bought some holy pictures from the priest to give out as gifts in India. I chatted awhile with some of the parishioners and then came back here about half past seven finish packing. I'd reserved a taxi to the airport for eight."

"All right, ma'am, we've already checked all this. Both your parish priest and the parishioners remember that you were there, and the taxi driver remembers you, too," said Teodori.

"You checked on my whereabouts?" she asked resentfully.

"We had to. Elisa Sordi was killed, not on the premises, during that time. She punched out at six thirty," Teodori explained patiently. "In these cases we confirm everybody's stories."

It was Gina Giansanti's look that gave me the first sign of alarm. The second came from inside my body, from a hidden corner of my brain where I'd wanted to bury all my doubts. My eyes traveled beyond the kitchen window toward the pavement stained with Ulla's blood. The blood was there; we couldn't go back. The invisible blood came from wounds in the soul.

Gina Giansanti's words came from a great distance away, like the first breath of wind that precedes a storm.

"No, that's not right. Elisa Sordi left while I was getting into the taxi to the airport, at eight that evening."

The coffee cup slipped from Teodori's grasp and dropped onto the tiles, where it shattered, along with our certainty.

. . . .

We had her repeat her story three times. The taxi to the airport, as the taxi dispatcher confirmed, had been booked for eight sharp. Gina Giansanti was keeping her eye on the green gate from the kitchen window. At five to eight she saw Elisa Sordi coming from Building B, crossing the grounds in a hurry and then leaving through the gate on Via della Camilluccia. She didn't see if anyone was waiting for her. She only noted that she was moving in a hurry and assumed she was late for the game. Five minutes later her taxi arrived—a fact we'd already checked. Gina checked in at Fiumicino at eight fifty two and got on the last flight to London, and from there she took the flight to Bombay at six the following morning.

There were no doubts of any kind. At five to eight Elisa Sordi left from Via della Camilluccia, just before Manfredi got in. It was ruled out that the long business of her death could have taken place in a few minutes in the middle of Via della Camilluccia while it was still daylight.

We'd had it: me, Teodori, the chief of police, the minister. Ulla killed herself through our blundering. Through my blundering, because of my certainty. The count would destroy us; he'd annihilate us all.

. . . .

"Where's your car, Balistreri?" Teodori asked me. We got into the Duetto. The rain was pounding down.

Teodori took out his pipe and lit it. He seemed calm, lost in his thoughts.

"I'll tell the chief of police you didn't agree with me," I promised, knowing it wouldn't be enough. He was the boss; there was no way I could save him. They would force him out with a dishonorable discharge.

He looked at me with his yellow eyes and smiled. He was only a humble bureaucrat and not that smart. But I had solved the biggest problem in his life for him. And he was a good man.

"You can't save me, Balistreri. I outrank you. Besides, I'm the one who demanded Manfredi's arrest. You weren't even there."

"But I was the one—"

He interrupted me with a gesture. "I took all the credit for the investigation. I said I had the idea of consulting the records of the gym's electricity consumption, and I was the one who explained everything to the prosecutor, the chief of police, and the undersecretary. I never mentioned your name; I took all the credit. So you're not a factor—you haven't done a thing."

I stared at him in amazement. Now I understood. "You weren't a hundred percent sure, and so you kept me out of it."

He avoided my eyes. "That was my mistake. I had some doubts and I shouldn't have arrested Manfredi. The countess would be still alive."

"You had doubts," I muttered, bewildered.

"I have a daughter, Balistreri; I know things you couldn't know. Elisa Sordi would never have gone down to the Tiber with Manfredi of her own free will. With another man, yes, but not with him."

I was appalled. It was a simple explanation. And true. "But you can't assume responsibility for my mistakes, Superintendent Teodori."

He now looked at me more firmly. "I'll say it was all my idea and you were against it from the start. I'm old, and I have hepatitis that's turned into cirrhosis. In exchange, you can do me another favor, the biggest one I can ask of you."

"Claudia?"

"Exactly. My daughter. I'll be dead before long; you must be a guardian and a friend to Claudia. I think you'll know how to protect her until she's more certain of herself. And you can do it far better if you remain a policeman."

"You trust me to do all that?"

He forced himself to smile. "Not entirely. You have to swear to me you'll never touch her. Look, you would be an excellent guardian but a very crappy boyfriend."

I was at a point in my life where I was fully convinced of what my father had said, which was that I'd never amount to anything good because I had no talent and no will, nor the motivation to change it. And I didn't really care at all—whatever happened to me from that day on didn't matter to me. It was for this reason I accepted Teodori's offer, not to save my own ass but because I was worn out. All I wanted was to say yes, and then float away and fall asleep forever.

2005

ANTONIO PASQUALI CAME FROM Tesano, a small town halfway up the mountains in Abruzzo. A photo of the place hung on the wall behind his desk at a respectful distance from the rigorously symmetrical ones of the pope and the president of the Republic. His office was a solemn place. It was an office worthy of one of the highest-ranking officers in the Italian police force. Not the highest ranking of all, but the most influential in the circles that counted.

As a boy, Pasquali had shown a marked talent for acting and for politics, and there was a great deal of overlap between the two fields. Young Pasquali divided his time between drama school and the local branch of the Christian Democratic party. His academic progress suffered a little as a result, but he made up for it with a lively intelligence and the help of his father, who had been mayor of Tesano for almost eight years. His teachers looked favorably and with understanding at the bespectacled boy, who was serious but sharp and witty when he needed to be. With his personal gifts and those of his family, it was clear to everyone that Antonio Pasquali would make a career for himself.

After graduating from high school, he spent several months in London studying acting. Then his father insisted he return to the real world. He earned a degree in political science in Rome and passed the police department entrance exam. After completing two years of the course for the rank of detective, his father spoke to the minister of the interior, who was also from Abruzzo and a fellow party member, who was able to confirm that the young Pasquali was a hard worker, decidedly on the ball, and a good communicator.

And so, in 1980, the Minister brought him to Rome as his assistant on secondment from the police and there Pasquali built the network of political contacts that would support him for his entire career. He had friends everywhere, from neo-fascists to the extreme Left, but he remained strictly a man of the center, a man for all seasons, ready to dialogue with everyone.

In the early 1990s, the prosecutor's office in Milan sprang into action with the *mani pulite* corruption trials. The Christian Democrats and the Socialists disbanded, and Italy's political system was left rudderless. One evening in 1993, Pasquali's father and his friend the minister were sitting in the drawing room of the family home in Tesano in front of an open fire, drinking a glass of the local liqueur. The two older men were discussing the by now obvious necessity of repositioning themselves politically. The Christian Democrats were splitting into two parties—one center-left, the other center-right—in order better to navigate the new majoritarian system that was being implemented. Young Antonio, who was rising quickly through the ranks of the rapid response team, proffered a solution.

"You should split up, one in each party."

The two looked at him in amazement. It was so simple. They agreed that would be best. They'd each join one of the newly formed parties, and then they'd wait to see which was going to dominate the new system. Everyone was well aware that the local electoral system of political favors, which had developed in the postwar period and had ruled for forty-five years, was now at risk of falling apart under the attack of the "Communist" magistrates in Milan and the new power of the media, and they had to find a place in both of the new alliances.

They discussed briefly who should go with whom, but the personal and political histories of the minister and Pasquali's father were identical. But here too the young Antonio found the solution. He took a coin from his pocket, turned to the minister—who, after all, out-ranked his father and was also the elder of the two—and said, "Heads or tails, Mr. Minister?"

Then his father asked, "What about you, Antonio? The police rely on political contacts, too."

Antonio was evasive. He said that in any future scenario it wouldn't be appropriate for a policeman to have any direct membership in a party; it would be more useful to have a simple sympathetic leaning. Nevertheless, he would think about it. What he didn't say was that he had it on good authority that there was a new political party brewing. It was going to be a party with limitless funds, and it would incorpo-rate sizable numbers of both Christian Democrats and Socialists and sweep the field. Antonio Pasquali wanted to keep his hands free: his youthful gifts as an actor would be appreciated in the new televised world of politics.

In 2000 he was transferred from the rapid response team to the organized crime division, where he conducted several brilliant busts that led to the arrest of longtime Mafia fugitives whose positions had been filled by other Mafiosi in the meantime. He was careful that no politician, present or past, of whatever persuasion, came to be involved. He was honestly convinced he was serving his country's true interests.

By the end of 2002, crimes committed by immigrants had become a high-profile political issue. Urged on by popular sentiment and vari-ous political parties, the government decided to create a special force to support the rapid response teams in the regional capitals in han-dling crimes committed by foreigners. The idea of naming Pasquali to oversee all the regional captains was suggested to the then-current minister of the interior by both members of the majority coalition and members of the opposition. He was a candidate with support on both sides: a capable and well-balanced man, an excellent policeman who was attentive to the political world's demands.

Andrea Floris, Rome's chief of police, had been appointed to his position by those on the left. He was familiar with Michele Balistreri's neo-Fascist history, but he also knew that Balistreri—who was the same age as Pasquali—was better qualified for the post, having run

Homicide successfully for the previous three years. He asked to speak to the minister of the interior but was passed to the relevant undersecretary who in turn shifted him to his first assistant, a young man not yet thirty with a degree from a prestigious university, who maintained that, given his distant past as far-right activist working with the secret intelligence service, Balistreri's candidacy would cause incomprehension precisely among the center-left where the chief of police had his political support. Floris countered by saying these were events that went back thirty years and Balistreri had more than redeemed himself for them by serving and risking his life for the state, as well as keeping his distance from all political factions. But this was insufficient for the young man; indeed, keeping his distance from politics actually made him "suspicious." Balistreri still used terms like *fatherland, honor, loyalty*. This was baggage from the past, an obsolete language, and was indicative of an older generation, the young man concluded. Used to Rome's political theatrics by now, the chief of police gave in: the politicians didn't want anyone like Balistreri for the position—a man who didn't speak to them, didn't go to their dinners on terraces or in the most exclusive clubs, a man who never spoke to journalists, a kind of maverick already in decline.

But Floris did manage to secure one condition in return for his support for Pasquali: the special team on immigrants in Rome would be the most active one, and he wanted Michele Balistreri to run it. Pasquali didn't think much of Balistreri, but he agreed in order to ingratiate himself with Floris, whose support was certain to come in handy. At the same time, this meant he could take the opportunity to see that Balistreri did not move to the rapid response team's fourth section, which dealt with crimes involving property and where the most politically sensitive investigations into fraud, corruption, and false accounting were under way. So he entrusted Rome's unit dealing with crimes by foreigners to him in the hope that he would go up in flames, after which Floris could replace Balistreri with a more trustworthy person. But Balistreri's performance had been impeccable for two and a half years.

And then along came the case of the letter R.

JULY 23-24, 2005

SAMANTHA ROSSI STOLE A glance at the clock on the kitchen wall. It was half past eight in the evening. The last light of day was filtering through an open window on the second floor, along with the sounds of a few cars headed toward the beach or out into the country. It had been a long hot day, the end of an interminable week of work. She turned off the burner and ladled the soup into a bowl, then sprinkled on some grated Parmesan cheese. Only a little, because a cardiologist had told Assunta, the ninety-year-old woman Samantha looked after, that she shouldn't eat cheese. She placed the soup in front of Assunta on the chipped Formica table and slowly fed her, one spoonful at a time.

Usually, at exactly ten minutes to ten, Samantha would pick up her backpack and, having kissed Assunta, would run to the other side of the piazza to take the bus to the Termini station and then the Metro to Ostia. At eleven she would be home with her parents in their house by the sea.

. . . .

From eight onward the Bierkeller was a madhouse. It was where Roma from the nearby travelers' camps, together with those who lived in the poorest housing on Rome's east side, gathered. After spending a whole day under a blazing hot sun placing one brick on top of another, or at a crossroads cleaning the windscreens of the Roman motorist, they were thirsty. Very thirsty.

A man sat in the Bierkeller's most dimly lit corner by the bathrooms. He had long black hair. He wore a Lazio soccer team hat and large sunglasses, and he'd been sitting by himself for more than an hour. He'd had only half a glass of beer. In a white bag at his feet sat two unopened bottles of excellent whiskey that he wouldn't touch. In the pocket of his jeans were several plastic envelopes of cocaine he would never snort.

He lifted his beer glass and winked at three eighteen-year-olds from who were exiting the men's room. He could see they were the same nationality he was. All had shaved heads and were dressed identically in sleeveless white vests and jeans. Only the tattoos on their swelling biceps and necks differed: a little swastika, an eagle, a two-blade Fascist ax, a gladiator, crossed swords. They were perfect.

. . . .

Balistreri was having dinner at his brother's house with his deputy Corvu, his friend Dioguardi, and one of his brother's colleagues. It was a light supper of Parma ham, melon, and chilled white wine, ahead of the poker game to come. Balistreri had cut his smoking down to the strict limits dictated by his unhealthy heart and had almost completely stopped drinking. Playing poker was a substitute pleasure for the many others he had slowly abandoned over the years, and it was one of the few sources of excitement left to him.

. . . .

When Assunta had finished her soup, Samantha led her from the kitchen to the only other room in the apartment, a small sitting room and bedroom. At nine forty Samantha got ready to leave. She carefully checked Assunta's pills. Samantha had written Assunta a very neat schedule that showed her exactly when to take what. Copies of the schedule were taped to the wall in the bedroom, the kitchen, and the bathroom. She paused to ask the elderly woman one last question.

"Assunta, did the concierge pick up your blood thinner for you?"

The old woman smiled absentmindedly. "I forgot to ask her, Samantha, but don't worry about it."

At nine fifty Samantha raced out the door.

. . . .

At nine fifty, he escorted them out of the Bierkeller. The three young men were drunk and high. Not too drunk and high—just the right amount, meaning enough to be a little muddled, but still physically strong and ready for action. The lonely piazza with its gardens was deserted. They saw her running up in great strides like an athlete and then shooting past, leaving all four with their mouths open.

"Wow, what a piece of ass!" exclaimed one in Romanian.

. . . .

Dioguardi was winning. He'd won for more than twenty years. The fact that his blond hair was now peppered with gray and his blue eyes were framed with wrinkles made him no less childlike. He always apologized for winning, and every so often he lost so that his friends wouldn't be totally humiliated. Alberto played in his regular scientific manner and lost with the same regularity.

"He's bluffing," Balistreri said to his brother, who had just passed on Dioguardi's most recent raise.

"I don't think so," Corvu said. "He's got a sixty percent chance of winning the hand. I think Alberto was right to fold."

As usual, Dioguardi said nothing. He smoked and drank much more than he'd ever done in his youth, but his bluffs and non-bluffs remained a professional secret.

. . . .

Samantha saw them out of the corner of her eye as she went past. She could smell them, too: a pungent odor of alcohol and sweat. She could feel the eyes undressing her, then the arms that grabbed and held her.

While she was being dragged away struggling and kicking, she could see her bus. It was pulling out and turning around the piazza. One of the men immediately put his arm round her neck and pushed a dirty rag in her mouth to stop her from calling out. With her eyes staring wide, Samantha saw the bus pull away and its tail lights disappearing as many hands pushed her into the brushwood and bushes of the little gardens.

"Mamma!" she wailed. "Papa!"

. . . .

An elderly man walking his dog at midnight found the young woman's body near a garbage dump. The proximity of the Casilino 900 travelers' camp and other squatter camps of the Roma people meant that the Balistreri's special team was immediately contacted. He ended the poker game with his friends and, together with Corvu, rushed to the scene. When he arrived, the medical examiner was already there. But they didn't need an expert to see that the girl had suffered multiple rapes and had then been strangled.

In less than twenty-four hours, both the press and the city at large were convinced that the perpetrators came from the Casilino camp. The center-right opposition coalition had long used a zero-tolerance approach with the Roma, who received more benign treatment at the hands of the center-left city government that had ruled Rome for years. The murder of the young Italian student detonated a request for the immediate dismantling of all the travelers' camps and the forced deportation of all Roma people.

A gang of ultra-right youths attacked the inhabitants of a camp with clubs and knives, wounding several people, including a woman who tried to protect her husband. Though the Roma weren't strictly from Romania, Italians tended to conflate the two groups, and Romanian flags were burned in the streets. Graffiti cursing foreigners blanketed the city walls. A professional Romanian soccer player on one of the Italian teams removed himself from the roster after suffering terrible insults from the team's own fans. The press escalated things further. The Italian and Romanian prime ministers met with community leaders, and they promised to work together to weed out the few bad apples involved.

The mayor and his center-left party discussed the problem, but didn't come up with a solution. Now, with the opposition, the media, and public opinion putting their backs against the wall, they convened a meeting with Chief of Police Floris and Antonio Pasquali in an attempt to settle the issue as quickly.

Since the first day, the investigation had obviously been directed toward the travelers' camps. Balistreri was alone in refusing to follow that path to the exclusion of others. His reason was a detail that had been kept strictly secret, known only to the top ranks of the investigating team and absolutely unknown to the press and public opinion. On Samantha's back the letter R, a half inch tall and the same width, had been carved using a sharp blade. And to Balistreri, the carving of a letter on the victim pointed to a level of premeditation that didn't jive with the blind herd instinct of a group of gypsies, even if they were drunk and high.

Pasquali immediately grasped this as an excellent opportunity to damage Balistreri's very solid reputation. At the end of the morning, during a press conference with his colleague sitting beside him, he launched into an impromptu theatrical scene using his great talent for dialectical debate. "The head of the special team dedicated to policing foreigners seems to believe that the responsible parties may not be clandestine immigrants," he announced. He then handed Balistreri the microphone.

Balistreri's face went dark. "I have no comment at this time," he said, cutting things short and infuriating the journalists, particularly those in the media agitating the most for the removal of the travelers' camps and putting the blame on the Roma. The following day, headlines blared, CAPTAIN OF SPECIAL TEAM SAYS "THE ROMA AREN'T RESPONSIBLE."

. . . .

All through Saturday night and Sunday morning, the camps were searched. During a blitz by the Carabinieri in a squatter camp not far from Casilino 900, a bracelet with the initials S. R. was discovered hidden under a mattress in a caravan where three young Roma males were living, having arrived in Italy ten days earlier from the countryside around the Black Sea. They had neither jobs nor a residence permit. The DNA evidence was incontrovertible. The three were blind drunk when they were picked up.

After two hours of questioning, they confessed to everything. That evening they'd gotten drunk in a bar with a guy, a fellow Roma, who had also given them cocaine. They'd left the bar about ten and he'd gone up to Samantha, but she resisted, so they dragged her over to the garbage dump. There among plastic bags, table scraps, discarded syringes, and dog shit, they raped her. Taking turns, one held her by the neck, one held her arms and the other raped her. In the end, she'd fainted. Each accused the other of strangling her, then they said it had been this mythical fourth man they knew nothing about. But the traces of organic matter on Samantha's body were all from the three of them; there was nothing to indicate the presence of a fourth man. When they emerged from the carabinieri station, a crowd of thousands was waiting, howling for blood. The forces of law and order were barely able to hold them back; several officers had to be restrained as well.

The media attacked the Roma community and the police. They focused on the special team and its captain, Michele Balistreri, a former Fascist agitator who might soon be a former policeman as well. But Pasquali didn't strip Balistreri of his badge. He also knew that the three Roma boys could neither read nor write and were therefore incapable of carving a letter on the murdered girl's body. His instinct and his cautious nature kept him from acting. He had learned from the Christian Democrats that it was best to have a scapegoat in place and an escape route ready and waiting.

PART 2

THURSDAY, DECEMBER 29, 2005

Morning

BALISTRERI WAS AWAKENED BY the sound of someone cursing. He turned over in bed and looked toward the window. Dawn was breaking. He glanced at the alarm clock: five forty. He put his head underneath the pillow but couldn't fall back to sleep. His mind was racing.

This part of Rome was a mixture of heaven and hell. For three years he'd been forced to live here in the historic center, which he hated; it looked magical at night, but during the day it was smelly and chaotic. He lived in a building near the ministry of the interior reserved for members of its staff. The small apartment on the third floor overlooked a narrow street crowded with traffic and tourists in a shopping frenzy. Almost every evening he shut himself away with a CD or a good book, ever more rarely with a woman, and he closed the windows on the world outside. He slept little and poorly. Every sound seemed amplified. And he couldn't take sleeping pills because they interfered with his antidepressants.

There was the cursing again, more loudly this time. Resigned to being awake, he got up, opened the window, and looked down onto the street. Two guys who looked like immigrants were unloading goods from a white van and carrying them into the clothing shop below. The owner, an elderly Jewish man, was arguing with an enormous guy who had gotten out of an SUV as large as he was. The white van was blocking the SUV. The SUV driver swore a third time, gave the elderly man a push, and screamed at him in a strong Roman accent.

"Get these fucking gypsies out of my way!"

The two young guys stopped unloading the van and moved toward the SUV. Balistreri saw the man with the mouth on him reach a hand underneath his black leather jacket.

"Don't do that," he yelled down to the man. The four men looked up.

"Who the fuck are you? Mind your own fucking business and go back to bed," the man with the big mouth shouted at him.

"Just leave your gun in your jacket," Balistreri said. "There's nowhere to run here, and I happen to have a gun myself." He waved the fake .44 Magnum he'd been given years earlier when he took a course with the FBI.

The man took shelter below the main entrance, out of range. The elderly Jewish man remained in the middle of the road and looked up at Balistreri.

Balistreri said, "Mr. Fadlun, kindly ask these young men to drive the van around the block so this gentleman can pull out."

"The road is now free, sir; you can drive off, no worries," Balistreri said to the hidden thug.

The huge brute looked up uncertainly from his hiding place. "The pistol's a fake," said Balistreri reassuringly.

Upon hearing that the thug got his courage back. "Come down here and I'll break your fucking neck."

Balistreri smiled, but he didn't move. Sometimes he wondered if he was getting soft.

"Calm down," said the shop owner to the man as sweetly as he could. "This gentleman's a policeman; he certainly wouldn't fire at you."

The white van had gone around the block and was now behind the SUV.

"I am, and I'll shoot out the tires on your SUV if you're not out of here in five seconds," Balistreri warned him. He held up his unloaded Beretta.

The man jumped into the SUV and left. Balistreri shut the window and went into the kitchen to make coffee.

After a few minutes, he heard the doorbell ring. It was Mr. Fadlun. He was standing on the threshold with a package in his hand that smelled sublime.

"My wife has just taken this baklava out of the oven. I know you like it very much," Mr. Fadlun said, full of contrition. Balistreri had told him, he didn't know how many times, that he should unload after six a.m. like all good Christians did.

"Please thank your wife, Mr. Fadlun."

"Again, I'm sorry," said Fadlun, now smiling a little. They had known each other for three years. "It's business—what can you do? Over Christmastime you have to have plenty to sell."

Balistreri looked at the old man's wrist, where the number that identified him as a Holocaust survivor was clearly visible. He shuddered to think what the Balistreri of thirty years earlier would have done to this old man. He thanked him again and decided to let it go.

The last two weeks of the year had been impossible. As usual, the center of Rome had been full of people hunting for Christmas presents and had turned into a pit of hell that was impossible to live in.

Balistreri took his acid reflux pill and ate a piece of dry wholewheat toast while staring longingly at Fadlun's wife's baklava. Then he drank his decaf coffee, smoked his first cigarette of the day, and checked that there weren't more than five in the pack. His coffee was like his life: insipid. His Sicilian father had been fond of saying that drinking decaf was like pulling out or smoking a cigarette without inhaling. But Balistreri had wiped out the Sicilian half on his father's side, the part he detested and had forgotten about, in favor of the half he loved.

He took a shower and got dressed. His pants hung loose. He had lost some more weight and gained some more gray hair. He swallowed his antidepressant with the last sip of coffee. *Once I wasn't frightened of death. Now I'm reduced to putting it off for as long as possible.*

It wasn't yet seven when Balistreri left his apartment. He arrived at the office five minutes later. The guard at the entrance obsequiously rushed to open the elevator door for him. Balistreri disliked having people serve him, but the other high-ranking officials didn't feel the same way. After his fall from grace, he didn't have any latitude to criticize the system. In any case, it was a system he'd worked in for twenty-five years. He'd been an integral part of it for too long.

He went up to the fourth floor, where his team's offices were located. His office was in the corner, a large room with an eighteenth-century frieze in the center of the twelve-foot ceiling and a view of the Colosseum and the Roman Forum.

All the other offices were empty except for the cubicle that belonged to Margherita, the new switchboard operator and secretary. She greeted him with a smile. She wore no makeup and had the appearance of a good clean girl.

She could be my daughter. If I tried coming on to her, she'd laugh in my face . . .

Over the years, he'd gradually eased up on his womanizing. He no longer had the ability to thoughtlessly inflict wounds with no feelings of guilt. Slowly the number of areas he had forbidden himself had spread into almost all female categories: those who were married or engaged and singles young enough to still entertain the hope of marriage. As a result of these self-imposed moral limits and his physical and mental decline, the field was reduced to the occasional one-night stand.

He had a good half-hour before his two deputies, Corvu and Piccolo, were scheduled to arrive. He started in on his daily routine. He put an unlit cigarette in his mouth, switched on his computer, and checked his email. As he did every morning, he read only the two that seemed most important. The first, from Graziano Corvu, was an update on investigations. It was a summary of all investigations begun in the past two years that hadn't been solved, with the latest findings highlighted in red. There were only four cases. One of them was Samantha Rossi and the case of the letter R.

There was only one brand-new case: a young Senegalese man had been stabbed to death outside the Bella Blu nightclub a block from Via Veneto on the night of December 23, or rather, early in the morning on December 24. Papa Camarà was a bodybuilding instructor at the Sport Center gym. In the evening he also worked as a bouncer at the Bella Blu. There had been an argument at the club entrance between Camarà and an unidentified motorcyclist just before the stabbing, which took place about two thirty in the morning. The Bella Blu's manager was a lawyer named Francesco Ajello. He was the one who called the police.

Balistreri made a note on a Post-it, stuck it on his desk, and lit his second cigarette. He turned to Giulia Piccolo's email: new cases. The special team on foreigners dealt not only with serious crimes, but also with any offense or relevant aspects of any investigation that involved foreigners—assault with intention to do bodily harm, rape, missing persons. Over the holidays, Piccolo's emails had been short. Around Christmas nothing very serious happened: women's bags were snatched as they were out shopping, shop tills were robbed, and merchandise was stolen by bored young boys on vacation. Then there were the tramps found frozen to death and fights between relatives of different ethnic groups rashly gathered together for the holidays, and obviously road traffic accidents increased tenfold because of the number of Italians on the roads and the abundant drinking. It was all commonplace and you could live with it. Nothing that warranted his attention.

But that day there was something new. The morning before a Romanian prostitute had reported her friend missing since the night of December 24. Another Post-it.

Beyond the blinds, which Balistreri kept lowered, Rome was lazily beginning to wake up. He left his desk lamp on and turned over the overhead light, then put on a Leonard Cohen CD at low volume. His psychiatrist had suggested he stop listening to Cohen, Lennon, and De André for a while, but he couldn't. He stretched out on the worn and cracked leather sofa, a symbol of both his status and his state of mind, and dozed off. He dreamed he was lighting a cigarette.

Balistreri's two deputies entered his office at seven thirty sharp. Both were extremely punctual and absolutely dedicated to their jobs, but apart from that they couldn't have been more different.

Graziano Corvu came from a poor family in a small village in the Sardinian interior. He'd studied like crazy and earned a cum laude degree in math at the university in Cagliari. Once he was employed by the police, he enrolled in evening classes and earned a second degree in economics. The youngest of five sons, he possessed the innate skill of pleasing everyone and had friends everywhere for whom he had done favors. Corvu was the ablest analyst in the Rome police. His Achilles' heel was women. In this endeavor, the indefatigable Corvu was a mixture of awkwardness and bad luck, despite the advice and encouragement of an old hand such as Balistreri.

Giulia Piccolo had grown up in a small seaside town outside of Palermo where her ambiguous sexuality was a hot topic of conversation. She left as soon as she turned eighteen. She was almost six feet tall and muscular, attractive in an angular way. She had earned a degree in physical education in Rome and held a black belt in karate. There was no talk of men in her life, which—according to Balistreri—was a bad sign. She was perhaps too impulsive, but her apparent courage and uncompromising nature were the very qualities the head of the special team knew to be the ones that over the years he himself had lost.

"Good morning, sir." It had taken everything for Balistreri to persuade Corvu not to address him by his official title, Associate Deputy Police Captain. Corvu had agreed to call him "sir" only after Balistreri had appealed to his analytical skills, noting that his title contained two diminutives—"associate" and "deputy"—and was therefore actually rather insulting.

"You look tired, sir," Corvu observed.

They're worried. They've heard rumors in the corridors that I'm on the list for early retirement.

"This guy have any priors?" Balistreri asked Corvu, changing the subject.

"Both Camarà and Ajello have clean records—immaculate, in fact," Corvu replied.

"Have you checked with Interpol?"

"Yes. Nothing."

"Civil court?"

"Checked."

"And SISDE?" It was a rather impertinent question. Corvu didn't have sufficient authority to access the secret intelligence service computer records.

"Checked. Nothing there." Corvu looked away. Balistreri didn't ask how he'd managed that.

"Doesn't it seem strange to you that the manager of a nightclub with cage dancers and bouncers, who are most certainly paid under the table, doesn't have a record? I don't necessarily mean a conviction, but being reported for stealing apples, that sort of thing . . ."

"With a lot of cash lying around, there's always something," added Piccolo.

Corvu scowled. "Sorry, sir, I should have thought of that. I'll check with the revenue agency."

"Good, you can tell me what you find tomorrow. For now, tell me about the dead man."

"Papa Camarà started working at the Bella Blu in early September. His shift was from 10:00 p.m. to 6:00 a.m., when the club closed. He stopped any 'unsuitable' types from coming in, so Ajello said. There was an argument outside the club."

"And what do we know of this argument?"

"We've got a witness. An American tourist who turned up about two o'clock, saw Camarà arguing with a motorcyclist, who then sped off. Camarà was found dying on the pavement outside the club at two thirty. Stabbed in the stomach with a knife."

"Any description of the motorcyclist?"

"The American was drunk. But he did say the rider was wearing a full-face helmet."

"Okay, talk to him again. And find out more about the victim, Ajello, the money."

He turned to Piccolo, picked up the other Post-it, and passed it to her. On it he'd written, "28!?"

"You're right, sir. The girl waited four days. For a variety of reasons, she claims. I've got the statement she gave at the Torre

Spaccata police station yesterday. Name's Ramona Iordanescu. She only met the missing girl, Nadia, a month ago. She didn't even know her last name. They both came from small towns in Moldova near Iasi. She hadn't heard from Nadia since late afternoon on December 24."

With a gesture Balistreri held Corvu back from the torrent of clarification he was about to request.

"Can you just give me the nitty-gritty?" he asked Piccolo politely. He was always very polite with her, less familiar than he was with Corvu. She didn't seem to mind.

"Ramona Iordanescu, born April 4, 1986, in Iasi, Romania."

"You said Moldavia," Balistreri said.

"Moldova, sir, not Moldavia. It's a region of Romania," Corvu explained.

"Since December 1, 2005, she's been living in an apartment on Via Tiburtina owned by Marius Hagi, who's also the owner of the billiard hall next door and employer of a distant cousin of hers, Mircea Lacatus. She met Nadia on the bus she took from Moldova to Rome in late November. They liked each other and decided to share the room she was going to rent from her cousin Mircea's boss. Once they arrived in Italy, Mircea and another cousin, Greg, forced them into prostitution and threatened to beat them if they didn't comply. Usual 'place of work' was Via di Torricola, a long road out into the country between the Appian Way and Via Casilina. On December 24, Ramona went to the usual spot with Nadia about six. She got into a car with a john around six thirty. When she got back, Nadia wasn't there, and she wasn't in the room on Via Tiburtina, either, when Ramona went home early on the morning of December 25. They planned to go to Romania together for New Year's. Ramona says she didn't file a formal report before, because she thought her friend managed to get away from their pimps. She gave us a photo of the two of them."

Piccolo handed over the photo. It showed two young women with their arms around each other in St. Peter's Square. Someone had drawn a heart around them with a red pen. They didn't look any older than twenty. One was tall and dark, the other small, slim, and blond. Someone had written an R under the brunette and an N under the blonde.

"And so yesterday she decided to report her missing?" Corvu asked.

Piccolo read directly from the statement, "Iordanescu came in today, December 28, 2005, at 5:00 a.m. to make a formal statement because one hour later she was departing for Iasi by bus."

She looked up at Balistreri indignantly. "It seems no one ever dreamed of stopping her."

Balistreri showed no sign of annoyance.

Who do you think is going to give a damn about a Romanian prostitute, without a residence permit, who disappears?

Now the car horns were honking outside the window, you could hear them even through the double windows. It was raining hard, and Balistreri was glad.

Rain cushions life, like an antidepressant.

He looked at the time.

"It's ten past eight," he said to Piccolo.

"I asked about the change of shift. It's at nine o'clock." Piccolo was on her feet.

"Take the dwarf with you, and use the siren. Rome's a disaster area in the rain."

. . . .

Inspector Antonio Coppola was a fifty-year-old from Naples known for three things: his short stature, which had earned him the affectionate nickname "the dwarf," his way with women, and, lastly, his poorly concealed racism, typical of a Southerner who has been discriminated against himself. As a young man, he'd been married and divorced twice. Both women were better looking than he was, and both had kicked him out because he cheated. He said he was compelled to cheat as a way to compensate for the inferiority complex his height gave him. Then, twice-divorced, he married Lucia, who'd been his first love back in high school in Naples. Tall and beautiful, Lucia bore Coppola a son, Ciro, who was now a very tall sixteen-year-old and captain of a basketball team. Nowadays Coppola confined himself to flirting with beautiful women, without going on to taste the fruit.

Nevertheless, Balistreri was resigned to the need to keep him far away from any investigations involving attractive women. He didn't want to be either the cause or a witness to any romantic crises.

Coppola drove, siren blaring, while Piccolo filled him in on the case. He sped through the chaotic traffic as if he were driving alone on the Monza racetrack.

Eventually they left the city center, and beautiful ancient buildings gave way to the shabby towers of Rome's eastern outskirts, built during the speculative housing boom of the 1960s.

They arrived at the Torre Spaccata police station at a quarter to nine and approached the officer on duty. Giuseppe Marchese, a twenty-year-old with very short dark hair and watchful eyes, was dressed in civilian clothes. He addressed Coppola, ignoring Piccolo completely.

"What can I do for you?" he asked with a marked Sicilian accent.

"Inspector Coppola." Coppola flashed his badge. A long pause. The officer became flustered, as many did when they dealt with the special team. Then Coppola pointed to the woman beside him. "I'm here with Deputy Captain Piccolo."

"I'll call my superior immediately," Marchese said, reaching for the phone.

"No," said Coppola, brusquely stopping him. "It's you we want to talk to. Is there an office where we can do this discreetly?"

"To tell you the truth," said Marchese in a feeble attempt to escape, looking at the clock on the wall, "my shift's over in five minutes."

"Perfect, so no one will disturb us. Where should we do this?" Coppola persisted. He was a little conflicted. On the one hand, Marchese was a kid who'd left some village in Sicily and been assigned to a police station in one of the worst areas in the city. And on the other hand, he'd let Ramona leave. Anger won out.

Marchese led them to a little room off to one side. The officers for the next shift were already arriving. Some looked at them inquisitively, but Coppola shut the door in their faces. There was a table and two chairs in the room. Coppola offered the larger chair to Piccolo, who took it into a corner and sat down. Coppola leaned heavily on the desk.

"Sit down," he said to Marchese. The poor kid sat on the edge of the seat.

"Ramona Iordanescu. You took her statement, right?" Coppola said. Marchese shot to his feet. "Inspector . , ." he tried to say.

Coppola placed a hand on his shoulder and pushed the kid back into his seat. He was visibly uncomfortable. Piccolo had learned to recognize fear instantly. Even for an emotional young man, his reaction seemed too extreme. Of course, he was dealing with the special team and the dwarf's tough-guy attitude, but no one was accusing him of anything. She got up and stood in front of Marchese with perfect timing, while Coppola moved out of the young policeman's field of vision.

Piccolo squatted down in front of Marchese so that their eyes were at the same level.

"Giuseppe," she said calmly, "you've done nothing wrong. You're hardly responsible for the whole station at your rank." He looked at her as if she were Our Lady of Help of Sciacca and had come to save him. Piccolo gave him time to calm down, then in a low voice addressed him, Sicilian to Sicilian. "I just want to know one thing: Who told you to let her leave for Romania?"

The kid's eyes shot toward the door; voices could be heard outside. Piccolo glanced at Coppola, who went and stood in front of the door. Someone knocked. Coppola opened the door, left, and shut the door behind himself. The voices on the other side of the door were growing louder. She had a minute, maybe less.

"We're not back in our small towns in Sicily anymore," Piccolo said sympathetically. "They're not kidding around up here in Rome, so just tell me who it was or you'll be screwed."

"I'm screwed anyway. The little people always get the shaft," he grumbled. Then he whispered a name.

. . . .

In the corridor, all hell was breaking loose. Piccolo opened the door. A fifty-year-old deputy captain a good foot taller than Coppola was screaming in his face, "I'm reporting you to the disciplinary board! We're not in Chicago here. Just who the hell do you think you are?"

Piccolo stepped out and flashed her badge. The man said, "You can't just come in here and subject one of my men to an interrogation."

Then he whipped out his own badge in return: Deputy Captain Remo Colajacono. He was tall and fit, his long, thick gray hair combed straight back and held in place with plenty of gel; he had a boxer's nose and close-set, dangerous-looking black eyes.

"We can talk about it in your office, if you wouldn't mind, not out here in the middle of the corridor," Piccolo said politely.

The man turned rudely on his heel and showed her the way to an office in a corner. He took a seat below a crucifix and a photo of the president of Italy. Without inviting her to sit, he pointed to Coppola and said, "The officer has to wait outside." Coppola stepped out and closed the office door.

"All right, let's talk about Ramona Iordanescu," Piccolo began.

"She filed a report yesterday morning," he said quickly.

Piccolo restrained a smile. Violent men were often quick to react.

"No, the last time. Did you speak to her?"

Colajacono was uncomfortable because Piccolo wasn't easy to pigeonhole. For him, women fit into one of a small number of categories: mothers, sisters, whores, or murder victims. He was tall, but she was taller. He had quite a high rank, but so did she and on a high-profile special team. To buy time, he lit a cigar.

"Do you mind if I smoke?"

"No," said Piccolo. She got up as if she were at home and went to open the window.

Colajacono decided to take the approach that would give him the most control. "I spoke to her a few minutes that time. She came in midmorning on December 25. Officer Marchese told me there was a young Romanian girl who wanted to speak to the captain, but I took care of her instead. She told me her friend Nadia was missing. I asked her if her friend had a cell phone, and she said no, they couldn't afford phones. I asked her if her friend was happy working the streets and she said no, that she wasn't happy either. She said there's no such thing as a happy prostitute."

Piccolo said nothing, but her look became darker.

"I told her to let us know if her friend didn't show up," Colajacono finished. He visibly relaxed.

Piccolo raised an eyebrow. "Really? You were that vague?"

Colajacono gave her a piercing look with his cold black eyes. "I don't remember exactly what was said. We assumed that whore found some Italian sucker to be her sugar daddy and she stopped working the street."

"Do you think the prostitutes on Via di Torricola are allowed to just stop working?"

"You tell me. You seem to know everything," Colajacono answered sarcastically. He blew smoke in her face.

You can't lay a finger on him, Giulia. Not here, not now.

Piccolo got up.

"We'll start looking for Ramona," she said. Then, looking him straight in the eye with an angelic expression she murmured, "Let's hope nothing happens to her in the meantime."

She found Marchese in the corridor. He'd finished his shift. The two of them and Coppola walked out together. Despite it being almost half past nine, the traffic was still very heavy. They crossed the street at the crosswalk on the corner. Cars and mopeds brushed dangerously close to them. The bar across the street was crowded, mostly with office workers stopping for breakfast before starting their days at their desks. There were also some immigrants dressed for manual labor.

"Fucking Romanians, already drunk on beer at this time of day," Coppola said, not bothering to hide his contempt.

Marchese was more relaxed now that they had left the police station. He and Coppola stayed in the bar, but Piccolo went to the car and sat with the heat on. It was still raining hard and the street was blocked with cars moving at a crawl to get over some rut filled with ten inches of water. Get rid of the potholes and the Roma gypsy camps. That's what the opposition was urging the mayor to do. Potholes and Roma gypsies.

You could fill the potholes with Roma bodies. Many would agree with that. She called Balistreri and told him everything.

"All right, Piccolo. Bring Marchese here and I'll deal with Colajacono."

Piccolo smiled. Balistreri wanted to keep her out of trouble.

· · · ·

"Corvu, I'm meeting Linda Nardi after lunch. Top secret."

Corvu was shocked. Linda Nardi was a journalist, and Balistreri usually avoided journalists like the plague. Moreover, she wrote for a paper that often criticized the police. Balistreri didn't even read it anymore. Five months earlier, during the heat of the Samantha Rossi case, Linda Nardi had been particularly persistent in pointing out the many missteps made by the special team. She'd never joined in calling for Balistreri's head, though.

Balistreri lit his third cigarette of the day and thought about Linda Nardi. How old could she be? She had to be about thirty-five, even though there were days and moments when she looked ten years younger, and others when she looked ten years older. A good-looking woman, no matter her age. The face of a serious child, eyes that went from intensity to detachment in a moment. A woman as polite and open as she was firm in her opinions and uncompromising in making them known. Balistreri knew that they considered her indispensable at the newspaper for the interest her articles aroused in their readers, but also dangerous in the past for the trouble the same articles had caused within political circles, the extremist fringe of the Church, and with officials from several foreign countries.

Rumor had it that many men—including police and journalists—had tried without success to get her into bed. She was courteous, even kind, but she didn't respond to that kind of attention, sometimes with a bluntness that humiliated her would-be suitors.

One of them had been Balistreri's predecessor in homicide, Colicchia, a real Don Giovanni. Having a beautiful woman aound who wouldn't have sex with him disturbed his sense of equilibrium, partly because of his innate presumption and partly because he thought all women were easy. So Colicchia had sent Linda Nardi a bouquet of red roses and a card inviting her to dinner wherever she chose. She had politely declined, but when Colicchia had continued to persist, adding a veiled threat about cutting her off from privileged channels of communication, she finally accepted and had chosen Il Convento for their dinner. Colicchia, who was notoriously cheap, nearly had a heart attack: this was a restaurant with only eight tables where the food was heavenly but outrageously expensive, especially for an honest policeman.

But by then his reputation was at stake. He took her there and rattled off the usual selection of crimes he more or less romanticized and with which he usually impressed his prey, only to discover that Linda Nardi was as insatiable at the table as she was chased away from it. She ordered multiple dishes and the most expensive wines, which she barely touched. Then she began to ask Colicchia to tell her his bloodiest tales. In the end, when they were the only customers left, she began to tell him in all seriousness about her research into certain crimes committed in America by women against men. Tales of horrifying mutilation. In the end Colicchia who, like almost all of the rapid response team, suffered from gastritis and had been forced to drink all the wine she'd ordered and barely touched, had to run to the men's room and throw up, returning to the table as white as a sheet. So ended their night out.

. . . .

As usual, Balistreri decided not to use an official car. It was still raining, Rome was awash.

It was a little after nine thirty, and the city was waking up. Shop owners unlocked their doors. Office workers who were running late—and those who had punched in and then left for breakfast—finished their coffee. Government bureaucrats and messengers were everywhere. A sea of buses, taxis, official cars, and private vehicles with permits surrounded the ministry of the interior as half of Rome's residents tried to gain access to the historic center to get to work. They were all sounding their horns like crazy, as if the cacophony would help move the traffic jam along.

He walked to the Via Cavour subway station. The train was dirty and empty. As he exited the station, two African immigrants entered, jumped the turnstile, and ran down the stairs. Two transit workers shouted at them, and then one turned to the other and said, "Fucking black bastards . . ."

When Balistreri came out of the station, his BlackBerry buzzed with two messages from Corvu: the first contained information about some Romanians he was planning to track down, and the second was simply a place and a time and a pair of initials: *Sant'Agnese in Agone, 3:00 p.m. L.N.*

He took a bus the rest of the way. At least the traffic was moving here, unlike in the narrow alleys of the city center. But the stench of refuse was evident, the garbage collectors having been on strike since the day after Christmas. A private company had cleared the city center so the tourists wouldn't see the eyesore, but in the suburbs, the contents of the trash cans were spilling out onto the pavements and into the middle of the streets.

When he got off the bus, Balistreri saw two homeless people picking up wrappers from all the special Christmas cakes, hoping there might be something left inside. He passed them, noticing the smell of piss and alcohol. One of the two addressed him without ceremony.

"Give us a smoke, boss, will ya?"

Balistreri handed him a cigarette. So much the better—one less for him to smoke.

The billiard hall was located in a building that had seen better days. On the right was the main entrance to the building; on the left was the door to the billiard hall, which sagged half-off its hinges. Behind the bar stood a thin young man with his hair in a ponytail. Two Filipinos were playing the slot machines.

Balistreri ordered a coffee. The bartender poured it immediately and served it with a piece of chocolate. As in every bar in Rome, *Out of Order* was written on the restroom door—except that here, instead of a piece of cardboard, they had written on the door itself, thus making it permanent. Next to the restroom was another door that remained closed. Above it was written BILLIARDS ROOM.

A young thickset guy came in with a shaved head and three-day stubble, wearing a long black leather coat.

"Do you want a beer, Greg?" the bartender asked. He had an Eastern European accent. Greg nodded. He leaned on the bar and lit a cigarette right under the sign that read NO SMOKING. The Filipinos at the slot machines followed his lead and lit cigarettes of their own. "You can't smoke in here," Greg said.

The Filipinos dropped their cigarettes to the floor and stubbed them out with their toes, then started playing again. "Don't just drop your butts on the floor. What are you, animals?"

The younger of the two Filipinos turned around with an attitude, but the other stopped him. They picked up the cigarette butts and left.

"No slant-eyes allowed in here, Rudi," Greg told the bartender. He picked up his glass of beer, burped loudly, and headed into the billiards room. He closed the door behind himself.

"Where are you from?" Balistreri asked the bartender.

"Albania, sir," the bartender answered.

Balistreri flashed his badge, but not his special immigration team ID. "I'm looking for the Lacatus cousins."

"There's only Greg."

"His cousin's not here?"

"Mircea left this morning."

"I was supposed to meet him here," Balistreri said, feigning surprise. "When did he leave?"

"Actually he was here with Mr. Hagi. A half-hour ago he took the car and left. And Mr. Hagi went to Marius Travel, his travel agency."

"What kind of car does Mircea drive?"

The kid thought for a moment. "I don't know, but I paid for the registration, so I have the license plate number." He reached under the counter and took out a piece of paper.

Balistreri typed the number into his BlackBerry and sent it to Piccolo with an order to stop the car and come to the bar as soon as possible. Then he changed the subject.

"Do you know Ramona and Nadia?"

The kid from Albania looked nervously toward the door to the billiards room.

The first difference between the gophers and the real villains: the former look upset, the latter don't give a shit.

"I'll take care of them. I can put them away for a long time. You'll be far away from here before they have a chance to hurt you."

The kid snorted. "In this country? They'd be out before I got to the bus stop."

He's pretty on the ball.

"If you tell me the truth—everything—I'll help you."

"You can't keep me safe," Rudi said.

"Hey, asshole, bring me another beer," Greg boomed from the other side of the door.

Balistreri quietly walked over and locked the door to the billiards room. Then he returned to the bar.

"I want a lawyer," the young bartender said.

Balistreri shook his head. "You're not being accused of anything."

The doorknob began to rattle. Greg was trying to get out.

Balistreri led the bartender outside, turning the sign on the door of the bar to CLOSED on the way. They couldn't hear Greg's threats out there, but Balistreri was pretty sure that by then he'd called someone on his cell phone to come let him out. He sent Piccolo a text message, telling her to get there fast and bring backup. Calmly, he turned to the bartender.

"What's your name?"

"Rudi." The kid relaxed a little. He took a pack of cigarettes and a slim blue lighter out of his pocket. "You want one?"

"No thanks. I've got my own."

Rudi lit a cigarette, his hands trembling. "Greg and Mircea brought them back here at daybreak."

"Was Hagi involved?" Balistreri asked.

"No. Mr. Hagi's different. He pays me and gives me a place to stay. He doesn't live here, but he comes by every morning."

"Where do the girls live?"

"They have a room in an apartment on the second floor. Greg and Mircea share one room. I'm in another, and the two of them are in the third. They went out every day at five. Sometimes they'd have a private client and go out later, but Mircea always took them to meet the private clients."

"Do you know where he took them?"

"No. I asked Ramona once and she said she couldn't tell me."

"Do you remember the last time Mircea went out with them?"

"Yes, December 23. He only took Nadia. Ramona went out at 5:00 as usual. He picked up Nadia at eight thirty. Ramona came back early that night. She wasn't feeling well. It was midnight. The bar was already closed. A little later Mircea came in with Greg, but no Nadia. They stayed down here and played pool. I went upstairs to the apartment and I found Ramona throwing up. So I came back down and made her some tea with lemon, but I didn't tell Mircea and Greg that she was back. We had a toast at midnight with the hot tea because we wouldn't be able to on the twenty-fourth."

At that moment, two young men in leather jackets and jeans pulled up on a motocross bike. They parked the bike and walked toward Balistreri.

"Hey, faggot, what are you doing out here? Blowing old men during working hours?" the taller one said in a strong Eastern European accent. He was beefy and hairy, with tattoos covering his neck and shoulders.

"They're going to tear you a new one, faggot," said the second one, a short guy with yellow teeth. "Did you lock Greg inside so you could suck this old dude's dick?"

Balistreri tried to look humble. "Sorry, sorry. It's my fault. I asked Rudi—"

The larger of the two said, "Fuck off, Grandpa. Go find someone else to suck your cock." He spat on the ground.

Two unmarked cars pulled up and parked. Piccolo and four detectives stepped out. Balistreri nodded to them to enter the bar. They did, and the two Romanians went in as well, followed by Rudi and Balistreri, who locked the door behind them.

"What the fuck you think you're doing?" asked the big guy. Piccolo showed him her badge, and the four plainclothes cops opened their jackets and revealed their guns.

"Hands in the air," Piccolo ordered. A search found that each was carrying a switchblade. Very good.

Piccolo read them their rights and declared them under arrest. Then she handcuffed all three of them, Rudi first.

Then they pulled Greg out, who was beside himself. He had a plastic bag of coke in his pocket. Seeing he was about to jump on the policeman who was searching him, Piccolo delivered a single blow to the solar plexus that made him fall to his knees, gasping for breath. A perfect blow, because it leaves no marks. While Greg was flailing, they handcuffed him. Balistreri shot Piccolo a warning look.

She's just like I was. I'll have to teach her to be a bit more careful.

Piccolo had already called for more cars from the closest police station. They sent the three men in to be booked. Balistreri turned to Rudi, who stayed behind.

"Who's in Ramona and Nadia's room now?"

"No one. I've got the keys. I do the cleaning."

Balistreri winked at Piccolo. They were pushing the envelope.

"Maybe the door's unlocked," Piccolo suggested with faux innocence. "Is it unlocked, Rudi?"

The young guy was sharp.

"Well, now that I think about it, I believe it is."

"Piccolo, go up with Rudi and take a look."

"I'll call Corvu and have him relay custody orders to the prosecutor," she suggested.

Balistreri nodded. "All right. Remember that the sanitation workers are on strike."

Piccolo found Rudi instantly likable. He was polite, helpless, and also, she was surprised to find, very handsome.

When they left the bar to slip into the entrance next door, she kept the handcuffs on and gave him a vicious push.

Just in case one of those shitheads happens to be looking.

They entered using Rudi's keys. The apartment had three rooms with two single rusty iron-frame beds in each, a kitchen, a bathroom, and no living room. The furnishings were basic, mostly junk. In the first room, which belonged to Mircea and Greg, there was a television and a DVD player. The one in the middle was for Rudi and any occasional guests. The last room at the end belonged to Ramona and Nadia, an illegal extension common throughout Rome: a lumber room knocked into a balcony and finished off with aluminum and plastic sheeting. Two ramshackle beds, an old chest of drawers, no closet. Patches of dampness showed through the walls. The bathroom had no windows, no toilet seat, and only the most basic in the way of sink and shower. There was a smell of cigarette butts and ammonia everywhere.

Rudi was growing agitated.

"Ma'am, thank you for leaving the handcuffs on me."

"Please don't call me 'Ma'am.'"

"Officer?" he asked hesitantly.

"I'm a deputy captain, actually," Piccolo told him.

Both beds were made, but one was perfectly neat, while the other was rumpled.

"Which one is Nadia's?"

He pointed to the neat one.

"Mircea told me to change the sheets."

"When?"

"On December 25 about six in the evening, after Ramona went to work. I was down in the bar. He told me to come up here and clean up."

"Clean up what?"

Rudi ran a hand through his hair. He was obviously uneasy in that room.

"Um, it was a mess. There was stuff all over the floor. Clothes. Nadia was messy, and some of it was hers. But Ramona was usually neat, and there were her clothes, too. And Nadia had never been that messy. Then I changed the sheets on Nadia's bed and made Ramona's bed, too."

"Have you been in the room since then?" she asked.

Rudi was trembling.

"Can we get out of here?"

"No problem. Let's go."

They went down to the bar. The detectives were standing outside. Piccolo entered and went into the billiards room with Rudi. Two billiard tables, a foosball table, two card tables, two more slot machines, a phone on the wall. Three black garbage bags closed with twist-ties had been tossed in a corner. *Remember that the sanitation workers are on strike.*

"What are those?"

"Mircea told me to throw the bags that smelled onto the curb and keep the others in here until the strike ended. But I'm sure there were only two. Don't know where that third one came from."

Piccolo called one of the detectives and had him open the three garbage bags. The first two were full of beer cans and bottles, cigarette butts, newspapers, magazines, and other trash. But the third contained a red raincoat, two T-shirts, two polyester miniskirts, a pair of jeans, a pair of beat-up sneakers, a blue sweater, and several pairs of stockings, as well as bras and panties. The underwear fell into two categories: half the kind of showy stuff appropriate for a prostitute and the rest cheap cotton things for a normal teenager.

Rudi burst into silent sobs. Piccolo placed a hand on his shoulder.

Rudi pointed to a bunch of gossip magazines in Romanian that had spilled from one of the bags.

"Those are Nadia's too," he said.

Piccolo bent down, picked up a magazine and started to leaf through it. A card fell out and fluttered to the floor. She picked it up. It was a ticket. *Rome—Iasi. Stazione Tiburtina. December 29, 2005. 6:00 a.m. Seat 12.*

She stepped outside thinking about that empty seat on the coach back home.

· · · ·

It had stopped raining, the sun had come out, and the pavements were gleaming. Traffic was flowing now, too. There was less traffic and so Balistreri took a taxi back to the station.

He looked out the window at the outskirts of Rome: pedestrians, potholes filled with rainwater, garbage everywhere. The taxi driver was unloading on the mayor.

"Look at those potholes. I have to change my tires every two months. You think they had potholes under Mussolini? No way. Politicians don't give a crap. They're only in it for themselves. We're the ones who have to drive around San Basilio, Tor Bella Monaca, Tor de' Cenci, and Quartuccio at night. I'd like to see that Communist prick of a mayor live in one of our neighborhoods with the blacks and the Romanians."

As they approached the center of the city, the refuse grew less and the street life began to change. They passed the Coliseum and the Roman Forum, bursting again with happy tourists.

He arrived back in the office in time for lunch and asked Margherita, the new switchboard operator, if she wouldn't mind picking up lunch for him from the café downstairs. Five minutes later she came back with a bottle of beer and a slice of pizza bianca split in half and made into a sandwich generously stuffed with prosciutto and buffalo mozzarella.

"Margherita, you're a mind-reader. You brought me just what I needed."

The woman blushed and left the room.

That's all that's left to you, Balistreri. Double entendres.

As Balistreri ate his sandwich, he read Piccolo's e-mail about what she'd discovered. Just then Corvu came in, a satisfied smile on his serious face.

"What is it, Corvu?" Balistreri didn't invite him to sit. Corvu liked to move around as he talked.

Corvu glanced at the notepad in his hand. "Something new on Ajello, the lawyer who's manager of the nightclub where the Senegalese man was killed. The Bella Blu belongs to a company called ENT, and we've got something new from the revenue agency."

"Hold on a minute. Tell me about Marchese first. Where is he?"

Corvu looked unhappy with the interruption.

"He's in my office, but you told me not to question him."

"Officially," Balistreri said, "but I can't believe you just sat there and stared at each other without speaking."

"We talked about our native islands."

Balistreri went quiet and Corvu continued, a little uneasily. "He said the Sardinian sea seems more beautiful in appearance because it's more transparent, but the really beautiful sea is Sicily's, which has more soul—"

"He didn't mention Ramona?" Balistreri asked impatiently.

"I'm getting there." Corvu searched for the right words. "Marchese said it's the same with women. Sardinian women seem easier, but, ultimately, Sicilian women—"

"Just tell me what you talked about. What did he say about Ramona?"

At that moment, Piccolo entered before Corvu could reply. "We brought them all in, Captain, including Mircea."

"Tell Mastroianni and Coppola to get ready. We'll need four of you, since there are four Romanians."

"Five," Corvu corrected him. "Marius Hagi is coming in this afternoon with his lawyer."

"I'll question Marius Hagi when you're done with those four."

"There's also the Albanian kid."

Piccolo said, "We have to protect Rudi. I brought him in. Right now he's locked in my office."

"Let's leave him alone for now," Balistreri said. He swigged from the beer bottle, but it was empty. "Corvu was just about to tell me what he got out of Marchese."

"I'm sorry, sir. As I was saying, Marchese said that Ramona was different from Sicilian women, who . . . who are . . " he stammered again, looking desperately at Piccolo, his face burning.

Before Balistreri went completely ballistic, Piccolo finished what Corvu was trying to say: "Saints on the outside and sluts on the inside! Sicilian men are so full of shit." Then she remembered her boss's origins and looked out of the window.

Balistreri broke the silence, pretending he hadn't heard the last part.

"So according to him, Ramona Iordanescu is a saint."

"Yes, a saint," Corvu said. "She had the courage to go back a second time for her friend after Colajacono told her that if he ever saw her again he'd bend her over his desk, fuck her up the ass, and then throw her in prison."

Balistreri saw the muscles in Piccolo's face grow tense.

Trouble ahead. Have to keep her under control.

Afternoon

Balistreri was happy to go on foot to Piazza Navona even though it was full of people, as it always was toward New Year's.

He walked past the stalls, the street performers, the artists drawing caricatures, and the people collecting for charities as he headed toward the church of Sant'Agnese in Agone. Linda Nardi was already there. She had extraordinary eyes, wore no makeup, and dressed like a fifty-year-old. Balistreri had noticed a vertical line that sometimes appeared in the middle of her brow and ran to the bridge of her nose. One day, during an interview, he had stared at her breasts. They were well shaped, not huge but promising, so he certainly wouldn't have embarrassed her. And yet that furrow had appeared straight away. This frown was as inexplicable as the woman herself, who was far too detached in a way that was so different from all the other women he'd known. In a world where the gentler sex could obtain a great deal by seduction, she could have put her good looks to use in so many ways. But Linda Nardi wasn't trying to seduce anyone.

"Ms. Nardi, thank you for agreeing to meet me."

"No problem. I'm a little surprised, though. You're not in the habit of seeking out journalists."

"No, not really," he agreed.

"We'd better go inside before somebody sees us."

The silence in the church was in direct contrast to the noise in the piazza. There were many tourists wandering silently through the aisles, and several Italian families with children pulling at their parents to make them leave. Mass was about to start.

Linda pointed to the pews in a quiet corner. She looked about calmly, as if they were actually there to attend Mass.

"Do you know the story of Saint Agnes, Captain Balistreri?"

"Why don't you tell it to me?" He wasn't particularly interested, but he hadn't quite worked up to asking her for what he wanted.

"The Roman prefect's son had a thing for this Christian girl, Agnes, but the feeling wasn't mutual, and the pain of rejection made him sick. So what do you think the prefect did?"

Balistreri joked, "Fell in love with her himself?"

Nardi shook her head. "To get back at Agnes, who had taken a vow of chastity, the prefect ordered her to be cloistered with the vestal virgins of Rome's patron pagan deity."

"But she wouldn't go?"

"Exactly. Agnes refused and the prefect locked her up in a brothel. Am I boring you, Captain Balistreri?"

He didn't like the story, and the way she was telling it seemed to indicate that she thought he was on the side of the prefect.

"Agnes refused to go to bed with clients?" he asked, knowing that wasn't the story.

"Women can refuse to do almost anything, but they can't defend themselves against men's physical violence. Agnes was lucky. Everyone knew the reason she was there, and for a long time no client dared touch her. Then a man said to be blinded by an angel fell in love with her. Agnes tried to intercede with the Lord to restore his sight and was accused of witchcraft," Linda continued.

"That was her big mistake, don't you think? A vain attempt to challenge authority, an act of pride. Did she want to cure a blind man who loved her or show off the power of her God to the people?"

Linda looked at him for a long time in silence, but without hostility. She seemed to be trying to get to know him better through his reactions to the story. Then she went on.

"Perhaps Agnes didn't want to heal the blind man as much as to bring to light the weakness of the powerful and the strength of the persecuted. Anyway, she was stripped naked and killed. They slit her throat and bled her out, like slaughtering a lamb."

Nardi told the story with little inflection, but her eyes were dark and serious.

"I'm investigating the possible disappearance of a young Romanian prostitute," Balistreri announced without ceremony.

"I'm sorry, I don't understand. Is this the same captain who once said that when it comes to illegal immigrants there's no difference between criminal and victim?"

The words escaped my lips during a heated press conference after dozens of stupid questions from you journalists.

"That's not exactly true. Or maybe I said it, but you're taking it out of context and making it sound xenophobic."

"Your boss, Pasquali, certainly wouldn't approve of the head of the special team wasting his time like this," she cut in.

"That's why I need you to do something for me. But I can't offer you anything in return."

She considered that for a moment.

"I won't do anything illegal."

"I'll be committing a small infraction. You won't run any risk at all."

"And you trust me?" She sounded sincerely surprised.

"I have to trust you. But I'm telling you upfront that this doesn't mean I'm going to give you information about the investigation."

"I didn't ask for any. I wanted to speak to you about something. But not here. If you're free, we can do it one evening over dinner."

From Linda Nardi's lips it was different from how any other woman would have said it. There was no shade or play of meaning. A working dinner. He remembered poor Colicchia.

She read his thoughts, knowing that he and Colicchia had been great friends.

"It'll be on me."

Balistreri looked straight at her.

"I'm still not giving you any information."

"You already said that, Captain. I heard you loud and clear. Are you going to tell me what you want me to do?"

So he told her. She listened in silence until he'd finished speaking. Then she shook her head as if to say no, but at the same time she said, "Okay, I'm in."

· · · ·

Officer Marcello Scordo was a young man in his thirties from Calabria whose movie-star looks had earned him the nickname "Mastroianni," after the famous actor. He was closely attached to a woman from his native region and faithful to her—despite the fact that many beautiful female colleagues had come on to him, sometimes quite openly—so in many ways the nickname was ironic.

"Giorgi and Adrian have regular residency permits and are employed by the travel agency Marius Travel," Mastroianni reported. "They say Marius Hagi is an excellent boss—kind and honest."

"I get it. He's next in line to be pope," Coppola said sarcastically.

"Giorgi and Adrian don't know anything about the girls. On December 24, they left the travel agency with Hagi, Mircea, and Greg. They took the subway straight to Casilino 900 and got there at six. They were together the whole time, and by ten o'clock they were in St. Peter's Square. They weren't the ones who picked up Nadia."

Coppola shook his head. "I'm sure those bastards hang out in St. Peter's Square all the time, praying and meditating."

Balistreri turned to Corvu. "What have you got on Mircea and Greg?"

"Greg and Mircea Lacatus are from Galati's poorest suburbs in Moldova, near the Black Sea, where Marius Hagi is from originally.

He brought them here at the end of 2002. They've got clean records in Italy, but we're checking in Romania. They're on the books as employees of Marius Travel."

"What do they say about the girls?"

"According to them, Nadia and Ramona were prostitutes by choice. They wanted to whore themselves out in order to make money as quickly as possible and get back to Romania. Mircea and Greg found them a place to stay for free at Hagi's. In short, these two were regular guardian angels."

Balistreri turned to Piccolo. "Rudi told us that on the evening of December 23, Nadia didn't go to work on Via di Torricola because she went out with Mircea."

Piccolo nodded. "Mircea says he took her to a restaurant and nothing more. After dinner they argued, because she didn't want to have sex, so he left her where she was and went back home with Greg, who was in the area. Rudi confirms that they were both there at midnight and didn't go out again."

"Corvu, get a printout of the records from the phone company," Balistreri ordered. "Find something that will let us hold them for forty-eight hours. As for Rudi—"

Piccolo raised her hand. "Rudi needs to be somewhere safe before they get out."

Balistreri smiled. "All right, you can see to that. Mastroianni, go to Via di Torricola. The prostitutes should be there soon. Pass yourself off as a client."

Corvu said, "Captain, Mastroianni's hardly a credible client. Maybe we should send someone else." He pointed to Coppola.

Coppola was pissed. "Listen, Corvu, if anyone needs to pay for it, it's you."

Balistreri calmly cut off the argument. Over the years he'd learned the art of mediation.

"Okay, Mastroianni's not a great choice. You go, Coppola, because I need Corvu elsewhere," he said. "Corvu, can you reach out to your Romanian contacts and ask them to speak informally with Ramona in Iasi tomorrow morning? I think there's still time to get on the last flight to Bucharest."

While the others were exiting, Corvu was diligently taking notes. Then he looked at Balistreri. "Mastroianni's going to question Ramona, right?"

Balistreri stood up. "Yes. Do you have anything on the killing of the Bella Blu bouncer?"

In his hand Corvu held two printouts. Balistreri stared at them in disgust.

"Listen, Corvu, we'll do it this way. Just fill me in on the conclusions to your analysis. If I have any doubts, then we'll look at the sheets of paper."

Corvu got to his feet. "Do you mind if I move around?"

Balistreri imagined Corvu out to dinner with a girl, with a stack of papers in front of him full of figures, diagrams, and formulas. She asks him a question whose answer isn't on the sheets of paper. He gets up and starts walking around.

"Corvu, just sit down."

Corvu perched on the edge of a chair and glanced sideways at his notes.

"Well, the Bella Blu's part of a chain of nightclubs, betting parlors, and arcades that belong to a company called ENT. Ajello's been the main shareholder since the end of 2004, when he took over ten percent of the stock from the heirs of a previous shareholder and director, a certain Sandro Corona, who died in an accident at the end of October 2004. The remaining ninety percent of the company, since it was constituted in the middle of 2002, is in the hands of a trust."

"Which means we need a judge and a valid motive to find out who's behind it," Balistreri said.

"Ajello has an immaculate record, but ENT makes a huge profit, five million euros, half a million of which go to Ajello."

"And we have nothing on ENT?" Balistreri asked.

Corvu consulted his notes. "Yes, proceedings on a charge from the finance police in September 2004. They found electronic games in one of the arcades that weren't properly registered and taxed. But ENT was run by Corona back then, not Ajello."

"All right, Corvu, we'll get back to this later. Hagi should be here by now."

Balistreri had known Hagi's lawyer, Massimo Morandi, for more than thirty years. They had met in 1971, when they were students at Rome's Sapienza University and active on opposite political fronts. Morandi, an acknowledged leader of the far left, was giving a speech, and a group of right-wing students led by Balistreri stood out in the hall with bats and crowbars and created a disturbance. Morandi and Balistreri ended up sharing a jail cell, where they passed the night exchanging insults. These days, Morandi was a left-wing senator who made millions in fees defending CEOs accused of false accounting. Less frequently, he also defended immigrants, but only those like Marius Hagi who had the means to pay his exorbitant fees.

When Balistreri and Piccolo entered the room for the informal questioning they had no idea whether to expect a kind of senior underworld boss or someone like Greg. Hagi was neither. He was extremely thin, almost ascetic, with short black hair, hollow cheeks scored with deep furrows, and black eyes set below thick eyebrows and with dark bags underneath. He was dressed in an almost nondescript fashion, and was resting against the chair with his bony hands placed loosely and calmly on the table. He didn't seem worried, as if the matter was nothing to do with him. He had a weary air, a sharp cough, and the rough voice of longtime smoker.

Morandi said, "So, Captain Balistreri, what's the charge against my client?"

"Nothing, officially. We're asking for his help," Piccolo answered.

"I assure you he knows nothing," Morandi said. He didn't even look at Piccolo.

"He knows nothing about his three employees who were armed, one of whom was in possession of cocaine?" Piccolo said.

"The cocaine was not in Mr. Hagi's possession and he knew nothing about it. And the two men with the knives weren't even in the bar."

"We'd still appreciate your client's cooperation in this matter," Piccolo said evenly.

"Be more specific."

"We have some questions. How does a legitimate businessman come to have two prostitutes as houseguests? How does he come to employ people who go around armed with knives and with cocaine in their pockets?" Piccolo asked.

Morandi didn't even look at her. He gave a little laugh and addressed Balistreri. "Do you really think I'd let my client reply to questions of this kind without any corresponding charge? I want to know now, right now, what this is about. You're the special immigration team, not a local precinct."

"You're absolutely right, sir," Balistreri replied. "One of the two young Romanian women living in Mr. Hagi's apartment on Via Tiburtina disappeared on December 24, and the second young woman reported the fact only yesterday, December 28, and as soon as she did she took off for Romania. We have reason to be concerned about the missing woman and the possible involvement of your employees."

Hagi turned deep black burning eyes on him. He spoke in the hoarse voice of a smoker.

"Do you suppose all Italians are honest? There are many prejudices against Romanians, although the majority are normal, inoffensive people. Among those I help, giving them a home or work or a gift, there are extremely honest people and also some young men who are difficult. It would be easy to wash one's hands of them, but then what help would it be if I abandoned precisely those who needed help the most?"

"So, you know about their illegal activities," Piccolo said. Hagi didn't look at her either.

"If by illegal activities you are referring to the fact that Nadia and Ramona sell their bodies on the street, yes, I do know, as do the Italian police, who see them on the street every night. Except that I don't earn a single euro from it, whereas I cannot say the same for your police."

Morandi shifted uneasily.

"They're all employed by your travel agency, aren't they?" Piccolo asked.

"Yes. And they work hard, at least twelve hours a day. I often send Greg and Mircea to Poland and Romania to check out new hotels and restaurants. Giorgi and Adrian look after the office in Rome."

"And they need to be armed with knives to do that?" Piccolo asked.

Hagi smirked. "They live in the Casilino 900 camp. If you lived there, you'd need more than just muscle for protection, too."

"Are you telling us they're good guys?" asked Balistreri. Hagi had another coughing fit and followed it with a weak smile.

"Are Greg and Mircea good guys? No. Honestly, they're terrible people. But their parents helped me escape from Ceausescu's Romania when I was young. In 2002, they told me that Greg and Mircea had moved on from dealing contraband goods to dealing drugs. They asked me to take them to Italy and find work for them. I did. I couldn't deny the people who saved my life. I set down clear rules for Greg and Mircea. I told them they were going to work hard, and they couldn't have weapons or get involved in crime."

"Aside from a little cocaine and prostitution," Piccolo said. Balistreri shot her a warning glance.

"If they push so much as one gram of cocaine I'll send them back. They know that. They probably had it for personal use. Plenty of Italians do the same thing, including the police and politicians."

Balistreri caught a trace of deep embarrassment on Morandi's face.

Balistreri said, "What about Ramona Iordanescu and Nadia? First, do you know Nadia's last name?"

"No. She was a guest and paid no rent, therefore I wasn't obliged to report her presence."

You're almost as good as a lawyer yourself, Marius Hagi. This country's brought you up well.

"The girls were there almost a month and you never saw them?"

"I don't live there, and we had completely different schedules."

"But you knew that Nadia was missing and Ramona was about to leave?"

"Greg told me Nadia might be missing on the evening of December 25. Mircea told me today that Ramona left."

"What do you make of that?"

"Of what?" Hagi seemed genuinely surprised by the question.

"Nadia has been missing for five days. What do you think happened to her?" Piccolo asked.

"I haven't the faintest idea."

"All right," Piccolo said, pressing forward, "let's go back to December 24. We're interested in what happened from six o'clock onward."

Morandi raised a hand for them to pause and whispered something in his client's ear. Hagi shook his head calmly and replied.

"At six o'clock I left Marius Travel with the other four. We took the subway to Via Togliatti. From there, they went to Casilino 900 and I walked to my house to pick up presents for the children. I put the presents in my car and drove to Casilino 900. We celebrated Christmas there with sparkling wine and panettone, and the children opened their presents. At half past nine I went home. The others went to St. Peter's Square."

"Why didn't you go to St. Peter's with them?" Balistreri asked.

"I was tired. My health isn't what it used to be. I go to bed early these days." After a long pause, he added, "And because if God existed, I'd be more likely to find him in Casilino 900 than in St. Peter's Square."

. . . .

Pasquali's secretary, Antonella, was a Mediterranean beauty of forty. She and Balistreri had slept together a few years earlier, but it had never been anything more than physical. He had subsequently lost interest and the sex had grown less frequent until it disappeared altogether. However, in its place a friendship was born in which Antonella was able to lavish her maternal instinct on this man who had so little enthusiasm for life.

She ushered Balistreri into the small meeting room, which was decked out like a room in a stylish apartment with an ultra suede sofa and armchairs, a marble coffee table, and a nineteenth-century bar cabinet in one corner. Out on the balcony stood a sculpture of an angel surrounded by allegorical figures representing the fine arts. Pasquali called it his guardian angel.

"Pasquali's with the chief of police. They'll be here soon. Would you like coffee?"

Balistreri knew he couldn't smoke and that coffee would make him want a cigarette, so he declined.

On the one hand, the chief of police means problems, but on the other there are advantages.

A telephone and a few magazines sat on the coffee table. Balistreri glanced at the cover of a magazine with a photo of Casilino 900 and the headline "Europe's Gift to Italy."

The scent of expensive aftershave announced Pasquali's arrival. He ushered in the chief of police. Pasquali's dark-gray designer suit was impeccable. His gray hair was perfectly styled, and he wore a pair of glasses with sleek titanium frames. In comparison, the chief of police looked like a country bumpkin, and Balistreri a homeless man plucked from the street and rinsed off with a hose.

Pasquali's greeting to Balistreri was cold and formal, but the chief of police shook his hand and smiled. Floris belonged to those leftists Balistreri had fought when he feared them. Nowadays, when he found them as inoffensive and confused as a ninety-year-old in the middle of traffic, he looked at people like Floris with more objectivity. Floris was no genius, but he was a good man.

Over the years he had had to learn to live with people who were incapable as well as those like Pasquali, who were capable of anything.

The inevitable compromises, as my papa used to say. The ones that make a child into a man.

Pasquali offered the chief a seat in one of the two large armchairs, while he took the other. Balistreri grabbed the sofa.

Pasquali turned to Balistreri. "So, the chief of police is present at this meeting for two reasons: one urgent, the other more basic."

"Urgent things first," Floris said.

Although it was obvious that the balance of power tilted toward Pasquali, there were appearances to keep up: rank, age, hospitality. All things in which Pasquali was a master. He spoke affably.

"The chief of police has received a telephone call from the commissioner's deputy prefect." Pasquali paused. Balistreri sensed that he was searching for any sign of guilt, fear, or embarrassment on his face. Pasquali really was a master of the pause, the meaningful silence, and the unexpected question. He was a very talented actor.

"It seems that one of your deputies, together with a colleague . . ." Floris's voice trailed off as he searched for the right words.

"Created a disturbance in a police station," Pasquali finished for him.

Balistreri raised an eyebrow and frowned, as if he were trying to remember something. He turned directly to the chief of police.

"Did the prefect really use the word *disturbance*?"

"No, no," Floris said. "They're alleging intimidation of Deputy Captain Colajacono and seizure of an officer inside the station."

"Did they use the word *seizure*?" asked Balistreri with an even more bewildered air.

"The word choice really isn't important," Pasquali said. "We're here to ask *you* some questions and receive an explanation. And when I say 'we,' I mean the two of us plus the prefect." His voice was soft and calm. He was a man who didn't need to raise his voice for his orders to be obeyed.

Balistreri stood up. He knew his attitude would irritate not only Pasquali but also the good nature of the chief. It was essential, however, that some time should elapse. He went to the bar cabinet and chose an unopened bottle of Delamain cognac and twisted the cap. He turned to the two men. "Excuse me, but I need a drink."

Balistreri sat down with his glass of 1971 cognac. He needed another forty minutes. He spent thirty of them relating the story of Nadia and Ramona.

"And where are Marchese and the Albanian now?" the chief asked.

What a good man you are.

"No need to worry," Balistreri reassured him. "They're both safe in our offices."

"Was the officer arrested?" Pasquali asked.

"Of course not. He's with us of his own free will."

"But you did question him?" Pasquali asked, not bothering to hide his irritation.

"He chatted a little with Corvu, one of my deputies. They talked about Sardinian women versus Sicilian women."

He turned to Pasquali with a submissive air. "I was planning to tell you. I'm certainly not hiding anything. I want to proceed with the arrest of Deputy Captain Colajacono."

Pasquali was truly a cold-blooded animal. Balistreri watched as he paused to reflect, weighing the pros and cons—the political implications, of course, not anything to do with the investigation.

He was being forced to think on his feet and answer in front of the chief of police.

"First the chief of police and I will have a word with the prefect. In the meantime, you will refrain from taking action of any kind."

There was no hint of menace in his voice, but without question it was an order. With two sentences, he had re-established who was in command.

The telephone on the table rang. Pasquali answered and said, "Antonella, during meetings like this I don't want—"

He was suddenly quiet. "Put her through to my office," he said. Something serious. Not only was he interrupting a meeting with the chief of police, but he didn't want to be overheard.

Balistreri decided it was time to visit the angel. He would allow himself his fourth cigarette of the day, and he knew that Floris always kept a half-smoked cigar in his pocket. He nodded and indicated the door to the balcony with a tilt of his head. They stepped outside.

Up on the fourth floor, the sound of the traffic was a little muted. The well-lit streets were full of shoppers. It was cold but no longer raining. The balcony was dirty; the rain had turned the dust on the railing to muck.

"Your relationship with Pasquali seems a little strained," Floris said apropos of nothing.

"I'm working to improve it," Balistreri said obediently. His fate depended on the chief of police. Pasquali didn't have the authority to demote him.

Floris took a puff on his Tuscan cigar. "It's a shame. Until the Samantha Rossi case came along, the two of you saw eye to eye." Floris was one of the few people familiar with the details of the case.

"But ever since you've had my back. Why is that?"

The chief mulled that over. "First of all, I happen to think you're one of our best men. And second." Floris paused.

Balistreri drew an R in the wet grime on the balcony railing. "It seems easy enough, but you have to know how to write," he said.

"Exactly. And we've arrested three illiterates."

. . . .

Pasquali reappeared in the room. He started tapping his fingers on the arm of the chair, which for someone like him was a sign of deep agitation.

"We have a problem," he said to both of them. "That was Linda Nardi, the journalist. My secretary told her that I wasn't available to speak to her and she told her to give me a message, immediately."

"What message?" Floris asked.

Pasquali's eyes met Balistreri's. "Her message was 'the Torre Spaccata police station.'"

The chief of police looked startled. Pasquali kept his eyes on Balistreri.

Yes, you know I'm capable of it. But you can't do a damn thing. Not now.

Balistreri looked interested and at the same time concerned. He had to be very careful not to overdo either his indifference or his concern.

If the chief of police had the slightest inkling of what Pasquali suspected, he was in trouble.

"What did you say to her?" Floris asked Pasquali.

Pasquali grimaced. "She told me that an informant told her there was a fight of some kind in the Torre Spaccata police station this morning."

Pasquali paused, clearly waiting for Balistreri to speak. But Floris spoke first. "That's hard to believe. Who would be talking to her?"

Balistreri said, "There were a lot of officers in the station, and plenty of civilians. Any one of them could have called her. Unfortunately, Colajacono made a real scene. Piccolo escorted him to a private room, but he was a little out of control."

"Fucking moron," Pasquali mumbled. Balistreri had never heard him swear before.

Pasquali continued, "Nardi sent one of her reporters to the station, and a policeman told her that the fight occurred between members of the special team and Deputy Captain Colajacono over a report made by a friend of the missing Romanian woman."

"What does she want?" Floris asked. He looked as if he were already picturing the headline to a damaging front-page article: POLICE RIFT OVER RECENT DISAPPEARANCE. That was the best-case scenario.

And so they might have got away with it. But Linda Nardi wasn't the kind of person to stop there. Unlike her colleagues, she wasn't after any scoop, but something far more dangerous: the truth. He would have to warn the mayor and ask him to call the newspaper's managing director, or better still the owner.

Now, with a touch of sadism, Pasquali landed the chief of police with what Linda Nardi had said on the telephone. "She's filing a request to get access to the missing persons report. She wants to see the original, no copies."

Balistreri had difficulty holding back a smile. The bit about the original was Linda Nardi's touch.

"We can't do that," Floris said.

"If we refuse, she'll just print an article in the paper tomorrow saying that we refused her request," Pasquali said.

Floris poured himself a generous shot of Delamain. He sank into an armchair and relit his cigar without asking Pasquali's permission. Balistreri could read his thoughts. The article comes out, the entire press demands an explanation. We refuse on the grounds that an investigation is underway. But we can't be sure whether the person who spoke to Nardi told her that Colajacono sent Ramona packing the first time and discouraged her from coming back. If that got out, it would spell trouble for everyone, starting with the chief of police.

Pasquali had already arrived at the same conclusion. "I told her I wasn't aware of any fight, but an investigation is underway about the way the report was filed, so I can't give it to her tonight but she can have it tomorrow."

"And she was okay with that?" Floris asked.

"She did ask me a question before she agreed. She wanted to know whether we were using this time to question Colajacono and the officer who filed the report." Pasquali looked at Balistreri. "Naturally, I said yes."

I know you'll make me pay dearly for this. But this evening we're doing it my way. And you can take it as you like, along with that guardian angel on your balcony.

Evening

Before he went out, he allowed himself a few moments' reflection. Panting a little with the effort, he climbed the last flight of stairs that led to the roof of the old building. He had the key to the unused terrace where washtubs once stood and the washing was hung out to dry. The building was at the top of a slope, and on the roof it appeared as if you were on a tenth floor. It was dark and the noise of the traffic was only a distant hum. To his right he could see the floodlit Quirinale with the Italian flag fluttering on it. In front of him stood the white marble of the Victor Emmanuel Monument and Mussolini's balcony on Piazza Venezia; to his left were the Colosseum and the Roman Forum.

This was the center of the new political power that had replaced the traditional parties after the Tangentopoli corruption and bribery scandal in the 1990s. New only in a manner of speaking, of course. The only new things were the issues: a country that was too well nourished and therefore lazy, too old and therefore weary. A country that needed young immigrants but was scared of them and had no system for integrating them or economic model to follow. In addition, St. Peter's majestic cupola reminded the city and the whole world that behind those walls was an immense power enclosed in less than half a square mile.

I thought I could change the world, at least a little. But the world wasn't in the least bit interested, and instead it changed me.

He'd witnessed the decline of the West parallel to the decline of his own body and spirit. The mistakes he made as a reckless and thoughtless youth had gradually turned into sins. In the cloud of remorse, his dreams had finally dissipated.

Slowly, inexorably, he had become what he had thought it was impossible for him to become: a bureaucratic old civil servant like his former boss, Teodori.

If I were offered the chance to be a child and start over again, I'd refuse. The effort would be unbearable.

. . . .

When he came down he found Corvu and Piccolo waiting outside his office. They had been worried about him for some time.

"Marchese says Colajacono offered to swap shifts with him and Cotugno on the night of December 24 as a favor, even though he was tired," Piccolo said.

"So who was on duty between nine on the night of December 24 to the morning of December 25?" Balistreri asked.

"Colajacono and his right-hand man, Officer Tatò," Piccolo said.

Corvu was impatient. "It's half past eight, sir. We have to get going if we want to catch Colajacono at the police station."

"You can see to Colajacono on your own, Corvu. His boss has already been informed by the chief of police."

I don't want Piccolo getting into any trouble.

"And What if he won't refuses to cooperate?" asked Corvu the rule-follower asked, ever attentive to the rules.

"Either he comes voluntarily or you arrest him for twenty-four hours. No interrogation tonight, nothing until tomorrow morning. Just make sure he has no contact with the outside world. He'll be very comfortable here in our guest room."

He turned to Piccolo. "You talk to this Tatò, Piccolo, but outside the police station. And one last thing."

"I won't lay a finger on him, Captain, not to worry," Piccolo said, holding her hands behind her back. He suspected she was crossing her fingers.

"Captain, today's Thursday," Corvu reminded him as he left.

Thursday. Dinner with Alberto. Poker.

He grabbed his cell phone to postpone.

His brother answered on the first ring. "Michele, I can't talk. I've got to keep any eye on the guanciale. I'm making a carbonara that will blow your mind."

· · · ·

Colajacono showed no surprise at seeing Corvu. His massive form filled the whole threshold to his office door. Smoothing his hair, he said, "Can I help you?"

Corvu introduced himself. He was tiny compared to beefy Colajacono. A twig next to an oak.

"I'd like to invite you respectfully to come to the special team offices for an informal meeting, not for questioning, and we'll put you up for the night."

"A night in the historic center in your fine establishment? That sounds nice, but I've got plans."

Corvu's steely Sardinian soul came to the fore.

"If you don't come tonight, I'll have to come back with a warrant tomorrow, and then everyone will know about it."

Colajacono spat. The gob landed a few inches from Corvu's feet.

"Okay, I'll come and sleep over. Is the room service any good in your hotel?" he asked in a nasty tone.

They went out along the corridor where several policemen were standing. Colajacono turned to them with a smile, his small eyes gleaming with irony.

"Boys, I'm just taking a stroll down to the offices of the smart police down in the city center. I'll be back tomorrow."

. . . .

EUR, south of Rome toward the coast, was a suburban area built in the Fascist era to house the 1942 Universal Exhibition in Rome, but then World War II intervened and the exhibition was cancelled. Work was completed after the war.

In the evening the district is almost deserted. The bars and restaurants that work frenetically until early afternoon for its thousands of workers are already closed by dinnertime. On the whole, the atmosphere is almost weightless, in contrast to the hubbub, chaos, and heat of the historic city center.

The villa where Balistreri's brother lived with his German wife and two teenage sons stood at the end of a narrow street. There was always a patrol car parked on the street, because an important politician lived there. For Balistreri that car's constant presence, even when the politician had no official engagements, was a sign of what Italy had become.

Alberto opened the door wearing a chef's apron. He was Michele's older brother, but he'd taken better care of himself. More exercise, no smoking, little drinking, a happy marriage, two fine sons, a career as a well-paid executive: the ideal outcome after he'd earned a bachelor's and a master's in engineering in the United States. His was a life full of plans and positive thoughts.

They embraced, then went into the kitchen. The house was hot. A halogen lamp lit the living room and the background music was the old Pink Floyd album *Meddle*. Along with Leonard Cohen and Fabrizio De André, it was one of his favorites.

"You've lost more weight, Michele."

Balistreri was aware that his clothes were now too big for him, but he didn't want his brother to worry. He'd done enough of that for a lifetime.

"I know, it's weird. I skip a meal now and then, but I do eat. Anyway, I'll make up for it tonight. What are you making besides the carbonara?"

Alberto pointed to his nose. It was his chef's obsession: you could tell good things by their aroma.

Balistreri sniffed. "Lamb," he said. "And I think I smell strudel."

Alberto nodded. "But we'll wait for Angelo and Graziano for dessert." He popped the cork from a bottle of Frascati. "The strudel's too hot to eat now. In an hour or so it will be perfect. Would you grab the red wine? That goes with the lamb."

Balistreri saw the empty bottle of Brunello di Montalcino that had been opened two hours earlier and decanted into a wooden Piedmont-style carafe. His brother really did love him: in order to serve him his favorite wine, Alberto was breaking one of his cardinal rules. The lamb was a Roman specialty, and Alberto was a fervid believer in pairing food with wine from the same region.

The table was laid for two. Balistreri wandered around the room. So many photos, a peaceful life framed in silver. Alberto, his lovely wife, two boys with open, eager faces. In the only wooden frame was a black and white shot taken on the shore in Tripoli. Alberto and Michele as children dressed in short pants and knee socks. Beside them stood their mother, Italia, and their father, Salvatore Balistreri, a captain of industry.

She was looking at the sky, he at the ground. Honor and strength. An obviously unequal duel.

Alberto interrupted his thoughts.

"Okay, Michele, it's ready. Angelo and Graziano will be here soon."

The carbonara was delicious. Crisp guanciale, perfectly cooked spaghetti, just enough egg to coat the strands. The chilled Frascati was the perfect accompaniment.

"I wanted to ask your opinion about the slot-machine market," Michele said.

"For investigative reasons?" Alberto was never happier than when he felt he was helping with a case.

The oven timer went off. "I'll go and get the lamb and we'll talk about it," he said. He disappeared into the kitchen with the empty white wine glasses.

When Alberto had returned and settled back into his seat, he said, "After an investigation into illegal video-poker games in 2004, the government decided to regulate things before the situation got any worse. Also, the national debt was growing so quickly that collecting that kind of money was going to come in handy."

"What kind of money are we talking about?"

"Fifteen billion euros a year from the legal ones," Alberto said.

"Billion with a B?"

"Billion with a B. About three quarters of the money goes back to the players in winnings. Let's say that the system keeps almost four billion euros and hands one and a half billion over to the government. Up until 2004, that one and a half billion stayed in circulation. Think what kind of fortunes were amassed from unregulated video-poker. And there are still two and a half billion floating around each year. That's not even counting the illegal games."

"Meaning what?"

"The games that still aren't plugged into the system so that taxes are collected. No one can seem to do anything about them. Even if the financial police find out about them, they can only levy administrative fines."

Balistreri made a face and sweetened his taste buds with the last piece of lamb and a sip of Brunello.

At exactly ten thirty the intercom buzzed. It was Corvu, who had been home to spruce himself up. Out of consideration to Alberto he was wearing a suit, whereas during the day he went around in jeans and a sweater. His hair was still wet from showering, but he would never have arrived late. He had brought along a bottle of homemade alcoholic cordial made from Sardinian bilberries. They put it in the fridge and Corvu sat down at the table with them.

"Have you eaten, Graziano?" Alberto asked him. He always addressed Corvu by his first name, which Balistreri couldn't bring himself to do, even when they were off-duty.

"I have, but that lamb smells amazing, Alberto," Corvu said. He gratefully accepted a plate. Then he turned to Balistreri. "Everything's in order. Colajacono's staying the night in our offices."

Their Thursday evening poker sessions had been going on for three years. Corvu had replaced Colicchia, Balistreri's predecessor, when he retired and moved away from Rome.

"Alberto was just explaining how bar owners make money off of their slot machines," Balistreri said to Corvu.

"What role does ENT play in the value chain?" Corvu asked. He must have picked up the technical term in one of his evening classes in economics.

"What the hell is a 'value chain'?" Balistreri asked.

The intercom buzzed again, and Balistreri went to open the door for Angelo. With growing irritation he heard Alberto explain the famous chain to Corvu and Corvu reply, "Oh yes, I see. That explains it all."

. . . .

Piccolo took advantage of the wait to call home. Rudi answered after just one ring.

"Deputy Piccolo's residence."

"Rudi, I told you to answer the phone only after three rings and then a hang-up. And not like Jeeves the butler. I don't want anyone to know you're there."

"I'm sorry. You have a beautiful apartment. I'm very grateful for your hospitality."

"No problem, Rudi. The fridge is full, so help yourself."

"No, I'll cook something and wait till you come home. I'm really good in the kitchen."

She saw Tatò coming out of the police station and ended the call. Tatò was a fat forty-year-old with thinning hair and rheumy eyes. She followed his car for a mile or two. The Capannelle racetrack was lit up, and the parking lot was crowded. Tatò parked on the sidewalk, and Piccolo was forced to do the same.

The stands at the track were almost full. She trailed him, trying not to get too close. Tatò sat at a table with three other middle-aged guys, clearly gambling men like himself. She saw him take out a wad of hundred-euro bills and speak animatedly. They were deciding where to place their bets.

She caught the words ". . . the jockey swears he'll go slow . . ." and Tatò saying "If he fucks up, he knows I'll arrest him, no problem."

Glasses of whiskey arrived while one of the men went off to the tote windows. Piccolo sat down nonchalantly in the vacated seat,

"That seat's taken," one of the men said.

Piccolo ignored him. "I need to speak to you," she said to Tatò.

There was no need to show her badge. He'd gotten a good look at her that morning in the police station.

He glanced around. He didn't want a scene. "I'm off duty, Deputy."

"So I see. Unless you moonlight here."

Tatò turned to the other two men. "I'll see you guys later."

They got up without a word, but the look they gave Piccolo clearly expressed what they would have liked to do to her.

Why don't you try it? You'd be in for a nice surprise.

"Can I get you anything to drink, Deputy?" Tatò had decided to take the path of politeness.

"No, thanks. I *am* on duty."

"What can I do for you?"

Piccolo got down to business. "Let's talk about the evening of December 24, when you and Colajacono were in the station in place of Marchese and Cutugno. Why did you offer to take over their shifts?"

"We felt sorry for them. They'd worked nine to nine every night during the holidays. They asked if they could at least spend Christmas Eve with their families."

"Cutugno and Marchese said it was Colajacono's idea."

Tatò looked slightly uncomfortable. "Well, maybe it was. I don't know who came up with the idea. I just know they were thrilled to have the night off."

"And Colajacono suggested that you and he take their shift?"

Tatò thought for a moment. "He suggested it to me on the morning of December 24. Colajacono's like that. He believes people at the top should set an example. Besides, neither of us is married."

"And neither of you went to midnight mass, I presume?"

"I went to Mass at six in the local parish church—it's next to the police station."

"And after Mass?"

"Colajacono was waiting for me outside the church. It was almost seven. We drove around the precinct. It was all quiet. Everyone was going home for Christmas Eve dinner. We stopped to eat something in the little restaurant across from the station; it was the only one open. We were back in the office just before nine."

That was a lot of things to check. Mass and the meal in the restaurant were easy, the drive around more difficult. The patience of Corvu would be required.

The roar of the crowd announced the start of the race. The group at a gallop was at the other end of the oval. Piccolo saw that Tatò was following the race with trepidation, beads of sweat forming on his forehead. The horses were approaching their part of the stands, and the crowd was on its feet. Tatò watched intently. In the home stretch, number six went ahead and won by a head. Tatò cheered.

Piccolo said, "Let's get back to December 24, after Mass. Did you drive past Casilino 900?"

Now that Tatò's horse had won, he was more relaxed. "There was no need. Everything was quiet. They were setting up for a party themselves. Even the gypsies celebrate Christmas, you know. They use all the money they steal from Italians."

Piccolo clenched her fists but remembered Balistreri's advice. "So, you have no idea where Colajacono was between six and seven while you were at Mass?"

Tatò nodded thoughtfully. People were moving toward the windows to place their bets.

"From nine o'clock onward you didn't leave the police station?" Piccolo asked.

"That's right, we didn't leave until the morning after."

"Neither of you went out?"

"No, neither one of us."

"How can you be so certain? You were together the whole twelve hours?"

Tatò let out a guffaw. "Well, not exactly. I don't know about you, but when I go to the John I don't like company."

Concentrate on the objective here. Don't let yourself be distracted by anger. Do as the boss told you.

She counted to ten, then started calmly again. "Apart from calls of nature, you were always together. Therefore you would be ready to swear that Colajacono was with you from seven o'clock until nine, and in the twelve hours from nine that night until nine the following morning he never left the station."

"Absolutely," Tatò said. "Now if you don't mind, I need to place a bet."

. . . .

Balistreri opened the door. There stood his best friend of more than twenty years. His only friend, really. Alberto was his brother, and Corvu was a colleague.

Angelo Dioguardi hardly looked any older, but he'd become a lot stronger over the years. Breaking off his engagement with Paola and resigning from his job with her uncle the cardinal in 1982 had changed him. Paradoxically, while Balistreri felt that his own life had been in decline since then, that was when things had started looking up for Angelo.

They had never stopped their endless nights of conversation about things great and small, but their roles in life had become reversed. Now it was Angelo who, not often but every once in a while, went after women in search of the ideal he never found, while on the same front Balistreri had retreated: endless repetition, the sense of guilt, and the lack of stimulating women had all played a part. And while Balistreri had become ever more involved in the mechanisms of networking and in the bureaucracy he had so hated, Angelo Dioguardi had become one of the ten best professional poker players in the world. He continued to donate a large portion of his winnings to charity, but he now oversaw their use directly.

While Alberto and Corvu were talking about balances and the damn value chain, the two friends went into the living room. Angelo lit his thirtieth cigarette of the day and poured himself a double whiskey; Balistreri lit his fifth and refilled his water glass. Whiskey upset his stomach.

"I have a question for you, Angelo. I'd like some information about illegal gambling. You must have seen some early in your career."

Angelo frowned. "Have they transferred you to the vice squad?"

"Don't be a prick. I just need some information."

"Michele, times have changed. Today there are high-stakes tournaments in private clubs, but it's all legal. They pay taxes and everything."

"What are 'high stakes'?"

"Depends on the jackpot. I think it's quite high in the midlevel tournaments. What exactly do you want to know?"

"I'm investigating a company that runs a nightclub and poker tables, slot machines, and betting parlors. It's controlled by some trust abroad."

Angelo thought for a moment. "I suppose you could use that kind of business for money-laundering. But for large amounts of money, you'd need something bigger."

"Such as?"

"I've ever been involved in anything like that. My poker winnings are more than enough for me."

"I know, you're a saint. I'm certainly not accusing you of anything. But if you were going to do something like that, how would you arrange it?"

"Serious money-laundering uses property, not in Italy, but in places where you can buy a skyscraper for cash in a week—the Caribbean, Dubai, Macao."

"And where does the money come from?"

"Criminal operations: drugs, arms dealing, prostitution. It's not just Italian criminals, of course. Even our criminals are falling behind the Russians and the Chinese. The Russians will fly in with a suitcase full of cash and buy a couple of apartment buildings during the course of a weekend."

"But even the Italians . . ."

"Sure. But Italian criminals tend to invest at least some of their money in Italy. Real estate, retail chains, hotels, the service industry, nightclubs. They want to create jobs here. That way they can sway votes, which means they can influence politicians."

"Are you talking about kickbacks?" Balistreri asked.

Angelo smiled. "Kickbacks no longer exist since the Tangentopoli trials, right? Look, anyone with his hand in the public purse is more careful these days. They prefer to sweeten a deal with a nice penthouse purchased in cash for the guy's children, or they'll renovate a country house. Someone small-time might get a hooker."

"Where does our slot machine and nightclub company fit in?"

"Right in the middle, most likely. It invests the illegal money that's been laundered abroad in Italy."

Angelo lit another cigarette. Balistreri watched him with envy. "How many do you smoke?"

Angelo shook his head. "That depends on my mood. One or two packs a day. Please don't lecture me. Not you, of all people."

"I've cleaned up my act, you know that. What about women?"

Angelo smiled. "It's a time of freedom, of transition. Anyway, it's not my fault I sleep around so much. I'd like to stay with the same women, but they all get bored with me eventually."

"It's your fixation with love. Why can't you be satisfied with a simple healthy fuck?"

"Look who's talking."

"I'm the opposite—I'm sick of feeling guilty because of women's illusions. The price to pay is too high."

Angelo thought for a moment, looking perplexed by the affirmation and sorry for his friend.

"Michele, you're confusing value with price."

"Comparing, not confusing."

"I wanted to say that some things are priceless."

He said it with the humility of an uneducated boy from the working-class slums in the face of an educated middle-class friend. For Balistreri that "I wanted to say," which Angelo sometimes used, almost to excuse himself when he wasn't in agreement, was the starting point for their great friendship and kept it alive.

Alberto called them to order. The card table was ready. Things went as they nearly always went. Angelo won, almost without wanting to. In all this time, they still hadn't understood when he was bluffing and when he had a good hand. In the end he won, and the winnings went to a nonprofit that ran homeless shelters.

As Angelo drove Balistreri home, Balistreri felt drained from the interminable day.

"I really need one," he said, pointing to the pack of cigarettes.

"Then I'll keep you company," Angelo said, lighting his fortieth of the day.

They ended up talking until four in the morning.

FRIDAY, DECEMBER 30, 2005

Morning

MASTROIANNI'S FLIGHT FROM BUCHAREST landed in Iasi at eight. The airport was small, but modern and functional, like many things built in Eastern Europe after the fall of Communism. A lanky young man in a jacket, tie, and jeans was waiting for him at the arrivals exit.

"I'm Florean Catu, deputy inspector of police," he said.

"Marcello Scordo. Do you speak Italian? My Romanian isn't very good."

Catu smiled. "My aunt lives in Florence; I visit her every summer."

They drove off in Catu's Golf. There were few people around. It was very cold, but the sky was clear. The city's architecture reflected successive periods in Romanian history: a few ancient buildings, the small low terraces from the years between the wars, stark monumental buildings from the Communist period, and last of all the post-1989 era, represented by modern buildings that looked like they'd fall over in a stiff wind.

"We're interviewing people in the country villages near Iasi to find out Nadia's last name. Maybe someone was waiting for her to arrive for the holidays and reported her missing, but I doubt it," Catu said, driving between the few vans and bicycles.

"Wouldn't her relatives be worried when they didn't hear from her?"

"You'd think so, but here we only start to worry after several months, not several hours. We're going to pick up Ramona near the university, but we can't force her to answer your questions."

"I'd like to speak to her alone. That way if there was a crime involved, the Romanian police won't know about it."

Catu appeared to be weighing the pros and cons.

"All right, but you'll have to question her outside the police station. There's a bar on December XIV Square that makes the city's best and most expensive espresso. Take her there."

. . . .

Balistreri had slept only a couple of hours, and in that brief time he'd had nothing but dreams full of unanswered questions. Exhausted, he ate a breakfast of decaf and whole-wheat toast, then walked to the office in a cold drizzling rain.

At seven thirty Corvu arrived punctually at his office together with Piccolo, who looked a little too subdued for her normal self.

"Did you find a safe place for Rudi?" Balistreri asked.

She flushed and looked at Corvu.

"The witness is receiving excellent protection. He's staying at Piccolo's place."

Balistreri felt a twinge of anxiety. He couldn't stop himself from being sarcastic. "Really? A homosexual linked to a criminal gang is sleeping in the home of a female deputy captain? Great idea."

You've become an old pain in the neck. And she's not your daughter.

"Precisely," continued Corvu. "Corvu said, "Well, we figured since he's gay, better Piccolo's apartment than mine." Before Balistreri could answer, he changed the subject. "Sir, Coppola's waiting. He's ready to report on the prostitutes he's questioned."

They brought Coppola in.

"Well," he began in embarrassment, "I'm sorry to say I found out very little."

"Well, let's hear it," encouraged Balistreri.

"I talked to the four girls who were there on the night of December 24 and who stood near Ramona and Nadia's usual spot. I asked for information about charges, services offered, and so on."

"Okay, Coppola," Balistreri said, "spare us the rates for their services. Did you get any useful information?"

"I learned two things. The girls watched out for each other. They took customers' license plate numbers. Second, the evening of December 24 was quiet. They didn't see Nadia go off with anyone and they haven't seen anyone acting strange. But one girl did mention a car with a broken headlight. She remembered because from a distance it looked like a motorcycle."

"Did she know the model?" Corvu asked.

"She didn't see it. Her cousin saw it. She was alone that night, so her cousin was there with her."

"Good. Bring her in and I'll question her and see if we can figure out the model," Corvu said. "Did the girls on the other side of the street see anything?"

Coppola shook his head. "They don't remember it."

Balistreri looked worried.

He persuaded Nadia to get in. He switched off the headlights. Bad sign.

. . . .

The area was full of young people on foot or on bicycles. While Mastroianni buzzed the intercom for Ramona a pair of female students gave him an inviting wink, which he returned with an inoffensive smile.

Ramona Iordanescu was good-looking—tall and dark, with a country girl's healthy face on a great body, as he'd already noted from the photo with Nadia. But she came down without makeup in baggy sweatpants, a shapeless pullover, and a black imitation leather jacket. She spoke decent Italian: without articles, but with the verbs more or less correct.

She was a little taken aback to see the handsome young Italian, and she was happy to be invited to the bar in the center. "That bar is very expensive. A German student took me there once, but he was rich," she warned him. A taxi got them to December XIV Square in ten minutes. The bar was on the ground floor of an ochre-colored eighteenth-century building; it was a beautiful, warm place with wood paneling and circular wrought-iron tables.

"What would you like, Ramona?"

"Very good cappuccino here." She hesitated, clearly wanting to say more.

"Would you like a croissant with that?" Mastroianni asked.

She nodded. "What's your name?"

"Marcello."

"Like Italian actor. You look like him." Their order arrived, and she smiled as she bit into her croissant.

Mastroianni said, "You had to report Nadia missing twice, right?"

"Actually, three times. First time was at dawn on December 25. It was seven in the morning. Police station seemed closed. I rang the intercom and that man opened for me."

"Deputy Captain Colajacono?"

"Yes," she nodded, finishing the last bite of the croissant. "I think so, but I knew his face, not his name."

"You already knew him by sight?" Mastroianni asked.

Outside the large window of the café, grandmothers were pushing bundled up babies in their strollers. A few brave cyclists chanced the freezing roads. In the bar, a romantic Romanian song began to play.

"That man has wicked eyes. Eyes that say you don't exist." She wiped away a tear. "For him I was a piece of meat."

Mastroianni felt terrible for her. "I'm sorry, Ramona. Not all Italians are like that."

She smiled at him. "Can I have another cappuccino?"

Mastroianni ordered another round, and she went on with her story.

"I met him in a nightclub, the Cristal, maybe ten days ago. Mircea bought me black leather pants and top. He told me to wait for him in the bar and left me cell phone. At midnight it rang and Mircea told me to come out. Outside was big policeman, Colajacono."

She paused, bit into the croissant, and made up her mind. She spoke very quickly, all in one breath, becoming agitated. "He asked me if I know how to use a whip and I say yes, even if not true. To get him excited I said I would be happy to whip him. He looked me with those evil eyes and gripped my arm with his huge hand. He asked me if he looked like the type to be whipped by a Romanian bitch, and I said it was a mistake and was sorry."

Mastroianni rested his hand on top of hers as a tear rolled down her cheek.

"Then the big policeman took me to a studio apartment on the second floor beside the nightclub. Big bed in the middle, big mirror on the ceiling. Whips, handcuffs, and dildos. He gave me house keys and said to leave them in the house after. Then he explained what I was to do. Go back to Cristal and sit at the bar. Wait for old, very well-dressed man. I had to say straight away that I wanted to be slave owner."

"And Colajacono left?"

"Yes. Then the well-dressed gentleman came and I did my work in the apartment. With whip."

"Did you ever see the man again?"

"No, never."

He had to get to the point. "And when you went to the police station in the early morning on December 25 to report Nadia missing, there was Colajacono."

"Yes, I rang and he opened the door. I was surprised and frightened. He asked what I wanted and then he laughed. Said it wouldn't be smart to piss him off."

"Was he embarrassed or surprised? He must have been shocked to see you there. It meant you knew he was a policeman."

She seemed to think about that for a moment. "He didn't care at all. For him, I was nothing."

"So you went back to your room?"

"Yes, to see if Nadia had come back. She was not there, but she wasn't with a client. She left the clothes there."

"Are you sure her clothes were there?"

"Yes." Ramona smiled at something. "Nadia's clothes were all over floor and on the bed, as usual. She was messy. Rudi cleaned up after Nadia, so she gave him little presents."

"You went back to the police station later. Weren't you afraid of Colajacono?"

"Yes, but it was almost eleven. Nadia had not come back and I was worried."

"Why were you worried, Ramona?"

"We never got into a car with a customer unless the other was there."

"I don't follow," said Mastroianni.

"We stood in pairs. We never get into a car unless a partner took license plate number. Customers saw and were afraid to do bad things."

"Very clever. But what if a customer comes while one of you is working and the other's standing there alone?"

"We made him wait. It doesn't take very long." She gave a little laugh.

"And you went off with a customer and when you came back Nadia wasn't there?"

"Yes, it was six thirty. There were few customers because at Christmas Italian men do not go to women on the street. I went with a client, she wrote the number. When I came back, Nadia was no longer there."

"You were only gone a few minutes?"

"Well, a little longer. He had trouble getting hard."

"All right, now tell me about when you went back to the police station."

"It was almost eleven. I could do nothing. I looked in the police station and saw there were people. I had to be brave. I rang the intercom and a young policeman opened."

"Marchese?"

"I don't know his name. The young man took me to Colajacono in his office, then went away. He said I am a whore, Nadia is a whore. He said he would put me in prison if I came back. Coming out, I saw the time sheet and saw Colajacono didn't come to work until nine."

She was brave and smart, too. Colajacono had been unlucky. Most girls wouldn't have dared to return, but Ramona was different. She seemed to read his thoughts.

"Not because I am brave," she said. "Nadia was like a sister to me." She burst into tears.

"Was Nadia upset the day before? Had anything happened to her?"

Ramona paused to consider this. "Not upset, no. She was more happy than usual. She didn't talk much, but she was happy."

"And why was she happy?"

"I do not know. That night she came back very late. I had been sick. I asked her what had happened, and she said that things were looking up."

"Can you tell me about Nadia's clothes?" Mastroianni asked.

"The afternoon of December 25 I went to work and the clothes were still there on bed. When I came back the morning of December 26, everything was tidy. The clothes were not there, and Nadia's bed had clean sheets." She was speaking softly.

"And then you decided to report her missing and leave?"

She shook her head. "No. I went to work as usual on the evening of December 26. Then when I came back on December 27 that thing happened. Mircea said that if Nadia had left me something, I must give it to him immediately. But Nadia had not left me a letter, a note, nothing. I said that, but they did not believe me. They said they would beat me to death. I was crying, not understanding what they were looking for. Then . . " Her voice trailed off. She was staring at the next table where a young man was sitting by himself, reading a newspaper and smoking.

She rose abruptly. "That's enough now," she said sharply. "You pay and we should go."

Mastroianni paid and they went out into December XIV Square. It was extremely cold, a freezing wind was blowing in from the Urals and the pavement was icy. The shops still had their lights on although it was now half past nine. They walked in silence to the taxi stand. When they found one that was free, she told him, "I'll take the bus."

"Why?" Mastroianni asked.

"Good-bye, Marcello," she said quietly. A bus pulled up at the stop, and she whispered, "Be careful." Then she jumped on the bus. The doors closed behind her.

Puzzled, Mastroianni turned back to the taxi stand. There he saw the young man who had been in the bar at the table next to theirs. His newspaper was sticking out of his pocket. It was an Italian newspaper.

. . . .

A beep on the computer signaled Mastroianni's e-mail with his report from Romania, which was in a different time zone and therefore one hour ahead.

Balistreri read it out loud. "Nadia's clothes left in a mess and then they disappeared. That follows." Then he looked at Piccolo. "But it's Ramona's clothes that I don't get. You told me that Rudi said . . ." He didn't finish the thought.

There was Colajacono to question. He decided to take Piccolo along. With him she was under control and a little provocation would be helpful.

Colajacono was waiting for them where they'd questioned Marius Hagi. He was rested and shaved, his thick gray hair slicked back with gell. He watched them in silence, a sly look in his small closely set eyes.

His lawyer was sitting beside him. He put out his hands, palms up. "My client is here to make a voluntary statement. If this takes a turn I don't like, we'll stop immediately. Or you may proceed to charging him formally and taking him into custody."

He was using Morandi's technique. He knew they didn't have the authority to arrest Colajacono. "Well then, let's hear what the deputy captain has to tell us voluntarily," Balistreri said.

"With regard to what?" Colajacono asked.

"Ramona Iordanescu," Piccolo said.

Colajacono didn't even look at her. He continued to address Balistreri. "About her two visits to the police station?"

"Three visits," Piccolo said.

Colajacono had a boxer's crooked nose, and the nostrils flared now. His thin mouth stretched into a sneer. He turned slowly to Piccolo.

"That's right, that fucking Romanian whore. She came three times, as if we had nothing better to do."

"Tell us about the first time," Piccolo said evenly.

"She came early Christmas morning. It was still dark; Tatò and I were there alone. I opened the door and this whore started jabbering away about some other whore who hadn't come back. I didn't give a fuck, obviously. I didn't even let her into the station. I had bigger things to worry about."

"On Christmas?" The disbelief in Piccolo's voice was plain.

"Listen, sweetheart, we deal with scum like her every day at our station. We've got Casilino 900 with six hundred and fifty of them, and it's not the only camp in our precinct. These people are criminals. They're animals. If we didn't watch them day and night, they'd be attacking all the women, children, and elderly in the neighborhood. We've got our hands full."

"Still, you should have let her file a report," Piccolo insisted.

Colajacono shot her a scornful look. "You have balls to sit here in your fancy office in the center of Rome and tell me what I should have done. Litter's the worst crime you see here. Street sweepers in paradise, that's you." He spat on the floor. His lawyer whispered something in his ear.

"Tell us what you felt when you opened the door and saw Iordanescu there," continued Piccolo.

He looked at her in annoyance. "What did I feel? What the fuck should I have felt?"

"I don't know," Piccolo replied. "Surprise, fear—"

"Fear?" Colajacono interrupted, and his lawyer placed a hand on his arm. "Me, scared of a whore?"

Balistreri stuck a half-smoked cigarette in his mouth. It was the signal agreed with Piccolo. It was time to hand over.

"You weren't surprised to see the young woman at the station?" Balistreri asked.

Colajacono looked at him and for the first time hesitated. In the end he decided that it was wise to have an escape route ready.

"Well, a little, yes, in the moment."

"And wasn't the young woman surprised to see you there?"

Colajacono's lawyer interrupted. "Captain, this conversation is taking a cryptic turn that I don't like at all. Just be direct with your questions."

"The question was crystal clear, but I'll repeat it: given that Deputy Captain Colajacono wasn't surprised to see Iordanescu, even though he'd already met her, we were wondering whether Iordanescu was surprised to see him there in uniform, having met him a few days earlier in plain clothes outside a nightclub."

The lawyer quickly turned to Colajacono. "Don't say a word." Then he turned back to Balistreri. "The voluntary statement session is terminated. If you want to ask additional questions, follow the proper procedures."

Colajacono raised his huge form up and, standing a few inches taller than Balistreri, placed himself in front of him, staring at him with open disdain.

"Well, are you going to arrest me, or am I free to go?" His breath smelled of garlic and whiskey.

Balistreri lit his cigarette. The interview was over. What disturbed him more than Colajacono was the clearly visible Italian newspaper mentioned in Mastroianni's report. He knew what it meant.

. . . .

As a youth, Coppola had been a warehouseman at the NATO base in Naples and had learned a little English. So for him to be given the job of asking a few questions of the witness who had observed the fight outside the Bella Blu between the bouncer Camarà and the motorcyclist was a gratifying recognition of his linguistic ability. Thus he switched from Romanian prostitutes to a young American professional who worked for a multinational, a category that in Coppola's mind consisted only of superior beings.

Midmorning, the bar in Piazza di Spagna was full of the citizens of Rome who were both wealthy and idle. The north wind had cleared the sky, which was now an intense blue, and you could look down below on Piazza del Popolo, filled with tourists. They sat outside under the veranda next to a gas heater that made the temperature acceptable.

Fred Cabot was in his thirties, a young man with a likable manner. Coppola immediately reassured him that he was fluent in his language. "I speak American," he said.

Cabot ordered a juice and Coppola ordered a cappuccino and a cream-filled pastry.

"I love Rome. Houston, where I come from, is very modern. Everything is so old here."

Between Cabot's Texas accent and the fact that, as Coppola was quickly realizing, his English was pretty rusty, Coppola could only understand half of what Cabot was saying. He pulled out a sheet of paper. He'd written out the questions with the aid of a dictionary. The waiter brought their order.

"Please tell me about the night of December 23."

"Well, you know, it was late. I'd been to a bunch of clubs and I was drunk. *Ubriaco, sì*? I wanted one last drink."

"And some girls?" Coppola asked with a wink.

The American laughed. "Yeah, but a drink first."

"What time did you arrive at the Bella Blu?"

"I think it was two o'clock, maybe a little later. This black guy was at the door and he wanted to pat me down. He was just starting when a motorcycle stopped in the middle of the road and the rider yelled something, and then he rode away."

"What did he say? What language?"

"I don't really know. Italian or Spanish, I guess. It was something bad, though, because the black guy was angry," Cabot recalled.

"Where did the motorcycle come from?"

"Well, I'm not sure, but my impression is that it was just around the corner. I heard the engine starting."

"Did you see the person?" Coppola asked.

Cabot thought about it. "The guy wore a helmet."

Not having understood a word, Coppola held up a hand in desperation to stop him. He pulled out a pocket dictionary and with a melancholy air looked up "whore." With surprise he found it meant "prostitute." A prostitute in a helmet, that is, a crash helmet. And then he seemed to recall that "queer" meant a homosexual. This was a real tangle—a prostitute in a crash helmet on a bike with a gay guy.

"But how did you know she was a prostitute?"

Cabot looked at him as if he'd just swallowed the cup as well as the cappuccino. Then he burst out laughing.

"No, no," he said, trying to contain himself. "'Wore' is the past tense of 'to wear.' He had on a helmet."

"Okay," Coppola said, not fully understanding, "so this person yelled at the black man. The black man yelled back. He got on a motorcycle and went away."

Cabot nodded.

"And do you remember the motorcycle?" Coppola asked.

"It was a nice bike. Fast. But it was kind of strange."

Coppola shook his head sadly. His English needed refreshing. He'd understood that the bike was large, but for the rest he needed a dictionary. With some relief he said good-bye to Fred Cabot, who was leaving for the United States the following day, yet with the clear feeling of his having missed something important.

. . . .

Giulia Piccolo was unsettled. The decision to bring Rudi home had been made on the spur of the moment. Now, in the cold light of day, the positive side to it was still there but the problems had also become clear. The most troubling of these wasn't what other people might think, but why she had made the decision. She felt lonely, that was true. Indeed, she was lonely, and had been for a long time, ever since the moment Francesca had left. And Rudi was excellent company—sensitive, witty, gay, and very handsome.

Where does a good-looking Albanian homosexual fit into the mess your life's in? Serious wounds can't be healed by the dying. Neither one of us is what we'd like to be and together we're even less where we'd like to be.

She arrived at the restaurant around ten. She'd telephoned the manager to make sure that he'd be there at that unusual time with the waiter who'd served Mircea and Nadia. She was greeted by a well-dressed man in his forties in a jacket and tie, whose shoes were in need of cleaning. The waiter, on the other hand, was nearer seventy than sixty, and below his slightly greasy white jacket the zipper of his black pants was open.

"I'm Carpi. I've been waiting for you."

The restaurant was quite large and had two dining areas, one for smokers. The menu was translated into English, French, and Japanese. In other words, it was a typical tourist spot in the historic center. The walls were lined with photos of actors and actresses who had probably never set foot in the place.

Carpi pointed to the waiter. "Tommaso here served them. He recognized the couple from the photos you sent."

Piccolo turned to the seventy-year-old. "Did you recognize him or her?"

"I remember the girl very well. She was pretty."

"All right," Piccolo said. "Now tell me everything you can remember from the moment they came in, starting with what time it was."

"I'm not sure of the exact time, but they had a reservation. He said he'd booked a table in the smoking section, and he made a stink about it. Luckily we're never full, so I was able to accommodate them."

"And where did they sit?"

Tommaso led her to the smoking section and pointed. "I offered him a table in the middle and he said he wanted to have his back to the wall. Like a Mafia don or something. You know how Romanians are."

Piccolo could have done without the commentary. "What did you do?"

"I switched tables and gave him the one he wanted. Then I took their order. She spoke in Romanian and he translated. He ordered penne all'arrabbiata, but she didn't order a pasta course."

"You remember an order from a week ago?"

"He busted my balls about that, too. He said the penne weren't spicy enough. Basically, he did nothing but complain from the minute he set foot in the place."

"Did they talk to each other?"

"He did all the talking, but they were pretty quiet."

"Anything else unusual that you remember?"

"Well, yes. To begin with, he was taking it really easy—they were here for more than two hours. You know, couples usually only stay here a short time; they eat and then go off to—"

"Tommaso!" said Carpi, rebuking him.

"But the guy went on sipping away at the wine until he'd finished the bottle, while the girl drank only water. Then he ordered dessert, then coffee, some bitters, then a whiskey. And then in the end he raised his hand to her. You know how those Romanians treat women. These people really don't know how to treat a lady. An Italian would never dream of—"

"Did he actually hit her?" Piccolo asked.

"Not exactly. I was in the other room, but I heard him yelling at her, and then a loud sound, like a slap. So I went in and she was holding her face in her hands and everyone at the other tables was looking at them. And the man turned to the other customers and said, 'Mind your own fucking business.' Then he left two fifty-euro bills on the table, got his leather jacket from the coatroom, and left."

"And the girl?"

"She sat there for a while, as if she didn't know what to do."

"How much was the bill?" Piccolo asked.

Tommaso looked at Carpi. "I don't recall."

"More or less," Piccolo insisted, "given that the girl ate little and drank water . . ."

"Probably around seventy euros," Carpi said.

"Did you bring her the change?"

"Yes, I remember she left a good tip."

"All right." Piccolo turned to Carpi. "Would you have a look through the receipts for that evening?"

Useless question, Piccolo. Imagine them giving an official receipt to foreigners.

After a moment, Carpi came back with a receipt for eighty euros.

"Tommaso, what time did the Romanian leave?" Piccolo asked.

"About eleven thirty."

Piccolo held the receipt out to Carpi and pointed to the date and time: *December 23, 10:15 p.m.*

"Couldn't you find something a little more believable?"

The manager blushed and returned to the cash register.

She asked the waiter, "Did you escort her to the door?"

"I saw her leave. She was wearing a raincoat that was too long for her—it touched the ground."

Nadia didn't own a coat. She'd borrowed Ramona's.

"And did you see which way she went?"

"She stood outside and looked around, as if she was thinking about where to go. Then she nodded to someone and turned left toward Piazza del Popolo."

. . . .

Corvu was worried about Balistreri. After the Samantha Rossi business and the stuff about the camps, now there was Colajacono, too. The possible indictment of a deputy captain of police who was extremely popular with his colleagues and locals was not going to go over well.

He had checked and everything was confirmed. On December 24 the four Romanian employees had left Marius Travel and arrived at Casilino 900 a little after six. But Hagi had stopped by his house to pick up presents for the children. Colajacono's alibi checked out, too, but in both men's stories there was a gap of one hour—enough time to pick Nadia up on Via di Torricola.

Corvu was dissatisfied though. Investigative work was undertaken with one percent intuition and ninety-nine percent sheer analytic drudgery. You could only develop an intuition on the basis of analysis, and the facts were so damned few.

At ten o'clock he was told that the Ukrainian prostitute who had seen the vehicle had arrived. Corvu had permission to use Balistreri's office instead of his little glass cubicle when he had to make an impression on anyone brought in for questioning.

The girl was slender and petite, with a lively little face that was both kind and makeup free under straight black hair with purple streaks. She looked even younger than her twenty years.

"What's your name?" Corvu felt a little embarrassed. He had been expecting a slut and she was more like a schoolgirl.

"Natalya. What's yours?"

Suddenly taken aback by her familiar manner, Corvu blushed and stammered as he said "Graziano."

He offered her the armchair in front of Balistreri's desk and sat down in the one next to it. He didn't want to sit in Balistreri's swivel chair and intimidate her.

"How long have you been in Italy, Natalya?"

"Only two months."

"Where did you learn to speak Italian so well?"

She smiled. A beautifully genuine smile. "I've had an Italian boy-friend for three years. I came to Italy to be with him."

"And this boyfriend forces you to work as a prostitute?"

She burst out laughing, displaying two neat rows of white teeth. "I'm not a prostitute," she protested, still laughing.

Corvu didn't like surprises. "Then what were you doing at night on the street?"

"Graziano, I was just there that day, and it wasn't at night. I was there for about two hours. Then I went to work."

"What kind of work do you do?"

"I'm a waitress in a snack bar. Breakfast, lunch, and dinner."

"So what were you doing on Via di Torricola on December 24?"

"It was Christmas Eve. I went to keep my cousin company for two hours. She was on her own until eight. Unfortunately, she does work as a prostitute."

"Weren't you afraid when she got into a car with a man and left you there alone?"

"It only happened once for ten minutes. Luckily no one stopped. Anyway, we'd agreed that I'd play for time and would wait until she came back."

"And during those ten minutes when you were alone, a car that was missing a headlight drove by." Fate had spared Natalya and chosen Nadia.

"Yes. I was frightened then. I thought it was going to stop for me, but instead it slowed down, passed close by, then sped up again."

"Did you see what kind of car it was?"

Natalya shook her head. "No, it was dark. But I think I might be able to recognize the model. My brother sells used cars in Ukraine. It was familiar, I think."

Now was his chance to show her what he could do. "Natalya, I have a computer program with the various parts of all kinds of cars: hoods, doors, roofs, everything. If we go over these together, do you think you can identify the ones that are most similar to the car you saw?"

She was sharp and thoughtful, an excellent witness. They were both involved in examining the particulars of the cars closely. When the Janiculum cannon went off as it did every day at noon, they looked at each other almost guiltily, like two high school students caught smoking in the bathroom. Two hours had passed.

"Oh my God, it's so late. I have to go to work," she said.

"We're not even halfway through," Corvu said.

"I work until five today, Graziano. Then I have a haircut appointment, and then I'm free. I can come back then and we can finish. All right?"

"All right," Corvu agreed quickly. Then, as she was leaving the room, he blurted out, "I hope your boyfriend doesn't mind you spending so much time with me, Natalya."

Have you gone crazy, Graziano? What the hell are you saying? Who do you think you are, Brad Pitt?

He blushed at his own audacity and then, closing the door sharply behind Natalya, barricaded himself in Balistreri's office.

While he caught his breath he heard her cheerful voice from the corridor.

"I don't have a boyfriend anymore. See you later, Graziano."

Corvu was overcome with embarrassment.

. . . .

After the meeting with his team and the interview with Colajacono, Balistreri was even more out of sorts. He wanted a smoke, but he was already one cigarette over his daily ration. He wanted a coffee, but his stomach was too upset to drink it.

In the meantime, Margherita announced that Pasquali expected him at one thirty sharp. The man certainly wasn't going to feed him lunch. Pasquali was a workaholic who barely ate. He needed a break.

In the outer office, Margherita was tapping on her keyboard.

"Can you help out with an investigation?"

She stared at him, clearly surprised.

"Of course. I'm all yours." She said it without looking away from the screen.

In an earlier era, that "I'm all yours" would have carried other meanings and led to certain consequences. These days, though, young people called him "sir" and "Captain." He was always a little surprised to hear those terms of address, but they didn't bother him the way they once had—without physical attractiveness, the only power he possessed these days was conveyed through his position.

Having pondered these thoughts, he wondered if by chance he'd forgotten to take his antidepressant. This could have been a direct consequence of the depression. The sufferer can become self-destructive. The psychiatrist had mentioned this after Balistreri's last visit, while he was writing a hefty check.

They went into his office and Balistreri closed the door. The wood was thin, so he could hear Coppola's comment clearly.

"What the hell is going on around here? You're shacking up with an Albanian faggot. Graziano's mooning over a Ukrainian hooker, and the boss is screwing around with Margherita."

Balistreri opened the door to his office. Piccolo looked ready to murder Coppola, but Balistreri shot her a look and she backed off.

"Don't you have anything better to do, Coppola?" Coppola didn't meet his gaze. At least he had the good grace to be embarrassed.

"I'm meeting the girlfriend of that Senegalese guy at the Bella Blu in the gym where Camarà worked during the day."

"Get going then. But before you do, what were you talking about just now?"

Coppola turned pale. "I apologize, sir. I was out of line."

"Not about me, about Corvu."

"I told you Corvu had to pay for sex, didn't I?" he said triumphantly.

Balistreri had already heard Corvu's report and knew Natalya was no hooker. "Don't go shooting your mouth off, Coppola," he warned.

When they left, he shut the door again and turned to Margherita.

"Margherita, I've got a problem that a beautiful young woman such as yourself can solve for me."

She turned bright red.

Old games I no longer have any use for.

"It's to do with work, Margherita," he explained, trying to reassure her. "You have to imagine that you're a prostitute who works as a pair with a friend and is waiting for customers on a dark street."

"With a friend? You mean they do it together?" she asked.

This conversation's becoming embarrassing; the girl's too awkward.

"Not exactly. When one of you gets into a car with a john, the other one writes down the license plate number," he explained.

Margherita settled down. "Okay, I get it."

"So, you and your friend are on a dark street and there are no houses around. Just other prostitutes, the closest about fifty yards away from you. One gets into a car with a customer and the other takes down the number."

"Okay."

"A car stops, your friend gets in. You get the number. They drive off. You're alone. You can see the other prostitutes, but they're too far away for you to talk to each other. Two minutes go by. A car with only one headlight on—the other one must be broken—drives up and stops. What do you do?"

She looked at him a little uncertainly. "I take my time. I start chatting while waiting for my friend to come back."

"He's in a hurry. He tells you to get in," Balistreri insisted.

"I continue to stall for time," she repeated, not knowing what to say.

Balistreri got up and pulled down the blinds. The room was dark.

"Close your eyes. Place yourself in the scene."

She looked at him uncertainly, but then her respect for authority and the desire to help kicked in. She closed her eyes and sank back into her chair.

"Now think about it, Margherita. He's pushy. What's going to happen?"

"He gets out, drags me into the car."

"No, if he got out of the car you'd scream and the others would hear you and get suspicious. You get in."

She was breathing heavily now. Concentrating.

"He knows my name," she whispered.

Balistreri nodded. "Yes. He addresses you by name and asks you to get in. You go up close to get a better look. The car's interior light comes on. Can you see him now, Margherita?"

Her voice was monotone, as if she were hypnotized. "Yes, I recognize him."

"He smiles at you, beckons to you to get in. And you do. Why?"

"He's someone I trust," she whispered. "I was waiting for him."

Balistreri's voice seemed to come to her from far away. "He's promised you the world, hasn't he? And you know what he'll give you instead, don't you?"

Suddenly Margherita saw the face of her Latin teacher at school who'd invited her to take a ride. She let out a scream.

Five seconds later the door flew open. Giulia Piccolo was there—five foot eleven inches of muscle ready for action. Corvu was behind her.

"Come in and close the door," Balistreri commanded, calmly switching on the light. Margherita blinked slowly. Balistreri put his hands on her shoulders. "Excellent job, Margherita."

Piccolo and Corvu looked suspicious. They'd heard Margherita scream and seen the blinds lowered.

Balistreri could read their suspicions. Was it possible he'd fallen so low in their esteem?

He brought them back to reality. "Nadia recognized him and was waiting for him. It was all prearranged."

Afternoon

The gym was on the ground floor of an office building near Via Veneto. When Coppola arrived at the entrance to the gym at one o'clock, several people could be seen through the windows working out on the equipment, lifting weights, and cycling on stationary bikes. Others were dancing to deafening thumping music around a large swimming pool. Professionals, well-heeled women, and some high-class villains, for sure.

Carmen was waiting for him. Like Camarà, she was of African descent. Her face wasn't particularly pretty, but she had a trainer's well-developed body.

"I'm from Miami," she said in perfect Italian.

Coppola felt a sense of relief. His English couldn't have withstood another test. She led him into a tiny cubicle that must have been her office. On the wall was a photo of her and a large-muscled black man standing in front of the gym.

"Were you good friends?" Coppola asked.

"We'd been together for three months," she said. "Papa was a real sweetheart."

"Was there anyone who held a grudge against him? Had he argued with anyone?"

Carmen shook her head. "No. It was that awful man on the motorcycle. I'm positive."

"We know that they'd had words just before. We have a witness, an American from Texas," Coppola added to give it more credibility.

"You don't say," she added scornfully. "A lying Texan, just like our president."

"The witness states that they yelled at each other," Coppola went on.

"The motorcyclist started it. Papa just told him to fuck off."

"How do you know that?"

"Because he called me right after and told me about it. We talked a bunch of times that night. He wasn't feeling well. We were passing a urinary tract infection back and forth."

Coppola had checked the phone records. Camarà had made a call to Carmen's cell phone at two fourteen, right after the altercation with the motorcyclist and right before he was found dead. That call lasted two and a half minutes.

"What did he say?"

"He called to tell me he was okay. He was peeing a lot, but no temperature or anything. Then he told me about this guy on a motorcycle who'd screamed at him for no reason."

"Had he ever seen the guy before?"

"No, that's why it was so strange."

Coppola lef the gym with the renewed conviction that urinary infections were common among people of African descent. He was too distracted to notice the man watching him from the opposite pavement.

. . . .

A little before one thirty Balistreri went on foot to see Pasquali. He realized he was short of breath and decided he ought to cut out even his last few pathetic cigarettes.

"He's waiting for you in his office," Antonella said. "Can I bring you a decaf?"

He nodded and thanked her. She really did watch out for him.

Pasquali was sitting at his imposing eighteenth-century desk. The little glasses on the end of his nose gave him the look of an intellectual. He could have been a harmless retired schoolteacher. Instead he was the ministry of the interior's most influential official.

"Take a seat," he ordered. "I have to be with the undersecretary in ten minutes, so I'll be brief. We don't like this business at all."

He put an emphasis on the "we" without making it clear who else he meant. The chief of police, prefect, minister of the interior, his father. . . . But the mention of the undersecretary was not by chance. Balistreri said nothing.

Pasquali continued calmly. "It's out of the question for you to bring charges against Deputy Captain Colajacono. You have nothing on him. He sent away a Romanian prostitute who didn't know where another Romanian prostitute was. Is that really a crime? It barely qualifies as an oversight. Colajacono is respected by his colleagues and the locals."

"And he's respected by the residents of Casilino 900. Or maybe feared."

"You and Colajacono are of like mind about Casilino 900."

Balistreri shook his head. "No, we're not. Colajacono wants to dismantle it, arrest everyone, and then deport them. I'm concerned about the safety of our citizens. Those camps are a time bomb waiting to go off. They should be moved outside of the city."

"We need political consensus for that. We're getting there."

"All anybody cares about is getting reelected. On the left, they're clueless. And on the other side they know only too well: procrastinate and let trouble brew, so in the meantime we have an increase in kidnapping, rape, and car theft by drunks who run people over. And perhaps with this tactic next year we can say good-bye to this mayor and one from the other side can take over."

"It's a complex problem, Michele. We need time and broad consensus. Any new camps need to comply with European regulations. And the Roma also have to be willing. The Vatican and the center–left coalition that's in power aren't going to agree to a forced move."

Of course, let's be patient until someone gets killed.

"Look," Pasquali continued, "sometimes Colajacono's methods are heavy-handed. As a policeman and as a Catholic, I don't agree with them. But you can't hang any charges on him."

"He knew the Iordanescu girl and didn't mention it."

"He'll just deny it, and then you've got the word of a highly esteemed deputy captain against that of a streetwalker."

"Ramona says Colajacono wasn't at all surprised to see her outside the police station."

"Precisely, Michele. Because he'd never seen her before."

"Look, imagine for a moment that the Iordanescu girl is telling the truth and they already knew each other. What does it mean that he wasn't surprised to see her there on Christmas morning?"

Pasquali remained impassive and silent, only a slight frown betraying his concern. Then he pushed the thought away, as if it were a warning of bad weather for the weekend that he didn't want to believe.

"He didn't know her, Balistreri. End of story."

The switch to his surname signaled the end of the discussion. Taking his time, Pasquali smoothed his gray hair. "There's another thing," he said. "There's the problem of Linda Nardi. We promised her the Iordanescu girl's statement today."

"Let her have it. There's nothing compromising in it."

"I know. I already authorized you to give it to her. But she asked me something else on the phone yesterday in exchange for keeping quiet about the fight in the Torre Spaccata police station."

And you didn't want to mention this in front of the chief of police. It must be a serious problem for you, then.

Pasquali looked out the window toward the dome atop St. Peter's as if searching for divine inspiration. "She wants to know what we're hiding on Samantha Rossi."

So now you're starting to worry about the R carved on the poor girl's back.

"All right, I'll see to it, Pasquali. I'll try to see her this evening."

"I'm sure this Nardi woman will be happy to see you again—it's been so long since you last saw each other," he concluded icily.

. . . .

Right after lunch, Corvu went to ENT headquarters. The offices were in what had once been a large apartment in the city center. Hardwood floors, expensive carpets, photos of casinos, old pinball machines, and period jukeboxes. Even the receptionist was elegant.

Avvocato Francesco Ajello, the lawyer who was ENT's director and manager of the Bella Blu nightclub, was very different from what he had imagined. He looked nothing like the owner of a casino or even a gambler.

Instead, he was tall and well-dressed, hands manicured, hair recently cut, his face fresh from a day spa, his body trim from the gym, a wonderful tan from a sunlamp.

Behind him hung his law school diploma. On his modern desk were photos of a refined-looking blonde and a muscular adolescent. He was clearly a successful man with an aura of utmost respectability.

"We're all so sorry about the death of that young man in our employ," Ajello said. "So senseless to die because of a silly argument. Of course, that's what's wrong with the world today." He glanced at his son's photo.

"An unfortunate occurrence, but not an unusual one in the modern world," Corvu agreed.

"So, what can I do for you?" he asked, checking the Rolex on his wrist.

"If you have a moment, I'd like to ask you some questions about Bella Blu and ENT."

Ajello raised one eyebrow. "I assumed you wanted to ask me about the night the young man was killed. What does ENT have to do with anything?"

"The young man could have made enemies, either in the gym where he worked or at the club. Someone who couldn't get in or lost money on the slots."

"Do you really think this was premeditated? I thought the American tourist indicated there had been an argument with a motorcyclist."

"At the moment we can't rule out anything. Could you explain to me exactly what it is you do?"

"ENT was created in 2002 by a group of shareholders and owns nightclubs, arcades, and betting parlors. I own ten percent. I bought my stake in late 2004 from the widow of the previous shareholder, Sandro Corona, who had died a couple of months before that."

"Corona was the manager when there was trouble with the finance police?"

Ajello shrugged his shoulders. "No big deal—a fine for tax evasion. Slot machines had just become legal. During an inspection they found some that weren't properly wired into the tax system."

"Which meant people could play them without paying taxes," Corvu clarified.

Ajello made a little face of disgust, as if mentioning tax evasion was the equivalent of uttering a vulgarity. "Shall we say revenue that wasn't in the books?"

"Who are the shareholders who hold the other ninety percent?"

"I don't know them and I don't think they want to be known, otherwise they wouldn't use a trust. I'm only in touch with their trust manager."

Sure, and without just cause no judge would force a trust company to reveal the names of its partners. And there's no link between ENT and Camarà's killing.

"All right. Now let's talk about the night Camarà was murdered. You were at the Bella Blu, weren't you?"

"Yes, there was a private party in one of rooms. I arrived at the club about one thirty. I let the party guests in the back and took them to the room they'd booked."

"You came from another club?"

"Yes, we have a nightclub in Perugia where there was another private party. It was a birthday party for someone I know. I stayed there until he blew out the candles on the cake at midnight and then I slipped away."

"And you made it to Rome in an hour and a half?"

"I travel on the company plane. I couldn't do without it given the number of clubs in different cities I have to visit in one evening."

"And later?"

"Later, about two thirty, I heard shouts. I rushed outside and found the American standing there. Camarà was lying in a pool of blood. Then I called the police."

Corvu had nothing more to ask him. He nodded to one of the photos on the desk. "A fine young man, that—my compliments."

Ajello smiled at the photo with evident pride. "Yes, it was actually Fabio who introduced me to Camarà; he was his bodybuilding trainer at the gym."

While he was on his way out, passing the secretary, Corvu saw a light on the phone come on. It was Ajello's private line.

. . . .

The south wind had veered to the southwest and huge black clouds were filling the sky. It was still afternoon, but the shops had already switched on their lights. Balistreri took the bus to Casilino 900. Marius Hagi was waiting for him at the entrance. He was alone, which was the deal they'd made with his lawyer, Morandi.

Hagi was wearing a gray flannel shirt, corduroy pants, and a black wool sweater. Despite the cold and damp he wore neither a coat nor a hat. He still had that cough. It seemed to have gotten worse.

Balistreri held out his hand.

"Good afternoon," Hagi said, but he didn't shake. His attitude wasn't hostile but neither was it friendly.

"Thank you for coming, Mr. Hagi—as you know you're under no obligation to talk. I wanted to have a little informal chat and take a tour of the camp with you."

Casilino 900 had existed for more than thirty years and housed about seven hundred people, mostly women and children: Romanians, Macedonians, Bosnians, Kosovars, Montenegrins. They went in the main gate. A police car was parked outside. Between the shipping containers and makeshift huts that served as residences, the camp's unpaved roads were full of muddy puddles and strewn with garbage.

As far as the eye could see there were laundry lines, and old rusted out cars. There was no running water or gas supply. Some of the huts had dubious looking electrical cables hanging off of them. Candle-light flickered from others, dangerously close to plastic and other flammable materials. Port-a-potties were the only toilets, and they gave off a smell of sewage and chemicals. Hagi and Balistreri walked among the huts. Children and adults were selling all kinds of items, probably the profits of dumpster diving and picking pockets. A group of children were playing a game of soccer. They shouted and laughed as they chased the ball around the puddles.

Beyond the confines of the camp, Balistreri could see the dump where the remains of Samantha Rossi's tortured body had been found. Behind the dump at the time had been a small unofficial squatters' camp, since cleared, where the three Romanians had been discovered with Samantha's bracelet.

Hagi caught Balistreri looking in that direction.

"You'll release them after a few years for good behavior. In my day in Romania they would have been impaled."

Balistreri wanted to tell Hagi that there might be more such animals among the men Hagi was protecting, but he was there to talk about Nadia, not Samantha Rossi.

"We try to be a civilized country, Mr. Hagi." He said it without much conviction, a conditioned reflex of the institution he represented.

"Look, Balistreri, the severity of justice is a measure of civilization. You're not civilized—just cowardly. Your tolerance is based on the need for home healthcare aides, prostitutes, and people to pick the tomatoes in your fields. If immigrants weren't of use to you, you'd take any immigrants who stepped out of line and nail them to crosses along the road, just like they used to do in ancient Rome."

While Hagi led him through the huts, Balistreri noticed that dozens of eyes were watching them. Word must have gotten around that a policeman was visiting.

Hagi noticed, too. "You're safe here, don't worry," he said

"Because I'm with you?"

"No, because no one's stupid enough to lay hands on a policeman inside the camp."

At that moment an old Roma woman came up with two steaming tin mugs. She offered them to Hagi and Balistreri. They thanked her and sipped the tea. Hagi smoked continuously, lighting a new cigarette from the butt of the last one, despite the fact that he was wracked by coughing. His thin face was pale, but his black eyes were dark coals below his thick eyebrows. The circles under his eyes accentuated his Mephistophelian appearance.

They stopped near a trailer that looked a little better maintained than the rest. Someone had written the number 27 on it with a marker.

"This is where Adrian and Giorgi live," Hagi said.

Behind the trailer a motocross bike was chained to a bench. The inside was bare, but relatively clean. Hagi and Balistreri sat down on the only two chairs, which were set around a rusty table.

"Your good little boys will be released tomorrow, Mr. Hagi."

"If you'll bear with me, I'd like to tell you something."

Balistreri lit his fourth cigarette of the day. "Be happy to hear it."

Hagi began to tell his story, interspersed with bouts of harsh coughing. "I'm forty-six years of age. I was born in Galati near the Black Sea. My brother, Marcel, and I were already orphans by the time I was twelve and he was sixteen. We moved to Costanta on the Black Sea, where we both found work in the port. We slept at the port inside a warehouse. We were, as you would say, good little boys."

"But you managed to put that difficult childhood behind you."

"No, it got worse. My brother was a great soccer goalie. In early 1978 he was hired by a first-division team in Bucharest. They gave him a small salary that allowed him to take care of me. He hired the team's accountant to teach me math. One day in May 1978, in the national championship final, Marcel saved a penalty kick. His team won the championship, and they beat the team that was managed by Ceausescu's son."

Hagi paused, overtaken by yet another bout of heavy coughing. When he had finished, he continued.

"Two bastards from the secret police came to the room where we lived and broke Marcel's fingers one by one. Then Marcel did something crazy. He went to the police and reported them. A few days later, when I came in, the room was turned upside down, blood all over the place. They'd cut off his hands. Marcel had bled to death on the floor."

Hagi stopped to light another cigarette, then went on with his story. "I was saved by pure luck. Some friends of mine knew a guy in Krakow, so I went there. I was nineteen, and I met Alina. More luck. She was only sixteen and an orphan, living with her uncle, a priest who'd worked with Wojtyla and ran an orphanage. When the pope invited him to Rome six months later, Alina and I got married and came with him. We arrived in April 1979, and Alina got a job right away through her uncle."

"And with your knowledge of Eastern Europe you became a businessman."

"I knew very little about anything, but immediately discovered that Italians like Eastern European girls a lot. They would set off for Warsaw, Belgrade, and Budapest with suitcases full of nylons, jeans, and beauty products. I used my contacts with friends in Poland and started to organize these pleasure trips. There was nothing illegal about it—I simply put two parties together to their mutual satisfaction. Then I opened bars and restaurants. I became a wealthy immigrant and respected member of the community."

"Italy has been good to you. Have you been happy here?"

Hagi thought for a moment.

"Italy's made me rich, but it's made me unhappy. It took the thing I loved the most. Alina died in 1983, when she was only twenty."

Balistreri had read all about it in his file. A moped accident. But a moped accident was one of the most common causes of death for a young person in Rome. Why did Hagi blame Italy for his wife's death?

"Cardinal Lato, who helped you come here, filed a report. He claimed Alina was running away from you when she had the accident."

Something gleamed behind Hagi dark eyes. "Alina was like a daughter to him. He was crazy with grief."

"In his statement, Cardinal Lato said that you beat her."

Again that slight shudder like the shock wave of a distant earthquake. Then Hagi replied coldly. "The statement was withdrawn of his own free will after a month, when Monsignor Lato calmed down and reason prevailed over grief. And now enough about that—it's all beside the point."

"All right. What happened to you after your wife died?"

"I went on with my business activities for six years, but I had no enthusiasm for them. Then in 1989, when Romania was freed from that monster, Ceausescu, I sold everything I had in Italy and went back there. I used my savings to purchase property that's now worth more than ten times what I paid. I've got bars, restaurants, real estate agencies, and travel agencies in Bucharest. I go there twice a year."

"You sold everything you had in Italy?"

"I still have the little house where I live, some apartments, the Bar Biliardo, and the travel agency Marius Travel. I use them to provide employment and a place to stay to my fellow Romanians. I help young people settle into the community, and I give a hand to the Roma that you herd into these camps and treat like animals."

"Do you know a Deputy Captain Colajacono?" Balistreri asked.

Hagi grimaced and suffered a bout of coughing. He immediately lit another cigarette.

"I know who he is. Everyone in here's acquainted with him, some of them to their own cost."

"You've never met him?"

"Once, here in the camp. They were carrying out a search and found a working moped in the middle of the scrap heaps of cars, and he wanted to know who'd stolen it. It was Adrian's moped. He'd bought it with cash from a scrap dealer. That was what he rode before he got the motocross bike that's parked outside."

"What happened?"

"I told Adrian to explain that it was his. He and Giorgi went outside. I watched and listened from this window here. Colajacono and another guy brought them into the trailer, and I hid in the back. Colajacono wanted to see the registration, but of course Adrian didn't have it. Then the other policeman said it was stolen. They threatened to confiscate it and arrest Adrian."

"Do you remember what this policeman looked like?"

"Short, fat, and balding. He asked Adrian to hand over the keys to the moped and Adrian said 'Like hell I will,' and the guy smacked him on the shoulder with a rubber nightstick. Then they beat both of them. They took the keys and confiscated the moped. They never filed charges or anything. Adrian found the moped busted into pieces outside the camp. That's the closest I've come to meeting Colajacono."

"Colajacono's the man who took the Iordanescu girl's missing persons report about Nadia."

Hagi seemed to have lost interest in the conversation. He said nothing.

"Yesterday I asked you whether you had an opinion about Nadia's disappearance. Do you think Mircea is capable of doing something stupid?"

A light flashed in Marius Hagi's eyes. "My employees know not to get out of line like that. They know I'd be furious."

You happen to be a benefactor of the destitute, but it's not wise to rub you the wrong way.

"I'd like to ask you one last thing about your wife Alina."

Hagi stared at him in silence. He said nothing. In the end he got up. The conversation was over.

. . . .

Coppola went by streetcar. He was early for his appointment with Sandro Corona's widow. He used the time to look in the elegant district's shop windows and lingered in front of a shoe store. There were several extremely nice pairs with high heels that were well disguised. He looked at the price tags and turned pale. And yet the shop was full of people trying shoes on and making purchases. The most he could have afforded were the heels alone.

The glass reflected a passing face. He had a fleeting feeling of unease. He continued his stroll, stopping in front of other windows. Nothing came to mind. It was only just before he arrived at the front door of Mrs. Corona's apartment building that he placed the face. It was the boy who had been sitting in a corner of the streetcar.

He sent Balistreri a text message, informing him that he was being followed.

The concierge in Corona's widow's building was the suspicious type. Coppola had to show his badge.

"Did her husband live here with her?" he asked the concierge when she was finally satisfied.

"No, she bought the apartment six months ago. Her husband was already dead."

"Does she live by herself?"

The concierge looked at him askance. "I mind my own business. But yes, she lives by herself."

Ornella Corona was a deluxe model, just like the costly apartment she'd bought. She was younger than he'd pictured. Her late husband had been nearly sixty. She looked thirty-five at the most. She had manicured nails and her toned legs were discreetly displayed in black leggings. But her eyes were bored and distant. The photos on the wall featured a younger version of her on the catwalk, modeling clothes by Valentino, Yves Saint Laurent, and Dior. She was clearly used to the finer things in life.

She showed Coppola into a living room full of expensive furniture. "Would you like something to drink? An aperitif? Grapefruit juice?"

Coppola went for the juice. He couldn't take his eyes off her, and he was certain she was aware of it. Luckily she sat down, sipping a grapefruit juice. "What can I do for you, officer?"

"A young man was killed at the Bella Blu, a nightclub run by ENT."

"I know all about it. I knew Camarà from my gym. I take spinning classes there."

Coppola was surprised. "You knew Camarà?"

"Well, I didn't exactly know him. I knew who he was. Then a few days ago I read that he'd been stabbed during a fight outside the Bella Blu."

"Did you know he worked there?"

Ornella Corona had a way of crossing and uncrossing her legs that was distracting, to say the least. Her wristwatch kept attracting his attention, too—its black face was a winking feminine eye with long eyelashes.

"He wasn't working when my husband was there. Then in late 2004 I sold my ENT stake. I haven't had anything to do with the Bella Blu since."

"You sold the shares to Mr. Ajello?"

She made a face. "Yes, that's right."

"And you bought this apartment with that money?"

She was paying attention to Coppola for the first time. She thought about it, then made up her mind. "I suppose it's pointless to ask you how you know that I just bought this apartment. But what does this have to do with Camarà's death?"

"To be honest, I don't think it has anything to do with it. Forget I mentioned it. Would you rule out the possibility that your husband knew Camarà?"

"I absolutely would rule it out," she said. "Can't you tell me why you're asking these questions about me and my husband? Perhaps I could be of help if I knew what was going on."

I can't think straight. Come on, Coppola, buck up and don't make a mess of it.

"We're just looking into Camarà's place of work, where the crime took place."

"But I read that there was a fight with a customer."

"There was some kind of fight. It might have been a previous employee at the Bella Blu, though. Did your husband ever mention anyone violent there?"

"Well, there was the bartender, Pierre. I think he's done time," she admitted readily. She got up to pour herself some more grapefruit juice and Coppola found himself with his eyes inches from her round, tight rear end.

"I think my husband would have left ENT anyway, even if he hadn't had that accident." She turned around and caught him staring.

"He would have left ENT anyway, even if he hadn't had that accident," Coppola repeated. He was blushing. He felt like a thirteen-year-old who'd been discovered leafing through a *Playboy*.

She continued. "He wasn't earning enough to make it worth the trouble, including the trouble with the other shareholders."

"Do you know them?" Coppola asked.

"No. Well, I did hear one of them on the phone once. A call came to the house. The man said my husband's cell phone was off and asked me to tell him to go to Monte Carlo that evening. He didn't say please or thank you, only to pass the message on. I objected that it was already five o'clock in the afternoon, and he said that was why they had a private airplane. Then he hung up on me."

"Was he Italian?"

"Yes, he was Italian. An Italian used to giving orders."

"Was your husband angry?"

"More than angry, he seemed puzzled about why they'd called our home number. It had never happened before, and from then on he began complaining about the job, saying there was too much pressure."

"In September 2004 your husband was hit by a truck while he was walking in a crosswalk."

She didn't ask what that had to do with anything. "The traffic cop said the driver might not even have realized he'd hit someone. The investigation was endless."

She sighed dramatically, crossing her legs once more. Then she leaned toward Coppola to pick up a cigarette case from the table. The low neckline of her T-shirt sank even lower. Coppola almost had a stroke.

He took his leave in a hurry. As soon as he was out of the building he contacted Balistreri. He gave a meticulous account of the facts, at the same time omitting any description of Ornella Corona.

"Coppola, the investigation into Corona's death is fishy. It took twice as long as normal. Any idea why?" Balistreri asked.

"I told you everything I know, sir. I'll go to the traffic department and ask."

"What's Mrs. Corona like?"

Coppola wondered if he'd given himself away.

"Typical widow," he said. He thought he heard Balistreri laugh.

"Are you sure?" Balistreri asked.

"Uh, yeah. Nothing special."

"Really? Should I come over myself and verify that?"

"Unbelievably gorgeous," Coppola admitted.

Balistreri laughed. "Her photo's in the file. One last thing, Coppola, from a purely investigative standpoint: top or bottom?"

This came from one of Coppola's vulgar remarks for men only about a very beautiful woman under investigation. Balistreri had redeemed the remark from its vulgar meaning, using it to refer to the character of the woman under investigation and thus giving it true investigative weight.

"Bottom, sir, one hundred percent. She'd let you do whatever you wanted, but she'd just lie there, filing her nails and then applying polish. Even her watch winks at you."

. . . .

Corvu tidied up his cubicle before Natalya arrived. While he was polishing the glass walls, Margherita approached. They had been friends since she'd first arrived. Margherita leaned against the door.

"Graziano, I'm worried about something."

Corvu finished polishing the glass and moved on to dusting his computer keyboard. "What's wrong?"

"Nothing's wrong, but I wanted to speak to you about that witness who's coming in again."

Surprised, Corvu stopped cleaning and looked at her. "Natalya? What is it?"

"Well, I don't really know how to say this, so I'm just going to come out with it. Are you really interested in a prostitute?"

Corvu explained Natalya's situation, and that he, too, had been surprised.

"Oh, good. She really likes you," Margherita said with relief.

Corvu blushed. "How do you know?"

"I'm a woman. And as she was leaving she told you she doesn't have a boyfriend. She wants you to ask her out. You should go for it."

"You know I'm terrible at that kind of thing," Corvu said.

"I've got a brilliant idea," Margherita exclaimed. She hurried off to her own office and returned shortly with a framed photo of a good-looking blonde.

"Isn't that your sister?" Corvu asked.

"We'll put this here," Margherita said, placing it on a corner of Corvu's desk. She nodded with satisfaction.

"Why would I want to have your sister's photo on my desk?" Corvu picked it up and handed it back to Margherita, who promptly placed it on his desk again. They went through this routine a few times. Finally, Balistreri came in.

"What's going on here?"

"Nothing, sir," Corvu said.

"I'm trying to help him out," Margherita said. She explained the situation with Natalya.

"Corvu, I order you to leave the photo on your desk," Balistreri commanded.

"With all due respect, sir, this is a private matter. You can't order me to do that."

"You're right, I can't order you to put the photo on your desk, but I can assign the questioning of Natalya to someone else. After all, you got nowhere with her before. We need someone with a real grasp of female psychology," Balistreri said. He turned to Margherita. "What shift is Mastroianni working tomorrow?"

Before Margherita could answer, Natalya knocked on the glass. Balistreri waved her in. Margherita still held the photo in her hand.

"Please sit down," Balistreri said. "We're almost finished. Deputy Corvu tells me you've been a great help."

"It's easy to help when the police are so kind." Natalya shot a smile at Corvu, who turned red.

"Excuse me, Deputy Corvu," Margherita said, placing the photo on the desk. "I replaced the broken glass in the frame. I apologize again for my carelessness." She turned to Natalya and said, "Unfortunately, Deputy Corvu's fiancée passed away last year."

Balistreri said to Natalya, "Can you go over for me again everything from the evening when you saw the car with the single headlight?"

Natalya said, "As I told Graziano, I was alone. My cousin was working. It was well past dark, and I thought it was a motorcycle. When it came up to me it slowed down as if to stop and I realized it was a car, and then it sped up and turned the corner in seconds."

You didn't tell me, Corvu, that it slowed down so much. And you didn't wonder why?

"I don't suppose you got a good look at the driver," Balistreri said.

"He was wearing a hat and dark glasses," Natalya replied.

Balistreri looked at Corvu. His face was so mortified that Balistreri could only think of excusing himself from the room to save him from embarrassment.

If I hadn't popped in here by chance I'd never have known. Look what a disastrous effect a young girl can have on this chump here! Hat and dark glasses in a car in at night.

Evening

Balistreri had almost an hour to spare. It was enough to get him to Trastevere on foot. He felt the need to walk, and all the better through the steady drizzle that seemed determined to last through the end of 2005.

He went down Via Nazionale. The shops were about to close and customers were leaving, while restaurants were opening and filling up. Money was shifting from clothes to food.

While he was crossing the Tiber—from the dark city center lowering its rolling shutters, over to Trastevere lit up by its restaurants—his mood darkened, as it did every time he put the river between himself and the capital's temporal power and came closer to the Vatican's spiritual one.

He whose judgment no one escapes.

The doubt had been growing slowly inside him since 1982, inexorably and against his will. It was the revenge of the Catholic education that he had rejected as an adolescent.

He suddenly found himself in front of her. Linda Nardi's profound and distant beauty was, as usual, equaled by her total lack of interest. The contrast was as irresistible as it was permanent.

It's as if she were a nun from a cloistered order temporarily visiting the outside world.

Balistreri had booked a table in a pizzeria popular with young students and families. They ordered. When he ordered himself a beer, she told him she didn't drink. So those costly wines had served only to teach Colicchia a lesson.

For a while they chatted about Christmas shopping and other inconsequential topics. Then Balistreri began to fill her in on the developments in Nadia's case. She expressed little interest.

It was very warm in the pizzeria. Linda took off her jacket. Balistreri was unable to resist glancing at her breasts. And then the vertical line appeared down the middle of her forehead.

They were quiet for a long time, until the arrival of the *tiramisù*. Only in front of the dessert did Linda relax again, taste it, and give the waiter a satisfied smile, asking him to pass on her compliments to the chef. After a while the chef came out in person. He was a young Egyptian man.

"You are very kind," he said humbly.

"And you're an excellent chef." She got up and hugged him briefly.

Balistreri watched with some surprise.

Unselfish kindness, tenderness toward the weakest. A distant memory.

When the chef had returned to the kitchen and she sat back down, he said, "Okay, there must be something you wanted to know. What is it?"

"You're under no obligation to tell me," she said. She was so unfailingly polite that it was almost irritating.

"I really appreciate your making that phone call to Pasquali. I gave you the information on Colajacono and the Iordanescu woman's report, and I can guarantee you'll be the first to hear of anything else that happens."

"I'm not here to talk about future crimes." She said it flatly, with no aggression.

You're not interested in the next crime. You want to speak about the one before. But I don't.

"All right. What do you want to know?"

"You're not convinced. I want to know why."

He was taken aback. "What are you talking about?" he asked.

"Those three Roma boys and the fourth man they implicated."

"What makes you think I'm not convinced?"

"Because you can't stop thinking about it and it shows."

"Ms. Nardi, there's been no miscarriage of justice in that case. Those in prison are guilty, without a shadow of a doubt."

"But maybe not everyone who's guilty is in prison, right?"

"The case is closed. It's over." He heard the doubt in his own voice.

"What about the fourth man?" she asked.

Don't get yourself involved in this business, Balistreri. This woman has things in her head you don't fully understand. Things that could cause you a great deal of harm.

"I'll get the bill," Balistreri said.

She said softly, "What if he carves up another girl?"

She wasn't expressing a challenge or an accusation, only a concern, and even appeared apologetic about making him feel embarrassed by the question.

Balistreri, who prided himself on his control, on thinking before he spoke, visibly lost it. He was a little frightened at himself, hearing his own voice before having thought what he was going to say.

"I'm going to figure out who passed information to you, and when I do I'm going to destroy him," he said, his voice rising.

"Best of luck with that, Captain Balistreri." There was no challenge or trace of arrogance in her voice.

As if I'd made her a promise, not a threat.

Linda Nardi got up, left money for the bill, and made her way out.

.   .   .   .

An analytical appraisal of the risks and advantages should have put her off, but Giulia Piccolo wasn't Graziano Corvu. They had nothing at hand to ask for a search warrant of Mircea and Greg's flat before they were released.

"Don't worry, we're going there to pick up your things and take them to my place. Ten minutes at the most."

"What if someone comes in?"

"Mircea, Greg, and the other two are being held until tomorrow. Don't worry."

"Why don't you call a couple of uniformed guys for backup?" he suggested.

She suddenly realized that Rudi was afraid for her safety as well, because she was a woman among a bunch of beasts.

"Don't worry, I have my gun for backup." She smiled and pulled back her jacket to reveal the holster.

The policeman they had put on guard on the street confirmed that plenty of people had come and gone in the building, but not Marius Hagi. Piccolo had wanted to put the officer on the landing outside, but Balistreri had said no.

It was already late and only a few windows were lit up. They used Rudi's keys to enter. The apartment was completely dark, with no light coming in from the outside.

"Didn't we leave some of the blinds open yesterday?" asked Rudi.

Piccolo took the gun from her holster and motioned to him to stand close to the door of the first room and stay still. She moved silently along the hall with the gun in her hand. When she came to the third door, the one to Ramona and Nadia's room, she quickly switched on the light. The room was in chaos: mattresses ripped open, drawers pulled out—even the radiator had been wrenched from the wall.

Slowly, she turned toward Rudi's room. She stopped in the doorway and switched on the light. This room looked even worse. Rudi's things had been scattered about. She could hear him breathing quickly behind her. "Stay here in the hall," she whispered. The doors of the wardrobe were closed. She went into the room and approached it, gun in hand. As she reached to open it she heard Rudi cry out. There was a thump, and then a door slammed shut. She rushed to the door and almost fell over Rudi, who was lying on the ground and moaning, his hands cupping a bloody nose.

She rushed to the window and called down to the officer on the street, "Someone's coming down—stop him!"

Then she ran down the staircase. The policeman said, "No one's come out."

Piccolo went back in followed by the policeman. "The basement," she said, pointing to the stairs. "You stay here and keep an eye on the front door."

"But . . ." he objected. She was already on her way down the stairs.

You're crazy, going into an apartment building full of sleeping families with a gun in your hand. And what if the guy also had a gun? Would you blaze away in there like a "Gunfight at the OK Corral"?

The cellar was a real labyrinth. She switched on the light and followed the passages. Nine floors, four apartments per floor, thirty-six storerooms. Thirty-six locked metal doors. He could be behind any one of them. The light, on a timer, went out, and she couldn't find the switch. In the dark she felt the sweat trickling down her neck. She performed a breathing exercise her karate teacher had taught her. Her anger was stronger than her fear. The bastard was in here, a few meters away.

She waited in absolute silence. Several minutes went by. The policeman called to her from the top of the stairs. She made no reply. Then a gust of cold air wafted through. Piccolo held her gun with both hands and released the safety. In the dark and total silence she heard rustling. She heard footsteps coming toward her. She aimed her gun in that direction.

"Stop where you are and put your hands up," she called out, her voice shaking slightly.

"Deputy, it's me." The policeman turned the lights on. Piccolo lowered her gun, but she could see that he'd been thinking the same thing she was—another few seconds and she might have shot him.

They went up to the ground floor. Piccolo phoned Balistreri, who was walking back from Trastevere. She told him everything briefly, including the fact that she had been about to shoot a fellow officer. Balistreri listened without interrupting.

When she had finished, he said, "Piccolo, the person driving the car was wearing a hat and sunglasses." This news shut her up, as he had hoped it would. They hung up, and Rudi came down the stairs holding his nose, his face and his sweater covered in blood.

She put an arm around his shoulders and led him to the car. The uniformed officer returned to his post.

"Get in the car and tilt your head back," she said to Rudi, handing him a pack of tissues. Then she opened the trunk, took out a canvas bag, and went back into the building.

She said to the policeman, "Check anyone who comes out. Call for backup if you need it."

Without another word she went back down into the basement of the building. From the bag she pulled out a crowbar and a pair of cutters. It would take a couple of minutes per door.

A half-hour later, Balistreri arrived. By then she was almost halfway done. It was hard work, and she was sweating and cursing.

"Twenty to go," she said.

"You can stop. He's not here," he said.

"Where the fuck is he then?" she hissed.

Balistreri looked up. "In order to have a storeroom, you'd have to have an apartment."

She dropped the cutters and cursed loudly. Breaking open the doors of thirty-six storerooms was one thing, but searching thirty-six apartments without a warrant was something else entirely.

Balistreri picked up the cutters. "If we're going to pass this off as a robbery, we'd better open all of them."

He gave her a little pat on the head and immediately regretted it as being too affectionate.

You'd be a real disaster as a father.

Piccolo then went back to breaking open the storeroom doors. When she had them all open, Balistreri told the policeman to go home and make no report until his boss had spoken to Balistreri.

Balistreri asked Piccolo for a lift back to the office. Rudi was asleep in the passenger seat, so Piccolo gently fastened his seatbelt and Balistreri got in the back.

"I know the captain in this precinct. He's a good man. I'll sort things out," he said to her.

They drove in silence. Before he got out of the car, she mumbled, "Thanks."

. . . .

He imagined no one would be up on the third floor, it was almost midnight and he was exhausted, but as soon as he entered the corridor he heard giggles.

Then he heard Corvu's voice coming from his office. "Don't worry, we'll find it."

Balistreri peered around the corner. Corvu and Natalya were at his desk. Two empty pizza boxes sat in front of them. They were staring at the computer monitor with their heads together. Each held a can of beer.

When he tapped on the glass Corvu leaped up and the can fell into his lap, spilling beer onto his crotch.

"We were, we were . . ." he stuttered, trying awkwardly to wipe away the foaming beer.

Natalya began to laugh, then she took out some tissues. "Can you do it, Graziano?"

"Yes, better let Graziano clean himself off, unless we want to see him have an attack of something," said Balistreri sarcastically.

When Corvu had regained his composure somewhat, Balistreri joined them at the computer. There were several images of a car on the screen.

Corvu explained, "We began by reconstructing the rear of the car that Natalya saw for a few seconds as it drove away. She's almost certain it was white or gray—anyway, it was a light color."

Balistreri refrained from asking why they'd accomplished so little in all this time. He was happy for Corvu, even though he didn't want to admit it.

First of all, he's not your son. Second, he'll never be able to pull off a relationship.

All of a sudden he felt very tired and very old.

"I think we should call it a night," Balistreri said. He quit the application, and his desktop came up. The background was a photo of a young Balistreri posing with a group of other young officers in front of his first police station.

"Look how handsome," she exclaimed.

Corvu's face clouded. Natalya moved closer to the screen and pointed her slender finger at the police car in the photo.

"That's the car. I'm positive. I recognize the long taillights."

Balistreri and Corvu looked at each other, then back at the screen. The car was an old model, an Alfa Romeo Giulia GT.

SATURDAY, DECEMBER 31, 2005

Morning

THE SEARCH FOR A light-colored Alfa Romeo Giulia GT 1300 with a broken headlight began immediately, but the night of December 30 nothing turned up.

Corvu slept in Balistreri's office at his insistence. He hoped Natalya would stay over with him. Then Balistreri went home to get some sleep.

When Balistreri came back at seven, he found his deputy asleep on the worn sofa. Naturally, he was alone.

He went down to the cafeteria and ordered a cappuccino-to-go in a glass and bought a still-warm doughnut. He went back up and put the hot cappuccino under the nose of Corvu, who woke instantly and dragged himself up in embarrassment.

"Sir, I'm sorry, I couldn't manage it." Balistreri put the cappuccino and doughnut down for him.

"Mastroianni e-mailed from Romania," Corvu said, biting into the doughnut. "In 2002, before Hagi brought Mircea and Greg to Italy, they were acquitted of a charge of double homicide on the grounds of insufficient evidence and thanks to the best defense lawyer in Romania. Anyway, Mastroianni's on his way home now."

He continued, "I've gone through all the vehicle databases. Fortunately, there are only a few of those cars still in circulation, only fifty-two in Rome. Twelve of them are registered to immigrants. Apparently they're into fast cars."

"Do you have the names and addresses?"

"Yes. Of course the records might not be up-to-date. They could have been sold off without the registrations changing, and some of them may not be registered at all. With cars that old, there are no guarantees."

"All right, run them down by phone. But divide up the twelve cars that belong to immigrants between yourself and Piccolo and Coppola and Mastroianni. Work in pairs, not alone. And take care of it today."

Once he was alone, Balistreri turned on the radio and lit his first cigarette of the day. He took another pill to stave off acid reflux so he could drink at the New Year's Eve party that night at Angelo Dioguardi's apartment.

The mail with the press cuttings came in, and contained Linda Nardi's article. A front-page headline: SAMANTHA ROSSI: IS THE CASE CLOSED? Below the headline was the girl's photograph, the one every Italian had known for months. A gleaming smile in front of a sailboat.

Reluctantly, he forced himself to read the article. No hint at all about the carved initial or the fourth man. The main point was all in the question that concluded the piece.

Are we looking at the chaotic fury of someone who lost control or the premeditated barbarity of someone in full control of himself?

The question caught him off guard—which happened only rarely, yet always with this woman.

Fury or premeditation? Linda Nardi's question brought back a particular unease, something whose roots were sunk in well-hidden depths.

Piccolo came in punctually at seven thirty. Balistreri could sense a new disquiet in her that left him feeling anything but easy. He was hoping she would have calmed down with regard to the previous night, but that wasn't the case. On top of her anger there was a determination that was too personal, and experience had taught him that in you could a lot of damage in that frame of mind.

"How's Rudi?" he asked her.

She smiled weakly. "He's sleeping on my couch."

He struggled to find the right words. "Piccolo, I don't want to intrude, but are you involved with Rudi?"

"We're not having sex, not that it's any of your business, and he had an HIV test last week that came back negative," she said flatly.

Balistreri's phone rang. Relieved, he answered. "Alberto, are you up already? You're not working today, are you?"

"No, but I'm going on vacation with my family, remember? We leave for the Maldives after lunch. I wanted to wish you a happy new year."

"That's right, the big diving trip."

"Have you read the papers?" Alberto asked. His brother was worried about him.

"I read them. I spoke to Linda Nardi yesterday. I had a feeling she'd write something like that."

"Really she's saying you're right to have doubts."

"But I don't. I did before we found the three Roma, but once we did I realized I was wrong."

They both knew he didn't believe what he was saying.

"Why are you on antidepressants then? Because you're positive you didn't get justice for Samantha Rossi."

"You're the religious one, Alberto. You should understand regret and self-flagellation."

It was a gratuitous, wicked comment dictated by frustration. But his brother pretended to take no notice.

"No antidepressant can treat regret, Michele. You repent, make a confession if you believe, and then atone for your sins if you can."

"I've tried that. It doesn't work."

"Mike, not even the truth can close certain wounds. Not on this earth."

. . . .

At lunchtime, Balistreri called Angelo Dioguardi on his cell phone. They were planning to usher in the new year from his small penthouse on the Janiculum Hill. From up there they'd have a sweeping view of Rome and the midnight fireworks.

"Are we going to play poker after we pop the cork on the champagne?"

"No poker game. Your brother's away, and Corvu says he's not available."

"I bet he's spending the evening with a woman," Balistreri said, pleased to hear it.

"I hope so, for his sake. There will be plenty of women at my place tonight, too."

"I'm a little old to be getting it on at midnight," Balistreri said.

"Some old-fashioned recreational sex would be good for you."

"I think you're the one who needs some old-fashioned recreational sex, no strings attached for once in your life. Might help you to see women a little more realistically."

"You know, you were more fun when you were a cynical woman-izer. A cynic who doesn't get any action is just sad."

They bantered for a few more minutes, then said good-bye.

Balistreri called Coppola. "Any news?"

"Actually, there is some interesting news."

"Did you find out what kind of underwear she wears?"

"No, but I did find out why the investigation took so long. There was a life insurance policy on Sandro Corona."

"Let me guess—his attractive wife was the beneficiary."

"Exactly. She got three million euros thanks to that policy."

"Thanks to an unknown truck driver, you mean."

"Maybe she was involved in her husband's death somehow."

"Where are you now, Coppola?"

"Out with Piccolo. We've got eight names on our list. Mastroianni just landed at Fiumicino, and he and Corvu are going to handle the others."

"Okay, get busy. And keep an eye on Piccolo to make sure she doesn't do anything stupid."

Afternoon

The office was quieter than usual. The year was dragging slowly to a close. Balistreri settled down to the inevitable wait. He was in pain because he couldn't smoke. He looked at the drawn blinds outside which the rain was pelting down and thought of the stalemate he was in: no brainwave from which to launch a fresh initiative, only the hope that the dragnet would come up with a bigger fish.

The hours passed slowly. Margherita popped in a few times to ask if he wanted a sandwich, a beer, or a coffee.

He politely declined. His mind was full of memories he was trying to resist. They were bouncing off the walls of his brain.

Summer 1967. Summer 1970. Summer 1982. Summer 2005.

Every so often he heard a phone ring somewhere and a voice answer it. Then even those sounds stopped. Everyone was leaving. At six o'clock Margherita stopped by to offer her best wishes. He watched her as she left and wondered who would be taking her out that evening.

Certainly not you, Balistreri, but perhaps someone her own age.

That reminded him of Ramona's story, relayed to him by Mastroianni, of the client who couldn't get it up. The bastard with the broken headlight had gotten lucky—he'd gained extra time. Anyway, Nadia had gotten into the car with him without making a scene because she knew him. She was waiting for him.

The room was far too hot. Balistreri opened a window to let in some fresh air. The sound of fireworks mingled with the sound of thunder. In the distance, beyond the Colosseum, a bolt of lightning split the sky. Finally, the year was coming to an end.

Evening

Stores were locking up and everyone was rushing home to get ready for the big night. But Piccolo and Coppola were soaked to the skin, cold, and bone-tired. Piccolo felt like she was getting a fever. Occasionally, she shook with chills. The red taillights of cars reflected off the wet pavement. They sat in their car and studied their crumpled, wet list.

"Finished," Coppola said. "And we haven't accomplished a fucking thing, pardon my French." Coppola didn't like to swear in front of women, but the many hours he and Piccolo had spent questioning people mystified by their interest in old cars, while all around them the New Year fireworks were starting to go off, had frayed his nerves. He wanted to get home to Lucia and Ciro and help them prepare a celebratory dinner. Instead, they'd wasted time questioning eight people in the rain.

"All right, Coppola, let's go home. We've seen seven vehicles, headlights intact, although lights might have been replaced. All the owners have solid alibis for the evening of December 24. Then there's the Egyptian guy who sold his car to an Eastern European whose name he doesn't know without changing the registration. But the headlights were working."

"A complete waste of time. Let's go home. And you should take an aspirin and get into bed," he said.

"I'll drop you at yours, then go on with the car from the pool."

When they got to his apartment, Coppola invited her in. "The wife'll make you a steaming hot mug of milk—you look feverish."

She shook her head. "There's something I have to do, but thanks anyway. Give my best to Lucia and Ciro."

Coppola looked at her suspiciously. "Are you sure?"

"Don't worry, I'm going home. Happy New Year."

At half past eight she pulled up outside the Torre Spaccata police station. There was hardly anyone still there—everyone was at home getting dressed up for the evening. Piccolo let her phone ring the agreed number of times, then hung up and called again straight away.

"Hello?" said Rudi.

"What are you up to?"

"I'm cooking. You said you didn't want to go out tonight, so I thought I'd make us dinner here."

"Did you go to the grocery store? I told you not to go out."

"Just to the supermarket downstairs. And I put on one of your hats and pulled it over my eyes."

Piccolo felt her own forehead. It was burning.

"Listen, Rudi, don't go out again, but eat without me. I'll be back late."

"No, I'll wait for you. I bought some sparkling wine, too. With my own money," he clarified.

She could picture him standing over the stove, stirring and tasting. She wanted to be in the warm kitchen, in the company of this good-looking man. A man who was gay, she reminded herself.

"All right, but I might be pretty late. Promise me you won't go out."

"Not until next year," he said.

Piccolo grinned. "If you do, I'll arrest you."

"I've got to get back to the lentils," he said.

Her head and her throat were both sore. She fished around in her pockets and found a hard candy. Then she settled back to keep an eye on the entrance to the police station. She wanted to turn on the heat in the car, but she didn't want to run the motor. The exhaust would be visible in the cold air, and she didn't want to be seen.

Colajacono and Tatò, both out of uniform, came out. They got into a car, and Tatò took the wheel.

She followed them at a distance. They went down a long boulevard with high rises, then turned off to an unlit area. The roads became ever more desolate until they came to one with no houses or street lamps, open countryside to the right. The road went up and down following the curves of the hills. Piccolo switched off her headlights and followed Tatò's tail lights at a distance of a hundred and fifty feet. Every so often on the right, dirt roads wound steeply up the hill. The countryside beyond the city stood out under the lights of fireworks and flashes of lightning, although a couple of kilometers away on the left the illuminated outlines of the outlying high-rises were visible.

At a certain point the red lights slowed down then shifted over to the right and went out. It was a rest area at the top of a slope, totally deserted in the freezing rain.

Piccolo stopped immediately. She couldn't stay there in the middle of the road. Thirty or so feet back she'd seen a metaled road on the left, so she reversed to it and put herself out of sight. A flash of lightning lit up Tatò's car parked in the rest area.

Will I see them if they get out in this dark and this rain? Keep calm—they can't see you.

Piccolo felt for the pistol in its holster. In the silence she could hear only the constant beating of the rain and the intermittent noise of the fireworks. She was stretched out almost flat so as not to be seen. Feeling herself begin to shiver, she was tempted to switch on the heater, but resisted. She zipped up her jacket and tried to breathe through her nose. Every so often she cleaned the condensation off the window with her sleeve. The lightning allowed her to keep an eye on the other car. Two glowing red butts told her that Tatò and Colajacono were having a cigarette in the car. The time passed—ten o'clock, eleven— and she was growing steadily colder.

They're waiting for someone or something. But who or what? Should I tell Balistreri I'm following two policemen without any reason after what I got myself into last night? First we'll see what happens, and then I'll tell him.

She decided to call Rudi again, but there was no signal. She saw the glow of a cigarette as someone got out of the car, and a flash of lightning illuminated Colajacono's grotesque figure taking a piss in the rain with the cigarette in his mouth.

Her headache was worse, her throat burning. What she needed was to lie down, warm and peaceful, and have some of Rudi's lentils. In the distance, she saw a motorbike headlight coming toward her.

The headlight turned down a dirt road. Then another flash of lightning lit up the scene. It wasn't a motorcycle at all. It was a Giulia GT, struggling up the hill with only one headlight. Tatò's car turned and began to follow it at a distance.

.   .   .   .

Half an hour before 2005 ended, Angelo Dioguardi's penthouse was overflowing, with about two dozen people squeezed into seven hundred square feet. A cold north wind was blowing. Balistreri and his host stood on the glassed-in terrace.

"Graziano called. He wants to play poker after all. He'll join us around two with a friend, so there'll be four of us."

"That's too bad. I guess he's not getting Natalya into bed tonight after all."

"Graziano takes his time."

"That's your bad influence, Angelo. The ideal woman is an immature delusion."

It was one of those cutting remarks that Balistreri had made on many occasions, but this time Angelo took issue.

"At least I have my delusion, Michele. You don't even have that much."

Balistreri looked at him in surprise. It wasn't in Angelo's character to criticize. In fact what he read in Dioguardi's eyes wasn't an accusation, it was his sorrow for a friend who, while still alive, was already dead on the inside.

. . . .

You make certain decisions in a moment and they stay with you for the rest of your life. Piccolo was twelve years old on the beach at Palermo when she dived into the waves to save a little boy. She was fifteen when she flattened the best-looking guy in the school with a karate blow for copping an uninvited feel. She was seventeen when she first went to bed with a girl. Now she'd brought a male homosexual home and, with the onset of a fever, was about to face corrupt policemen and potential killers.

She drew her gun from its holster and placed it on the seat beside her. She started the car and turned to follow Tatò's car, which she could only manage to see when the brake lights came on. There was no way they could see her. The important thing was not to lose them.

They turned where the Giulia GT had turned. The dirt road, all mud and puddles, wound around the dark hillside. Piccolo's car slipped and went off the road, but she managed to get back on track.

Every so often she touched her gun for reassurance. She was breathing heavily because of her temperature and the tension. They passed several curves, then a crossroads. Now the potholes were enormous. She dropped back farther so they wouldn't hear her car. The whole time she kept her eyes trained on the lights in the pitch black. Then all of a sudden the car ahead of her stopped abruptly. She braked and switched off the engine. The tail lights she'd been following completely disappeared and the darkness became total. There was only the wind whistling in the night and the distant sound of fireworks. It was biting cold and the dampness chilled her to the bone, but at least it was no longer raining. She looked at her watch, the only weak light in all that surrounding blackness: five minutes to midnight.

A flashlight came on and moved away from Tatò's vehicle. Piccolo got out of her car. It would have been better to turn it around so that it was facing down the hill in case she needed to make a quick getaway, but there was no time. She grabbed her gun and began to follow the light of the flashlight. She slipped and fell into the mud, banging her knee.

She got to her feet and pressed on. She was dog-tired. Her legs felt like lead and her head was on fire, but she was determined not to lose them. One last bit of hill, and she arrived. The Giulia GT was parked on a patch of grass near an abandoned farmhouse. She could see the flickering light of an oil lamp inside, and she could hear male voices. She couldn't make out what language they were speaking, but they were probably foreigners.

The flashlight had been switched off. Piccolo had no idea where Colajacono and Tatò were. Gripping her gun, she hid behind the last tree next to the clearing where the farmhouse stood. She covered her nose and mouth with her jacket to hide her breath as it condensed in the freezing air. Fireworks went off in rapid succession. She huddled behind the tree.

Her head was throbbing, her legs weak. She had to make a decision; she couldn't stay here forever. She held her gun with both hands and ran behind the farmhouse. As she paused for breath, a hand was pressed over her mouth and an arm came around her from behind. Instinctively, she jerked her free hand back. She heard the cartilage of a nasal septum breaking and a curse in Roman dialect. She pointed her gun at Tatò, who was on his knees and groaning with a hand cupped over his nose.

The farmhouse door opened and two men stepped out carrying the oil lamp. One was armed with a knife and the other with a club. Piccolo moved behind Tatò and pointed her gun at them.

"Drop your weapons," she ordered.

"Who the fuck are you, bitch?" the one with the club shouted in a heavy Eastern European accent.

"Police," Piccolo shouted. She tried to keep her eyes on them and also look around for Colajacono.

The two men nodded at each other, then started to walk toward Piccolo.

"Stop or I'll shoot," she warned.

Fifty feet away. They hesitated a moment, then resumed walking forward. Once they got within fifteen feet of her, it was all over. She had only a few seconds to decide.

She fired a single shot in the air. She couldn't spare any more than that. The two men hesitated again.

"On the ground, now!" Colajacono shouted. The two men jumped at the noise.

They turned to face Colajacono, who stood with his legs apart and a gun held in both hands, his arms tensed. They looked at each other and began to run toward the path. Piccolo heard a shot and saw the Roma with the club fall over, holding his leg. The other one stopped.

In that moment Piccolo realized the not-too-distant sounds she heard weren't fireworks, but the blades of a helicopter that was hovering over them. A spotlight illuminated the scene from above, while a voice from a loudspeaker warned the escaping man to stop and put his hands up. Sirens squealed and tires screeched as police cars raced up the hills. Their headlights lit up the road.

Colajacono turned to Tatò. "You'll have to get your nose fixed thanks to this stupid bitch."

Piccolo saw the slap coming. Under normal circumstances she'd have parried it with one arm while striking with the other. But the fever, the tension, and the cold had made her sluggish. The blow sent her reeling into the mud.

SUNDAY, JANUARY 1, 2006

Early morning on January 1

BALISTRERI RECEIVED A PHONE call just after midnight. He listened in silence, then called Corvu and ordered him to take Natalya home and pick him up in a police car.

At one o'clock they were on top of the hill. Floodlights powered by photoelectric cells lit up the scene. As they drove up they met the ambulance taking away the shepherd wounded by Colajacono; the other was in handcuffs guarded by two policemen. A paramedic was taking care of Tatò's nose.

Balistreri found Piccolo wrapped in a blanket and sitting in a police car.

"Corvu, go check out the farmhouse. Do you have your equipment?"

"Yes, sir." He went off to get the gear he needed to analyze the scene without contaminating it.

Balistreri slipped into the backseat of the car, sitting next to Piccolo. He saw she was trembling, but didn't ask her anything. She told

him everything freely, except for the slap she received from Colajacono. She'd decided to think about that for awhile.

"I'm sorry," she said. "I was afraid they'd get away and I didn't
know if Colajacono was on their side or ours."

That was going to be hard to explain to Pasquali. Even harder to
explain than Tatò's nose.

"I'll get someone to take you home," Balistreri said.

"Let's look for Nadia first," she replied.

"We'll look for her. You're going home right now. I'm getting
someone to take you." It was an order that brooked no discussion and
several minutes later Piccolo was in a car finally taking her home to
Rudi's lentils.

Balistreri turned to Colajacono.

"I'm sorry about Tatò's nose. Anyway, there'll be time to talk about
that and what you were doing here."

Colajacono looked at him with undisguised contempt. "Whenever
you say, sir. Then you can explain why that crazy bitch was following us."

Balistreri didn't bat an eye. "In the meantime, why don't you tell
me what you two were doing here."

"The farmhouse is occupied by one of the Roma—that one," he
said, pointing to the young man in handcuffs. "They herd sheep out
here. We got an anonymous tip that there was a Giulia GT with a
broken headlight up here. The car is his."

"Do you follow up that swiftly on every anonymous tip?"

"I told you, Captain Balistreri, we're not in a fancy office like yours.
We can't afford to fuck around."

Balistreri remained calm. "What about the other guy?"

"Another shepherd. He lives in a different abandoned farmhouse,
on the other side of the hill, a mile or so away. They figured everybody
would be out celebrating tonight, so they broke into a house nearby
and stole a television, a stereo, a video camera, and some silver. It's all
in the trunk of the Giulia GT. This one's name is Vasile Geoana. He's
Roma."

Balistreri approached the shepherd. He was thin and bony and
had a long beard. He wore a leather jacket over a T-shirt and jeans. He
smelled like sheep and alcohol.

"Do you speak Italian?"

With a hard, sly look he nodded.

"Is that your car?"

"Yeah, mine." His voice was rough, his accent guttural.

"Who did you buy it from?"

"Egyptian who makes pizza. Two hundred euros."

"With a broken headlight?"

"What's a 'headlight'?"

"Front light."

He shook his head. "No, got broken after. It was fine when I lent it, broken after."

Corvu came out of the farmhouse. He went up to Balistreri and showed him two long blond hairs in a plastic bag. Balistreri showed them to the shepherd.

"Where's the girl?" Colajacono asked him brusquely.

Vasile stared at the ground.

"What girl?"

"This girl," persisted Colajacono, pointing to the bag with the hairs.

"I bring whores here sometimes."

Colajacono placed his enormous hand around the shepherd's handcuffed wrist. He howled in pain.

"The girl you picked up in your car on Via di Torricola. Where is she?" Colajacono asked. He squeezed the man's wrist. Vasile screamed in pain, his face contorted. A gust of icy wind swept across the field. Tears were streaming down the shepherd's face.

Balistreri turned to Colajacono. "Leave him alone," he ordered.

Colajacono didn't even look at him. His face was twisted in a grimace of cruel satisfaction.

"I don't know," the shepherd groaned. "I don't know where she went." He was on his knees.

"Leave him alone or I'll place you under arrest," Balistreri warned Colajacono.

This time Colajacono turned and looked at him mockingly.

"Oh, really? You think these animals who screw Italians over should be treated with kid gloves, do you?"

He spat on the ground. "Street sweepers in paradise. That's all you are."

Giving the shepherd's knee such a powerful kick that he fell face down in the mud crying, Colajacono turned to Balistreri with a defiant air.

"I'll leave him to you, Balistreri. See what you can do with all your nice ways of protecting civil liberties, your DNA, and your big words . . ."

Balistreri managed to keep himself under control—there were enough problems already.

Or perhaps I know that you're partly right.

The ground was a mixture of water and mud. Going over it by the light of photoelectric cells would be difficult, but it had to be done. It was one thirty and dawn was five hours away. Balistreri gave instructions to Corvu to call for the dogs and make a start.

He lit his first cigarette of the year. He looked over the city, lit up by the last fireworks. He wanted to be sitting in Angelo's warm apartment, playing a game of poker. Or else with Linda Nardi.

He drove the thought of her away angrily and set off through the freezing rain.

Morning

By dawn on the morning of January 1, they had found nothing. The wind had died down and the sky was a dense iron gray. Nevertheless, its light would help the search. The area was half deserted; the police were all out on the hill. As soon as Forensics had completed their examination, Balistreri went into the farmhouse with Corvu and the shepherd.

The place was a dump. It was rank with the smell of alcohol, sheep, and shit. An empty whiskey bottle and a half-full one sat next to a broken armchair. There was a stained mattress in a corner of the room. A television set and a satellite dish sat next to it.

"Tell me about the girl," Balistreri said to the shepherd, who was still moaning and rubbing his wrist.

"I don't know anything."

"In Sardinia, we feed people like you to the pigs," Corvu said.

Balistreri looked at him in surprise.

Hagi would have had them impaled; Colajacono would have liked to break every bone in their bodies; even the usually shy Corvu was talking about feeding them to the pigs. But Balistreri still felt that something was off.

They had examined the car. Besides the stolen goods there were more blond hairs, a hat, and a pair of sunglasses.

"Listen, Vasile," Balistreri said, "this girl was seen getting into your car. You were wearing the hat and the sunglasses we found in your car."

"Not my stuff. Girl was here, waiting for me."

"She was here, waiting for you. When?"

"When I come back from house of friend. The one you shoot."

"Why did you go to his house?"

"Afternoon I leave sheep with him. He has sheep pen and dog. Then we drink something and we talk. I come back always at seven."

"You always come back at seven exactly?"

"*L'Eredità* television program start then. I always watch."

Marvelous. The wonders of assimilation.

"And the girl was already here by seven. What day was this?"

"December 24. He said present for me."

Balistreri decided to ignore the "he" for the time being and concentrate on the gift part.

"Why did he give you a present?"

"For the car," Vasile replied quickly.

Balistreri pointed to some rags in a corner. Underneath them was a bucket with a rope attached to the handle.

"Is there a well here?"

"Yes, near my friend's house, but well is not good now, water is not good."

Corvu and Balistreri exchanged looks. Corvu hurried out the door.

"All right, Vasile," Balistreri said, "a present in exchange for the car. Explain."

"I lend him car, he give me one hundred euros and a whore to fuck."

"And what did he do with your car?"

"He was moving a bed. My car has a luggage rack."

A fast car, not registered to its actual owner, ideal for a robbery. And Vasile knew that. He also knew that he didn't run much of a risk because the car wasn't registered in his own name. It was a good deal: one hundred euros and a good time simply for lending his car.

"Where did you hand over the car to him?"

"No, I left it here unlocked with keys inside. He said he'd come and pick it up and then bring it back that evening."

"So you never met this man?"

"No, he called my cell, offered deal. I said yes."

"When did he call?"

"Day before—December 23."

"Was he Italian?"

"He spoke Italian with Italian accent."

"Then what?"

"On the evening of December 23 I come back and find one hundred euros here, as he promised. Then the morning of December 24 before I go out with sheep, I leave car with keys and when I come back at seven car is here, blonde whore is here. As he promised. She has two bottles of whiskey because he break light on car. We fuck. I drink a lot. I don't remember when she go." He pointed to the bottles on the floor.

"And the man who borrowed the car?"

"Nothing. He disappears."

Balistreri heard Corvu's footsteps approaching. He looked at Corvu's face, and he knew.

"Come on," Balistreri said to the shepherd, and they set off along the path behind Corvu. The three of them walked single file in silence through the mud. It was raining again. In the distance sheep were bleating. When they came within sight of the well surrounded by police, Balistreri stopped. He met Colajacono's stare. "Stay close to this piece of shit here," he told Corvu, pointing at Vasile. "No one lays a finger on him."

Nadia's body was in the water forty feet below. It was Corvu who climbed down the ladder. They hauled the body up with a rope. The girl was naked. Her legs jutted out at strange angles; they'd probably broken when she hit the bottom of the well. She looked as if she'd been there for a while, possibly a week. There were cuts and cigarette burns on her arms and thighs. The letter E, one inch high, had been carved in the middle of her forehead.

. . . .

At seven on the first morning of 2006, while they were returning to the city, Rome was deserted under a leaden sky and drizzle.

Balistreri called Pasquali on speakerphone. "The girl's dead," he said. Silence. Pasquali was waiting for the rest. "We have a suspect," he added.

"How long has she been dead?" Pasquali's voice was a whisper. First of all, of course, he was concerned about possible comments on their efficiency.

"Judging from the state of the body, several days. She was probably killed the evening she disappeared."

"Thank goodness," Pasquali said.

"It was a Roma shepherd in the country illegally."

"More problems for the mayor," Pasquali muttered. He would be happy that this news would damage the city's center-left government.

"There's something else," Balistreri added.

Pasquali was silent.

"She had the letter E carved in the center of her forehead," Balistreri said.

There was no sound on the other end. Pasquali was probably getting up and walking silently into his well-appointed bathroom. The letter E reopened a door that he thought had been shut tight.

Pasquali spoke, no longer whispering. "Michele, I'll inform the chief of police, and you inform the public prosecutor. We'll put out a short press release in the early afternoon. Meet me in my office in one hour."

. . . .

At nine o'clock Rome was dull and deserted, the roads wet and covered in trash from the New Year's Eve festivities. Despite the fact that it was a holiday and the office was half-empty, Pasquali was wearing an iron-gray suit with a blue polka dot tie, impeccable as usual and having already been to Mass.

Floris, the chief of police, was dressed less formally. Balistreri was still wearing what he'd put on the night before to go to Angelo's. He was unshaven and his shoes were covered in mud.

They sat in Pasquali's lounge. Balistreri gave a thorough recounting of events. It wouldn't have helped to hide anything, as Colajacono would have ensured they knew everything anyway.

"How is Tatò now?" Floris asked.

"They're resetting his nose this morning. It's nothing serious."

"Nothing? Deputy Piccolo attacked him," Pasquali said.

Balistreri shook his head. "She didn't attack him. She was in a dangerous situation. She reacted out of instinct. Tatò acted in an imprudent manner and was struck."

"If Tatò was imprudent, what does that make Piccolo? She failed to inform her superiors of her activities."

"There was no reception out there, Pasquali. She couldn't inform anyone."

"She wasn't using her head. I'd like to know why she was following Colajacono and Tatò."

"Because she had doubts about them, as I told you yesterday."

Pasquali said, "And now we know she was wrong to doubt them. We have the vehicle, the girl's body, and the guilty party thanks to Colajacono and Tatò who, as true professionals, radioed headquarters before going up that hill."

"How did they know where to look for the car?" the chief asked.

Balistreri made a face. "An anonymous phone call came in about half past eight last night. Some guy had seen the Giulia GT with a broken headlight coming down the hill a little earlier. It was Vasile and his friend going off to commit a burglary. End of story. If we believe the story, that is."

"We certainly do believe it," Pasquali said. "Deputy Piccolo should stay out of this case from now on, for her own good."

Balistreri said nothing. Pasquali looked a little nervous. He was twirling his glasses in his hands. Linda Nardi's request had made him nervous.

"Let's talk about the letter E," Floris said. "And about the R, naturally."

Pasquali straightened the knot in his tie. He must have already weighed the political pros and cons.

"We should reopen the Samantha Rossi investigation, which was never officially closed anyway," he said, as if this were the truth. "But no press and no official link between the two cases."

"The E on Nadia will get out—it was pretty visible. Anyone who was there when she was pulled out of the well saw it, and everyone in Forensics," Balistreri said.

"But no one knows about the R in the Rossi case. And who says they're linked?" Pasquali replied.

"We have the same M.O.," Balistreri said. "The guilty Roma served up on a platter and another person who disappears."

"Are you saying there's some kind of plot against the Roma?" Pasquali asked sarcastically.

"Apart from the Roma, we have a serial killer who carves initials on his victims. First an R, then an E. Maybe he's writing a word," the chief said.

"There are major differences between the two crimes," Pasquali said.

Balistreri preferred to let this theory run its course without any rebuttals from him.

"Differences in the modus operandi," Pasquali continued. "Samantha was attacked and raped by persons unknown to her. Nadia got into the car of a person she knew and went of her own free will to have sex with a Roma shepherd. That's assuming the autopsy doesn't reveal any violence."

"There's another difference," Balistreri said. "Samantha Rossi was an Italian student, and Nadia was a Romanian prostitute."

"Exactly," Pasquali said. "They could be two unrelated cases and the letters purely a coincidence. Or else the three Roma boys in the first case knew this Vasile and they told him how they'd murdered a girl and carved a letter on her before we arrested them. And then he imitated what they did."

Balistreri shook his head. "Vasile's only been in Italy since September, and the three Roma in the Rossi case were in prison by August."

"When you interrogate Vasile more thoroughly, you can determine whether he made it all up," Pasquali said. "This story of lending his car sounds like fiction. He picked up Nadia for sex and instead of paying her, he threw her down the well. The end."

"Except for the E carved into her forehead," Balistreri said.

Pasquali got up. "We'll put out a short press release in the early afternoon that doesn't mention the letter. It's not a high-profile case. A Romanian prostitute, a Roma shepherd. We have everything—let's close the case there. Officially. But unofficially we'll continue investigating the Samantha Rossi case."

It was a reasonable solution. It could even hold up if the letters were kept secret.

And if the murderer had finished writing.

. . . .

Corvu had called Piccolo and told her about Nadia. She related the story to Rudi. He cried for a long time. Then he got up and prepared a cool compress for her.

Piccolo was lying on the sofa in her pajamas. She had a high temperature. It was hot in the living room, and Rudi insisted on opening a window to let in fresh air.

He placed a compress on her forehead.

"I'll squeeze some more fresh orange juice for you," he told her. He'd been taking care of her since she returned that night; they had grown closer than ever.

"You've already made me two glasses."

"You have to drink. Liquids and vitamins."

"I haven't tasted the lentils you made for New Year's Eve yet," she said weakly.

"Nor the boiled sausage that goes with them. But tonight you'll feel better and then . . ."

"I've messed up for two nights running, one after the other, doing really crazy things."

"Well, all things come in threes. Today you're not going out, so you can do crazy things at home, if you want."

She recognized a slight hint and was surprised to feel a certain pleasure.

Dim midmorning light filtered in from outside. Piccolo didn't want the lights on—they hurt her eyes. Rudi was sitting on the floor at the foot of the sofa. He hadn't gathered his hair into a ponytail and he looked even more handsome than usual: slim, angelic, and kind. But still frightened.

"If you know anything, you should tell me, Rudi. Help us find the person who did this to Nadia."

He shook his head. He was trembling. They heard the first muffled sounds of people waking after New Year's Eve. Chairs moved in the apartment above. There were voices, a television being switched on. While the world was waking to the new year, Piccolo finally began to drift off to sleep.

But then Rudi began to talk. His voice sounded distant, as if it, too, came from one of the neighboring apartments. "Mircea and Greg were in Ramona's room. They were yelling at her, pushing her around. I was in bed, scared out of my wits. I could hear they wanted something from her, but I couldn't understand what. Then Mircea came to get me."

Piccolo's head stopped throbbing, and she felt a little less weak.

"Ramona was crying. The room was a mess. Greg said that if she didn't help them, they'd take it out on me, but she begged them to leave me alone and promised she'd do anything she could. But she didn't have what they wanted. So Mircea went to get the broom."

Piccolo felt him take her hand. Half asleep, she heard him still talking, now closer. He went on for a long time, lying next to her. Then she began to feel his light breath on the end of her nose, his lips brushing against hers. She became aware that it was her very own hand that was guiding Rudi's under the elastic of her pajama bottoms, then lower down inside her underwear. Then everything became mixed up in her sleep.

The last man who had tried to touch her had been that guy at school. He'd been awkward and rough. Rudi was the exact opposite.

The violence of that time, all the violence of all the men in the world, faded, and she melted under those delicately exploring fingers. She gave into the pleasure, and it grew more intense and unstoppable.

When she woke many hours later, her fever had broken.

. . . .

Balistreri knew the Samantha Rossi file by heart—every name, every photograph, every timeline. But he wanted to read it again now that he'd seen the E on Nadia's forehead. He opened the window to fresh air, silence, rain.

First, the autopsy. Multiple blows to the body and sexual violence. Then strangulation. Then the incisions. He lingered over the description of the actions that had been the cause of her death. Prolonged pressure at the base of her neck. Thumbprints. Strong hands with firm and deadly intent.

He moved on to the confession made by the three young Roma men. They had come to the bar early and only had money for beer. Inside the club, coming out of the bathroom, they met a man. He spoke Italian and was rolling in money, but he had no friends and wanted to have some fun. He'd given them a hundred-euro note so they could drink to his health. Then he disappeared and they drank like fish for an hour. At a certain point he showed up again. He led them into the men's room to do some coke. They lost sight of each other and then at a quarter to ten he was at the entrance to the bar. He called them over. "Let's get some women," he said.

They thought he meant to pay for some whores to go along with the booze and the coke, so they eagerly went with him. As soon as they were outside, the fourth man offered everyone more cocaine. Then a girl ran toward them. The piazza was empty; there was no one at the bus stop. He grabbed the girl. They helped him drag her into the bushes as the bus went past. He delivered a sharp blow to her head and knocked her out. They threw her into the dump. He passed around a bottle of whiskey. Then the girl came to, and they began to beat her. None of the Roma could say exactly what they or the fourth man had done. One of the three said that he'd stood off to the side, watching and smoking. When the girl fainted again, he was no longer there. They went back to their trailer. They didn't even remember taking the bracelet, never mind carving the R on the girl's back. They'd been given a handwriting test. None of the three could read or write.

Balistreri moved on to the part that interested him more: the identikit of the fourth man. Unfortunately, the three Roma had supplied only vague details. Indistinct features, long straight hair over forehead and cheeks, hat, large glasses. They were even more confused when it came to his height: one said medium, another very tall.

He looked at the picture. It could have been anyone. The hair was probably a wig, the glasses too large. Like the hat and sunglasses worn by the driver on Via di Torricola.

He reread the last part of the description. The fourth man hit Samantha Rossi first, but then he moved aside, falling further back into the dark shadows until he disappeared altogether.

Vasile the shepherd had said the same thing about the man who'd borrowed his Giulia GT. The man who'd sent Nadia to him along with two bottles of whiskey. Two very similar men. Or else they were one and the same.

The thoughts clashed with one another in the mix of facts. It was useless trying to find the end of the thread to untie all the knots—the tangle seemed too complicated.

While he waited, Balistreri drank water and listened to music, shut in the silence of his office in the early morning. He was waiting for inspiration.

Sure enough, a thought began to take shape slowly in his head: the Invisible Man.

. . . .

Balistreri walked by just before lunch. He saw Linda Nardi coming out of the newspaper offices. She looked well rested, as if she'd gone to bed very early, skipping the festivities. Perhaps after reading a good book and sipping a cup of herbal tea.

"I was just going to have coffee across the street," Balistreri lied shamelessly.

She didn't seem to realize it was a lie, nor was she angry with him. Instead, she seemed happy to see him, as if that contentious dinner had never happened. But she was still extremely polite.

"I heard about it on the radio a little while ago," she said bluntly.

"The newspapers published the details of the vehicle we were looking for, and Colajacono received an anonymous call about the Giulia GT."

Linda Nardi stared in silence.

"I'm happy to give you some answers. I said I would, in return for your calling Pasquali."

She asked "Who is Marius Hagi?"

That wasn't the question he'd been expecting. He was quiet for a moment. Then he told her about Hagi, Greg, Mircea, and Nadia.

She listened without saying a word. When he was finished, she posed another unexpected question.

"When did Hagi's wife, Alina, die?"

"In 1983," he replied. He had no idea what was behind her questions, but he liked talking to her. It was like walking on a thin sheet of ice toward the gates of paradise.

Linda Nardi traced the line of a drop of coffee with her finger on the steel counter. He watched her as if she were a fairy that had stepped out of a children's book.

Afternoon

Corvu must have had time to relax; he was dressed casually, a dark-green shirt hanging out of his jeans and a good amount of gel holding his short black hair in place.

When Coppola saw him, he started to whistle the theme from *Love Story,* and Corvu gave him a fierce look. They were sitting at the table in Balistreri's office.

Mastroianni was recounting all the details of his talk with Ramona.

"What did she tell you about the bachelor pad where she took the distinguished-looking customer?" Balistreri asked.

"In what sense?" Mastroianni asked.

The guy was handsome, but he wasn't as quick as Balistreri would have liked. Or maybe he was just jaded by his many years on the job. "The bedroom, Mastroianni. Where was it? How was it set up?"

"She told me there were sex toys, dildos, whips, handcuffs, a big mirror on the ceiling."

No, you couldn't trust him. Unless I'm the one who's too much of an expert in these things. A mirror on the ceiling, a video camera.

Mastroianni went on. "Then I went from Iasi to Galati to check on Mircea and Greg. They have serious records. Premeditated double homicide."

"Who did they try to kill?" Corvu asked.

"Two retired ministry officials. A couple of friends who were former colleagues. They'd bought a small farm outside Galati with their severance and their pension. They went to the market one day and sold thirty lambs for cash. Our two suspects attacked them on the way back to their farm with the intent to rob them. The two retirees put up a fight, and the other two simply cut their throats. A witness saw them walking away from the farm just after the crime. They were arrested, but two days later a high-profile Romanian lawyer took on their case. He got them released from custody and their passports were returned. After that, the charges against them were dropped."

"I take it we don't have any idea who paid this lawyer," Corvu said.

"No idea," Mastroianni said.

Corvu said, "There are more pressing issues anyway. First an R, now an E. What if that's only the beginning?"

"But they might not be related. Samantha Rossi was a respectable Italian student; the other victim was some Eastern European whore," Coppola said.

"Aren't you ashamed of what you've just said?" exploded Corvu, stammering with emotion.

Balistreri decided it was time to end the meeting.

Evening

He kept imagining conversations in which they spoke different and incomprehensible languages, but where she understood everything and he nothing.

A different level of understanding. A level that I recognize and that scares me. That of total trust.

In order not to think about Linda Nardi, he made a decision.

"Margherita, today is New Year's Day and I don't want to eat dinner alone."

She hesitated for a moment, but then her innate trust and desire to please prevailed.

"Thank you, Captain. It would be an honor to have dinner with you."

He took her to a well-known and crowded little restaurant near Piazza Fontana di Trevi. Margherita kept on calling him "sir." She certainly had no fears about her old boss coming on to her after dinner.

At one time I'd have had her in my Duetto as soon as we came out of the restaurant, or perhaps already on the way there and saving on the money for dinner.

Margherita was staring at two old Japanese tourists. She watched as they threw coins into the fountain. "They're holding hands, so sweet."

"They're probably wishing for another hundred years together," Balistreri said sarcastically.

"Don't you believe in love, Captain?" She blushed after she'd said it, as if she'd gone too far.

"In what sense?" he asked.

"Don't you believe that a woman could come along and change your life?"

Balistreri was about to say something, but he was interrupted by a familiar hand on his shoulder.

"Michele." It was Dioguardi with his usual open smile.

"Angelo, what are you doing here?"

"I started the new year with a high-stakes online poker tournament. And I came here to celebrate my first win of 2006."

On his own. As I would be were it not for this little angel, Margherita.

"Sit down with us and have coffee with us," Balistreri offered immediately, happy to have him there.

Angelo sat next to him and facing Margherita. He always looked like a great big kid. His hair was disheveled, his blond beard unshaven. He turned his blue eyes to Margherita.

Clearly, she liked him. She bombarded him with questions about his career as a professional poker player. Balistreri mentioned the charity work Angelo financed with the winnings. Angelo said nothing. He was looking at Margherita while Balistreri regaled her with stories about the early days of their friendship, their evenings together, the women they'd loved and lost, and how Angelo had been transformed from office worker to world poker champion, while the Balistreri was growing old and gray in an office. Then he told her about the first time they'd met in Paola's apartment, when Angelo gave everything he had in order for Balistreri to get a woman into bed.

Margherita laughed. "Angelo, shame on you."

"He was engaged," Balistreri said. "And unlike me, he's always believed in love."

Angelo looked startled, as if he'd been accused of something.

"And did you ever find love?" Margherita asked.

Balistreri listened to them absentmindedly, as if he were sitting at another table. They liked each other, obviously. He feigned a call from the office and left the restaurant. He knew where he wanted to go.

Now he was on the hunt for murderers, not love.

. . . .

It wasn't far away. He was happy to walk in the cold evening to the pavement outside the open nightclub entrance. It was here that Papa Camarà had died, his stomach slit open by a knife. He recognized the corner from where the motorbike had emerged. Forty feet. The rider had waited with his engine just turning over before the insulting the Senegalese. And then, perhaps, he came back to kill him. A murderer who was very stupid. Why insult him precisely at the moment when there was a witness?

It was early; there were still few customers at the tables. The waiters were chatting quietly among themselves. He ordered something to drink, then called the bartender over to his table. Pierre wasn't frightened by his badge. He was a laid-back guy with a pleasant manner, and he showed no surprise when Balistreri told him he was there about Camarà.

"Did you have any reason to speak to him that night?"

"No, some other cops already asked me. I bumped into him a couple of times when he was going to the restroom and coming up the stairs again in a hurry. Ajello—the manager—likes to have the main entrance covered at all times."

"Is there another entrance?"

"Yes, in the alleyway. But it's always locked; the manager's the only one with the keys. He uses it to let in the guests who go to the private lounges. There's two of them, one large and one small."

"And that night?"

"There was a party in the larger one after one o'clock. Friends of the manager's son, who was also there. The manager came from Perugia to welcome the guests and let them in the rear entrance."

"Whose party was it?"

"Some rich girl from Rome celebrating her eighteenth birthday. She's friends with Fabio, Ajello's son."

"I understand you had a different manager before."

"Yes, Corona. Poor thing. It was horrible the way he was killed. Not that he had a happy life."

"What do you mean?"

"Are you married? He was, and it wasn't a happy marriage. Because of that bitch of a wife he lost everything."

"You mean this place?"

"Not just this place. Corona was stockholder in a company that runs a whole bunch of nightclubs. She wanted him to make more money, and she didn't care how he did it."

"So he did things a good manager shouldn't do," Balistreri said.

Pierre nodded. He looked sad, sincerely upset about Corona.

"He was in trouble with the finance police. Some business over slot machines that weren't registered properly for tax purposes. The problem was that the money ended up in Mrs. Corona's account, not in the shareholders' account," Pierre explained.

Then the bartender stiffened. A well-dressed and distinguished looking forty-year-old was approaching the table where they sat.

Pierre made the introductions. "Mr. Ajello, our manager. Captain Balistreri, police."

The man held out a freshly manicured hand. A gold Rolex, diamond cufflinks, a Marinella tie, a custom-monogrammed shirt, clearly expensive shoes.

Ajello said to Balistreri, "If you're not in a hurry, why don't we have a drink in the private lounge?" He wanted to get away from Pierre.

They walked down a long hallway at the end of which was a bath
room and a security door. On either side were the two private lounges.
They entered the smaller one. Leather armchairs and sofa, bar, DVD
player, and video projector.

"Very nice," Balistreri said. "I'll just take a glass of water."

Ajello pointed to one of the armchairs and brought him a glass.

"This room is reserved for our most important guests. People too
well-known to mingle with the general public in the main room."

"Actors?"

"Soccer players mostly, some television personalities, politicians
seeking privacy," Ajello said with ill-concealed disdain for such
people. "People who don't blink at spending five thousand euros on
champagne in a couple of hours."

"Was there someone here the night Camarà died?"

"No, only the large room was occupied. A party for one of my son's
friends."

On the glass coffee table sat a huge ashtray and a large wooden
box. Ajello opened it.

"Cuban cigars. Real ones," he said, pointing to them. "I don't
smoke them myself, but they tell me they're very good. Help yourself."

Balistreri shot a glance at the box's contents. There were five com-
partments and five cigars, each cigar attached by a silver thread to a
small pocket lighter with a stylized dancer in blue, the nightclub's
logo. A gift for customers.

"I'll stick to my cigarettes, thanks. Is there something you want to
tell me?"

Again he flashed that condescending smile. "To be frank, Captain
Balistreri, I found your officer's curiosity a little over the top. It was
like being interrogated by the finance police. Thousands of questions
about ENT, its shareholders, the previous manager. Nothing serious,
but a little strange for a murder that has nothing to do with us."

"Mr. Ajello, I don't think you've taken into consideration the fact
that Camarà's killing could have something to do with the Bella Blu,
or its business associates, or the previous manager, or yourself."

"We have no enemies. We're extremely careful to do everything by
the book."

"But the finance police found unregistered slot machines here."

Ajello waved his hand as if brushing away a fly. "An oversight by Sandro Corona, the previous manager. He left several slot machines unregistered back from the time when there were no regulations. Nothing serious, Captain Balistreri. Don't tell me you're one of those narrow-minded puritans who thinks anyone who doesn't pay every cent he owes should be in jail? Corona failed to pay a little money, completely by accident."

"So tax evasion only counts when there are millions of euros at stake?"

Ajello maintained his composure. He stared at Balistreri as any wealthy lawyer with good contacts would stare at an ill-dressed, aging civil servant.

"Corona didn't understand life, Captain Balistreri. And in order to live life well, you need to understand it."

"Or maybe he did understand it, but someone close to him was putting pressure on him," Balistreri said.

Ajello looked at him more closely.

"Do you know Mrs. Ornella Corona well, Mr. Ajello?"

Ajello weighed the question. "I knew her well when I acquired the ENT shares she inherited from her husband."

"So you knew her before that, but less well," Balistreri said.

Ajello shifted uneasily. He stalled by getting up and going to the drinks cabinet.

While he poured out a whiskey, Ajello spoke with his back to Balistreri. "We used to go to the same gym."

Well done. All doors now open. We went to the same gym, and we didn't so much as say hello to each other. Or else we went to the same gym and frequently fucked in the bathroom.

They said good-bye with feigned politeness. Outside the Bella Blu he called a taxi, noticing a gray saloon car parked on the corner. Two men were calmly smoking cigarettes inside, totally uninterested in him.

They know their presence is enough to let me get the message, because I know the house style.

. . . .

He was at Piccolo's before midnight. Rudi came to open the door wearing a sweatsuit twice his size bearing the initials G. P.

"The officer resting on the sofa, sir." Balistreri tried to suppress his annoyance at the protective tone.

Rudi seemed different. He looked ridiculous in Piccolo's sweatsuit, but seemed more at ease, no longer afraid. Balistreri tried to show his indifference.

Piccolo also seemed to be calmer. The latest events must have worn on her. Instead she was only sad for Nadia. Otherwise she seemed rather pleased with herself, like a schoolgirl who had just received a perfect report card.

"Rudi is making me rest on the sofa all day, even though I could go out. I don't have a fever anymore."

"In Albania you only go out after a whole day without a temperature," Rudi said, sounding like a wise old aunt.

"Yes, but we're not in Albania, and I have things to take care of in the office," Piccolo said.

"You need some rest and some time to think," Balistreri said.

"Captain, would you like something to drink? Rudi, get him a glass of mineral water."

"How do you like it here, Rudi?" Balistreri asked.

"I like it very much. But I also have to get back to work, and not at the Bar Biliardo."

"Because of Marius Hagi?"

"No, I already told you, Hagi has never done anything to me. But Mircea and Greg are a different story."

"They beat him up, the bastards," Piccolo put in.

Balistreri shot her a questioning look.

"The morning before Ramona left. They wanted something from her, but she didn't know anything. They beat up Rudi to get her to talk."

Rudi served Balistreri a glass of water and sat on the sofa next to Piccolo. He was smoking nervously.

"They said Nadia had stolen something valuable. They were sure she'd given it to one of us because they hadn't found it in the apartment," Rudi explained.

Balistreri nodded. "Look, Rudi, you've already told us that—unlike Nadia—Ramona was very tidy. But when you went in everything was a mess."

"Mircea and Greg were looking for something."

"And they didn't tell you what it was?"

"No. I don't think they even knew themselves, but they were convinced Nadia had stolen something valuable."

"All right. Now listen, Rudi, you used to clean up after Nadia, right?"

Rudi gave a sad smile. "Yes, she was really messy. I'd put her things away, and she called me her little brother."

"And she gave you presents."

"No, Nadia didn't have money for presents. But she was nice to me, as was Ramona."

"She never gave you anything? Maybe something she'd picked up somewhere?"

Rudi seemed to remember something. "But Mircea said it was something valuable," he murmured.

"Maybe not valuable in economic terms, Rudi. Valuable because of its meaning."

Rudi went pale and put his hand in his pocket. He handed something to Balistreri.

"Jesus Christ," exclaimed the head of the special team as he took the blue lighter from Rudi's hand. The stylized dancer on the side of the lighter winked at him.

MONDAY, JANUARY 2, 2006

Morning

"THAT'S INCREDIBLE," CORVU SAID.

"Isn't it?" Balistreri agreed, lighting his first cigarette of the day and opening the window on the cold morning of the first work day of the new year. "Well, it seems incredible, but I don't believe in coincidences. Rudi had completely forgotten about the lighter, because it wasn't really worth anything. Nadia gave it to him on December 24. He thought she'd found it lying around and given it to him as a present in exchange for the favors he did for her."

"But we can't rule out a coincidence," Corvu said. "Nadia could have gotten the lighter from a client who went to the Bella Blu."

"That wouldn't explain the frenzied way Mircea and Greg were looking for it, and someone was still searching for it in the Via Tiburtina apartment when they were surprised by Piccolo and Rudi."

"Captain Balistreri's right. Nadia must have picked it up at the Bella Blu herself," Piccolo said. "Except those freebies are only handed out in the private lounges, not the club itself. They're attached to the

Cuban cigars reserved for important customers. Therefore, Nadia was in Bella Blu's private lounge on the night of December 23."

"It could have happened before December 23," Corvu said.

But Piccolo had all the answers. "In that case, Mircea and Greg would have gone looking for it earlier. No, Nadia comes out of the restaurant alone around eleven thirty, and then later she's in the Bella Blu's private lounge, where she pockets the lighter, which she then gives to Rudi."

"Maybe Mircea was waiting for her outside the restaurant and they went to the Bella Blu together," Corvu suggested.

"No," Piccolo said. "Rudi told me that the night Mircea came back with Greg just after Ramona, who was feeling ill. That was around midnight. That means he left the restaurant and went straight home."

"So someone else picked up Nadia," Corvu said.

"They were sitting at the table for two and a half hours. Mircea kept on ordering drinks. That's a bit odd for an uncontrollable guy who's in a hurry to get into bed with somebody," Piccolo said. "Then he hits her because, he says, Nadia won't have sex with him. He gets pissed off and leaves. Does that seem credible?"

"So you think Mircea wanted the waiter to remember he was there and then left? Why would he want to kill time like that?"

Balistreri had let his two deputies continue back and forth while a dark cloud was gathering in his mind. "In order to deliver the girl to someone else," he said.

The two of them looked at him in surprise. They'd all but forgotten about him in the heat of the discussion.

"In order to deliver her to someone who took her to Bella Blu," concluded Corvu logically. "But how did they knew about the disappearance of a lighter? It's almost impossible."

"It's perfectly possible," explained Piccolo. "I went to Bella Blu early this morning and talked to the cleaning woman. The private lounge runs like a hotel minibar and has to be refilled. She checks it every morning and makes a list of what needs to be replaced. And she clearly remembers that on the morning of December 24, a cigar and its lighter were gone. It's written down on the stock sheet."

"Who gets the stock sheet?" Balistreri asked.

"Pierre the bartender restocks the lounges. But anyone can get a look at the sheet."

Silence. Each of the three was considering the consequences of this line of reasoning and coming to the same inevitable conclusion.

Someone had noticed the stock sheet. Someone who knew that the private lounge had been occupied the night before and knew Nadia might have taken the lighter. So Mircea and Greg were told to look for something, but not exactly what, because they couldn't be allowed to know the whole story. And they couldn't know about the Bella Blu.

Piccolo finally spoke. "Someone who didn't want to run the risk of any link being found between Nadia and the Bella Blu."

Corvu added, "Someone who knew that Nadia was already dead."

Balistreri's thoughts wandered darkly further back and further forward in time. Something had begun a great distance away and was slowly, but inexorably, coming closer.

. . . .

Linda Nardi was about to do something that her editor would not have encouraged and that Balistreri wouldn't have approved.

She crossed the sunny center of the city on foot around noon. She came to the Trevi Fountain, which was packed with tourists. Graffiti covered the surrounding walls, and there were political posters pasted up all over. A small truck parked next to the fountain displayed a smiling face and the words *Augusto De Rossi for Deputy Mayor* next to an image of Casilino 900 and the words *Only integration can stop the violence.*

At the restaurant, she took a good look around. Nadia had left the place before midnight on December 23. According to what Balistreri had told her, the waiter had said she'd wrapped herself up in a raincoat that was too big for her and then waited outside for a bit. Did she not know where to go? It was possible, but the large sign of the Piazzale Flaminio subway station was visible a few yards to the right. Instead, after a while she'd gone toward Piazza del Popolo, where there were taxis, but no subway stop. Could she have taken a taxi?

Nardi stepped inside. An elderly waiter came up to her and she showed him her press card. "Are you Tommaso?"

She noticed the waiter's gaze falling on her breasts and tried to suppress her annoyance.

"The police have already been here," he said.

"I need you to try to remember something," she said, handing him a fifty-euro note. He quickly tucked it into a pocket.

"What do you want to know?"

"I want you to tell me exactly what the girl did after the Romanian guy left."

"How should I know? There were other people around. I was covering all the tables."

"Can you remember for her sake?" Nardi asked gently.

"After that piece of shit had left, I thought she'd leave, too, but instead she went into the ladies' room. When I saw her again she'd already gotten her raincoat from the coatroom and put it on."

"Did she have a purse?"

"No, a small knapsack."

"You don't remember anything else?"

Tommaso looked at her with a half-smile. "You know, I think she'd changed. Her clothes, I mean. In the bathroom."

"She changed her clothes? How could you tell if she was wearing the raincoat over them?"

"Well, I'm not sure. I just had that impression."

"Do you remember what she was wearing when she came in?"

"Torn jeans."

"All right. And on top?"

Tommaso thought for a moment, and then his face lit up. "That's why I said she'd changed. When she came in she was wearing a big baggy turtleneck sweater."

"And when she left?"

"Well, there was no turtleneck poking up out of the raincoat, and no jeans showing at the bottom. Also, before she went out she put on a pair of gloves, which seemed odd to me because it wasn't cold that night."

She'd changed into a low-cut shirt and a miniskirt to go to a nightclub. She was dressed for somebody's pleasure.

Linda Nardi felt both better and angry when she left the restau rant. She looked toward Piazza del Popolo. That was where Nadia had gone that night. She'd gone to meet whoever was waiting for her.

Going out to meet her fate.

. . . .

Margherita appeared stood at in the doorway slightly out of breath. "Excuse me, but I have to take the afternoon off. May I?"

Balistreri could see she was nervous. "No problem, but would you slip downstairs and get us two coffees first, please? Make mine a decaf."

"No coffee for me," Corvu said. "I'll have a grapefruit juice."

Balistreri gave him a disgusted look. "Grapefruit juice? Before lunch? You'll burn a hole in your stomach."

"I've given up coffee," he said firmly.

"All right, Margherita, a coffee and a disgusting grapefruit juice. Can you send Coppola and Mastroianni in and ask them what they want from downstairs as well?"

Coppola and Mastroianni listened closely to the latest.

"We should talk to Ramona again," Mastroianni said.

"And Ornella Corona," Coppola said.

"Mastroianni, arrange to get the Iordanescu girl back to Rome— we'll pay her airfare. I'll take care of Ornella Corona."

"I don't see why I can't," Coppola objected.

"Because you have to talk to the American tourist—Fred Cabot."

Coppola didn't like the idea of another conversation with the American and the linguistic humiliation that went with it.

"Cabot's back in America by now," he objected again.

"We've got his number. Call him up."

Cursing silently, Coppola nodded.

"And there's another thing I want to know from Carmen, the victim's girlfriend. What kind of urinary infection did he have?"

They all looked at him in amazement.

"Captain, there's no way I'm asking personal questions like that!"

"Very well, you can go and question those shepherds in prison," Balistreri suggested.

Coppola said, "All right, I'll get in touch with Cabot and go and talk to Carmen."

"Good. Corvu and Piccolo will question the two shepherds, along with the public prosecutor."

Corvu raised a hand. "We have authorization from the judge to get the names of ENT's shareholders from the trust administrator now that there's a direct link to the crime."

Afternoon

Corvu was in a very good mood. It worried Balistreri to see him so happy and confident, as if his deputy's reliability depended on insecurity. Falling in love might make him take his job less seriously.

They were early for the appointment, which was for two o'clock, so they mingled with the people swarming toward St. Peter's Square, bought two slices of pizza, and made their way toward the great dome, which stood out against a sky that was finally blue after so much rain. Young Roma women with their children were chasing after the tourists. The citizens of Rome recognized them instantly and steered clear.

The main office of the ENT trust was on the third floor. There was a nameplate on the door, and a pale secretary led them into an imposing office.

A gentleman of a certain age, who introduced himself as Davide Trevi, was waiting for them. On his business card he was identified as CHIEF ADMINISTRATOR. The card provided a telephone number and an e-mail address, but no cell phone number.

"Naturally, gentlemen, we are willing to cooperate. If you'd like to explain what you need, within a few days I'm sure we can provide it."

Corvu shook his head. "We need something very simple—just one thing. But we need it now."

"As you can imagine, we have our protocol to follow."

"Mr. Trevi," Corvu said, "one of the nightclubs run by ENT is linked to a murder, possibly two murders. We need to know the names of the shareholders."

"I understand, but you are aware that we have the right to see any official request before supplying the documents requested. With all due speed, of course."

Balistreri stood up and went to collect his raincoat from the hallstand.

This shit is accustomed to all kinds of problems and to resisting them, procrastinating. We won't get anything in the normal way.

"You say that you need some time, Mr. Trevi. Very well, please take it. However, these two murders could be linked to a previous one and the sequence could well be followed by another."

Alarmed, Corvu shot him a glance of strong disapproval.

"Captain Balistreri means to say that we can't exclude the risk of a recurrence."

"I mean to say," Balistreri said, interrupting Corvu sharply and staring into Trevi's eyes, "that if by any chance there is another victim and we ascertain any link whatsoever with ENT, then we will rigorously check how you used the intervening time."

Like Pasquali, Trevi was used to weighing the pros and cons. Unlocking a drawer, he took out a gray file with ENT written on the spine and drew out a sheet of the trust's white letterhead.

"This is our authorization to act as agent," he explained, "There's only one shareholder who's entrusted us with ninety percent of the ENT shares. The authorization is tacitly renewed every year in the absence of a written order rescinding it."

"And who is this shareholder?" Corvu asked.

Trevi allowed himself a little smile. "ENT Middle East, a company registered in the Dubai Free Zone, United Arab Emirates."

Balistreri and Corvu looked at each other, stunned. "But there must be a name on the authorization," Corvu insisted.

"The ENT Middle East administrator is Nabil Belhrouz, a Lebanese man. Here is his contact information in the Emirates."

"His address is a post office box," Corvu protested.

"That's how they do it over there, but there is the name of the company's sponsor, Free Zone Media City. We have the address for that."

"And how often are you in touch with Mr. Belhrouz?"

"I've never seen him or spoken to him," Trevi said. Then, seeing their faces, he added, "That's actually very common. Trusts are employed by people who don't want to be known. No client comes here to us. Mr. Belhrouz's signature was obtained by an Italian notary who has a counterpart in Dubai."

They made a photocopy and left his office. As they passed by the secretary's desk, Balistreri saw the light for Trevi's external phone go on.

. . . .

Linda Nardi was walking in the cold air of the early afternoon, lost in her thoughts. The lives of these women meant nothing to anyone. She knew this scenario very well. The politicians never gave a damn about any Italian deaths, let alone a Romanian prostitute. And the police cared even less.

And Balistreri, an ex-Fascist now working for justice? Can I trust him?

Graffiti was beginning to appear on the walls saying ROMANIAN MURDERERS, ROMA GO HOME, LET'S BURN THE TRAVELERS' CAMPS. No distinction between the Roma and the Romanians. Rather, the fact that the victim was Romanian and the presumed murderer a Roma gypsy only served to link them in people's opinion. And the political party posters had already leaped into the argument, milder in tone but the same in substance. The opposition laid all the blame on the city council and promised they would dismantle the camps as soon as they were in power. The mayor's party underlined what had already been done and what would soon be done. Faces and names of senators, MPs, city assessors—all had something to promise. The electoral implication of these circumstances was a juicy bone for some, a bitter pill for others. No doubt there were those among the politicians who were hoping cynically for another Samantha Rossi.

At the newspaper offices, Linda learned there would be an important city council meeting the following day. For the first time, a majority was prepared to vote to move the camps outside of Rome immediately. If the mayor and the council wanted to avoid an electoral massacre, they had no choice but to go along with it.

She was now about to do something that both her editor and Balistreri would not only have disapproved of, but forcefully deplored.

She was prepared, having brought along something to use as a weapon, but it was still a dangerous business. This was a part of her she knew well, ever since she was a girl asking her mother questions she couldn't answer.

Linda demands the truth, even when it could do a great deal of harm.

The Marius Travel office was closed for lunch. Behind the glass door she could see two young men, who had to be Mircea and Greg, eating sandwiches and drinking beer. Two ordinary employees. No one would have thought they were exploitative pimps or perhaps worse.

When she knocked on the door, the taller of the two glanced at her, sizing her up. She smiled winningly.

Mircea opened the door, then locked it behind himself after he'd let her in. They looked at her with condescension.

"Actually, we're closed," Greg said, "but for you we'll make an exception."

Linda flashed her press card. "I'd like to speak to Mircea."

They stiffened a little, but then Mircea snickered and signaled to her to take a seat in front of the desk at the back of the room. Linda was aware they couldn't be seen from outside, but there was nothing else she could do. Mircea sat opposite her and Greg at her side, blocking any escape route. She saw the key was no longer in the lock.

"What is it?"

"I'd like to ask about your dinner with Nadia on December 23," Linda said calmly. She was not afraid.

"What will I get if I talk?" Mircea asked, staring at her breasts.

"If you provide useful information, I'll give you a present."

"What kind of present? Money?"

After a huge effort, she managed to give that smile again.

"All right then," said Mircea. "It's very simple. Me and Nadia went there on the Metro, about nine. We ate, argued, I left there and called Greg, who was nearby in an arcade. We took the Metro and were at the Bar Biliardo by midnight. You can ask the Albanian bartender and the other girl, Ramona, who were there."

"What were you arguing about?"

He looked at her in a provocative manner. "Nadia had said she was tired and that I'd promised her a night off. So she didn't want to have sex. And I don't waste my time with women who don't want to have sex."

"Why did you take her out to dinner then?" Her tone was polite, understanding, as if she were speaking to a child who had confessed to eating chocolate in secret. She knew Mircea was only voicing what most men thought.

"If I'd known I wouldn't have wasted my time and my money."

"So if you hadn't known she wasn't willing to have sex with you, you would have skipped dinner and taken her straight to Piazza del Popolo at eleven thirty." She said it softly; she knew she was courting danger.

Mircea hesitated and glanced at Greg. His chair squeaked.

"I don't know what you're talking about," Mircea said at last.

"Are you familiar with a nightclub called Bella Blu?"

Mircea's face relaxed and he looked relieved. "Never heard of it," he said.

"Okay, tell me about Cristal. You know that club, right?"

"Yes," Mircea replied. "Greg and I go there once in a while."

"Some beautiful pieces of ass there, like you," Greg said with a wink.

"You took Ramona there," Linda said to Mircea. She could feel the danger clearly as she got close to the crucial area, but she had to press on. She tried not to look at the door and confined herself to taking out her cell phone with its send message ready and pressing it as she transferred it from her bag to her pocket.

"Maybe. I don't remember." Mircea gave her a threatening look; Greg was so close to her that he was almost on top of her.

"You had to introduce her to a policeman, Colajacono, and he had to introduce her to someone else," Linda said.

Greg was on his feet. He walked over to the glass door and drew the blinds.

"Does Marius Hagi know about Cristal and Bella Blu?" she asked, looking Mircea straight in the eye.

Mircea grabbed her hand and squeezed hard. "Fuck you, bitch."

She stared back at him. "Let go of me," she said flatly, and he did.

Quickly, she reached into her bag and aimed a can of pepper spray at Mircea. She pressed the button, and sprayed it in his eyes. As Mircea staggered back screaming, someone began knocking energetically on the glass door.

"Who the fuck's knocking like that? Fucking . . ." swore Greg, pulling back the blind.

He instantly recognized the mountain of muscle with the pistol in her hand and jumped back a step. He still remembered the blow she had landed on his solar plexus. He pulled out the key, quietly opened the door, and let Linda Nardi go over to Giulia Piccolo's side.

. . . .

While they were walking back to the office after the visit to the trust administrator, Corvu called Media City in the Arab Emirates on his cell phone. He got Belhrouz's number and asked to be put through to him. Not only did Belhrouz answer his phone, but he spoke surprisingly good Italian and said that it would be no problem to meet them in Dubai the following day.

Soon after, Corvu's cell phone rang. He lowered his voice as he answered. "Yes, of course, but I can't take you to the amusement park tonight. I'll see you later."

"Was that your niece?" Balistreri asked sarcastically. Corvu blushed and said nothing.

Balistreri stopped in front of a shop window to tie his shoelace. "You've got a good memory for faces, right, Corvu?"

"Of course. I never forget a name or a face."

"Then take a look."

Corvu looked in the direction indicated by Balistreri and was appalled to find himself staring into a window display of sexy lingerie. "What am I supposed to be looking at?"

"Check out the reflection," Balistreri said, turning to the other shoe. "Across the street, next to the lamppost."

Corvu stiffened. "The guy with the newspaper?"

"Yes."

"He was outside the pizza place when we bought two slices."

Balistreri nodded and set off at a brisk pace.

"Coppola had a feeling he was being followed when he visited Ornella Corona," Corvu recalled. Plus there was that gray sedan Balistreri seen outside Bella Blu, but he didn't mention that.

And I saw a gray saloon outside Bella Blu. And other little things . . .

"All right, let's leave it there," he said. "You head back to the office."

"Aren't you coming?"

"I'll see you there later. I have to go see Pasquali and explain why we're going to Dubai. But first I have to make the acquaintance of an attractive woman."

. . . .

Bottom, one-hundred-percent. A woman who'd let you do anything you wanted while she filed her nails and then, when you're finished, she'd start to polish them.

One glance at Ornella Corona was enough to confirm for Balistreri that Coppola was infallible reader of people.

Her dark black hair, smooth and shiny, was gathered in a ponytail that fell to her hips. Her distant and bored eyes regarded him without curiosity. The watch with the eye and eyelashes winked from her slender wrist.

"Are you sure you're the famous Michele Balistreri? You don't look like a supercop." She wasn't the least bit sarcastic.

"Shall I show you my badge?"

"I believe you. You just don't look like a hard-boiled detective, or a character out of one of those British mystery novels."

"You were expecting someone with a pipe and mustache?"

Instead you get someone who looks like a retired punch-drunk boxer.

Ornella Corona smiled and Balistreri could easily imagine how many men she had knocked out with a smile like that. It wasn't a real smile, more like "I'll let you play with me awhile if you like, but when I get bored, you'll be dismissed."

She moved like a former model when she brought him something to drink and when she bent down to sit on the large sofa, folding her long legs sheathed in leggings beneath her. She wore no bra under the baggy cotton shirt.

"You can smoke if you like, Captain Balistreri."

"Do you smoke?"

"That's one bad habit I don't have, but I don't mind the bad habits of others."

All right. Let's play. Just for a while.

He could smell nail polish in the air, and the fingernails on the middle finger, index finger, and thumb of her left hand were painted dark purple. "I interrupted your manicure," he said.

Ornella Corona didn't even look at her hands. She said, "Every couple of weeks I change the color, but I only paint some of my nails."

"I see that," he said, indicating her left hand with his chin.

"I'm left-handed," she said, holding up her hand, "so I use these three fingers for creative things. Holding a paintbrush or a pen."

Balistreri tore his gaze away. He wondered what he would have done at one time with a woman like Ornella Corona and her three purple fingernails. Various hypothetical activities came to mind, none of which attracted him at that moment.

I've become a sinner in thought and omission. How sick . . .

She was going on in the same tone. "That man of yours who came to pay a visit, the little one."

"Detective Coppola."

"Yes. He asked an awful lot of irreverent questions."

Damned maniac . . .

"My apologies for him. Sometimes when he sees a beautiful woman, Detective Coppola sometimes—acts less than professional."

She laughed. "Silly me. I meant to say 'irrelevant.' I get all mixed up sometimes."

Balistreri said, "I have a question for you that I'm pretty sure he didn't ask."

"Is it relevant or irreverent?"

"Relevant. We now have reason to believe that it was no accident that the crime took place at Bella Blu. And therefore any questions regarding Bella Blu are relevant."

"But I haven't been there in ages," she protested, suddenly serious.

"Not since you sold your ENT shares to Mr. Ajello?"

"Even before that, even when my husband was still alive. I can't stand that place."

Ornella Corona stood up. She walked gracefully to the bar cart and poured a glass of grapefruit juice with her back to him. The leggings fit her toned backside like a glove.

You have to turn around. I want to see your face, not your behind, when I put the question to you.

She sat down again, and she leaned forward toward Balistreri. The baggy shirt sank lower, and he was offered a clear view of the sight that must have tortured Sandro Corona and plenty of other men.

"Did you already know Ajello before your husband died?"

"Yes," she replied immediately. Then, after a short pause, she added, "That is, I knew Fabio Ajello, the lawyer's son. We took spinning classes together at the Sport Center."

Balistreri nodded. "You met Fabio Ajello through his father, I imagine."

"No, the opposite. It was Fabio who introduced me to his father when he came to lunch at the Sport Center."

"How old is Fabio?" Balistreri asked. Immediately he regretted the question. He'd given her the reaction she wanted.

Now she's laughing at me. An old fool who's thinking the unthinkable. And she's amusing herself by having me think it.

"Nineteen, or so. He finished high school a year late and is still trying to decide which university course he should take. He's not a minor—I'm sure of that," she finished, giving him with the most innocent look in the world.

He had one more chance.

"How long have you been going to the Sport Center?"

"Five years."

"And Fabio Ajello?"

A slight hesitation. To lie or not to lie. She decided not to. The gym would have log books, of course.

"He's a member of the water polo team. I think he's been on the team since he was a little kid."

"How did you get to know a little kid when you were a young married woman?"

"I knew his mother, Mrs. Ajello, and I met Fabio through her. Then Fabio grew up and gave me swimming lessons. Then one day he introduced me to his father."

"The father who some years later acquired your husband's ENT shares."

She remained silent. That was her way. Evasiveness instead of a lie—only a few privileged people can allow themselves to do this in a relationship where the powers are unequal. Balistreri imagined the good soul of Sandro Corona in this woman's grip and felt sorry for him.

"Ajello's been in the business a long time. Was he the one who got your husband involved with ENT in the first place?"

He cursed himself straight away. His best card, the only ace left in the pack, played far too soon. And all because of male solidarity with a dead man he'd never met.

Morally done in by this siren. Perhaps physically as well.

Ornella Corona was no longer smiling. She was considering her options. She could have told him to get lost, but she was too clever to fall into that trap. One was obvious. She could say "It's none of your business, Captain Balistreri. What's all this got to do with Camarà?"

Naturally she was too clever to make a mistake like that. So she chose her usual tactic, evasiveness. Finally she said, "I haven't the slightest idea."

She wasn't confirming she'd known Ajello before 2002, nor that she had introduced her husband to him. She hadn't confirmed it was Ajello who had introduced Sandro Corona to ENT. Nor had she confirmed it was Ajello who had suggested the life insurance policy that had allowed her to buy the very nice apartment where they were sitting.

Her answer neither denied nor confirmed anything. He could now ask more detailed questions, go deeper, dig further, back her into a corner. She knew this, so she was cannily showing him her breasts. And he was looking at them, though he was thinking of Linda Nardi and the vertical crease that etched her forehead each time he let his gaze wander in that direction.

She got up unsteadily. "My head's spinning, Captain. I'm going to lie down in my bedroom. You can come in and talk to me there if you like."

He followed her. He had a good idea of what the room would look like. A large circular bed, an enormous mirror in front of it. Back in the day he would have handcuffed her in front of the mirror, taken her leggings down to her knees, and thrashed her with his belt until he drew blood. Which was what she wanted.

He stopped on the threshold.

"I'll let you rest, Mrs. Corona. Please don't bother to see me out."

Ornella Corona was only a fork in a road that started from very far away. And only when he was outside once again and saw the posters with the face of the deputy mayor, Augusto De Rossi, preaching the words *Only integration can stop the violence* did he feel certain of it. The man with the newspaper who was leaning against a traffic light and calmly smoking a cigarette was watching him.

. . . .

"They're all in there questioning the shepherd. The public prosecutor is in there and so is his lawyer," Margherita said.

A flower sat in half a glass of water on her desk.

"All right. And Mastroianni made the travel arrangements for Ramona?"

"He's come to an agreement with the Romanian police and Iordanescu. She's flying back to Italy and should arrive the day after tomorrow."

"Any news from Coppola?"

"Detective Coppola's also in there for the questioning. He hasn't managed to track down the American tourist."

"And what about Carmen, Camarà's girlfriend? Has he found her?"

"He already sent you a report by e-mail."

When he was alone, he lit a cigarette and opened Coppola's e-mail.

Subject: Camarà's urinary tract infection. After several requests, I received a copy of the file from the doctor who treated him. Symptoms: itching, burning, swelling, urgent and frequent micturition. Diagnosis: acute prostate inflammation. Therapy: systemic and local antibiotics. P.S. A friend of mine who specializes in men's health says urinary tract infections are common among men who practice unprotected anal intercourse. Black people's poor hygiene makes them more susceptible.

Presumably, the racist comment came from Coppola, not the specialist. But Balistreri was starting to connect the dots. Camarà's infection and his subsequent increased urge to urinate and Nadia's small theft had upset the murderer's plans.

He called in Corvu and Piccolo. "Let Coppola and Mastroianni finish questioning Vasile."

He read them Coppola's e-mail.

"I don't see what that has to do with it, sir. We already have the lighter to link Nadia to Bella Blu," Corvu said.

"Exactly, but the lighter doesn't link Nadia to Camarà. Why was he killed?"

As usual, Piccolo was faster. "Because he saw Nadia that night."

"I don't think so," Corvu said. "Nadia entered the private lounge directly from the back alley."

Balistreri said, "True, but Nadia saw Camarà when he went to pay an urgent visit to the bathroom, just as Nadia was coming in from the back alley. The doors are all along that same hallway. Unfortunately for Camarà, Nadia wasn't alone. Someone else saw him."

"But why? It doesn't hold up," Corvu protested. "You don't commit a murder for something like that," Corvu protested.

Giulia Piccolo got it. She said, "Unless the bastard knew he was going to murder Nadia the following day."

Keep your cool now, girl. With prejudices and a hot head you only make grave errors.

There was another point that needed immediate clarification. The most dangerous connection. All three went into the interrogation room. After greeting the public prosecutor and the appointed defense lawyer, Balistreri noted the plaster cast on the wrist Colajacono had crushed. He asked the prosecutor for permission to ask a question and turned to Vasile.

"When they brought the Giulia GT back to you, was it any different apart from the broken headlight?" he asked.

"No," murmured the shepherd.

"Did it smell any different?"

"Smelled of cigarettes more than usual. I smoke, but not very much."

"Were there any cigarette butts?"

Vasile shook his head.

"I figured," Balistreri said, "because smoke doesn't yield DNA results, but cigarette butts do."

Corvu swore in Sardinian. Balistreri said to the public prosecutor and the lawyer, "Please excuse the interruption."

His deputies followed him back to his office.

"I can't believe I overlooked that," Corvu said.

Balistreri could believe it all too well. Natalya was affecting Corvu's concentration. He felt sorry for Corvu, but he had to tell them. "One of the three Roma said the Invisible Man was smoking while they were raping Samantha Rossi."

Corvu and Piccolo looked shocked.

"You don't think it's the same killer, do you?" Corvu asked.

The three folders were still on his desk: Samantha Rossi, Nadia X, Marius Hagi.

We're only at the start of the game. These are only the first three cards on the table. The decisive ones are yet to be revealed.

Evening

Balistreri decided not to bother Pasquali. He was afraid that a wrong move might lead to cancellation of the Dubai trip. So he didn't tell him that he suspected he was being followed, and he didn't mention the links between the murders of Samantha Rossi and Nadia. The Bella Blu lighter, however, was enough to justify the short visit.

Antonella greeted him with a decaf and made a slight fuss over him, as a sister would over her unruly brother.

"You look tired, Michele. You should get some rest," she said.

She ushered him into the less well-appointed meeting room. That meant Floris wasn't coming. Pasquali, even more impeccably dressed than usual, rushed in a minute later. His hair was fresh from the barber and he wore a new made-to-order suit. He shot a slightly disapproving glance at the sleeve of Balistreri's jacket. If he knew that breaking into the cellars of an apartment building under investigation had caused the tear his disapproval would have been more evident.

"I know you and Corvu are leaving tonight for Dubai," he began. Of course, all requests of this nature passed across his desk, even if Balistreri had his own independent budget.

Balistreri explained the link between Nadia, Bella Blu, and ENT, including the outcome of the visit to the trust administrator. He had to give credit where credit was due: Pasquali was an excellent listener and asked pertinent questions.

"Where does ENT fit in with Nadia and Camarà?" he asked.

"Camarà was killed there—at the time that was all we knew. But Nadia was in the private lounge the night before they kidnapped her. We can't exclude the possibility that she might have been with one of the ENT shareholders. If we don't investigate we may miss an important lead."

"Isn't there a less costly method for finding out the names of the shareholders?"

"It would appear not. Corona's dead. Ajello says he's never met them and his only contact is with Trevi, who deals only with the Lebanese lawyer, Belhrouz. Mrs. Corona once spoke with one of them on the telephone, but she didn't know who it was."

Pasquali stared at him. "Do you really think there's a link between the murders of Nadia and Camarà?"

It's no use, he's too sharp.

Balistreri knew how slippery the ground was, but under those inquisitive eyes he had to answer truthfully. Pasquali would catch on to any possible lies immediately.

"Perhaps Camarà unwittingly saw the person who was planning to kill Nadia."

Pasquali fiddled with his glasses while he weighed his reply. "And after a few hours, this person dressed up as a motorcyclist, faked an argument, and then killed him."

"Not exactly," Balistreri said.

"I don't follow," Pasquali said.

"Let's say that this character, let's even call him the murderer, already intended to kill Nadia out of some sadistic sexual compulsion. But at that moment he hadn't killed anyone yet. Does it seem logical to you for him to improvise something so complicated in order to protect himself against a crime he hadn't committed yet? And what crime? Killing a Romanian prostitute? He could have just killed a different one three days later."

You're an idiot, Balistreri. Pasquali's managed to get you to reveal your innermost thoughts. And now you can see something in his eyes you don't understand.

He immediately backtracked. "Naturally, there are more plausible explanations. This character wanted to kill Nadia specifically, her alone. Perhaps he was a stalker."

Pasquali peered at him from behind his glasses.

Okay, we both know this is bullshit. I'm asking for a truce. Let me have it and let me check things out in Dubai. Pretend you believe me and let's postpone the Samantha Rossi problem.

Pasquali stole a glance at his expensive Piaget. That meant the truce was granted.

"One last thing," he said, stopping Balistreri before he could leave. "Linda Nardi."

Since Balistreri was a boy he had learned how to sniff out real danger, so he said nothing.

Pasquali wasn't even looking at him. He was staring at the computer screen. "A very intelligent woman. Dangerous for us and for you. Be very careful, Balistreri, and keep as far away from her as you can."

· · · ·

Angelo offered to take him to the airport for the night flight to Dubai. He was both cheerful and thoughtful at the same time.

"Michele, you're not upset that I'm seeing Margherita, are you?"

"Not at all, Angelo. I've already fucked her up, down, and sideways. Your turn."

Angelo's knuckles tightened on the steering wheel. Then he burst out laughing and playfully punched Balistreri.

"Lying bastard. Margherita wouldn't sleep with you if you were the last man on earth."

"If I'd wanted to, she'd have let me. But I'm no longer interested in cradle-snatching."

"No, I'd say Linda Nardi is just about your age."

Balistreri was taken aback. "How the hell do you know about Linda Nardi?"

"Graziano told me. It slipped out—don't be mad at him."

"I'll kick that guy so hard he'll land back in Sardinia with his goats. Corvu's in love, and he's lost his mind. The usual story."

"He thinks of you as a father figure. He wants you to be happy. We all do. And he says Linda Nardi is just your type."

Balistreri interrupted him with a threatening gesture. "You can stop all this bullshit. The Nardi woman's an arrogant and presumptuous shit—lesbian or frigid, I don't know, and I don't want to know. I wouldn't touch her, not even—"

Dioguardi burst out laughing.

"What the fuck are you laughing at, Angelo?"

"Nothing. It's just that I've never heard you talk like that about a beautiful woman before. This must be serious."

TUESDAY, JANUARY 3, 2006

Morning

BALISTRERI DIDN'T SLEEP A wink on the flight to Dubai. The seats were small and uncomfortable. Business class was only for politicians and executives, not for someone doing something as inconsequential as tracking down a bunch of murderers. Beside him, Corvu was playing video poker on the small screen.

He fell asleep exhausted during the last hour of the flight when they were already over the Arabian Peninsula, music from the headphones still penetrating his ears.

The Ottoman servant had her face half-covered, but her body was draped in transparent veils. When his eyes fell on her breasts a vertical line furrowed her brow. He murmured words of apology, but couldn't manage to shift his gaze and realized with horror that his hands, which were no longer linked to the control of his brain, were loosening the knots and progressively revealing the girl's nakedness. She let him do as he wished, silent and unmoving. Her eyes stared at him from the opening in her veil. It's your choice, they were saying.

He awoke bathed in sweat when the undercarriage hit the runway. When they disembarked, Corvu turned out to be fully prepared: map of Dubai, address in Media City, Nabil Belhrouz's telephone number, passport, landing card, sunglasses, baseball cap, Lacoste shirt, and light cotton trousers.

The airport was aggressively modern and full of noisy stores. Courteous officials in long white robes led them through the arrival process.

Huge hoardings advertised new residential centers in the middle of the sea in the shape of palms. A cluster of drivers stood holding cards. One card read MR. BALISTRERI—MR. CORVU.

"He must be from the hotel," Corvu said.

The driver in a dark blue suit was a young Pakistani. He led them through a forest of big cars and SUVs to a limousine. It was air-conditioned, with a bar and a television in the back.

Before Corvu could pass the address to the driver, he said, "Media City, correct?"

The traffic was heavy. The driver explained that Dubai was sprawling and it would take a while to get downtown. The limousine moved slowly amid Porsches, Ferraris, and Lamborghinis. The number of cranes and construction sites was incredible. They crossed the bridge over Dubai Creek, which divided the city in half, and entered the modern side.

Gleaming glass skyscrapers soared in the air. Corvu enthusiastically played tour guide.

"It's the emirate nearby, Abu Dhabi, that has the petroleum. But Dubai has skyscrapers, seven-star hotels like the Vela, shopping centers out of a sci-fi movie, a ski slope covered in snow right next to the beach. Alcohol, nightclubs, girls."

They took Sheikh Zayed Road, which led to the recently developed area along Jumeirah Beach. They arrived in Media City at ten o'clock. Balistreri insisted on wearing his jacket and tie, though he thought longingly of Rome's rain and cold as he sweated through his shirt.

The driver dropped them in front of the main door to the building that housed the offices of ENT Middle East. A Filipina secretary greeted them and accompanied them to a meeting room on the third floor. The wide window offered a view of the green sea furrowed by motorboats and catamarans.

Nabil Belhrouz was a handsome man with gleaming black hair and a sunburnt complexion. He was thirty-five at the most.

"We can speak Italian, if you prefer."

Balistreri accepted his offer, relieved not to be forced to serve as Corvu's interpreter.

Belhrouz served them cups of American coffee. He said, "You're probably surprised to see how young I am, but Dubai offers a world of opportunity for the young."

Balistreri took an instant liking to Belhrouz. Corvu seemed a little sullen, however; perhaps he was envious.

"Mr. Belhrouz, we're here because one of the ENT nightclubs in Rome, the Bella Blu, was the scene of a crime before Christmas," Corvu said.

"Yes, I read your e-mail and I'll give you any information I can. I don't exactly understand the connection with the crime, though."

Corvu ignored that and continued. "We know that ninety percent of ENT's shares are held by an Italian trust that receives its orders from ENT Middle East. We need to trace the ENT Middle East shareholders."

"Of course," Belhrouz agreed. "Being Italian, I presume you'll understand that there are certain issues. Anonymity is totally protected here."

Balistreri and Corvu exchanged a worried glance.

"I mean," Belhrouz explained, "that here in Dubai you will never be given the first and last names of persons residing physically in Europe."

He handed a sheet of paper to each of them. It was a shareholders' register, certified in the Media City Free Zone for the Dubai Chamber of Commerce. On it was the name of the sole shareholder of ENT Middle East: ENT Seychelles with headquarters in the Seychelles.

Corvu gave Balistreri a skeptical look. "I should have known," he muttered.

"This trip has been a complete waste of our time," Balistreri said in Arabic. Belhrouz looked startled. He replied in Italian.

"Not entirely. Yours is a difficult request and this is a difficult world, almost impenetrable for various reasons—nearly always for tax reasons, but sometimes for more or less legal reasons. As far as I know, everything is absolutely legal in the case of ENT. I'd like to help you, however."

He was a likable young man, clearly well compensated to act as front man and ignore any seamy traffic underneath But Balistreri could see that he was concerned. He wasn't a citizen of the Emirates, and a murder investigation wasn't a joke. Italy had an embassy in Dubai and even a polite protest over less than satisfactory cooperation could cause him problems. The sheikhs wanted to live in a clean, orderly, and civilized country. A young Lebanese lawyer could be expelled, even if he wasn't guilty of anything.

"There are no nighttime flights to Italy, so I imagine you'll be leaving early tomorrow morning. Which hotel are you staying in?" Belhrouz asked.

"The Hilton Jumeirah."

"Excellent. You have the whole day free. So please enjoy the sunshine and I'll pick you up at seven. We can talk in a less formal way over dinner."

So, he didn't want to talk in the office. They had no choice but to accept. Before leaving, Balistreri said, "Thanks for sending the car to pick us up from the airport."

Belhrouz looked bewildered. "I didn't send a car."

Balistreri had a disturbing thought. "Then it was our own travel agency. We'll see you this evening."

Afternoon

They had arranged to meet at the café the day before, as they stood and talked outside Marius Travel.

"I could have managed with my trusty pepper spray," Linda Nardi said, "but thanks all the same for your help. I imagine you'll have to tell Captain Balistreri about this."

Piccolo smiled. "I was following you after I heard about your visit to the restaurant. But Balistreri wouldn't approve. It's best we keep this to ourselves."

"I have a proposal for you, Giulia."

Piccolo looked at her. Linda Nardi was beautiful, intelligent, sensitive. But it was also clear she had no sexual interest in her whatsoever. She listened to the proposal in silence, not letting her excitement show.

An older sister. More sensible than I am, but prepared to do anything, like me.

"Aren't you afraid?" Piccolo asked, for the sake of hearing her say what she wanted to hear her say.

And Linda said it, with her peaceful look. "My only fear is that this is going to keep happening."

. . . .

The well-organized Corvu had brought two pairs of swim trunks, one for himself and one for Balistreri. They stayed on the hotel beach until five o'clock. Every so often Corvu phoned Natalya and told her what he was doing. He took pictures with his cell phone and sent them to her. He went parasailing. He tackled the ski slope. He swam for over an hour. Balistreri slept on the beach, where he had a dream in which Linda Nardi spoke to him in a language he didn't understand.

Evening

By the time Belhrouz picked them up in his Audi A8 it was dark, but a light breeze was blowing and the temperature was mild and pleasant.

The restaurant was on a dock that jutted out into the sea. They sat by the water illuminated by the lights from the skyscrapers. The average age of the diners was about thirty. The women were gorgeous, and the prices on the menu were outrageous. He ordered tiger prawns.

During the meal Belhrouz talked about his family, who were of Palestinian origin: his grandparents had been driven out by the Israelis, and his parents had escaped the Lebanese Christian army in 1982 in Shatila. The young lawyer drank white wine and kept his eye on the attractive women surrounding them.

Dinner ended with scotch on the rocks and good cigars. As they puffed and sipped, Belhrouz said, "Dubai is one huge game of chance.

You see, here it's the same as in your Gospels—the loaves and fishes get multiplied every day. Real estate, finance, tourism, everything."

"Because no one asks where the money comes from," observed Corvu.

"Exactly. The Russians, Chinese, Iraqis, Iranians, Saudis—all come with suitcases full of cash to buy skyscrapers. No one asks where the money comes from. Manufacturing or contraband weapons? Supermarkets or traffic in human organs? No matter, the money is always good."

"What if the economy slows down and the government cracks down on money laundering for tax purposes?" Corvu asked.

Belhrouz pointed to the magnificent silhouette of the world's most elegant hotel.

"Those suites cost a minimum of four thousand dollars a night and are booked for the next two years. But that could change in a matter days. And I'd go back to East Beirut," he concluded with a sad smile.

Balistreri decided it was time to pick up where they had left off that morning. "What would we find if we went to the Seychelles?"

Belhrouz smiled. "More beautiful beaches. Another useless name. And so on."

"And if we kept going?"

Knocking back his fourth whiskey, the young lawyer leered at the tight rear end of their waitress.

"In the end, Captain Balistreri, you would find yourselves back where you started in Italy. The truth lies there."

"But how can we—"

"Listen to me," Belhrouz said in a low voice. "You seem to be a serious man. I only need your word on two things."

"I'm listening."

"You must never mention my name."

"Okay. And the second thing?"

"My sister's studying in Italy, at the university in L'Aquila. Once when I was staying with her, she answered my cell phone by mistake and it was one of the ENT shareholders calling. I might need your help sometime."

"You have my word."

Belhrouz drained his fifth whiskey and paid the bill. He was drunk. He handed them a business card. "I don't want to talk here, and I have to go by my office to pick up some papers for you. We'll see each other at my house in one hour. Give the taxi driver this card. That's my home address."

They accompanied him to the exit. The valet brought his Audi. As he got into it, he called out, "See you later, my Italian friends!"

Balistreri watched the car as it headed in the direction of Sheikh Zayed Road. A huge SUV set off behind it.

He took out his cell phone, called the hotel, and spoke to someone at the desk.

"I wanted to know whether our car service to and from the airport was included in the price of the hotel."

He heard tapping on a computer keyboard. "No, sir, that service was not included in your room rate."

He shut his cell phone and ran toward the taxi stand. Corvu followed him.

They jumped in a cab. Balistreri gave the driver fifty dollars and pointed to the Audi A8 and the SUV two hundred yards ahead of them. As they sped to catch up, the taxi's alarm indicating that it was breaking the speed limit beeped continuously. The driver looked at him in the rear-view mirror. "We'll go to prison if this continues, sir."

Balistreri handed him a hundred-dollar bill and the driver accelerated. The taillights of the SUV and the Audi were zipping around the curves ahead of them and heading straight for an overpass.

"Have you got Belhrouz's cell phone number?" Balistreri barked at Corvu.

"Yes."

"Call him and hand me the phone."

Belhrouz answered on the second ring, his voice thick with drink.

"My Italian friend," he said happily.

"There's an SUV on your tail. Slow down and try to stop."

"What do you mean?" Belhrouz laughed.

Balistreri saw the SUV accelerate and swerve alongside the Audi.

Belhrouz exclaimed, "What the hell?" Then came the metallic clash of the two vehicles as the Audi was rammed. It careered to the right, hit the guardrail, overturned, and skidded back to the far side of the lane, where it hit the other guardrail and reared up over it. Then it fell over the side of the road.

. . . .

Pasquali's secret cell phone rang three and a half minutes after Belhrouz's Audi A8 crashed along the Sheikh Zayed Road and burst into flames. Pasquali had just arrived home and was greeting his wife. When he heard that phone ringing, he knew he had to get to someplace where he could be alone. Only one person had that number: a person Pasquali both respected and feared, a person he trusted.

Lord, I did it for the good of the country, perhaps for power, but not for money . . .

He went into his study and called back but didn't speak a word.

The familiar voice spoke. "Serious steps had to be taken."

Pasquali heaved a deep sigh and said nothing. This really was unexpected. But protesting was as dangerous as it was useless.

"We don't want any problems here when your man returns. Please take care of it," the voice said.

The call ended. Pasquali had not spoken a word. Before leaving the room, he turned to the crucifix on the wall and bowed his head.

. . . .

As expected, Colajacono left the police station at nine. Piccolo had let the news that Giorgi and Adrian had spoken about him filter down to him so that the information could not be traced back to her. They saw him enter Casilino 900; he was in uniform.

After a few minutes, they followed him in. They were dressed like two Roma women, and no one asked them any questions. The camp was dimly lit by oil lamps in the shanties; few people were outside in the cold. The smell of garbage and sewage was overpowering.

They went further, following Colajacono at an appropriate distance.

"Stick with him—I'll be behind you," said Piccolo. "If Colajacono sees me we've had it."

Linda continued on, trying not to lose sight of Colajacono or lose her way in the maze of huts and piles of garbage.

I learned what fear was many years ago. But since then I've wiped it out.

Colajacono entered a trailer. "That one belongs to Adrian and Giorgi," Giulia Piccolo told her.

Linda positioned herself under a half-open window.

"I'll tear you to pieces with my bare hands!" Colajacono sounded furious.

Linda crouched down, knowing she had to be patient. She prepared the small portable infrared video camera she'd brought.

She heard the first slap, then the second. The two Romanians protested feebly.

"Now tell me the truth or I'll cut off your balls and stuff them down your throat!"

It was time; she breathed deeply and rose to her feet, ready to film. The scene was perfect: two young men on the floor and a uniformed policeman pointing a gun at them. She filmed for a few seconds before Colajacono saw her. He ran outside, and she threw the camera to Piccolo, who hid behind a nearby shanty.

Colajacono was swearing and waving his gun. "Come here, you little bitch."

His backhand swipe caught Linda on the cheek, sending her to the ground.

The violent are so predictable. Capture it all, Giulia.

"You gypsy bitch, give me that video camera," Colajacono said.

"I'm an Italian journalist," she said. She stood up and wiped the blood trickling from her split lip. He stepped back, confused, then stared at her press card. Recognition flashed in his beady eyes.

"If you don't hand it over, I'll have to pat you down," he said, prodding her with the gun into the trailer where Adrian and Giorgi were still sprawled on the floor.

Piccolo continued to film, torn between her satisfaction over the plan that was working and the desire to intervene. But Linda had been insistent: "Only when I give you the signal." She moved closer to the trailer.

"Okay, where's the camera? I'm guessing you've shoved it between your tits, and I'm going to have to reach in there and search for it."

All three men were laughing. Linda shook her head. She was telling Piccolo to wait.

"We all enjoy a good search and seizure every once in a while. When I'm done you're going to give these two blow jobs for good measure." He turned to the two men. "Never say I never did anything for you."

Piccolo kept filming, though she was shaking with rage. Colajacono stripped off Linda's coat, her sweater, and then her blouse. She stood there in her bra.

Colajacono said, "Should I check between your tits first or between your legs?"

"Wait," Linda Nardi said. "I'll tell you where it is."

This was the signal. Piccolo stashed the video camera under the trailer, took out her gun, and opened the door.

"Hands in the air, all of you," she said.

Don't shoot them, Giulia, don't shoot. We can fuck them over better alive.

Incredulous, Colajacono hesitated a moment, glancing regretfully at the pistol he'd laid on the table. But the look on Piccolo's face dissuaded him from lunging for it—it was clear she was dying for an excuse to shoot him. The realization that he was in deep shit seemed to sink in, and his face went slack.

"Now lie down on the floor," Piccolo ordered. Linda pulled on her clothes and left.

Piccolo let several minutes pass, giving the journalist time to get out of the camp with the video camera. In the meantime, she listened in amusement as Colajacono swung from swears to threats and back.

"You're finished, Colajacono. We've got it all on film, including the attempted rape of a journalist."

"You fucking whore. You filthy dyke."

Piccolo laughed. "You shouldn't bother provoking me. I won't lay a finger on a piece of shit like you. I'll let your cellmates see to that. Do you know what they do to police officers who end up inside? You'll spend a few years sucking cock and taking it up the ass. Now get up."

Colajacono stood. He was trembling with rage.

"The video camera's outside the camp. In fact, it's already on its way to the newspaper. You have until midnight tomorrow to tell us who was with Nadia in the Bella Blu private lounge on the night of

December 23. If you tell us we'll check it out, and If it's true things will end there. Otherwise, you'll see yourself all over TV and the Internet."

Colajacono looked at her, sincerely bewildered. "How the fuck should I know who Nadia was with at Bella Blu?"

"Ask your friend Mircea—he knows. He took her out to dinner and handed her over to someone who took her to Bella Blu and then killed her."

"You're a fucking moron. It was that shepherd, Vasile."

Piccolo shook her head. "Give us the name. Otherwise, you'll be the star of the most watched video on YouTube."

She left him there to think things over.

WEDNESDAY, JANUARY 4, 2006

Morning

THANKS TO THE THREE-HOUR time difference, they were back in Rome before lunchtime.

The night before in Dubai, Balistreri had decided not to go after the SUV. The taxi driver was already terrified, even though he didn't know exactly what had happened. A car chase along the roads of Dubai wasn't a good idea. It could have ended in a shooting, which would have turned into a diplomatic incident. He had ordered Corvu to write a report saying only that Belhrouz had had a fatal accident after getting drunk at dinner. No mention of the meeting at his house, the hit-and-run SUV, or the driver who mysteriously picked them up at the airport.

It wasn't only Belhrouz's accident that was troubling him. He was also worried about the driver who knew about their arrival and intended destination. We always know where you are, who you're with, and what you're talking about. Certainly their conversation with Belhrouz either at the ENT offices or at dinner had been heard. And it had decreed the young lawyer's fate.

A warning—a card dealt—from someone who feels untouchable. They knew he would recognize the style, because he had practiced it for years. The threat was real, concrete. Whoever entered the circle was at risk. It was essential not to involve others in the game. It was now necessary to choose between his life or finding out the truth.

Once I wouldn't even have given it a thought. But today I don't want anymore regrets, any more sins to atone for.

Piccolo met him at Leonardo da Vinci airport with Nadia's file. She seemed excited about something, which to Balistreri always spelled trouble. As they drove toward the center of Rome, there was none of the usual traffic. Schools were closed, offices were operating with smaller staffs, the well-heeled were skiing in the Alps, and others were vacationing in the Roman hills.

Balistreri gave Piccolo the short version of the Dubai events. Then she reported on what had been happening back in Rome.

"The autopsy indicates that she died quickly on the night of December 24. Sexual intercourse, no signs of violence. Then strangulation. The other shepherd confirms Vasile's version of events. And now that he knows we're dealing with a murder, I don't think he'd lie. Vasile didn't pick up Nadia on Via di Torricola."

Corvu said, "Which means someone else picked Nadia up, took her to Vasile, who was drunk, they had sex, and then he strangled her."

"There's only one problem with that," Piccolo said.

"Vasile's left wrist," Balistreri said.

Piccolo looked at him in surprise. Corvu said, "Colajacono sprained it, so what."

Balistreri shook his head. "No, when Colajacono grabbed Vasile's wrist, he squealed like a stuck pig. Vasile must have already been injured."

"Maybe he sprained his wrist in the act of strangling Nadia," Corvu said.

"Unfortunately, that's not the case," Piccolo said. "The doctor who examined him said the sprain was at least ten days old—you can tell by what's left of the swelling. Vasile maintains that he injured himself playing soccer with some friends, and the other shepherd confirms it. He says that during the recent burglaries he had to do the driving and heavy lifting because Vasile couldn't."

"That's not possible," Corvu burst out. "That means Vasile didn't kill her. Whoever picked the girl up killed her, too."

"Yes," Balistreri agreed.

Corvu was skeptical. "But, Captain, that would mean this hypothetical killer goes to great lengths to get himself a Giulia GT that can't be traced to him, then he picks up Nadia without being seen. He takes her as a present to the shepherd so he can have sex with her. He waits there until the shepherd's finished, and then strangles her?"

"Well, before he strangled her, he waited for Vasile to get good and drunk and fall asleep," Balistreri said. "Does that remind you of anything?"

Piccolo and Corvu stared at him incredulously.

"I know who it was," Piccolo said.

"Me too," Corvu said.

"Not me, and I bet you two will come up with different names," Balistreri concluded.

Our preconceptions, our certainties. Disaster's taught me to be wary of them.

. . . .

Pasquali was less impeccably dressed than usual. The difference lay in the details. One shirt cuff protruded more than the other from his jacket sleeves. The part in his hair was crooked, as if he'd combed it hurriedly after a night of adulterous sex, thought that could almost certainly be ruled out in Pasquali's case.

He listened in silence to Balistreri's report, which omitted being tailed, the driver at the airport, Belhrouz's promise of help, and the SUV.

"Are you asking to go to the Seychelles now, Balistreri?" He wasn't sarcastic—just sour.

Balistreri shook his head. "It's a dead end. We'll never find out who the real ENT shareholders are."

"It may not have any bearing on the crimes against Nadia and Camarà anyway," Pasquali said.

Balistreri refrained from pointing out that there were three crimes. Talking about Samantha Rossi to Pasquali would only create more problems.

He changed the subject. "Pasquali, I know that this evening there's an important council meeting and that you'll be seeing the mayor and the chief of police. Could you please explain things to them?"

Pasquali nodded and made a face, as if he'd just bitten his tongue.

"The time frame in politics isn't the same as the time frame for police work. To move Casilino 900 and the other camps would require a kind of bipartisan agreement that doesn't exist right now. And the Vatican is opposed to it. Would you prefer us to take the Roma out to the middle of the Mediterranean and drown them?"

"Pasquali, it's gone okay this time because the victims were a Romanian prostitute and a Senegalese bouncer. If it had been two Italian girls from good families we'd be in deep trouble."

Pasquali brushed the image away with a brusque gesture, as if to exorcise it.

"That's what we need men like Colajacono for. No one's going to be lynching any Roma."

Balistreri shook his head. Pasquali couldn't possibly believe what he was saying. Another crime linked to the Roma would become a political football.

"Pasquali, with all due respect, I wouldn't be too sure. Someone has an interest in stoking the fire of intolerance. And racism in Italy does exist. Take a tour of the schools or the tiers of certain stadiums."

"Nevertheless," said Pasquali, cutting him short, "the outcome of this evening's meeting is truly in the balance. It only needs one vote more or less on one side or another."

"Listen, Vasile did not kill Camarà. He wasn't at the Bella Blu on the night of December the 23, he was with his three accomplices emptying the villas whose proprietors had left for the Christmas holidays."

"And you believe people like that?"

"No one is going to lie for someone like Vasile and run the risk of being charged as an accomplice to murder."

"But he killed Nadia."

Balistreri told him about the sprained wrist.

"That doesn't make a big difference," Pasquali said. "They're all in it up to their necks: Roma, Romanians, Casilino 900. You should be investigating those people."

Balistreri felt a vague sense of unease. Pasquali was pushing the absurd. And when an intelligent person did that, it meant he had a hidden agenda.

Afternoon

The telephone call from Morandi came out of the blue. Hagi wanted to have an informal talk with him. They agreed to meet at Bar Biliardo immediately after lunch.

On the bus to Via Tiburtina, Balistreri realized that it had been less than a week since his first visit. And yet the neighborhood looked different. The Christmas decorations had been taken down, and the political posters had been put up in their place. He saw them from the bus as it drove past. Attacks on the council, the mayor's labored and heartfelt defense. Everyone blaming each other, everyone saying that the integration model was the wrong one, no one coming up with a solution. They were even prepared to speculate about more deaths.

The strategy of tension was the product of lofty minds. This was a tactic of mediocre ones, a real mixture of the incapable, the profiteers and the common criminal.

He looked around him in the bus and saw only old people and non-EU immigrants. No one suspicious was tailing him. He concluded that they knew who he was going to see and that the trail had no interest for them. It was ENT that was the sensitive issue, certainly not the Bar Biliardo and Hagi and his acolytes.

There was a new bartender. Hagi was waiting for him with Morandi in the billiards room, which was closed to the public. He was coughing more than usual, but he looked happy. He made no mention of Rudi's disappearance, and he offered Balistreri a coffee. They sat down by a billiard table.

"Do you play?"

"When I was a kid we played in Sunday school, but only with our hands—playing with cues was forbidden."

"In my country, back in Galati, we thought playing with your hands was for queers."

Hagi was in no hurry and Balistreri didn't want to pressure him. Besides, the ENT trail having proved a dead end, they were waiting for the autopsy results and for Ramona Iordanescu to come back to Italy.

Hagi spoke first. "I'm worried about Mircea. You think he may have had a role in Nadia's death. Can I ask you why you believe that to be the case?"

And can I ask you your motive for asking me? Is it part of your mission as protector of those two delinquents?

"First I want to ask you something. If you answer honestly, I'll answer your question."

"Fire away, Balistreri," Morandi said, stroking his gold Rolex. "I'll decide whether my client will reply or not."

Balistreri turned to Hagi. "Mircea and Greg were accused of two murders in Romania the year before you brought them to Italy. Two retired employees of the ministry of the interior."

Hagi remained silent.

"They were released from prison thanks to the best lawyer in Romania and then acquitted. I was wondering who paid that lawyer."

Hagi didn't wait for Morandi's go-ahead. "Obviously it was me. As I've already told you, I owe my life to their parents. And when they asked me to help their sons it was my duty to intervene. It was a debt of honor that I had to pay."

"Even if it meant helping two murderers?"

"There was no evidence against them. Only a witness who said he'd seen them near the farm and then retracted his statement. They would have been set free anyway, perhaps after ten years in jail. In Romania we don't have any protection for what you call civil liberties."

As he was shaken by a cough, Hagi's eye peered into the soul of the special team's boss.

Balistreri remembered the last encounter with Linda Nardi and the Romanian's forbidden subject, so he asked: "Would your wife, Alina, have approved, had she been alive?"

Marius Hagi now wore a tougher expression. "I've already told you I don't want to talk about that."

"You're the one who asked to see me. And now we're no longer dealing with an investigation into a person's disappearance, Mr. Hagi. There's at least one murder involved."

The man squelched of his mocking laughs. "And what does the death of my wife in 1983 have to do with the death of Nadia in 2006?"

There was something in Hagi's feverish eyes that was difficult to decipher. It certainly wasn't fear. It seemed more like a mocking threat. Balistreri rose to leave.

"You didn't answer my question," Hagi reminded him.

"And you didn't answer mine."

"Then I'll just keep wondering. Good-bye, Balistreri." He coughed and lit another cigarette.

"I'll show you out, Balistreri," Morandi offered.

On the pavement outside the Bar Biliardo, among harmless housewives carrying shopping bags, Balistreri received confirmation of what he had suspected.

Morandi was smiling, almost friendly, as he shook his hand. "It's freezing here in Rome, Balistreri. You should have taken a vacation and stayed in Dubai a little longer."

. . . .

Piccolo was waiting for him not far from Bar Biliardo. It was cold and almost dark, but her leather jacket was unzipped.

"I hope you haven't been down in any basements," he said.

"I did better than that and worse, sir. If we can step into a café I'll tell you over a nice hot cup of tea."

When they were sitting down she pulled out a notebook. "I wanted to double-check a few things."

"About what?" Balistreri asked, feeling apprehensive.

"About Colajacono and Tatò."

Balistreri was relieved. The important thing was to keep his deputies away from any risk, and after Morandi's warning he was sure that those risks were serious. But they had to do with the investigation into ENT, not the world of prostitutes, pimps, Roma, shepherds, and violent, racist policemen. No one tailed them there; they could do what they wanted.

"All right, let's hear it."

"So, let's start with that fateful December 24. Before they finished their shift at nine on the morning of December 24, Colajacono told his men, Marchese and Cutugno, that as a reward they could skip that evening's shift. They accepted—a little surprised, but happy. Colajacono notified his right-hand man, Tatò, that they'd be standing in together for the two young policemen. Are you with me so far?"

"I have a few questions already, and I need a cigarette, but you can't smoke in here, so I'll just listen."

"Right. But why does he want to take their shift himself? In order to set an example, he says—to show the young policemen that their higher ups make sacrifices for them. True? Let's say it is—it fits Colajacono's personality. But why force Tatò, his faithful sidekick, to work on Christmas Eve? Because the two of them are bachelors, he says. And we can go along with this as well. What do you say, Captain?"

Balistreri really wanted to go outside and smoke. He urged her on. "Fine, Piccolo. Let's try another hypothesis. Colajacono has his own reasons for being on duty that night and also a reason why he wants Tatò there with him. However, we'd have to show that the reasons he's given aren't the truth, or find some evidence of the real reason."

"When I questioned Tatò he was worried, then relaxed, and then worried again at the end of the meeting."

"So you think he lied about something at the beginning and at the end of questioning?"

"At the start we were talking about Colajacono's idea of their taking the night shift. I checked the registry office records. Actually, Colajacono lives alone in Rome—his parents are already dead and his closest relatives live outside the city. But not Tatò. He's from the South, so his parents don't live in Rome, but he has a younger sister in the city who lives by herself. She works as a cashier in a supermarket."

"But we don't know if they usually spend Christmas together."

"We do now," Piccolo replied triumphantly. "Since Tatò move to Rome they've spent every Christmas Eve together. I sent Mastroianni to the supermarket where she works. She was really upset when her brother told her that he couldn't come over. They got into a fight."

Balistreri said, "I need a smoke—let's go outside."

He had two cigarettes left because of the flight—and he really needed them.

Outside it was almost dark; the lights were on in store windows. The Roman neighborhood was swarming with people coming and going in the supermarkets, shops, and bars. There were a large number of immigrants in the area, and there was angry graffiti about the camps on the walls. That evening the city council was expected to reach a decision with a very narrow margin.

His train of thought was full of heavy consequences that Balistreri had no wish to discuss at that moment. He limited himself to asking a question: "Why did he choose Tatò?"

"Because the alibi's false and only Tatò would go along with it," Piccolo said.

"What alibi are you talking about?"

"The one Tatò's giving Colajacono . . ."

"An alibi for what?"

Piccolo looked at him in surprise. "What do you think? For Nadia's kidnapping and murder."

"No, that doesn't hold up. You said yourself that Tatò was relaxed while telling you about it, so according to your interpretation, he wasn't lying."

Piccolo showed her irritation. "Not necessarily. Suppose Colajacono was in the Giulia GT on Via di Torricola at six thirty in a hat and sunglasses."

"That's precisely why it doesn't hold up."

Piccolo finally saw his point. "Shit, you're right. He would have said that Colajacono was at Mass too between six and seven to give him an alibi."

He let her chew on that for a moment, then he said, "I think both of them are lying. But we still don't know exactly what about. And we don't know why."

Piccolo looked as if she still had something important to say. She walked on in gloomy silence.

They found themselves outside the Torre Spaccata police station. "Did you bring me here on purpose?" Balistreri asked.

Now Piccolo avoided looking him in the face. "I've done something, Captain Balistreri."

Balistreri was seriously worried, but the reality was worse than anything he could have imagined.

He listened with growing horror to the account of the exploits of Linda Nardi and Giulia Piccolo at the Marius Travel agency and then at Casilino 900. He was angry, but what could he do? Slap her? He risked getting hit back. Send her packing from the special team? He'd lose a formidable member of the team. Giulia Piccolo was just like the young Michele Balistreri. Besides, Linda Nardi was the one who was really at fault. She seemed so polite and gentle, but she had a spine of steel. Finally, he realized that he was angry not with the two women, but with Colajacono, for what he had dared to do to Linda Nardi.

That pig had no right to go anywhere near her.

. . . .

He sent Piccolo back to the office and went into the police station. Colajacono's door was open. The deputy captain was sitting with his feet up on his desk; he was chewing an unlit cigar. He made no move to get up or offer Balistreri a seat when he appeared in the doorway.

Colajacono pointed at the piles of paper on his desk. "Look at this, Balistreri. More than one hundred crimes reported. Nothing a big shot like you has to worry about. Purse snatching, petty theft, a little breaking and entering, a few stolen cars. And in ninety percent of the cases the perpetrators are your friends the Roma."

Balistreri didn't respond. Colajacono swung his feet to the floor. "What do you want? I'm warning you right now, we're on my turf here, so don't piss me off."

He was very sure of himself. He must have found a way to solve the problem with Linda Nardi and Piccolo.

Balistreri stood right in front of him. "Someone on the morning of December 24 was scared. A small object from a nightclub had disappeared. Nadia had stolen it. So this person asked you to stay in the station and slow down the investigation into Nadia's disappearance. This person told you the girl had been with a politician as part of a blackmail scheme. You'd already helped out with something similar. But actually they were buying time to retrieve the object."

Colajacono shrugged, unmoved. "I don't know what you're talking about, Balistreri. If you have any proof, show it to me. Otherwise it's all hot air. Business as usual for you bureaucrats."

"By turning away Ramona Iordanescu, you held up the start of an investigation for several days. I have proof of that."

"Doesn't matter. Nadia was already dead. The autopsy report says she was killed before nine on the evening of December 24. It doesn't change anything."

"It might have made it easier to catch the killer," Balistreri said.

But Colajacono didn't bat an eyelash. "Vasile's the murderer. We've caught him and he's in prison. And it's thanks to my informants, certainly not yours."

He's being sincere; they've made an idiot out of him and caught him in a trap. He really believes it was the shepherd.

Images of Colajacono tearing the clothes off of Linda Nardi were torturing Balistreri. It had taken him many years and much remorse to manage his anger and become a good policeman, sensible and prudent. But that thought was too much for him.

He looked Colajacono straight in the face and said, "Vasile did not strangle Nadia."

Colajacono was taken aback for a minute by Balistreri's tone of conviction. Then he pulled himself together. "Yet more conjecture from an intellectual policeman, Balistreri. Listen to me: go back to your office in the city and thank God I'm not decking you right now."

He stripped Linda, this prick of a racist, this animal in policeman's uniform.

Anger prevailed completely over prudence. The words slipped from him without control, as they had so many years ago.

"Vasile's left wrist was sprained several days before Nadia was killed. That was why he screamed so much when you grabbed him. We have the medical report. There's not the slightest possibility that he strangled Nadia."

Madness, Balistreri, sheer madness. They should expel you from the force.

He saw Colajacono turned pale and suddenly get. He jumped to his feet and got in Balistreri's face. "What the fuck are you talking about?" he hissed, closing in.

Balistreri moved to the door. He could take Colajacono, but he hadn't regressed that far. A fight would have marked the end of the investigation, or at least his role in it. He chose to land a verbal upper-cut instead.

"You fucking moron. They had you stay here with Tatò so you wouldn't have an alibi for the time they murdered Nadia."

The effect was a lot worse than a physical uppercut. As he made his way toward the main entrance, he gave Colajacono a last look. He was as white as a sheet, leaning against the wall, staring into space. He had understood he was sitting at a card table where the stakes were too high for him.

. . . .

When Balistreri returned to the office late in the afternoon, Margherita told him that Corvu needed to speak to him urgently.

"Have him come into my office." He pointed at the flower in the glass on her desk and winked at her. She blushed.

Corvu had the agitated manner of a high-school student the day before final exams.

"Captain, I'm being followed."

Balistreri cursed under his breath and felt anxiety as well as anger growing inside him for the members of his team who were too enterprising.

"Followed where? Weren't you supposed to be in the office today?"

Corvu looked at the floor. Balistreri had come to expect this kind of loose-cannon behavior from Piccolo, but not from Corvu.

The deputy hastened to explain. "First, I analyzed all the data we have on Nadia. I spoke to Forensics and asked for any information. There were traces of bodily fluids that point to DNA from a single party. It's definitely Vasile's DNA."

He took Balistreri's silence as encouragement to continue.

"Then I compared the alibis of all the possible suspects between six and nine on December 24." He held out a chart.

Balistreri saw "solid alibi" written beside the names of Greg, Mircea, Adrian, and Giorgi and "incomplete or unsupported alibi" written next to those of Hagi, Colajacono, Tatò, and Ajello. The last name caught him by surprise.

"How do you know what Ajello did on the evening of December 24?" he asked. He didn't like seeing that name there.

"I called ENT and Ajello's secretary said that he was coming back from Monte Carlo this evening. So I said that we urgently needed to check the books of Bella Blu in order to get confirmation of the date that Camarà was hired. She got in touch with Ajello, who said it was okay."

"And you went over to ENT?"

Corvu was looking at his shoes. "With Mastroianni," he whispered.

Balistreri gripped the arms of his chair until his knuckles were white, and he clamped his lips so tight he crushed the unlit cigarette he had stuck in his mouth

Damn Corvu! And damn Mastroianni with his big-time Italian hot-shot looks!

When he felt he had regained control over himself and was ready for the worst, he said, "Tell me exactly what happened."

Corvu continued to address his shoes.

"We went there by bus. When we got to ENT I introduced Mastroianni to Ajello's secretary as an accounting expert. She had put Bella Blu's books in a meeting room. She offered us some tea, and Mastroianni left the room with her a couple of times on the pretext of making some photocopies. Then he asked her what some abbreviations meant. He kept talking to her. She was distracted and flattered, of course. I excused myself to go to the bathroom."

"And you checked his calendar." It wasn't a question.

Corvu nodded. "Ajello's last appointment in his office on December 24 at six thirty. Then the diary was empty until seven, when it said 'Grand Hotel: Cocktails.'"

Balistreri groaned softly. Then he waited in silence, resigned.

"I called the Grand Hotel and asked for the manager with the excuse that I was from the finance police and I was auditing a catering company. I asked if there had been a reception there in on the evening of December 24. They told me that every Christmas Eve there was a cocktail party at at seven for the members of a charity group that raised funds for a humanitarian organization. It'll be easy to check whether Ajello was there and whether he wrote a check."

Balistreri stood, and Corvu took a step backward. "Corvu, you will not do one more thing that involves ENT, Bella Blu, or Ajello. If you step out of line I'll send you back to the Sardinian mountains to count goats. Is that clear?"

"Yes, Captain," Corvu mumbled.

"Now tell me why you think you're being followed," Balistreri ordered.

"I noticed him when I was on the bus, coming back. He was the only one to get on with us. I didn't see him on the way there, but it was the same guy who was following us the other day."

Evening

There wasn't a minute to lose. The actions of Piccolo and Corvu and his own words to Colajacono had flipped the switch on a ticking time bomb. He summoned Coppola and Mastroianni.

"I want you to follow Colajacono and not let him out of your sight. Take turns and don't let yourselves be seen. Now get a move on."

"I wanted to tell you that I haven't tracked down Fred Cabot yet, but I spoke to Carmen again and she mentioned something strange," Coppola said.

"I don't give a shit, Coppola. One of you has to be outside the police station before Colajacono's shift ends, and it's almost eight."

Mastroianni raised his hand like an elementary school student with good comportment. "Coppola will have to go first. I need to be at the airport at midnight to bring in Ramona Iordanescu to spend the night for security purposes."

"But I've got my son's basketball game. Tonight's the championship," Coppola protested.

Balistreri tilted his head at him. "Coppola, there will be other games. Stick close to Colajacono and don't let him out of your sight. This is important."

Coppola reacted just as Balistreri expected. "Captain, you're right. Ciro will play in lots of championship games. I'll follow Colajacono to the gates of hell."

Left to himself, Balistreri went over again what they knew. Bella Blu had been chosen as a meeting place to introduce Nadia to someone. Then a real disaster happened. By pure coincidence, Camarà had a urinary tract infection and urgently needed to pee. He went down to the toilet. As he passed the private lounge, he saw Nadia with someone. The person who'd organized Nadia's death for the following day sensed he was in danger. And so he did away with Camarà, faking an argument with a motorcyclist.

But that wasn't enough. On the morning of December 24, the cleaning woman noted that a lighter in the private lounge needed replacing. They called whoever had been with Nadia in the lounge, but he didn't know anything about it. A link between Bella Blu, ENT, and a future crime was absolutely unacceptable. They figured they'd find the lighter on Nadia when they killed her, but they didn't. They panicked and called Mircea and Greg, figuring that Ramona must have it, but in order to protect Bella Blu they didn't say what they were looking for. Rudi would have given them the lighter if he'd known they wanted it.

What troubled Balistreri most was the inevitability. Up until December 23, nothing had happened that would compromise Bella Blu, ENT, or its shareholders. They could have waited. They didn't have to kill Camarà right away, or Nadia. They could have changed their plans. But it was as if there had been no other choice. Despite all the risks, the plan had to move forward. So Camarà died, Nadia died, and they beat up Ramona and Rudi in order to find the lighter. They continued to search for it in Nadia and Ramona's room and happened to be surprised by Piccolo and Rudi.

He was exhausted from thinking about it. He couldn't shake the powerful image of Colajacono trembling and pale as a ghost. He had to do something to stop what he himself had set in motion. He picked up the phone and called Linda Nardi.

. . . .

Both the police and the carabinieri armed themselves with the Beretta 92 nine-millimeter Parabellum. The gun was military issue and not available to civilians. The 92FS was the latest version; that was what most police officers with fewer than fifteen years of service carried. Balistreri had the 92SB, a model that was a little older but still in use.

Reluctantly, he took the weapon from his office safe. He cleaned it, loaded it, put the safety catch on, and slipped it into his holster, which he fastened under his left armpit. He'd learned to shoot when he was a kid, but guns weren't associated with happy memories for him. He hadn't touched a weapon with the intention of shooting it for many years. But now old ghosts, the dangerous crowd he'd run with before, were looming on the horizon.

He made his way through the city center on foot, while a few customers were leaving the shops that were about to close and people shivering with cold were beginning to slip into restaurants. There was a pleasant drizzle again, and when he got to the Pantheon his hair was wet and plastered to his forehead.

She was already there. She was wearing a dowdy raincoat and below it a sweater and baggy pants. The contrast between her childlike face and her old-lady clothes was greater than usual. Yet Linda Nardi was thirty-six, neither a child nor an old lady.

He got straight to the point.

"Are you trying to get yourself killed, Ms. Nardi?"

She considered that for a moment, as if it were a serious question. "Pretty soon no one will give any thought to Nadia, or Samantha, or the other young victims, or the family members who mourn them."

He stared at her. A beautiful woman, polite and kind, but incorruptible in her principles and therefore dangerous. In her eyes was the steady calmness of those who are right.

The eyes of someone I loved, the values that I lost.

The thought took him back forty years. Something collapsed inside him. It felt like the distant shock of an explosion at the bottom of the ocean when it finally reaches the shore.

"You're crazy."

They both knew what that "crazy" meant. The word that had slipped out was an impossible bridge over the raging torrent between them.

What do you think you're doing, Balistreri? You're an old man. Don't make yourself any more ridiculous to others than you already are to yourself.

She smiled at him, the first real smile she'd given him since they'd met.

"Finding out the truth is part of my life, part of what I am. I never knew my father, and I still don't know why. I was an aggressive child. I used to hit my classmates, boys and girls."

Balistreri said, "I don't believe you."

"I can show you pictures. I was an early bloomer, physically and psychologically. I was fully developed at age eleven. I went to a private middle school, the Charlemagne School. The upper school was there as well, the older boys. I didn't have a father, so I went looking for an older boy to take his place. At least that's what the psychologist said when all the trouble began."

"What kind of trouble?"

She shook her head, lost in an unwelcome memory. Balistreri knew how hard those could be to dispel.

"There was a problem and I had to leave the school. Fortunately, love heals all wounds. My mother's love, that is. She helped me get better. She took care of me until I was able to go back to school. And I got good grades once I went back. It turns out I really am intelligent."

"And it's precisely because you're intelligent that you should understand that tracking down a murderer isn't a journalist's job. Leave it to the police."

She nodded. "Colajacono is going to give me the name before midnight. I promise I'll give it to you immediately."

He paused. He really didn't want to ask for anything more, but he had to. "I need another favor."

This time again she listened to him without any interruption. She placed no conditions on doing what he asked. They left each other soon after in the Pantheon's deserted piazza. He had wanted to hug her in the rain but instead let her go with a brief good-bye.

. . . .

While he was walking home in the rain he was struck by a feeling of disquiet. Halfway there, he decided to stop in a bar that was still open near the Termini main railway station. It was full of foreigners. The Asians were crowded round the slot machines, the East Europeans were drinking shots of spirits, and the Africans were trying to sell counterfeit designer bags to the few passersby shivering with cold. All of them were smoking, not caring in the slightest that it wasn't allowed in the bar.

Balistreri lit his last cigarette of the day. The surrounding square was intermittently illuminated by the headlights of the few cars in circulation. It was a little after midnight.

He called Coppola. "Colajacono's still in the station. He went out to the little restaurant opposite with Tatò and then they came back. I promise I won't lose him."

"Thanks, Coppola. That's great."

Coppola added, "By the way, my son scored thirty-two points and his team won."

"Are you sure he's really yours, Coppola?" They laughed and hung up.

Then he called Mastroianni.

"I'm with Ramona. We're coming in from the airport now."

"Mastroianni, I want to talk to her immediately. Meet me at the bar on the Via Marsala side of Termini station."

. . . .

He had of course imagined a different and more private setting for questioning Ramona Iordanescu, but there was no time to lose. An official interrogation in the barracks or in the office was impossible without the public prosecutor present, so they found themselves sitting at a little table in the bar filled with people, smoke, and muffled voices.

The photo with Nadia taken in front of St. Peter's hadn't done justice to the girl's statuesque figure. The harsh features of her face were immediately belied by her adolescent's manners. She was making eyes at Mastroianni, which was no surprise. She asked for two cream-filled pastries.

"I just love these," she said, wiping a bit of the filling from the corner of her mouth.

"You can have as many as you like," Mastroianni said.

"All right," Balistreri cut in, "but meanwhile let's have a little chat."

Ramona nodded, her mouth full of cream and flaky pastry.

"You don't need to worry about this. Tomorrow we'll have a meeting with you and Deputy Captain Colajacono. Immediately after that, Mastroianni will take you to the airport and you can go back home," Balistreri said.

He read the fear in the young woman's eyes. "He'll go straight to prison on the charge of being an accessory to Nadia's murder and won't come out for many years," he said, trying to comfort her.

Mastroianni and Ramona both looked startled. "Accessory to murder, really?" Mastroianni asked.

Balistreri ignored him and spoke directly to Ramona.

"Tell me about the apartment near Cristal. Did it have a false ceiling or a real one?"

"I don't understand," Ramona said. Mastroianni explained the question to her.

"I don't know. How can you tell?"

"By the lights. Where the ceiling wasn't covered by the mirror was there a regular light fixture or spotlights?"

"Spotlights?"

Another explanation from Mastroianni.

"Yes, pink spotlights."

For filming from above. Real pros.

"All right, then what happened?"

"I did as Colajacono said. Well-dressed man at Cristal offered me a drink. We went to apartment. He wanted to be slave. I did my job. He was very happy and gave me hundred-euro tip, then went away."

"Would you recognize this man if you saw him again?"

"Every bit of him," she said. She giggled.

Balistreri took out his BlackBerry and looked for the e-mail Mastroianni had sent from Iasi. He frowned as he read.

"Ramona, you said that Colajacono wanted to convince you that Nadia was safe with the man she got into the car with. Is that exactly what he said?"

He felt Mastroianni was about to interrupt and signaled him to keep quiet.

"Yes, I'm sure. He said exactly that."

"And you told him that she had gotten into a car?"

Mastroianni was rhythmically tapping his cup against the saucer. Balistreri shot him a warning glance.

Ramona appeared to be making an effort to remember. "Well, I said that Nadia and I worked as pair, that we didn't get into car ever if other not there. Then I told him I was away with limp-dick client and on return I found Nadia gone. And that I waited and also asked other girls about her."

"Did you tell him what the other girls said to you?"

"No, he said not to piss him off."

Mastroianni was shifting in his chair. Balistreri, irritated, leaned over and whispered to him, "If you have to go to the bathroom, go ahead." Mastroianni stood and left the table.

"What's happening?" Ramona asked, disconcerted.

"Nothing. He has to go to the bathroom. So, you hadn't told him about the car."

This is what happens when you delegate questioning to the inexperienced and you sit in your comfortable office and read about it via e-mail. You're a fool, Balistreri. And stupid Mastroianni thinks he can get the right answers from a woman without asking the right questions.

Then he remembered the mess Corvu had made, and Piccolo. In the end, the only one who hadn't messed up was Coppola. He really should have thanked Coppola rather than teasing him. He picked up his cell phone to call Coppola, but at that moment a loud cry of joy rose up from the Romanians. They began cheering and toasting each other.

Balistreri turned to look at the television, expecting to see a replay of a goal in a soccer game. Instead, the face of a news anchor filled the screen. He managed to hear the closing words.

"By only one vote, the city council has postponed moving Casilino 900 and the other camps, committing itself however to seeking a path forward with all the concerned parties having input. The council has received the Vatican's approval."

He leaned closer to catch the interviews that followed. The mayor said that he had been pleasantly surprised by De Rossi's unexpected vote against the move. A brief interview with De Rossi followed.

"Deputy mayor," the journalist said, "the vast majority of voters, including those you represent, did not wish to see the move postponed."

"Each one of us must answer not only to voters, but to his own conscience," De Rossi said pompously, staring into the television camera.

Now even more furious, Balistreri turned away and found Ramona opposite him looking at the screen in astonishment.

"But that—" she stammered, pointing to De Rossi—"that's my dirty pig from Cristal."

Balistreri was already dialing Coppola's number. Coppola answered immediately. His car engine was audible on the other end.

"Where are you?" Balistreri shouted so loudly that the whole bar turned to look.

"Take it easy, Captain. Everything's okay. I'm following those two bastards."

Balistreri took a deep breath, trying to control himself. "Can you tell me where you are?"

Coppola's voice was just above a whisper. "Colajacono and Tatò are driving to the shepherd's old farmhouse, where we found Nadia. I can barely hear you. I'm losing you."

The line went dead. Balistreri felt a sharp pain in his chest that left him breathless. He leaned against the table, his sight dim and his hands trembling.

What an inglorious death, Balistreri. A heart attack in this shithole. Maybe you'll crap your pants as you go.

But he didn't die. Mastroianni came back. Balistreri said, "Give me your keys—I need a car with a siren. You can call a taxi. Take Ramona to the station, and don't either one of you move from there." Thirty seconds later he was driving at breakneck speed through the pouring rain toward the city's eastern outskirts.

He was there in twelve minutes, at ten to one, consumed with anxiety. He parked in the same place as Piccolo did on the night of San Silvestro, halfway up the hill, where the potholed road became a boggy unpaved lane. Coppola's car was now parked up there, and a little ahead, in the same place as a few nights earlier, was Colajacono and Tatò's car. He tried calling Corvu's number. There was no signal. He swore—Piccolo had already told him about that. The nightmare was repeating itself.

It was a good thing Coppola always had his gun. He remembered what Coppola had said on the subject: "It makes me feel taller. Plus, my son thinks I'm important when I come home and take my holster off from under my jacket."

Balistreri had no flashlight. He took off his jacket and his holster and began to run up the hill with his gun in his right hand and his cell phone in his left to light the way. His shoes slipped in the mud. Drizzling rain wet his forehead and the leaves on the low trees scratched his face.

He realized he was afraid, and the thought made him even more afraid. He was afraid for Coppola and for himself. He was afraid of dying too soon, before he had atoned for what he'd done wrong.

He was about to start up the hill toward the clearing when he heard Coppola's voice at the top.

"Put your hands up."

There was total silence for a few seconds, then all hell broke loose, with gunshots and shouting. He looked toward the clearing, which was dimly lit by an oil lamp. Tatò was lying on his back by the door. The shots were coming from inside the farmhouse and behind it and from an oak tree twenty yards ahead on the left. That had to be where Coppola was. He made it up there and saw Colajacono, terrified and in handcuffs, taking refuge behind the trunk of the huge tree.

Mircea was giving orders in Romanian—he heard him calling out to Greg, Adrian, and Giorgi. He managed to understand what he was saying—"There's only one." He was tempted to call out to Coppola, but that would have been doubly damaging, revealing not only that he was present but exactly where he was.

A burst of gunfire sounded from inside. Then he saw the silhouette of Adrian, who run off behind the old farmhouse, firing like crazy.

Balistreri came out into the open, taking advantage of the element of surprise, but his hand was moving in slow motion, a last show of resistance before he squeezed a trigger after so many years. Coppola came out from behind the tree, took two quick side steps and, holding his Beretta in two hands, opened fire as they had taught him at the police academy. Adrian fell with his arms open as Coppola quickly took shelter again.

Giorgi came running and shooting at Coppola from the other side of the building, while Mircea covered him from inside.

Balistreri felt his own hand stiffen on the trigger while Coppola shouted at him to take cover. He stood rooted to the spot in a daze, watching Coppola come out into the open. He fired a single shot that struck Giorgi in the head.

"Captain, get behind the tree!" Coppola shouted at him. Balistreri shook his head and started to run. He was almost there when Mircea's bullet hit him in his left side, making him twist in a half-pirouette. As he limped forward, he saw Greg coming toward him under Mircea's covering fire.

Who would have thought you'd die like this, petrified with fear?

Coppola went down on one knee and rolled toward the oak tree, firing like crazy. Greg fell face up in the mud, shot through the heart.

Your son will be so impressed. You'll never have to wear lifts in your shoes again.

Coppola quickly got up to return to safety. The bullet hit him between the shoulders. He fell forward and began to crawl toward the oak tree.

Balistreri swung toward the spot where he thought the shot had come from. As he hesitated, another bullet from Mircea in the farmhouse hit him below his right knee. The tree was only two yards away, but he would never get there with his leg broken and his side split open. In that moment, he met Colajacono's eyes.

"Help him," he ordered, pointing to Coppola lying on his back on the ground. Despite being handcuffed, Colajacono dragged Coppola behind the tree as if he weighed nothing. Then he came out into the open again and with more effort dragged Balistreri behind the tree, too. Oddly, the shooting had stopped.

Coppola's wide-open eyes were staring at him and a stream of blood was trickling from his mouth. "You're a big man, Coppola. Ciro will be proud of you," Balistreri told him. Coppola nodded in agreement, then closed his eyes.

Balistreri was losing a lot of blood. He knew he was going to faint at any moment. He tried not to lose consciousness and to control the savage hatred coursing through his veins.

Now I'm going to kill these fucking animals. Colajacono's right. We need to clear this scum out of Italy.

Suddenly, he was not afraid. His mind was clear, conscious that there was only one thing he could do.

"Haul me up and hold me by the waist, without blocking my arms," he said to Colajacono, who nodded in a daze.

The deputy captain held Balistreri upright while he leaned all of his weight on his left foot. Despite the handcuffs, Colajacono's strong arms managed to keep him balanced.

He steadied himself. He knew he had only one shot. With Mircea hidden and himself in the condition he was in, he would have no more than one chance. He saw the flickering light in the farmhouse and Mircea's shadow falling across the wall in the shelter of the corner next to the window. He weighed the rock, calculating the distance: twenty or twenty-five feet.

He needed a loud thud. Strength in the right hand, accuracy with the left. As a boy in Africa he had won shooting contests firing from his left hand because with his right there was no question, it wasn't even fun.

Picture the target your mother gave you as a present when you were seven. The bear's head appeared only for a moment in the little window. And in that moment you went pow! You only know how to shoot and punch, Michele. Just like your father used to say.

The pain was getting worse; the bleeding wouldn't stop. He felt his head spinning and knew it was now or never. He gripped the Beretta in his left hand. He pushed forward and let fly, as he did when he was a boy to get the crows out of the eucalyptus tree. The rock drew a perfect arc in the air and hit the farmhouse wall right next to Mircea's head. He jumped forward in surprise. The bullet went straight through his eye. Balistreri saw Mircea's shadow totter and fall.

Colajacono could no longer hold him up. Balistreri collapsed on the ground, and in the last moments before losing consciousness he thought he saw a shadow come out of the woods and slowly approach him. His eyelids were open just a slit. Through that slit he could see Colajacono's boots in the sloppy mud. He wasn't sure if it was real or a dream. The deputy captain's voice came to him from a thousand miles away.

"Get these fucking handcuffs off me."

The other voice was a whisper. "Don't worry, officer, it's coming now."

"What are you talking about? What's coming now?" Colajacono hissed.

The whisper grew fainter as Balistreri lost consciousness. "Your death."

Balistreri fainted before he could hear the shot being fired.

THURSDAY, JANUARY 5, 2006

THE MORNING PAPERS WERE published too early to cover the killings, but they were full of news of the city council's decision not to move Casilino 900. There was a short article by Linda Nardi with the headline IF A POLICEMAN DIES. It was a strange coincidence that few seemed to notice.

But the unhappy coincidence of the postponement of moving the travelers' camp and the shootings in which three brave policemen—Colajacono, Tatò, and Coppola—met their deaths, and the head of the special team, Michele Balistreri, was gravely wounded put the mayor and his supporting majority out of the limelight. It also created more embarrassment for the Church, which had staunchly defended immigrants and their rights. Accusing voices were raised even in parliament and the Senate, which, usually silent, were now explicitly clear about the Vatican's interference. While the Church had hoped for tolerance by conviction rather than convenience, several political groups were cynically riding the events for their own electoral ends. Someone openly floated the idea of reviewing the Concordat between the Vatican and the Italian government.

Appearing on his balcony in St. Peter's Square for the Angelus, the pope decried the violence and put out a call for mutual understanding. When he said that he would pray for the dead and that intolerance had already been the cause of too much damage, Italians in the crowd whistled to indicate their disapproval. Italian television channels cut that moment from the footage, but CNN and the Internet broadcast it around the world.

Linda Nardi was able to see all the footage, including what was censored by Italian television. Later she heard that, after operations on his spleen and tibia, Balistreri was out of danger. At that point she bought lots of food from the supermarket and retreated to her apartment. Then she called her editor-in-chief to tell him that she would now be working from home.

At dawn she went down to the newsstand below to pick up the papers and then returned to her living room. She read all she could— picking things out, cutting out, underlining, and cataloguing. She made a sizable synthesis of everything on her computer and saved the file in a folder that already existed, *Michele Balistreri*.

She named the file "For When You're Well."

TUESDAY, JANUARY 10, 2006

CONFINED TO BED IN the hospital, Balistreri had time to reflect. The seriousness of his condition gave him six days to prepare himself properly for the first round of questioning.

He asked a nurse to get him a copy of the January 5 edition of Linda Nardi's newspaper. He had seen the title of the short article IF A POLICE-MAN DIES and made his decision. Belhrouz, Coppola, Colajacono, and Tatò were dead. He didn't want to endanger the life of anyone else, least of all Linda Nardi. And that "least of all" worried him. A woman he didn't know had wormed her way into his thoughts against his will.

He had spent years becoming a rational adult, aware of duties, risks, and wrongdoings. This was the moment to bury the young Michele Balistreri, the adventurer who knew no fear or compromise, who was arrogant and cared only for himself. He had several deaths on his conscience other than the most recent ones. And there was no way at all he could wipe them from it. He could only try to move on, limiting the damage and asking forgiveness for his mistakes.

Truth had a price and in this case it was too high. He made a silent agreement with the Invisible Man. He would give up looking for him if the killing would stop. The manhunt was off.

The questions put to Balistreri by the public prosecutor and Pasquali were almost too easy to answer. The events had already been reconstructed and were clear. Colajacono and Tatò had their informants and had gone there to find something. They had been surprised by the four Romanians, the Lacatus cousins plus Adrian and Giorgi, the ones who had kidnapped Nadia and taken her to Vasile, who had later strangled her with the help of the other shepherd. Colajacono and Tatò had been handcuffed and killed in cold blood. The heroic and unlucky Coppola had followed Colajacono on Balistreri's orders, and Balistreri himself had raced over there when Coppola had contacted him by phone. The questions were a mere formality, intended to confirm what they already had determined.

Neither of them asked him if he had seen anyone else in addition to the four Romanians. Besides, there appeared to be no other traces and the shots to the bodies of Coppola, Tatò, and Colajacono and the ones that had nearly killed Balistreri had all been fired from the six guns found beside the four Romanians. The public prosecutor and Pasquali complimented him on the way he had taken out Mircea. No one asked him how he had managed to save his own skin alone under those conditions.

Because the Invisible Man didn't want to finish me off. He wanted me like that, permanently defeated.

. . . .

Linda pored over all the old newspapers she had brought home, the oldest from 1970. She knew that up to the summer of that year, Balistreri had been living in Libya, but she'd found nothing about him in that period. Then, in the fall of 1970, he showed up at the university in Rome.

A young Balistreri, looking very full of himself, appeared with groups of other equally proud young men full of conviction. Rallies about honor, loyalty, courage, the fatherland. Then the two-bladed ax, SS slogans, the Roman salute, black shirts, the wounded, police wagons, tear gas, and stones thrown inside the university and from the bridges over the Tiber. But he had never been linked directly to political crimes, atrocities, or acts of terrorism.

The Christian Democrat government disbanded the Ordine Nuovo at the end of 1973 and arrested its leaders. After 1974 there was no trace of Michele Balistreri in the newspapers or among the official records of the ministry of the interior. She could locate no home address or bank account for him during that time. Nothing.

Until June 1978—one month after Aldo Moro's death. At that point Michele Balistreri reappeared. He finished university and graduated with a degree in philosophy. He joined the police force and passed his captain's exam. As of 1980, he could be found in Vigna Clara, twiddling his thumbs in Rome's quietest neighborhood.

From one perspective, she found it easy to connect today's man to his past. Honor, loyalty, and courage were still a part of him, but they were hard to make out under the thick glue of reality. It was easy to imagine the Balistreri of 1970 with a gun in his hand, but the Balistreri of today must really have been forced to shoot at those Romanians on the hill.

She wondered if it would still be possible to lead that man back to his old nature in order to drag the evil out of hell and annihilate it.

FEBRUARY–MARCH 2006

BALISTRERI'S BROTHER, ALBERTO, TOGETHER with Mastroianni, Piccolo, Corvu, and Angelo Dioguardi, had organized things so that he was never alone during visiting hours. In the middle of February they were able to convince the head nurse to allow them afternoon poker sessions in Balistreri's room, but despite Mastroianni's seductive powers, she would not let him smoke. They played with the window open, even though it was cold outside, so that he could sneak a few drags. No one mentioned the crimes that had been committed, ENT, or work.

Balistreri hadn't heard from Linda Nardi, but it was as if her occasional articles were always addressed to him. Their fresh composure and irrelevance were a message. Empty articles, waiting for them to be able to talk. And on this imagined promise Balistreri built his hopes. *Take time to heal, Michele. I'll be waiting for you.*

When the doctors decided it was time for him to go home and continue with his physical therapy beyond the hospital, Balistreri felt almost lost. He had become used to the place where only muffled echoes came in from the outside world, along with the good things brought to him by his brother and friends.

The thought of going back to his apartment filled him with anxiety, as did any direct contact with the city. The hospital walls provided the ultimate cop-out. Inside them, he could do nothing. Once outside, it would be his choice alone whether or not to engage with the world and its friction.

Only one thing about leaving the hospital appealed to him, and that was that he would be able to see Linda Nardi again. His mind refused to obey: the more he told himself not to think about her, the more he came back to her. What worried him were the conversations he imagined between them and the apparent absence of physical desire. He had never felt more old.

On the morning of March 15, the date set for his discharge, he opened the windows to find a radiant day, one of those special ones that in Rome give a taste of the spring ahead. He was sitting in his armchair signing the papers for his discharge, when the nurse came in and said he had a visitor.

Linda Nardi had grown much more beautiful.

That's because I'm seeing her for the first time with new eyes—those of a soldier coming back from war, defeated but alive.

She stood still for a moment, then held out her arms. He rose up tottering, then, leaning on his crutches, allowed himself to be embraced. It was a silent embrace, perfectly still, that emerged from somewhere far away.

SPRING 2006

FROM THAT DAY ON, Linda supported him like a third crutch. They didn't talk about it, or make a conscious decision. It simply happened. She set him up in the guest room of her small top-floor apartment. In the morning she took her car out of the garage in her building and drove him to his physical therapy sessions, and in the afternoon, taking advantage of the Roman spring weather, she insisted on long walks through the streets of the historic center and Trastevere, even though they were crawling with young people and tourists.

When he was tired they went home and sat on her plant-filled terrace with its view of St. Peter's dome, and there they enjoyed the dinners she made for them. They never spoke of the night Michele Balistreri almost died, nor of the crimes that had been committed. He never mentioned them, and she avoided the subject completely.

Linda met his friends and his brother's family, and so they undertook the kind of humdrum bourgeois home life that Balistreri had always imagined he would detest. Several couples came to visit them: Alberto and his wife on Saturdays, Angelo and Margherita almost every evening. Corvu and Piccolo often came by after work. They even resumed their weekly ritual of poker, and on those evenings Linda usually went out with Margherita.

They were an ordinary couple, except for the lack of sex. At midnight they went their separate ways, each going to his or her own room to sleep.

Am I in love with her? Then why do I feel as if there's an insurmountable barrier?

Days passed, and one evening at the end of May, they set two chairs near each other on the little terrace facing St. Peter's.

In those ten weeks of living together, many things had become important to him. Now all he wanted was silence and Linda. He felt just as he had thirty-six years earlier on that beach on the other side of the Mediterranean.

His arm slipped around Linda's shoulders. She turned slowly toward him, her face a few inches from his. There was no furrow in her brow; her eyes were clear and calm.

It's your decision, Michele.

He remembered the silent pact he had made with the Invisible Man on that distant night.

The manhunt is off. But you have to stop.

He was just an old cop protecting something valuable, something that should never suffer even the slightest harm, something he had to protect from everyone, beginning with Michele Balistreri, his sins, and his remorse.

Because you can't harm the fairies in a nursery rhyme . . .

The moment passed as the thought came to him. Linda rested her head on his shoulder and fell asleep.

The following evening they were there again, not saying a word, enjoying the warm sunset that marked the beginning of the long Roman summer. Balistreri was scheduled to return to work the next day.

"Michele, I have to ask you something personal." Linda's tone was odd; direct questions were not a part of their everyday life.

"That sounds ominous," Balistreri joked.

But she was serious, clearly unhappy about asking the question. "I'd like to know whether, when you were involved in politics, you caused anyone's death."

Balistreri was struck by the roundabout way she phrased the question.

When you were involved in politics . . . you caused anyone's death . . .

He was certain she knew that, up until November 1973, Michele Balistreri had been a Fascist agitator and a leader of Ordine Nuovo, which was later dissolved by government decree because it had been accused of being a new incarnation of the old Fascist party. And, being a good journalist, she must have wondered why he hadn't been arrested and put on trial along with the movement's other leaders.

"Would it change anything between us, Linda?"

She thought for a while. "I need to know who you are today, Michele, and in order to know that I have to know something about who you were back then."

Balistreri didn't ask why. He trusted her and her good intentions in asking him.

"I never killed an innocent person nor ordered any innocent people to be killed. In my group, though, there were people who thought that bullets and bombs were the only means for engaging in the fight."

"And you?"

"After Ordine Nuovo was disbanded, I tried to make the group a political one again, but they only wanted armed struggle, and I lost."

"Where were you from 1974 to 1978?"

Her tone was perfectly friendly.

I was still part of that group, one of its leaders. But I'd agreed to spy on them.

"I can't tell you, Linda. It's for your own good."

She took one of his hands in hers. "I know you didn't kill innocent people. But when you found yourself next to people who wanted to kill innocent people, did you let them do it? Or did you stop them?"

I betrayed my former friends because they betrayed themselves, and because they thought combat meant putting a bomb in a dumpster in a crowded place.

"I did what I could, Linda—everything I could to combat what I thought was unjust and dishonorable."

"And you'd do the same thing again?"

Linda Nardi had a knack for asking questions that knocked him off-balance. Here was another one.

"Today I'd only kill someone if I were forced to do so. That happened five months ago up on that hill."

She nodded, but her eyes told a different story. She separated her palms, and Balistreri's hand was left free, light as a feather, and alone.

PART 3

SUNDAY, JULY 9, 2006

Morning

HE HAD BEEN BACK at work for a little over a month. It was a peaceful time. No one mentioned the shooting or the crimes. By now they were in hands of the public prosecutor's office and the killers were in prison. Vasile's accomplices, Hagi's four employees who had traded Nadia for a vehicle to use for a robbery, were dead. Camarà's killer was an unknown motorcyclist who had argued with him at the entrance to Bella Blu. There was no connection between the two cases. And even less of a connection between ENT and the secret intelligence service.

Balistreri was living with Linda, but also without her. With love, but no sex. He did things he had never done before, such as fixing a leak under the kitchen sink, watching a detective film on television, and attempting to play golf. He spent a whole Sunday in Linda's garage, getting oil and grease all over himself, trying to repair her old moped.

In the lazy days of summer, enthusiasm for the Italian national soccer team was reaching a fever pitch. There was a growing excitement in the air. Italy's march toward the World Cup final in Berlin was as unexpected and all-consuming as it had been twenty-four years earlier. There were Italian flags on balconies, and every evening the center was blocked by crazy traffic as Italians drove around rejoicing. In offices, churches, and hospitals and on the streets, the talk was of nothing else. Only "national" dishes were being served in bars and restaurants: salads of tomato, mozzarella, and lettuce, or watermelon, honeydew, and kiwi. The country chose to ignore Lombardy's talk of secession and dedicate its allegiance once more to the flag. In the hazy heat of a scorching July, Italians were caught up in their team's adventures on German soil.

Even politics and the great disagreement with foreign residents had been put on the back burner in the newspapers, on television, and in conversation. Indeed, many foreigners—some from conviction, others out of pure opportunism—had become Italian supporters, making a great deal of money selling counterfeit national team shirts on every street corner. People hugged each other in the celebrations after the games. No one could give a damn about killings anymore.

In the middle of the morning, Balistreri and Dioguardi were talking on the phone.

"While the match is on and the city center's empty, let's take Linda and Margherita for a nice long stroll," Balistreri suggested.

"Margherita really wants to watch the final. Everyone's going to Alberto's house. Your brother tells me he's even convinced Linda we should come. Apparently they all think we're antisocial."

"Then the two of us can go for a walk and they can join us later. Italy's going to lose. The center will still be deserted later."

"We're going to win, Michele, and Margherita and Linda will be out celebrating with everyone else."

"Linda would never go out celebrating, Angelo."

"Okay, but if Italy does win, it's going to take Linda three hours to get home from Alberto's."

They both had a sense of déjà vu, yet they both studiously avoided the subject. They had never spoken again of that night in 1982, but they'd both lost interest in soccer afterward. Together they came to the only possible solution: a walk through the deserted city center, and after the game another walk if Italy lost, or a strategic retreat to Linda's little terrace if the team won. Just the two of them.

. . . .

For Giovanna Sordi, it had been a Sunday morning the same as all the others for the past twenty-four years. The eight-thirty tram to Verano cemetery, because Sunday was the day she brought fresh flowers: tulips for Elisa's romantic heart, red carnations for Amedeo's socialist one. A brief moment of silence without tears and then she recited, "Eternal rest grant unto them, O Lord," in a whisper: twenty-four times for Elisa, ten for Amedeo. Then the tram again to the old house on the outskirts where she still lived. Midday Mass at the local parish church, and then confession, with no sins to list, just the usual plea, the one that the old priest no longer even heard and for which he granted absolution without penance.

Lord, at least tell me who did it.

Evening

Strolling through the center of Rome, they felt as if they were on the moon. Even innocent tourists who had never seen a soccer game in their lives had gathered in the squares where the final was being shown on enormous screens. Down the deserted streets, the total silence was broken by collective roars. It was impossible to ignore the game's progress completely, the result in the balance, the beginning of extra time. Along with the sounds, Michele Balistreri and Angelo Dioguardi were accompanied by an emotion that had nothing to do with the game. They walked along without saying a word, and the more they walked the more the memory wormed its way in gradually, subtly, inexorably. It grew very slowly, soft as a heavy snow fall on a winter's evening. For almost two hours they wandered around without exchanging a single word, surrounded by the historic center's overwhelming, incomparable, and silent beauty.

By the time the game reached the decisive shoot-out, they stood pale and exhausted outside the front door of Linda Nardi's apartment building. In the silence, as millions of people held their breath, they lit cigarettes and traveled back twenty-four years. Balistreri and Dio-guardi hurried up the staircase while the crazy crowds rushed onto the streets. They took refuge on Linda's terrace while the joy spread around them.

During an uproar like this, a monster cut Elisa Sordi to pieces while we couldn't give a damn.

Balistreri heard a whistling sound close by and turned to see the fireworks display. A line of white was running directly up into the sky; at any moment it would explode in a thousand colors. Instead, it reached a point in the sky, couldn't manage to go any higher, and fizzled out.

MONDAY, JULY 10, 2006

Afternoon

THE NIGHT OF WILD celebration was followed by a day of endless chatter and newspaper headlines, with T-shirts of the world champions on sale even outside cemeteries and in hospitals. Hardly anyone was working, and it would have been difficult to get anything done. To distract himself from the inane office chatter, Balistreri allowed Linda to persuade him to take a late afternoon walk.

After half an hour, his bad leg and his age made it necessary to rest. He also needed an espresso. They sat down at a café in Piazza Navona.

At the next table sat a couple with their two adolescent children. The mother read out loud from a guidebook. "Piazza Navona came into being in the first century AD, but as a stadium rather than a square."

With his mouth full of pastry, the son asked, "Did the Rome team play here?"

The mother carried on with the history of the fountain, the rivalry between Bernini and Borromini, and the raised hand on the Rio della Plata statue that blocks the view of Sant'Agnese. "Well, it is a pile of crap," the girl said, wiping a blob of pastry cream off her face with the back of her hand.

At a certain point the two teenagers got up without a word and went off to look in the store windows around the square that displayed designer clothes, iPods, and the latest cell phones. The mother put the guidebook down and looked at her husband, who was buried behind the edition of *Corriere dello Sport* that described the great Italian triumph in detail. "Do something, would you? They're your kids, too." He lowered the newspaper a little, looked over the top at her, and said, "You bring up the kids; I bring home the money."

Their two espressos arrived with two little glasses of water. By now there were very few cafés that kept up this tradition. Balistreri liked it. It reminded him of the *mabrouka* who performed the same ritual for his father when he was in his study. Papa thanked her with a little nod of the head without taking his eyes off his papers. He always took a sip of water first and then started on the coffee.

He glanced at the next table, where the father had spread the paper out on the table and was continuing to read. His eye fell on a headline buried among the interviews with the team's heroes. It was tucked in a corner, barely noticeable: A TRAGEDY OF TWO WORLD CUPS.

He got up and went over to the table. "Excuse me," he said.

The man raised a pair of hostile eyes, probably expecting to see an immigrant trying to sell him something, but when he recognized a typical Italian face, he softened a little.

"Yes?" he replied, irritated nevertheless.

"Forget about it," Balistreri said, having just noticed a newsstand at the other end of the piazza.

With Linda looking on, perplexed, he asked for the *Corriere dello Sport*.

The vendor laughed. "Sorry, all the newspapers were sold out by ten o'clock."

"Even hard news?"

"Even the papers that publish hard news are all about our champions today. All sold out."

Balistreri went back to the avid reader.

"Look, I need your paper. I'll give you ten euros for it."

The man shook his head. "I'm going to frame this and hang it on the wall."

"All right. Look, I just want to read a little piece that interests me there, and then I'll give it back to you."

The other man was now curious. "What do you want to read?"

Balistreri pointed it out to him. The man looked at it with a frown. "Why the hell would you bother with that on a glorious day like today?"

The look on Balistreri's face made him change his attitude.

"Keep that page. I'm not interested in it," he said.

Sitting with Linda in the joyful piazza overflowing with crowds of people, Balistreri read the article.

. . . .

A TRAGEDY OF TWO WORLD CUPS. Giovanna Sordi committed suicide yesterday evening by throwing herself off the balcony at her home. Just like her daughter, Elisa, who was brutally murdered twenty-four years ago on the day of Italy's World Cup victory in Spain, the elderly woman died as the national team was lifting its championship trophy. Was it a chilling coincidence, or did the latest national victory awaken unbearably painful memories for her? The Elisa Sordi case, which at the time was on the front page for weeks, has remained unsolved. No one has ever been formally charged with the murder. Unfortunately, what is a great joy for many is a huge personal tragedy for at least one family.

An extremely sensitive sub-editor, a piece that escaped the chief editor's notice.

A pang in the stomach, different from all the others he had felt for years. It didn't even seem to come from the usual point at the bottom of his esophagus, but somewhere deeper, distant, and clear.

He lit a cigarette and thought about Elisa Sordi's parents: humble origins, a worker in early retirement and a waitress. He remembered the couple's persistence—which he'd seen as overreaction—during the World Cup final, the desperation and restraint they showed after Elisa was found. He remembered how Amedeo Sordi came down to Homicide every morning to ask whether there was any news. He would sit in a corner and read *L'Unità*, remaining there in silence for hours. No one took any notice of him. He kept it up for two whole years until someone, perhaps his own lawyer, had gently let him know that it was pointless and that he was disturbing the police.

Giovanna Sordi had waited twenty-four years for someone to tell her who had taken Elisa from her and why. And when, after twenty-four years, World Cup champion Italy had replied no, she really couldn't know who'd done it, she had decided to end it all.

On impulse, he tried calling Angelo. Linda was watching him, the vertical groove clearly furrowing her brow. Angelo replied cheerfully after the first ring.

Balistreri read the article to him. A long silence followed. Finally Angelo Dioguardi hung up without saying a word.

TUESDAY, JULY 11, 2006

Morning

H E HAD WAITED TOO long to make the visit. It was Giovanna Sordi's
suicide that spurred him on to make it.

You can at least ask to be forgiven.

Linda offered to drive. It took less time to get from Rome to the
outskirts of Naples than from there to the center of the city. Balistreri took advantage of the delay to read the newspapers, avoiding
the sea of articles on the World Cup triumph. Several newspapers
remarked on how most immigrants joined in celebrating Italy's victory, as if that made them worthy of living there. Such was soccer's
power.

Linda drove calmly through hellish traffic in Naples while Balistreri
hurled curses at the cars beeping at them for stopping at red lights.
The city was even more strewn with flags than Rome, and hordes of
people were spilling out everywhere. They had told Lucia Coppola
they would arrive in the morning, but it was almost one o'clock by
the time they got there.

The apartment was small, but the entire bay was visible from its balcony. "It belongs to my parents," Lucia explained as she welcomed them in. "They're on vacation in Capri."

She was a good-looking woman, much better-looking than Coppola had been, and much taller. Inside, there were photographs of Coppola everywhere: photos of him with Lucia in high school, on their wedding day, on vacation, with handsome Ciro getting taller at every stage. Lucia was calm and relaxed, as if Coppola would be home from work at the end of the day. She showed them a photo she'd taken when they'd celebrated Giulia Piccolo's entry into the team. On the steps outside the offices, Balistreri was standing in the middle with Piccolo, Corvu, and Mastroianni, while Coppola was perched on the step above.

The table in the shady part of the balcony was set for four. The wonderful smell of pasta sauce and fresh basil drew Balistreri into the kitchen.

"Ciro's at practice; he'll be home any minute," Lucia told him.

Lucia and Linda were stirring the pasta when Balistreri heard a key in the door. He had prepared something to say, but he found words failed him when Ciro entered. The lanky teenager spoke first. He shook Balistreri's hand and said "My father found fault with everyone, but never with you."

At the table they talked about Italy's victory and the incredible fireworks display that had lit up the bay. Then Ciro told them about his successful trial period with the Naples basketball team. He would be starting on the team the following year.

"And school?" Balistreri asked, remembering Coppola's fixation with his son finishing high school and going on to study law.

Ciro's eyes sought his mother's. Lucia said, "It's been a difficult year, but he'll make it up."

After coffee, Lucia and Linda started to clear the dishes and Balistreri went along to Ciro's room. It was full of posters of star players and singers. Above the bed was an extraordinary photo of Coppola in a basketball uniform, completing a three-point shot at the hoop.

"He wasn't a bad player," Ciro said. "When he was young, he was a decent point guard."

They sat on the edge of the bed, one already an old man, the other still a boy. Without saying a word, they stared for a while at the photo that said so much. Then Ciro spoke. "My mother says you were absolutely not to blame."

Balistreri had no idea what to say.

The boy went on, smiling at him. "You were wounded going to help my dad."

Coming to Naples, he'd sworn to himself that he wouldn't tell this kid what violence could mean. But that photo changed things. He told him that his father had emerged from cover to save his life, rolling on the ground like a cop in the movies, and had scored a bull's-eye on the man who was about to kill him. He told him that they'd only succeeded in stopping him by hitting him in the back. Ciro's eyes glowed with pride.

As they were saying their good-byes, Ciro brought him a small flat packet. "Papa kept a calendar of his appointments at work—they gave it to us with his things. I want you to have it."

Looking at this gentle boy who would no longer have a father to applaud him as he scored three-pointers or praise his high grades, he felt a cold rage rising inside him—the rage he'd tried to put behind him and forget after that January night on the hillside outside Vasile's house. He feared that in twenty-four years, Lucia and Ciro still be waiting for justice, just like Giovanna Sordi.

Evening

When they arrived back at Linda's apartment, Balistreri opened Detective Coppola's diary while he drank a little white wine on the terrace and watched the sunset. As usual, Linda drank water and seemed lost in distant thoughts.

Coppola was a stickler for detail. Under each day he noted times and events. It was his diary for 2006, so it was new, yet in three days a good deal had happened. The last note was for 8:00 p.m. on January 4, jotted down immediately after he'd been sent to keep an eye on Colajacono.

Tell B. about Carmen. Call Cabot again. I spoke to Carmen again and something new came up.

Those had been Coppola's last words as he'd left Balistreri's office on that wretched evening. At the back of the diary were phone numbers. Balistreri immediately found the one he wanted. Still angry at the thought of Ciro and Lucia alone in that apartment, he dialed it immediately on his personal cell phone.

A foreign voice answered on the first ring. "Carmen speaking."

"Good evening. This is Balistreri from the police. I worked with Detective Coppola."

"I know who you are," the woman said. "The papers mentioned you a lot a few months ago. I'm sorry about Coppola."

"Thank you. Look, I could use your help. Coppola came to see you the day he died."

"He did. I remember he told me his son had a basketball game that evening."

"Right. Unfortunately he didn't have time to report what you talked about."

"I'm happy to help, but it's been a while. Anyway, nothing new came out."

Linda was listening in silence.

"Please bear with me and try to remember. I'd asked him to go over with you the phone call your boyfriend made to you that night, before the . . . before he was . . ."

"Before that bastard on the motorcycle killed him," she said.

"I wanted to be sure about the times."

"I've told you the same thing a thousand times. He called me at two forty five. It shows up on my cell phone records and his. He called to tell me how he was feeling. He said he had to urinate a lot, but he didn't seem to have a temperature. I asked him if it was a quiet night. He said it was, then he told me about this fool who'd gone past on a motorcycle and insulted him for no reason."

"And you asked him if he'd had any other problems with this guy?"

"I asked him, but he said nothing else had happened that night."

"Then what did he say to you?"

"Nothing. I can't recall anything else."

"The call lasted two and a half minutes. Did he describe the motorcyclist to you?"

A moment of confusion. "No, Coppola asked me that last time. Papa just said the guy was wearing a full-face helmet and it was strange."

"How could he see something was strange about the guy if he was wearing a full-face helmet?"

"It wasn't the rider who was strange. It was the bike."

"Strange? How do you mean?"

"He only said it was strange. Nothing else. And that the man was wearing a full-face helmet."

Balistreri said good-bye to Carmen and started to think. He quickly found the summary of Coppola's questioning of Fred Cabot on his BlackBerry. Rereading it, he realized it was highly condensed. Coppola had probably had difficulties with the language and had summarized a good bit. Cabot had spoken of a motorcyclist with a helmet and a big bike, one that was easy to handle and fast. That was a pretty full description. Either Coppola was exaggerating, or Cabot was a motorcycle enthusiast. He turned to the diary's last page. There were two numbers for Cabot, a landline and a cell phone. He picked one and dialed.

Cabot was a little confused at first, but he got up to speed quickly. Apparently the American newspapers had reported on the shooting of Balistreri and the deaths on January 4.

"I'm sorry about your guy. He was a good man."

"Thanks, Mr. Cabot. I just need to clarify something with you. In your conversation with Coppola you described the rider and the motorcycle, but Coppola translated it into Italian. Could you tell me what you originally said in English?"

A little embarrassed, Cabot explained Coppola's misunderstanding about a prostitute and a gay.

Balistreri couldn't help smiling quietly.

"Why did you say queer?" he asked.

"I said the whole thing was strange," he recalled.

There was that word again. "The rider or the bike?" Balistreri asked.

"I was thinking of the bike, not the rider. You see, I love motor-cycles—I collect them."

An expert, so the description was based on something more than just a simple impression.

"You said the bike was big, easy to handle, and speedy."

"No, no. It was easy and speedy, but it wasn't big. The detective must have misunderstood me. I meant that it was an unusual bike for him to be riding."

"Unusual in what way?" Balistreri asked, but then the truth dawned on him a second before Cabot's voice spoke it from the other side of the world.

"Well, it was a motocross bike. I was surprised to see one in the middle of a city."

. . . .

An evening breeze was blowing across the little terrace. Everything was as it had been for months. Yet everything was different, too.

"Linda, you asked me once about when Alina Hagi died . . ."

Linda was motionless, as if she were making a decision. She stared at St. Peter's dome. The vertical crease ran down the middle of her forehead.

Balistreri remembered her two questions at the end of their first dinner. *What about the fourth man? What if he carves up another girl?*

He couldn't bear the silence any longer.

"Who told you about the carved letters?" he asked urgently.

"No one told me, Michele."

"I don't believe you."

She stroked his hand. "Find the person who killed Nadia and Samantha and you'll find the person who killed Coppola."

Angry now, he jerked his hand away. "I'll find out who it was and when I do I'm going to throw him in jail."

She took the phrase in, as if it were confirmation of what she'd known for some time. Then she made a decision. She got up, went inside, and took a thick folder full of newspaper cuttings from a drawer.

Balistreri went over a little uncertainly. She held the folder out to him without saying a word. On it was written "For When You're Well."

Now that he was well, he could do what he wanted. But without her—that was the message.

"I'm not well, Linda."

She shook her head as he left. "You have to heal yourself."

Walking back to his own apartment, he thought about how she'd embraced him in the hospital, about the past months together, about the evening when he'd thought of kissing her and she had fallen asleep with her head on his shoulder, about the moped grease between his fingers.

There are no dreams without reality. There is no freedom without truth.

. . . .

Antonio Pasquali had taken a few days off and was relaxing in Tesano, his hometown, with his wife. His private cell phone vibrated briefly. He excused himself and went outside. When he heard the voice on the other end, he shivered with fear.

"Your friend has made two disturbing phone calls. There may be problems."

They had tricked him, dragging him into something so disgusting that he couldn't even have dreamed of it. He had believed he was serving his country better by helping them make sure an ex-Communist mayor lost the election, because he was convinced that the Communists could never change and with them in power Italy would be poorer and less free. But he had never imagined finding himself involved in anything like this and wouldn't tolerate anymore deaths among his policemen, least of all Balistreri's.

He gathered all the courage he could muster.

"Nothing drastic," he whispered.

"I beg your pardon?" The voice appeared to be mocking him and threatening him at the same time.

He didn't dare say anything more. It wouldn't have helped. He had to make a quick decision, a different one that would satisfy Balistreri, putting him out of danger.

"Keep an eye on him," said the voice, "and the woman, too. Don't ever forget about that article."

WEDNESDAY, JULY 12, 2006

Morning

CORVU'S RELATIONSHIP WITH NATALYA was having a rejuvenating effect on him. He'd changed his haircut. He'd bought new clothes. Even his poker strategy these days was a little more daring and less analytical.

"Alberto says no poker game tomorrow. Angelo can't make it."

"All right," Balistreri said.

He hadn't slept a wink. He'd tossed and turned all night thinking of Linda and that voice on the hill that had announced Colajacono's death. And a motocross bike.

"But Alberto's still expecting you for dinner around eight thirty."

"All right."

It was the second "all right" that aroused Corvu's suspicion.

"Are you okay, sir?"

Balistreri lit a cigarette, the first of his five for the day.

"Sit down, Corvu."

That "sit down" left no room for doubt. Playtime was over.

Balistreri pointed to the blackboard. It was an old habit. Sometimes, when an investigation had stalled, he asked Corvu to set his analytical gifts in motion and write all the important details on this board, where they stayed until the investigation was over.

"You can start writing," Balistreri said.

Corvu remained seated.

"What do you want me to write, sir?"

"Whatever you want. Details, questions, doubts," Balistreri said.

Corvu found the courage to look him in the eye. "Up there? After Dubai you told me that—"

"We'll keep the office locked."

Corvu went hesitatingly up to the board. "Let's do it like this," said Balistreri to encourage him. "Let's put down an exhaustive list of questions, along with any doubts. You do one, I'll do another, until we can't think of any more. We'll write the answers next to them as soon as we know them."

"What does the letter R mean? And E? Does it come after?" began Balistreri.

As he wrote this down, Corvu found renewed confidence and energy. They went on with growing enthusiasm for two hours. The blackboard was very large and Corvu's writing was tiny. By the end they were exhausted.

. . . .

What does the letter R mean? And E? Does it come after?

Why did Colajacono want to stand in for Marchese and Cutugno? Because he knew that Ramona might come in about Nadia.

And how did he know that? Mircea told him.

Why was Colajacono already dog-tired on the morning of December 24?

Why did Ramona offer her services to deputy mayor Augusto De Rossi? In order to blackmail him and make him change his vote.

Who blackmailed him? Mircea and Colajacono.

On behalf of whom and why?

Is there an Invisible Man in the Samantha Rossi case? Who is he? There is, but we don't know who he is.

Is he the same person who phoned Vasile to ask for the Giulia GT?

When was the Giulia GT's headlight broken?

Where was Hagi between six and seven on the evening of December 24 when Nadia was taken away? And then after nine?

Same question for Colajacono and Ajello.

Where was Hagi the night Coppola and the others died?

Same question for Ajello.

Were Mircea and Greg guilty of murder in Romania? And who were the two victims?

How did Alina Hagi die in January 1983?

Why did Colajacono want Tatò with him, even though he knew he intended to spend time with his sister?

Why did the Giulia GT slow down when the driver saw Natalya?

What was the relationship between Ornella Corona and Ajello and his son before her husband died?

Who suggested that she take out a life insurance policy on her husband?

How did Sandro Corona really die?

Why did Camarà die? Because he'd seen Nadia with someone in the private lounge on December 23.

Who owns ENT?

They decided not to write down the reply to the last question, nor to the question about the instigators of the Augusto De Rossi blackmail. The secret service would have been an inadequate reply, anyway. The question was who was behind it.

"For goodness sake," said Corvu, looking at the blackboard. "With all the things we don't know, it's a miracle we've got any guilty parties in prison."

"That's assuming they're really the guilty parties," Balistreri said. "I've got two more questions to add, but I'd rather you didn't write them down."

"Why's that?"

"Let's just say I'm superstitious. The first is this: Where was Adrian's bike on the evening of December 24 while he was at Casilino 900?"

Corvu looked at him. He paged through the statements made during questioning, then looked up again. "Why do we need to know that?"

"Because there are at least two things we don't know, and I'd like you to find out the answers. Where was that bike on December 23 when Camarà was killed? And where was it on December 24 when Nadia was kidnapped and killed?"

"I still don't get it. What does Adrian's motocross bike have to do with a guy on a motorcycle outside Bella Blu?"

Balistreri told him about his conversations with Carmen and Cabot. Corvu frowned. A second connection between Nadia and Bella Blu. Bella Blu meant ENT. And ENT meant big trouble, as Balistreri himself had made clear.

"What's the second question, sir?" he asked.

"There are too many invisible men in this case. The one who had the bike is the easiest one to find."

"Right. What do you want me to do?"

"Get ready to find the answers to these questions, except for the questions about ENT and Alina Hagi—I'll take care of those. And send Margherita in."

Corvu looked down, not meeting his eye. "Yesterday when you were in Naples she asked me if she could take the rest of the week off and I gave it to her."

"Is she okay?"

"Yes. I think she and Angelo are going away together."

Afternoon

The death toll from mopeds was seemingly infinite. No one gave a damn except the victims' parents. Everyone said that mopeds had been Rome's salvation, and that without them traffic would have ground to a halt twenty years earlier. The center could have been turned into a pedestrian-only area, but store owners wouldn't hear of it. Government offices could have been moved out to the outskirts, but public employees wouldn't hear of it. The roads could have been better maintained and the cobblestones paved over so that moped riders didn't bounce around as if they were in a pinball machine, but historic preservationists wouldn't hear of it. And so the death toll climbed higher.

Alina Hagi was just one of the countless victims. In Rome, a moped accident that cost a twenty-year-old her life was a purely routine case. Her accident might have had a few more details because it had been her uncle, Monsignor Lato, who filed the report, but there wasn't even a photo of her stapled to it. She'd died on a rainy night in January 1983, shortly after ten o'clock. Many witnesses saw her take the curve around the Colosseum at top speed, hit a hole in the road, swerve off to the side, and crash into a plane tree. Helmets weren't yet mandatory then, and she wasn't wearing one. No one had cut her off, and nothing unusual had occurred.

Balistreri read Monsignor Lato's statement, which the monsignor had later retracted. He said that a few days earlier Alina's arms had been covered in bruises. One of Alina's friends had told him that after the girl's funeral. However, there was no direct link between those bruises and the accident, and after a month Monsignor Lato regretted that he had mentioned it.

Linda Nardi's question nagged at him. *When did Alina die?*

The one-way roundabout suggested that Alina was coming from home and going somewhere in the dark after ten on a rainy January night, riding a moped at idiotically high speed. And Alina Hagi by all accounts had been an exceptionally sensible young woman, well-mannered, religious, and with a good head on her shoulders.

. . . .

He called Angelo many times that day, but his cell phone was always off.

He called Corvu and told him to track down Monsignor Lato. Corvu told him that he'd organized the investigation and set it in motion and that Piccolo was ready to jump in again. That enthusiasm worried Balistreri. The last thing he needed was a mountain of muscle ready to avenge wrongs against women.

The desire to call Linda came over him in waves, but he resisted. Not out of pride—there was no tug-of-war between them—but for a better reason: secrets are a barrier against complicity.

He spent hour after hour at his desk. He read all the statements again on his computer, then the list of questions on the blackboard.

He knew that the solution was there in the answers to those questions. He read the first one again.

What does the letter R mean? And the E? What comes next?
When did Alina die?
Linda's question bounced around in his head.
When? Why "when" and not "how"?

. . . .

Corvu called him around nine o'clock while he was walking home, alone, without Linda for the first time in many months.

"Monsignor Lato went back to Poland ten years ago. But he's alive and well, and I dug up his phone number."

"Excellent. You're still managing to get some work done." Corvu didn't catch his drift.

"I also contacted a friend of mine at the Vatican and found out where Alina Hagi worked. I sent you an e-mail about that."

"Good work."

"One more thing, sir. Natalya and I are going out for a pizza. Would you and Linda like to join us?"

"No, thanks. Not tonight."

He ended the conversation with Corvu. Now the desire to call Linda was irresistible.

Corvu's e-mail was very short. It began with the Monsignor's phone number in Poland and then noted in the driest terms that in 1982, Alina Hagi had worked in the San Valente parish on the Via Aurelia Antica.

I did it, memory says. I couldn't have done it, says pride. In the end, memory relents.

. . . .

Linda Nardi was looking beyond St. Peter's toward the river that now separated them.

She had tried with all her might to convince herself that he could understand or at least accept it.

But that wasn't the case. She knew that very well now, from that evening on the terrace. She spoke to her mother. She made the necessary phone call.

THURSDAY, JULY 13, 2006

Morning

FOR YEARS HE HAD avoided the stretch of the Appian Way that climbed upward as it passed the well-maintained low-rise housing hidden among the trees. It was an unconscious avoidance, as if his memory's immune system had driven his consciousness away from that place.

Because remorse has a face, a name, a habitation.

He knew that his old acquaintance, Father Paul, was in charge of the volunteer organization association whose headquarters were in San Valente parish.

Sunlight filtered through the trees. While he was parking, he noticed that very little was as he remembered. The squat church had been repainted, the greenery was thicker and better manicured, and at the end of the lawn the large house had at least doubled in size. He crossed the small square of grass. The place felt mature, as if it had passed from infancy to adulthood.

Father Paul had been informed of his arrival. He strode across the lawn to greet him. His red hair was tinged with gray, his blue eyes were more cautious, less open to the world. His handshake was firmer than Balistreri remembered, and it was obvious that the man in front of him was a lot more confident than the chatty young man he'd met years earlier. It was the first time he'd seen him without his priest's cassock.

Paul welcomed him warmly and led him to the back of the house. The tree where they had chatted the first time had grown. Under it were three chairs and a table set with glasses and mineral water. Beside the glasses were a BlackBerry and a pack of cigarettes.

"I never imagined you'd still be here after all this time," Balistreri observed as they sat.

"Do you mean here in Rome or here at San Valente?"

"Well, both, I suppose. I remember you as a young man who really wanted to travel."

Paul smiled. He no longer looked like a young American kid; he smiled like an adult who was sure of himself and his place in the world. And his Italian was perfect.

"You're right, Captain Balistreri. When I look back, I'm a little surprised myself. Every year I thought I'd move on, and every year they asked me to stay. And little by little, San Valente became the world I'd so wanted to se. Orphans and volunteers come here from all over. So I never needed to travel."

The chorus of birds in the trees mingled with the joyful sounds of children in the house.

"How many children are there?" Balistreri asked.

"We doubled in size ten years ago. At the moment we have thirty children ranging from ten to fourteen years old, and two volunteers who take turns covering the night shift. But we have dozens of houses like this on several continents."

"And you run all of them?"

"No, not at all. I'm in charge of selecting and training the volunteers, and I run San Valente."

Paul took a cigarette from the pack and offered one to Balistreri. "You smoke, if I remember correctly."

Balistreri looked at Father Paul, the typical Californian health nut, lighting a cigarette and inhaling with the relaxed and confident air of someone who had achieved what he set out to achieve. And he couldn't resist having a smoke with him, even if it was already his fourth of the day and his stomach was burning a little.

"And His Eminence?"

"Cardinal Alessandrini?" Paul smiled. "He's the driving force behind this miracle. Without him, not even the Vatican would have been able to save these children from the hell they were living in."

"Is he still in Rome?"

Paul pointed to the dome atop St. Peter's, visible in the distance. "Cardinal Alessandrini's never liked to be in the spotlight. He's always been happy to make decisions rather than make appearances. Today he's one of the new pontiff's closest advisers, but he still lives on Via della Camilluccia in the same place."

Paul enthusiastically set out the details of Cardinal Alessandrini's project: the number of children saved from terrible circumstances, the number of dictators bending under the influence and determination of this man of steel to allow exploited and abused children who were victims of corrupt and immoral regimes to be removed, and the huge influence he wielded with the current pope.

When Paul's BlackBerry rang he answered and spoke briefly, and then he turned to Balistreri. "If you don't mind, Captain, I have a little surprise for you. I told Valerio you were coming."

"Valerio?" Balistreri said. "Valerio Bona?"

"Yes. I don't know whether you remember, but he sometimes lent a hand here in the parish."

"I remember him very well. But I didn't think he was still living around here."

"Valerio graduated in computer science, worked a few years for IBM, and then came back to us. He runs our computer system."

Balistreri couldn't hold back. "But you two hated each other."

Paul said, "We weren't exactly friends, but 'hate' is too strong a word. Anyway, time sometimes works miracles."

Valerio Bona arrived with his uncertain gait. He seemed a little hunched, and there was no hair on his shaven head. He came up and offered his hand without looking Balistreri in the eye. The golden crucifix round his neck was the same one he had worn twenty-four years before.

Valerio had aged more than Paul. Time hadn't been kind to him. His eternally worried eyes now sat behind very thick glasses.

Balistreri said, "This really is a surprise. Do you live here, Valerio?"

"No, I work in the offices in a building near here, where I also have a small apartment."

"Are you married?"

"No, I'm not married. I live by myself." He said it evenly, but Balistreri caught a hint of regret.

Valerio told him about his computer science degree, the money he earned at IBM, and the feeling that his life was meaningless, until Cardinal Alessandrini suggested him for the job. In that way he could put his science into the service of his faith.

"He didn't accept right away when we offered him the job," Paul said. "I don't think he wanted to work with me."

Valerio gave a half-smile. "Maybe, but once I got to know you I was okay with it."

"You discovered I'd become much more likable! Captain Balistreri, I imagine you're here to discuss what happened on Sunday to Elisa's mother."

Hearing her name upset him. He quickly moved to change the subject.

"No, I'm not here about Mrs. Sordi's suicide."

"No?" Paul and Valerio exclaimed together.

"No. I'm here about a question from that time. But it has nothing to do with Elisa Sordi."

Valerio listened gloomily, Paul with curiosity.

"There was a young Polish woman working at San Valente back then," Balistreri said.

"There were lots of young Polish women working at San Valente then, after Wojtyla was appointed," Paul said.

"Her name was Alina. Alina Hagi."

The only sound was the singing of birds and the shouts of children. Paul lit a cigarette, and Valerio poured some water into a glass.

"You don't remember her?" Balistreri asked.

"Who could forget her?" Paul said, staring at the big white house. "Alina Hagi, the energetic blonde—you met her yourself."

A dozen children aged between ten and thirteen were playing soccer and a blond girl of about twenty was acting as referee.

He tried to draw on his photographic memory, keeping out the emotional one. "The girl who refereed the soccer and served at the food?"

"Yes, she was a force of nature. She'd been working with children for several years and the volunteers all went to her for help and advice."

"Did you ever meet her husband?"

Valerio shook his head. "Never, but I knew she was married."

"I saw him a few times," Paul said, "I think he was Polish, too."

"Romanian," Balistreri corrected him. "His name is Marius Hagi."

There was a long silence. Balistreri was aware that something in the air had changed.

After some time, Balistreri asked, "Do you know what happened to her?"

He met Paul's eyes and caught a look of disapproval bordering on harshness. The man was exhibiting a strength that hadn't existed twenty-four years earlier.

"I see you haven't lost the habit of asking questions to which you already know the answers," Paul said.

"Was Alina still working here when she had her accident?" Balistreri asked, ignoring the comment.

"Yes," Paul replied. "After Alina's death, Cardinal Alessandrini held a special Mass for her in the Vatican with all the children and volunteers."

"And were you here at the time, Valerio?"

"No, I was working for Count Tommaso dei Banchi di Aglieno while I went to college. After what happened, the count didn't want to employ me anymore, because of what I'd said about Manfredi, I think, and the fact that I was too close to the Catholic world."

He didn't say "after Elisa's death," as if her name shouldn't be mentioned.

Balistreri said her name, though. He said both names. "Did Alina Hagi know Elisa Sordi?" he asked.

"No way," Valerio said quickly. "Elisa never came to the church here, and Alina never went to Via della Camilluccia."

As these names and people slowly emerged from the past, Balistreri had the feeling that he shouldn't ignore them, although the people involved at the time were different now, and the connection between Elisa's death and the present was still murky.

"Does the count still live there?" he asked.

"He's never moved out of his penthouse. As you can see, we've all stayed put," Paul replied.

"Manfredi, too?"

Paul said, "No, Manfredi's the only one who went away. After Ulla killed herself, the count sent him to Kenya, where they have a huge estate. He earned a medical degree in South Africa."

"Does he ever come to Italy?"

"He comes to see his father every so often, but no more than once or twice a year. Cardinal Alessandrini tells me that the Kenyans see him as a kind of god, because he treats them free-of-charge and heals them. As you see, anyone can change," he said. He said it harshly, cruelly. Balistreri would never have expected that tone from him.

The person I was so sure was guilty has become a charitable doctor who heals the destitute.

"Was Alina particularly close to anyone?" Balistreri asked.

Paul and Valerio looked at each other, then Valerio spoke. "There was a tight-knit group of young people in those days. Alina was their leader."

"Did any of them mention that Alina had problems with her husband?" he asked.

Paul said, "We've already told you we didn't know her husband."

When Valerio spoke, his voice was dull. "These were good Catholic young people, Captain. Not like . . ."

Not like Balistreri and Dioguardi.

He decided it was time to leave. They said good-bye, but without any warmth.

Afternoon

Corvu, Piccolo, and Mastroianni were waiting in his office. They had brought in sandwiches, water, and beer for a working lunch. It was the first time they had done this since Coppola's death, and his absence hung heavy in the room.

"The first answers to the questions are starting to come in," Corvu announced with satisfaction as he approached the blackboard.

"But we have new questions to add," Balistreri said. He told them what he had found out about Alina Hagi.

Corvu scratched his head sullenly. "I'm not sure I follow. Are you saying there's a connection between this case and the Elisa Sordi case?"

"Not necessarily a connection," Balistreri replied. "But Alina Hagi's death twenty-three years ago, though it was certainly an accident, could be concealing something. And that something could be linked to today's case."

Corvu said, "We did find out something recent. Well, actually, it happened six months ago, immediately after the events of January 4. Then you got well and things changed." Corvu looked like he didn't know what to say.

Balistreri said, "Corvu, it's okay. You can say it—I wasn't interested in the case for a while. Now, tell us what this is all about."

"It's about Colajacono."

Piccolo smacked the table. "I knew it!"

Balistreri stopped them all with a gesture. "Listen to me very carefully," he said. "We've already had one death in the squad. Whatever we say, and I mean *whatever*, stays inside this room. I—and only I—will decide if and how it is to be acted on. I don't want any personal initiatives, in particular about Colajacono and ENT."

They were silent for a moment. Then, as if the words had been addressed to her alone, Piccolo said, "All right, I understand."

"Now let's hear it, Corvu."

"After the shootings on January 4, the newspapers published Colajacono's photo. And Pierre, the Bella Blu bartender, called me and told me he recognized him. I told him I'd call him back, but then you . . . anyway, I called him this afternoon."

Balistreri swore to himself and Piccolo started to say something, then bit her tongue.

Corvu continued. "I went to meet him. And now we have the answer to the fourth question on the list. Why was Colajacono already tired on the morning of December 24? Because he'd spent almost the entire night before at Bella Blu. Pierre's positive."

Piccolo couldn't contain herself. "The night of December 23, when Nadia went there and they killed Camarà. That bastard, he did it."

"That's enough, Piccolo!" Balistreri exploded. "I won't tell you again. Until we have proof to the contrary, Colajacono and Tatò were two policemen who were brutally murdered and then decorated for bravery after they discovered Nadia's killer. You broke the nose of one and the other you blackmailed with Linda Nardi."

"But I'm sure that—"

"Your intuition's not enough here—we need serious proof, which we don't have. And we'll never get it if, rather than looking for the truth, we look for confirmation of a story that happens to suit us."

Piccolo lost it. "Do you want it all to end with those four illiterate Roma in prison and those four animals you killed on the hill? And what about Colajacono, who was waiting for Ramona—or have you forgotten about that? And how about what they did to Rudi to get the Bella Blu lighter? And blackmailing the deputy mayor, De Rossi? Or do you believe the bullshit story that Colajacono and Mircea didn't know each other?"

Silence fell on the room. Only the sound of the new air-conditioning could be heard. After a while Balistreri stood up, dragging his bad leg, and went to the door of the office. He opened it and Giulia Piccolo left.

Balistreri then went back to his seat and addressed Corvu and Mastroianni. "Piccolo's out. You are not to share a single detail with her."

The silence of his team was clearly one of disagreement, but he decided to ignore it completely.

"Let's move on. What else have you got?"

Corvu was overcome by the whirl of events, so it was Mastroianni who continued. "I checked the alibis for December 24 and January 4. The night Samantha Rossi was killed is too far in the past."

"All right. Results?"

"We already know about Hagi on December 24. He has no alibi from six to seven, when he says he went home to pick up presents for the kids in Casilino 900. Nadia was presumably kidnapped around that time. And he doesn't have one after nine thirty, when the others went off to St. Peter's and he says he went home. And Nadia was presumably killed around that time. We don't know where Colajacono was between six and seven when Tatò went to Mass. After that, there's Tatò's word, which—if we believe it—gives Colajacono an alibi; if not, then he doesn't have one."

"And Ajello?"

"He went to the charity benefit, but nobody knows exactly what time he arrived there. The cocktail hour ended at eight o'clock with donors handing over their checks, and there was one from him. Afterward he went home and celebrated Christmas with his family. His wife and son are his alibis. But we haven't interviewed them."

"And the night of January 4 and 5?"

"Hagi says he was at home in bed. He was sick and asleep at that time. No alibi. We know where Colajacono was. We're not certain about Ajello."

"Why?"

"At nine o'clock he was definitely at the opening of a new ENT betting parlor in Florence. But we checked, and his private plane landed at Urbe Airport in Rome around eleven. He picked his car up there and went off, presumably home, because there's no sign of him at Bella Blu that night or in any of ENT's other nightclubs. We'll have to question him directly."

"Let's set aside Ajello and ENT for a moment. What about Adrian's bike?"

Corvu said, "We asked a lot of people at Casilino 900 who knew Adrian. That night he came on the subway with the others, without his bike. And he didn't have it when they went off to St. Peter's. Therefore, it's possible that it was used by Camarà's murderer on December 23 and then the day after it was ridden up the hill to Vasile's house."

"Good work. Now concentrate on Hagi and his past."

Corvu was obviously upset that Piccolo was being excluded from the investigation.

"Sir, may I say something?"

Balistreri's head was aching, as was his leg. And he missed Linda.

"Spit it out, Corvu. What is it?"

"It's about Margherita."

"Not now," he snapped, and he asked Corvu to leave.

. . . .

Alberto had set the table in the garden. Presented with a delicious plate of pasta and a cool glass of white wine, Balistreri managed to relax a little.

"I saw you hung an Italian flag on the gate out front. Aren't you ashamed of yourself?"

"If you had teenagers you'd understand. And once upon a time you were the big soccer fan."

"But then I came to my senses, while you've lost yours."

"Something positive has come out of it, you have to admit. Look how much calmer things are now that immigrants have been out waving the Italian flag and celebrating."

"You call that progress? We used to want to deport them for raping our women and murdering our policemen and now, after a game of soccer, we've decided they're assimilated into Italian society?"

"That's how Italians are. You know that. And the Roma situation is complex. It won't be resolved by issuing edicts. It's going to take cooperation, patience, and hard work."

"You sound like Pasquali. Alberto, everyone knows what needs to be done—move the Roma out of those filthy camps in the middle of the city."

"We'll have to wait and see what the next mayor does, whoever that is."

"I can tell you what he'll do. He'll move them out of Casilino 900 and we'll see his photos in the papers as he closes the gates. And he'll put them somewhere else. All things that could be done right now. Except that the politicians in this country are either useless or cynical. They don't give a damn who dies, unless they can use those deaths to win an election."

"Michele, there are plenty of honest politicians who are trying to get things done. I'm not saying that there aren't some who think only of their personal careers and getting votes. Votes still count, fortunately."

"Fortunately? You think it's fortunate to have a democracy where no one tries to resolve issues but instead concentrates on stealing and getting of votes?"

Alberto's face darkened a little. The words seemed to bring him back to the bad times with his brother, when he had been forced to make unpleasant compromises in order to get Michele out of trouble.

Alberto hadn't heard his brother say anything like this for years. It seemed he had become more prudent, or perhaps nothing mattered to him anymore. He figured it must have been Giovanna Sordi's suicide that brought all that aggression out.

"Michele, do you remember the senator, Count Tommaso dei Banchi di Aglieno? Would we be better off with people like him in the government?"

Balistreri sank into silence. The count was part of a whole series of memories of a time that had disrupted his life. He didn't want to answer his brother's question. He couldn't. He would have had to think about too many uncomfortable things: his father, his mother, the crimes that had never been solved, and those last terrible hours in Tripoli. Alberto seemed to read his thoughts, and he didn't press the point any further. He dished out the shrimp that sat on a platter between them and changed the subject.

"Have you heard from Angelo lately?"

"I've been trying to call him on his cell phone for days, but no answer. He must be at some romantic hideaway with Margherita."

"When he called me to cancel the poker game he told me he was going away. I don't know about a romantic hideaway, but they've definitely left Rome."

"I hope Margherita's a comfort to him," Balistreri said, thinking of Giovanna Sordi and the remorse he and Angelo both felt.

"And you and Linda?" Alberto asked. "Are we all going to get together this weekend?"

Balistreri shook his head, but gave no explanation. Alberto asked for none. After all these years he could feel the disastrous shadow coming back over his brother's spirit. He promised to pray for him again, and pray with fervor.

FRIDAY, JULY 14, 2006

Morning

MONSIGNOR LATO HAD BEEN told to expect the phone call. He had a warm voice and spoke Italian with a Roman accent.

"I read about your misfortune, Captain Balistreri. I hope you're fully healed."

"Thank you. I'm fine. I'm sorry to bother you, and to make you talk about something painful that happened a long time ago."

There was a brief pause at the other end of the line. Then he said, "Yes, I read in the papers that the men who shot you worked for Mr. Marius Hagi."

"They did," confirmed Balistreri. "But I assume you've also read that it's been proved that Hagi had nothing to do not only with that night's events, but also all his employees' illegal activities."

"Yes, and I'm not surprised." He heard a touch of sarcasm in Monsignor Lato's voice.

"You've known Hagi for almost thirty years," Balistreri said.

"Since 1978. That's when I saw him with Alina for the first time."

"Alina was your niece?"

"The only child of my sister, who died the year before that in an airplane accident with her husband. I took Alina with me to Krakow and helped her continue her schooling. That's when she began working with orphans. Alina was sixteen, but she was as mature as any adult. Unfortunately, she could also be very single-minded about things."

"Do you mean about Marius Hagi?"

The monsignor's voice grew bitter. "Alina had a very strict Catholic upbringing and a genuine vocation to help others. And she got it into her head that young Marius was a victim she'd saved from perdition."

"Did you try to convince her otherwise?"

"Unfortunately, I didn't understand the risk he posed right away. At first, they were just friends. Alina involved Marius in her work, and he really did seem like a lost soul. Then I was transferred to Rome after the election of Pope John Paul II. Alina and Marius came to tell me they were getting married. He wasn't the talkative type, but he was smart—maybe too smart. I could see in his eyes that the violence he had suffered had left its mark. But I couldn't stop the marriage. So I insisted they come to Rome with me. I wanted to keep an eye on the situation. Contrary to what I expected, Hagi accepted this idea enthusiastically. I even performed the marriage."

"And in Rome . . ."

"In Rome everything went well at first. Through Cardinal Alessandrini, I found a job for Alina at the San Valente orphanage. She adored the work, even though it paid very little. The orphanage had barely any funding at the time. After a short time, Marius started his own businesses—travel agencies, bars, restaurants. It was quite an achievement for a Romanian immigrant with no education, especially one who was so young. Whatever Marius touched turned to gold. They bought a house near the Colosseum. They had hundreds of friends."

"Alina was happy?"

"Yes, and very proud of Marius. And the orphanage was a focal point for everyone. It lasted almost three years. Then, I don't know exactly when, things changed. I used to see Alina and Marius every Sunday for the Angelus in St. Peter's Square. One Sunday she arrived by herself, and from then on Marius never came with her again. At first, Alina said he was busy with work, and after that she didn't say anything. I saw she was beginning to look unhappy and rundown. I tried to speak to her about what was going on, but I could see she didn't want to share her feelings. This went on for months; I didn't see Marius again until Christmas 1982, when there was a huge party in the parish. Marius came with dozens of presents for the children. I remember looking at Alina, hoping to see the old pride she'd once felt for Marius, but I saw only pain on her face. I cornered him and asked him if everything was all right."

"And what did he say?"

"He told me that both he and Alina had taken vows on the day they were married in church and they would never break them. I got the feeling Alina was his prisoner. I also got the feeling that she was suffering deeply."

"After Alina's death you lodged a complaint against Marius Hagi."

Monsignor Lato sighed. "It wasn't a real complaint, more of a statement. The circumstances of the accident were never in doubt—there were many witnesses. But it was clear Alina was running away. She died trying to escape from Marius Hagi."

"Did you have proof?"

"Indirectly. Alina was friends with several of the young women who worked at the orphanage with her. She was very close to one in particular. At Alina's funeral, this young woman was really upset. I took her out for coffee after the service, and she told me that a few days earlier she had walked in on Alina in the orphanage bathroom and found her applying ointment to her badly bruised arms. She asked her who had done that to her and Alina refused to tell her."

"But this friend thought it was Hagi?"

"Who else? If it had been anyone else Alina would have told her."

"The statement was withdrawn soon after."

Now Monsignor Lato's voice was full of bitterness. "I couldn't ask the young woman to testify. Who knows what could have happened to her? Besides, Alina was dead."

"There's one more thing I'd like to ask you, Monsignor, and that is the name of the young woman in question, your niece's friend."

"I don't think I ever knew her name, but even if I did I wouldn't remember it. This all happened such a long time ago."

"You have to help me, Monsignor. This tiny thread from the past is important. I have to know what took place between Alina and her husband."

"In order to do what, Captain Balistreri?"

Just like Alessandrini. The final judgment is reserved for God.

"My business is earthly justice, Monsignor, not divine. If you don't know her name, at least describe her. Then I can ask someone who was around at the time. I'll track her down one way or another."

Monsignor Lato gave a bitter little laugh. "I can do better than that. One day Alina and her friend asked me to take a photo of them."

Balistreri held his breath.

"I have a copy on my nightstand. I imagine that would be more helpful than a description."

"Monsignor, I don't know how to thank you. Do you happen to know what a scanner is?"

"Even the divine use technology, Captain. I'll scan the photo and e-mail it to you in a few minutes."

He spent those few minutes thinking about Linda Nardi.

You directed me toward Alina Hagi. What comes next?

He had the reply in minutes. A beep announced Monsignor Lato's e-mail. The photo was sharp. Two smiling girls were looking at the lens: Alina Hagi and Samantha Rossi.

. . . .

They met in Pasquali's office at mid-morning. As a child, Pasquali had learned—from his father and his Christian Democrat friends—to put off, to water down, and to soften things. He did so with a smile on his lips and rage in his heart, and with the consummate skill of an actor.

He adjusted his glasses and studied the photo Balistreri was showing him. "Yes, a remarkable resemblance," he said.

He added nothing further and waited to hear what Balistreri had to say. The head of the special team was holding out a photo that had appeared in the papers the year before at the time of Samantha's murder. It was of her mother, Anna, rigid with grief, as she walked behind her daughter's casket.

Pasquali said, "That could be Samantha's mother as a young woman, but it would be a remarkable coincidence."

"You find it a remarkable coincidence? Back in 1982 the wife of Marius Hagi, a man involved in two murders in 2005, was friends with the mother of one of the two victims, Samantha Rossi, and you think that's a coincidence?"

Pasquali assumed his most patient manner. "Keep in mind that Hagi hasn't officially been implicated in a murder. There's nothing linking him to the murder of Samantha Rossi."

"Unless he's the Invisible Man," Balistreri said, hoping to provoke a reaction.

Pasquali would not allow himself to be troubled, even by this. "The Invisible Man, as you call him, is so invisible that he's only been described by guilty parties attempting to shed themselves of part of the burden."

If I told you about the voice that announced Colajacono's death, would you say I was delirious?

"All right, but I'm going to speak to Samantha Rossi's parents."

"Fine," Pasquali said.

"And I want to question the three Roma who are in jail for Samantha Rossi's murder."

Pasquali pursed his lips. "The public prosecutor's office will want to know why."

"Because of the link with Nadia. It's a new lead."

"Link?" Pasquali didn't want to take the R and the E into consideration. "There is no link."

"There's another thing," Balistreri said.

Pasquali stiffened. He had a sixth sense for serious problems. Balistreri told him about the motocross bike at Bella Blu and the one in Adrian's possession.

Pasquali listened in silence. "So?" he asked coldly when Balistreri had finished.

"So, it could be the same bike."

"Or they could be two of the hundreds of motocross bikes circulating in Rome."

"I don't often see motocross bikes in the center of Rome or riding down the Via Veneto where the nightclubs are."

"But you do sometimes see one, Balistreri. And as a good cop you know that's enough."

As usual, the change to his surname was a clear message: that was enough. But it wasn't.

"Colajacono was at Bella Blu on December 23, the night Nadia went there and the night Camarà died."

Long moments of silence passed in which the things unsaid weighed as heavily as those said openly.

"I have something to say to you," Pasquali said at last.

Balistreri waited expectantly. He had a feeling he knew what it was going to be.

"I know you've gotten very close with Linda Nardi in recent months. I suppose you saw the little article that was published January 5."

Balistreri looked implacably at the paper Pasquali pushed toward him: IF A POLICEMAN DIES.

"Yes, I read it months later."

There was no need to tell him everything.

"And what did you think of it?"

"A remarkable coincidence," Balistreri suggested maliciously.

From the look Pasquali directed toward the stone angel on the balcony, Balistreri realized that his patience was wearing thin.

"If you read this piece in the light of what happened, doesn't it seem more like a warning than a theory?" Pasquali asked, shifting his gaze to Balistreri.

"If it was a warning it went completely unheeded."

"Who do you think was being warned?" Pasquali asked, staring directly at him.

Balistreri was aware of the danger, but he was no longer disposed to be cautious. It was as if his brush with death on the hill, Coppola's death, and Giovanna Sordi's suicide were dragging him back to his true nature, the one that the weight of remorse and time had crushed.

"Let's say, as a hypothesis, that the article was meant for whoever ordered the ambush on Colajacono and Tatò, except that it came outside the time limit," Balistreri replied.

Pasquali looked like a corpse. "Ambush? But if all the reconstructions say that Colajacono and Tatò decided to go to Vasile's farmhouse to find more proof and by chance bumped into the four Romanians that were there to make them disappear?"

"What if Colajacono and Tatò were two accomplices who had become inconvenient? They could have been lured there by one of their informants who wanted the four Romanians to kill them," Balistreri countered.

Pasquali gave him an icy look. "Did you dictate the article to Nardi?"

Balistreri feared what might happen to Linda if Pasquali thought it had been her idea.

"I suggested the idea for the article, yes."

Not a muscle moved in Pasquali's face. He was waiting for an explanation.

"I didn't explain the reasons behind my suspicions. She agreed to publish it in exchange for a future exclusive."

Pasquali picked up the telephone and spoke to Antonella. "Could you make me a cup of herbal tea, the one for an acid stomach, please?"

"I suppose you'd prefer something stronger," he said to Balistreri, pointing to the bar.

"When I was recovering I stopped drinking before dinnertime. If Antonella could bring me some tea, I'd appreciate it."

Pasquali called Antonella and asked her for another cup of tea.

It was as if Balistreri's confession had calmed their souls. Showing the weaknesses of their respective stomachs created a reciprocal act of trust, no matter how minimal. Two policemen who suffered from heartburn and fear.

"Colajacono was involved because he was useful, and then he became a scapegoat. But Coppola's unexpected appearance on the hill, and then mine, turned him into a hero," Balistreri explained.

"I can accept the first part," Pasquali conceded. "Someone got Colajacono involved because of someone. This someone wanted to be certain someone on his side would be inside the police station to greet Ramona if she went to report Nadia missing."

"Pasquali, here's what's really bothering me: the day I stopped by the station and confronted Colajacono, he was totally calm, even when I accused him of having taken Marchese and Cutugno's shift so he could delay Ramona's report. No reaction—he was imperturbable. But then I said something to him."

The two cups of steaming liquid arrived. Pasquali gestured to him to stop. "Let me have a sip of this herbal tea to settle my stomach before you tell me what you said to him. In fact, wait a second while I drink it, and I'll tell me myself."

He sipped at the herbal tea, then took off his glasses and massaged his temples. "You told him about Vasile's wrist."

You're a damned bastard, but you've got a great brain.

"When I told Colajacono about Vasile's sprained wrist, he shook with fear. He suddenly realized they were framing him. He had no alibi for the hour between six and seven, the hour in which they kidnapped Nadia, probably because someone had sent him somewhere else. He had only Tatò, who they suggested to him as company for the night precisely because he couldn't give a credible alibi. And he certainly didn't know that Nadia would end up dead. He must have thought it was another politician being blackmailed, just like the deputy mayor, De Rossi, had been blackmailed."

"You think they ambushed him on purpose?" Pasquali was shocked.

"Yes. First they told him Nadia was going to perform a little service for a politician. Then they told him that shepherd got drunk and killed her. They gave him enough information to track down Vasile, so he'd look good in the end. He was happy. But suddenly he realized that it hadn't been the shepherd. He knew very well who it was, but he also knew that he risked being framed himself. He'd already been forced to be seen with Ramona at the Cristal to blackmail Augusto De Rossi. Now we also know that they'd deliberately called him to the Bella Blu on December 23 when Nadia was there. You can imagine how Colajacono must have felt. They'd pulled the rug out from under him."

Pasquali frowned. "And you surmise that he turned on those who were giving the orders and they decided to silence him. Linda Nardi's article was supposed to help avert this situation, but there wasn't enough time. But you easily could have avoided telling Colajacono about Vasile's wrist."

Three policemen, including Coppola, are dead because I wanted to punish Colajacono for stripping Linda.

"They'd told Colajacono that all he had to do was stop the police from searching for Nadia for those two or three days when she would be used to blackmail a politician. I discovered his game and he called somebody. They arranged to meet him at the farmhouse to calm him and Tatò down. But he got there before the appointed time to look for evidence that would put the blame on someone else."

"Meaning what?" Pasquali looked pale, and his pallor worried Balistreri.

"Forensics found no tracks on the dirt road to Vasile's farmhouse except for those of the Giulia GT and the cars driven by Colajacono and Piccolo."

"So I read. Another reason for ruling out the Invisible Man. How would he have gotten away from there? Did he fly?"

"He could have walked down the hill, though it was dark and cold. But there was also the hill to climb to get to the Giulia GT. I agree it's too complicated."

"Therefore no Invisible Man—a mere invention of Vasile."

"So, if we count out Vasile because of his sprained wrist, who killed Nadia?"

"The other shepherd, his accomplice in the burglaries," Pasquali replied quickly.

"Could be, but then Colajacono wouldn't have been scared. Things went wrong and he knew it. He and Tatò went looking for the tire tracks from the motocross bike, but they were lying in wait to kill them."

Pasquali paused to reflect. "Forensics would have found the bike's tracks," he murmured, confused.

"Not if the bike went off the road. A motocross bike is handy that way."

"So your theory would be that the Invisible Man went up the hill on the morning of December 24 on the motocross bike, took the Giulia GT and left the bike, then came back around seven in the evening. with Nadia in the Giulia, killed her, and then departed on the bike."

Balistreri said nothing. There was an anomaly in that reconstruction, but this wasn't the moment to mention it.

Pasquali wanted a conclusion. "Where does all this lead?"

You know very well where it leads. To that wonderful example of integration, enlightened entrepreneur and benefactor of the destitute Mr. Marius Hagi.

Balistreri waited silently. It wasn't up to him to make the connection. If someone was resistant to logic, it mean he had a different agenda.

Pasquali was a man of great experience and great intelligence. He knew when the game was up and it was necessary to bow out without incurring catastrophic losses.

"I'll find a way to persuade the public prosecutor to let you speak to the three Roma who attacked Samantha Rossi. You go ahead and talk to her parents and find out whether there's a link with Alina Hagi. But don't mention the letters R and E to anyone, especially not Linda Nardi."

"I'll keep my distance from her." As he said it, he became aware that he had no choice but to keep that promise.

. . . .

He was glad Samantha Rossi's parents had moved away. His visit to San Valente had already reopened uncomfortable memories. Going back to see the house where Samantha was born and grew up wasn't top of his life's wish list.

They received him in the early summer evening, after working hours. It was a modern house: new, white, and clinical, like a hospital for anaesthetizing grief.

Anna Rossi was a good-looking woman in her forties. Samantha resembled her mother in her features, while she'd taken her height and bearing from her father. They welcomed Balistreri with cold politeness; after all, he believed the Roma boys to be innocent and had made the great blunder.

Balistreri knew he had to keep the visit as short as possible. His presence would only deepen their grief.

"I'm not here about your daughter, at least not directly," he said.

While they were looking at him bewildered, he placed the photo sent him by Monsignor Lato on the table.

Anna Rossi's sad look was lost in a memory that for a moment softened the bitter twist to her mouth.

"Alina," she said in a flash.

Her husband looked at her perplexed. "Alina who?"

She gave him an affectionate look. "She was my best friend at the beginning of the 1980s. I've spoken about her sometimes—she was the one who died on her moped a year before we met."

"And you saw Alina Hagi regularly at that time, Mrs. Rossi?" Balistreri asked.

Anna Rossi plunged into her memories.

"She was an extraordinary person. She looked like a fragile little doll with blond hair, but she was a bundle of positive energy. Alina could organize anything and get anyone to pitch in, from the orphans to us volunteers."

"How did you meet her?"

"I came to San Valente through my boyfriend, who was studying law and helped out with the orphans' immigration papers in the parish. He introduced me to Cardinal Alessandrini, who introduced me to Father Paul. That was in 1981, and Alina was my instructor in the training course. We became fast friends. She worked full-time there, but I only came when I had free time."

"Did you know her husband as well?"

"A little. He came to pick her up in the evenings. He was very serious, not very communicative, but he was smart and determined. Then I saw less and less of him. The last time was at Alina's funeral." A shadow crossed Anna Rossi's face.

"At the funeral you spoke to Alina's uncle, a priest. Do you remember?"

"Yes. I was shattered, and he consoled me. Then I told him about something that had happened a few days before."

"When you saw the bruises on Alina's arms."

"They were really bad. She said she'd fallen, but I knew it wasn't true. I asked her whether her husband had done it, and she denied it."

"Did Alina get along with her husband?"

"At the beginning, but it seemed to me that later the relationship fell apart. I don't know what happened, but as time went on she just didn't talk about him."

"Had you been in touch the night she died?" Balistreri asked.

"Yes, she called me. She asked if she could come and sleep at my place. She'd never done that, and I didn't ask why. She got into the accident on her way."

"Was she involved with someone?" Balistreri asked.

Anna Rossi laughed quietly. "Alina Hagi was a saint, Captain Balistreri, a very devout Catholic. She'd have died rather than betray her husband."

"Have you ever seen or heard from Marius Hagi?"

"No. When Alina died, it was as if I'd lost a sister. And then Samantha, too."

Her husband put an arm around her shoulders. He tried distracting her. "What's this about your old boyfriend?"

"Francesco? He was only a boyfriend, and he turned out to be up to no good. It was Alina who helped me see the reality; it was thanks to Alina I found the strength to leave him. We were a really good group of volunteers, you know? We were true believers. Francesco, on the other hand, was using the volunteer service as political leverage for his career, nothing more."

Impulsively, Anna Rossi got up, crossed the living room, and rummaged around in a drawer. "Here we are," she said, lifting out a photograph. "This is from 1982."

She handed a photo to Balistreri. There was the San Valente church in the background. He peered at the smiling group of young men and women. He recognized Father Paul, Valerio, Alina Hagi, and Anna Rossi. Next to Anna Rossi, with an arm around her shoulders, just as her husband's arm was around her shoulders now, stood a young man neatly dressed in a jacket and tie. He was younger then, but there was no mistaking Francesco Ajello, now an attorney and the manager of the Bella Blu nightclub and ENT shareholder.

Balistreri decided to keep his questions to a minimum.

"How did this boyfriend of yours become involved with the group of volunteers?"

"This boy here introduced him—they were friends."

Her finger pointed to the skinny figure of Valerio Bona.

Many remarkable coincidences, as Pasquali would have said.

. . . .

It was a Friday evening. Pasquali had probably already left to spend the weekend in his hometown, and there was no need to call him. Balistreri immediately ruled out the idea of contacting Corvu. Ajello's appearance on the scene put ENT at the center of the case again, and Ajello was ENT. And ENT was trouble. He had already lost Coppola, and Corvu had witnessed Belhrouz's demise in Dubai.

He knew the struggle between caution and the truth was the struggle between what he had become and what he had been. Now he had to find a way forward that left the living still living and brought justice for the dead.

He had taken Father Paul and Valerio Bona's cell phone numbers after their meeting. He called Paul first, since he thought he knew where he was.

"Captain Balistreri! We haven't spoken in years and now you keep calling me. Would you like to meet up?"

Balistreri could hear the voices of children in the background, along with the clattering of plates. They were sitting down to dinner at San Valente.

"Could I come by now?"

"We're about to eat. I'll set a place for you."

Paul greeted him in front of the large illuminated house. Several children were serving the dishes prepared by the cook in the kitchen. They were waiting for him to start. Paul pointed out an empty place between a little Asian boy and a small African girl who must have been between eleven and twelve years old.

They were serving delicious spaghetti with tomato sauce. The two children were joking between themselves and stealing sly glances at Balistreri. After a while, the little Asian boy plucked up the courage to say something.

"My name's Luk. What's your name?"

"Michele. I'm a friend of Paul's. You speak Italian very well."

"I've been here three years, thanks to Paul. He and the cardinal saved me."

"And where are you from, Luk?"

"Cambodia."

The girl tugged at Balistreri's sleeve. She was a beautiful child with enormous eyes. "My name's Bina. I'm from Rwanda, and I'm older than Luk."

They spoke to him of their lives in San Valente with no mention of the first part of their lives. Balistreri noticed every so often that Paul was watching him. For half an hour he managed to forget all about rapes, murders, Hagi, Ajello, and ENT. It was as if he'd been transported into another dimension where the miseries of everyday life had been wiped out by the innocence and happiness of these orphans. The chaotic passion of 1982 had been transformed into an efficient organization that dispensed only happiness. He could see why Paul was proud of the place, and deservedly so.

When fruit had been served, Paul signaled to him to move outside. They sat under the usual tree in the flickering light of a lantern. A girl of about thirteen brought over a tray with two cups of espresso. Everything at San Valente had changed; everything had grown, including Father Paul.

"Coffee and a cigarette?" Paul proposed, confirming those changes.

It wasn't decaf and it was excellent. Balistreri accepted a cigarette from Paul, his sixth of the day, after years of keeping to his limit.

"I went to visit Anna Rossi, Alina Hagi's friend."

Paul nodded. "I read about her daughter's death. Cardinal Alessandrini called to comfort her."

"Do you remember anything about Anna Rossi's boyfriend?"

A slight, barely perceptible shadow crossed Father Paul's face. "Francesco Ajello. He worked with Valerio for the count. He never came here; he worked in the office. He was studying law and helped the orphans get their papers."

"Did the count introduce him to you?"

"I think so. Valerio knew him—he introduced him to the count, who had a word with Cardinal Alessandrini about him. The same as Elisa Sordi."

"Did you like him?"

Father Paul lit another cigarette and Balistreri accepted his seventh without giving it a second thought.

"You tend to forget, Captain Balistreri, I'm first and foremost a priest."

"But you were a young man then, with likes and dislikes, same as anyone else. Don't you remember?"

Paul shook his head.

"What I said to you about Manfredi was poisoned by anger. I've lived to regret those words."

"Can you tell me anything about Francesco Ajello?"

"I was a confused young man. My opinion wouldn't be of much help to you."

Balistreri decided not to press him further. They were forecasting a night and weekend of warm temperatures. There wasn't a breath of wind in the dark of San Valente's garden. The children had gone to bed, the lights and the cries extinguished. Around the lamp fluttered a lazy moth.

He left Father Paul and that unbearable peace with the feeling of having entered the darkest of labyrinths.

SATURDAY, JULY 15, 2006

Morning

VALERIO BONA HAD ALWAYS loved the sea in Ostia, where Romans went to the beach. His parents had taken him there every summer since he was little. It was there that he had met Elisa Sordi in 1981, when she was seventeen and he was eighteen, a recent high school graduate who had just enrolled in computer science at the university. He wore his hair long that summer, down to his shoulders, and they frequently took long walks by the sea together. Then autumn arrived. Elisa started her last year of high school, and he was starting his first year at the university. Things changed. For him, the friendship had turned to love, but not for her.

Balistreri called him at eight Saturday morning. Valerio was preparing his dinghy for a solo outing, just himself and the sea. It was a moment of peace, when memory mingled with the lapping of the waves on the hull and the whistle of the wind. But Balistreri wanted to see him right away, and Valerio felt obliged to wait for him.

The weekend traffic was very heavy. Balistreri preferred to take the Metro line. He stepped out onto the seafront surrounded by bathers off to the beaches. Valerio was waiting for him on his moped. "I've got a helmet for you as well. Let's go to the harbor—we can talk in the boat."

Ever since the summer of 1970 Balistreri had avoided going out in boats as much as possible. He realized, however, that this would be the best place to talk to Valerio Bona. Valerio hoisted mainsail and jib and chose a close-reach course that allowed a little coolness and a seat in the shade of the sails. In ten minutes they were out on the open sea and the sounds from the crowded beach had become faint.

The cockpit was plastered with photos of Valerio at different ages at the helm of various boats. The two odd ones were one of Pope John Paul II and one of Italy's 2006 World Cup-winning team.

Valerio was relaxed at the helm. The gold crucifix hanging from a chain around his neck gleamed against his sunburned skin. He was completely at ease on the boat, as if he were inside a shell that still allowed him to control his surroundings. The insecure, awkward kid had been left on the shore.

Balistreri tried to relax, but the silence was broken by his worst memory. "So, here we are," he said. He was lighting a new cigarette every five minutes. The iron-clad rules he had set for himself were starting to rust and crumble.

"When you came to San Valente the other day, Paul and I were sure it was about Elisa's mother's suicide," Valerio said, looking out at the sea. "Instead it was about Alina Hagi. We were stunned."

Valerio Bona was incapable of forgetting. Inventing a new life is a justifiable defense after a great tragedy, and he had tried: his degree, IBM, and a career. But something had pushed him back; something stopped him from going too far away.

While Paul had been a kid back then and in time had matured into an adult, in 1982 Valerio Bona was already an adult, so he could only grow old.

"Do you both think I don't care about Elisa Sordi and her mother?" Balistreri asked.

Valerio seemed put off by Balistreri's directness.

"No, no," he murmured. "We were just surprised. But you're here about Alina Hagl, I imagine."

"And about her friend Anna Rossi and her boyfriend at the time."

A long silence.

"We're going to come about—watch out for the boom," Valerio said at last.

After the maneuver, Balistreri found himself with the sun in his eyes.

"You introduced Francesco Ajello to the count, right?" he asked, shading his eyes from the sun.

"Yes, I introduced him to the count, who offered him a position as an intern with the law firm that looked after his properties, the same one where I worked on the first PCs."

"Where did you meet him?"

"Right here in Ostia, during a series of regattas for two-man crews in 420s. He came from a wealthy family, had the nicest boat, and was looking for a good helmsman. The sailing club put us in touch and we tried several outings. It turned out we made a good team. We won eight of the ten regattas and the title in the summer of 1981."

"Why did you introduce him to the count?"

"Francesco was very smart and was studying for a law degree. He knew that the law firm that took care of the count's business was looking for an intern, and he wanted the experience."

"And after several months the Count introduced him to Cardinal Alessandrini?"

"Yes, the cardinal wanted a legal assistant to work for free on the orphanage's paperwork. The count introduced him to Francesco, who was more than happy to lend a hand."

"Generous of him."

"A lot of people, including Paul, said he was just a social climber. The fact is, he was very smart."

"And he had a girlfriend, Anna Rossi."

Valerio thought for a moment. "Francesco was pretty casual with women. Yes, Anna Rossi was his steady girlfriend, but probably not the only one. He was a certain type."

"Someone who tried to get every woman he met into bed? That type?"

"Only the attractive ones," Valerio said, almost admiringly.

"Was Elisa Sordi one of the women he tried to get into bed?"

Valerio lost control of the boat for a second. The sails lost wind and began to flap. The boat turned and the sun was no longer in his eyes, and when he looked at Valerio Bona he saw the deeply lined face of an old man.

Valerio got control of the boat and himself. "Elisa was off-limits. And I don't think she liked Francesco much."

Returning to Rome on the train, surrounded again by beachgoers, Balistreri fell asleep. The sun, the wind, the sea, and too many cigarettes had taken their toll. In his dreams, he met Linda Nardi in a place where there were families all around them. He looked at her breasts, and the vertical crease appeared in the middle of her brow, and then Linda Nardi's face was replaced by the sweet and childlike face of Elisa Sordi.

Afternoon

Balistreri was surprised that Count Tommaso dei Banchi di Aglieno agreed to see him right away. Either he didn't bear a grudge or he was simply curious. Most likely the latter. For his part, Balistreri would happily have skipped the meeting altogether, but it was unavoidable. He remembered the incompatible feelings of respect and repulsion the count stirred in him. Moreover, the man was the living memory of his most egregious investigative failure.

When it became clear the investigation had become a shameful mess, the count had taken his leave of him, along with his boss Teodori, with the same icy contempt he had shown for them from the start. It was a contempt mixed with the commiseration that superior beings absentmindedly display to imbeciles. The humiliation that accompanied that contempt had haunted him for years.

The residential complex on Via della Camilluccia was even nicer than he remembered. The trees had grown taller; the two buildings had recently been repainted.

The wide green gate through which Elisa Sordi had exited for the last time a little before the 1982 World Cup final was covered in ivy, as were the concierge's house and the gatehouse next to it.

Naturally, Gina Giansanti was no longer the concierge. Instead, the gate was manned by a young immigrant in uniform. It was hard to believe that this complex was located in the same city where Casilino 900 existed, the same city where Nadia's broken body had been hauled up from the bottom of a well.

Before entering, Balistreri smoked a cigarette. He remembered the strict ban on smoking inside that gate.

"The count is waiting for you, Captain Balistreri. You can park by the fountain," the young concierge informed him pleasantly.

Democracy has made its way inside. The count must have softened in his old age.

The sun illuminated the twin penthouses: the count's and the cardinal's. Balistreri drove across the grounds, circled the fountain, and parked his old Fiat in a shady corner beside an Aston Martin—a later model than the one he remembered. Behind the swimming pool and tennis courts sat Building B. The blinds on all its windows were closed. Balistreri's gaze fell on Elisa Sordi's window, and he quickly looked away.

He entered the small elevator in the lobby of Building A and pressed the button for the penthouse. On the landing, the gloomy prints of ancient Rome had been replaced by fine photographs: bright-green highlands, a lake that looked as broad as a sea, a river that was almost white.

The count's personal secretary, a young man wearing jeans and a Lacoste shirt, welcomed him. The residence that had always been dark, with its curtains drawn and the blinds pulled down, was now completely open to the sun. The heavy curtains were gone.

They crossed through two rooms. There was no trace of the black leather sofas and the disturbing tapestries—they had been replaced with modern furniture and mirrors.

The young man ushered him into a small air-conditioned sitting room furnished with two armchairs. The blinds were open.

"The count will be with you in a moment. May I offer you something to drink?"

Balistreri asked for coffee and sat down. He was breaking rules left and right, but decaffeinated coffee was no longer enough for him. The

French doors looked onto a large terrace. A table shaded by a large umbrella sat outside with a computer on it.

"Captain Balistreri."

He hadn't heard the count come in. Count Tommaso dei Banchi di Aglieno stood straight as a ramrod. His smooth hair, combed straight back, was only slightly thinner and sparser than it had been. A few gray streaks broke up the black. A short, well-trimmed gray beard had replaced his goatee. His double-breasted blue suit was impeccable. The surroundings might have changed, but the man himself looked the same.

"Count." Balistreri held out his hand, which the other man shook with the strong grip he remembered well.

"We'll be undisturbed here. Do sit down."

The count displayed not a bit of surprise, annoyance, or hostility. In front of him sat the man who, twenty-four years earlier, had unjustly accused his son of murder, causing his wife to kill herself. But nothing in his calm manner indicated that he was still chewing over the past. He was probably sick of thinking about it, though surely he was curious to know the reason for this visit.

"Thank you for seeing me on such short notice."

"I'm not as busy these days as I was back then, Captain Balistreri. Also, I hope the circumstances will be less unpleasant."

"I won't take up too much of your time."

"Please, it's not a problem. I'm a retired landowner. I keep a hand in things, but I'm officially retired. Also, I admit, I have something to ask you. The events of recent months interest me a great deal, although they don't come as a total surprise."

Balistreri decided to let that insinuation lie there, untouched.

"A war was about to break out between Romania and Italy," the count said, seemingly amused by the thought.

"And all it took to avert it was a soccer victory," Balistreri said.

The count nodded. "We live in a superficial world. This country's values lie buried under the garbage the sanitation workers leave in the middle of the street when they go on strike."

Things change around us, but not inside us.

"I know you haven't been involved in politics for many years."

The count smiled. He commanded the same respect as he always had, but not the same fear. He really did have the air of the retired landowner he claimed to be.

"After everything that happened in 1982, I gave up trying to bring back the monarchy to a country where no one would dream of being king. I was destined to fail, Balistreri."

"I can't believe you're afraid of a fight, Count."

"It was an unequal fight. The Christians were already democrats, the Communists have become democrats, and with the Vatican willing to turn a blind eye, everyone is democratically becoming wealthy. Too many challengers for an old aristocratic idealist."

Balistreri began to feel uneasy. It was annoying to share even a part of this man's ideas. Finding them in some way similar to his mother's was unacceptable and revolting. It was on these occasions that Alberto, always the respectful one, was the rebel.

Don't trust the Catholics. Theirs is a religion founded on resentment, bad conscience, and repentance. Don't trust the morality of the weak. It only distances you from life's joy.

The count was completely relaxed. He spoke as if they were old friends.

"I imagine you're not here to discuss politics with me, Captain Balistreri. The suicide of that girl's mother must have reopened a wound for you."

Here he was after twenty-four years, a few days after Giovanna Sordi's suicide. Father Paul, Valerio Bona, and now the count—how could they think he wanted talk about anything else?

"Actually, I'm here about another matter."

The Count politely raised an eyebrow. "Something to do with your recent adventures?"

"To tell the truth, at this point I don't know. Maybe."

The man smiled. "I see that time has given you the wisdom to accept doubt. That's one of the few advantages of growing older."

"I have to reconstruct several links from the past that partly concern you."

"Before you do that, Captain Balistreri, I'd like to understand how I can help you."

"I'm a policeman, Count. I'm conducting a very confidential investigation."

"But you know that I am a most confidential person. And I could help you better if I know what we are speaking about."

Balistreri decided that, leaving aside ENT and the incised letters, he could risk it.

"I'm trying to track down a ghost," he said.

"Interesting," the count said. He pressed the button on a remote control. "This room has a smoke extractor. Smoke if it will help you think."

The count enjoyed his astonishment. A little hesitantly, Balistreri lit a cigarette, nervously awaiting a reaction.

Instead, the count listened in silence to the summary of Nadia's kidnapping and murder. Balistreri carefully avoided any mention of ENT and Colajacono's possible involvement.

"It was Alina, the deceased wife of Marius Hagi, who led me back to the church of San Valente," Balistreri explained.

The count was silent, his deep black eyes unreadable.

"Yes, I remember Alina Hagi. Cardinal Alessandrini introduced me to her one day together with her husband, Marius. Two very special young people, both blessed with great energy."

Balistreri knew it would be useless to ask direct questions. He remained silent and enjoyed his cigarette.

"I'll have my accountants check my records for you. I think I gave Marius Hagi some work, as I did with everyone, perhaps too readily."

Balistreri shifted uncomfortably in his chair. It would be difficult to discuss Anna Rossi and Francesco Ajello without showing his cards.

"Do you happen to know whether Alina Hagi was particularly close to any of the volunteers?"

The count gave him another smile. "I never saw Hagi's wife again. As you know, unlike Ulla, I kept far away from San Valente and Catholic circles. However, I imagine you've already questioned Father Paul and Valerio Bona in this matter."

"Yes, I've spoken to them. And they mentioned a very close friend of Alina's whose boyfriend was one of your employees."

"What does that have to do with the death of this Nadia or with Marius Hagi?"

Balistreri said the only thing he could say. "We're not convinced that Alina Hagi's death was completely accidental. A few days before she died, her friend noticed her arms were covered with bruises. We don't know if Hagi was responsible, but if we find evidence of violence in Marius Hagi's past, that would support the theory that he was a party to the crime that took place this Christmas."

It was a logical explanation. It wasn't perfect, but it would do. The count mulled it over in silence, as if he were calling up a distant memory. Finally, he spoke.

"Captain Balistreri, if you're not in a hurry I'd like to show you something before we continue this conversation. Now that the sun is setting we can go outside."

The French windows that opened onto the terrace surrounded by tall plants were wide open, and the sun's setting rays fell on the parquet flooring. Outside, Balistreri saw the parasol, the work table with the PC, and the powerful shoulders.

A tomb on which I put a lid that was wasn't strong enough to last.

Hearing the sound of footsteps, Manfredi turned around. Balistreri turned into a pillar of salt. The disfigured youth was an adult with a normal face and calm demeanor. There was no angioma, no harelip, no swollen eyelid. His black hair had no need to hide anything. The plastic surgery had worked a miracle in aesthetics; the rest must have been worked by the medicine of the mind. Now Ulla's angelic face could be clearly seen beside the aquiline nose and features of the count. The slender lines of the scars could just about be seen, but the surgeons had done an incredible job. His powerful muscular structure was the same as it was twenty-four years ago, now it was covered with a suntan that must have been natural. The ugly duckling had become a normal man, handsome even in the contrast between his father's marked features and his mother's delicateness.

Manfredi rose to come and meet them. He had grown a little in height and was taller than Balistreri by half a head. He held out his hand, and Balistreri shook it in silence.

"I'm glad to see you, Captain Balistreri." His voice was quiet, soft and deep. He spoke soothingly, like a doctor with a good bedside manner. His eyes were bright and clear. His manner was unruffled, as if he were greeting an old acquaintance, not one of the pack of hounds that had once hunted him down.

Balistreri decided to be sincere. "I'm glad to see what I see."

The count said, "I'll leave the two of you to catch up while I go look for a few things in my records."

They sat down at the table. Balistreri stole a glance at the computer screen. *Paris: Tenth Conference on the Pathology of Infection. Presentation by Professor Manfredi dei Banchi di Aglieno, Nairobi University.*

"I'm presenting our latest research," Manfredi explained. "The Paris conference starts on Monday, then I have another in Frankfurt the following Monday. After that I go back to Africa."

"I understand you've been living in Kenya for many years now."

"Since August 1982. Our family has a large farm and estates on the border with Uganda. I got my degree in South Africa, and now I practice medicine in Nairobi. Look."

He clicked, and up came a photo that showed Manfredi in a white lab coat surrounded by hundreds of smiling people. He was standing in front of a new white building with a large pair of scissors, ready to cut the ribbon. The caption read, *Nairobi Hospital: Opening of the New Infectious Disease Unit. December 25, 2005.* That had just been a few months earlier.

"With my father's financial help, we've built a new unit for the care of infectious diseases. Unfortunately, in Africa diseases grow and multiply just as quickly as their trees and mosquitoes do. We're trying to turn things around there. Of course, when I have the opportunity to attend a conference in Europe, I make sure to stop off in Rome and visit my father."

The more Balistreri observed Manfredi, the more he wondered how such a transformation was even possible. Could a full-grown human being turn into a different human being entirely? Because that was what Manfredi was—an entirely different person.

Manfredi spoke evenly as he told his story. After Ulla's death, his father had sent him away from Rome to the family's estate in Kenya.

Subsequently, he had entrusted him to the care of the best psychiatrists and plastic surgeons in South Africa. Then he'd studied medicine in Cape Town. Upon earning his degree, he'd begun conducting research into diseases among the local populations in the desert and highland villages. There was no hint of any personal attachments in the story. He didn't mention a wife or children, only his father.

"I'm sorry to be so blunt, but the change is just amazing," Balistreri said.

"It's a miracle," Manfredi agreed. "And maybe if all those other things hadn't happened I'd still be up in my room in the dark with my posters, my angry music, and my disfigured face."

"You still paid too high a price," Balistreri said.

Manfredi let the statement pass by, along with flight of the swallows over the terrace lost in the greenery and last shadows of the dying sun.

"My mother was an unhappy person. Marrying my father had been a big mistake, but she was Catholic, so she wouldn't think of divorcing him."

"Your mother was a victim of several people, starting with me. Can you ever forgive me?"

Manfredi's blue eyes wandered over beyond the trees toward the twin building. The windows on the third floor were all closed. Balistreri tried not to look and lit another cigarette.

"I haven't forgiven you," Manfredi said. His voice betrayed a trace of the old arrogance. "What have you been doing all these years, Captain Balistreri?"

"Not sleeping well, that's for sure."

"What brings you back here on another search for the truth?"

"Giovanna Sordi."

"I figured. You owe her even more than you owe me."

At that moment the count came back with two pieces of paper. He handed Balistreri the first. It was an invoice made out to Marius Hagi.

"He worked for me only once, in the spring of 1982. He organized a visit to Auschwitz for my wife. Ulla had begun to study the persecution of the Jews. She was interested in understanding the role the Catholic Church played in either stopping or supporting the Nazis. Hagi had contacts in the area."

"Did your wife go?"

"Yes, in May. Anyway, we never used Mr. Hagi again. I suppose we had no reason to."

Balistreri glanced at the other sheet.

"Here's the information I've got about other person you wanted to ask me about," the count said.

"I didn't mention anyone else," Balistreri protested.

"There was no need to," the Count replied.

He handed him an account sheet for Francesco Ajello. It was a decidedly longer summary than the one on Hagi, with the description and date of every piece of work—all items regarding the count's property. Every so often a payment was mentioned. The work began in January 1982 and broke off in November 1985, after nearly four years. The count anticipated his question.

"Ajello graduated and went into practice for himself."

"And since then?" Balistreri asked.

"Since then, nothing on a professional level. Every year I get a Christmas card from him."

"Did he ever work here?"

"No, never. This is my home. As you know, I'm a private man. Ajello worked at the law firm that handled my business."

"Did you ever meet his girlfriend, Alina Hagi's friend?"

"No," said the count. "I never knew much about Ajello's personal life."

"I saw Alina Hagi's friend once." They both turned to Manfredi.

"You knew Alina Hagi?" Balistreri asked in surprise.

"Not really, but I ran into her here and she introduced herself. She was very kind. I think she was moved by my looks."

"And what was Alina Hagi doing in your house?" Balistreri asked.

"My mother had invited her over. She wanted some advice about traveling to Auschwitz. She was with another young woman—probably the friend you're talking about."

"Do you remember her name?"

Manfredi shook his head. "No, she never told me her name. But I remember she was the opposite of Alina Hagi. One was small and blond, the other tall and dark."

It was incredible. The one tenuous thread he had followed without much conviction was now unraveling into thousands of others all linked to a past that he had buried so deep. And those threads, shaped like a spider's web, were dragging him back in time toward a memory that he'd almost succeeded in blotting out completely.

The people in the present—Hagi, Ajello, Samantha Rossi's mother— were now getting mixed up with those in the past. He wondered where the line of demarcation was, if there was one. When he left the residential complex on Via della Camilluccia, he had the same feeling he'd had many years before—that the truth was at the same time both very close and very far away.

· · · ·

Returning home he passed through the center, full of people crowding into bars, restaurants, and theaters. It was a splendid Saturday evening in summer; everyone was out to have fun. He looked over at St. Peter's dome, toward where Linda Nardi lived. He picked up his cell phone then put it down for a while. Then he dialed Angelo Dioguardi's number. There was no answer.

Before going to sleep, he indulged in an old habit he'd broken many years earlier: a nightcap of whiskey, straight up, and a cigarette.

SUNDAY, JULY 16, 2006

Morning

HE SLEPT LITTLE AND badly, no more than two hours. It was the heat, the sounds of festive nights, the mosquitoes buzzing around, and the annoying thoughts he couldn't manage to eject from his mind. His stomach was burning from the whiskey. His head hurt from all of the cigarettes.

He got up at dawn feeling terrible. From Mrs. Fadlun's oven came the smell of baking cakes. On Saturdays Jewish people rested, but on Sundays they worked. He took a cold shower and gulped down a coffee with no sugar. He immediately smoked a cigarette, then got himself ready for the office.

His need for action increased at the same rate as he was physically and mentally tired, which was doubly dangerous.

At seven in the morning Rome was silent, full of sunshine, and absolutely deserted after a Saturday night of partying. Few bars had raised their rolling shutters at that hour. He bought a paper and drank another coffee, sitting down at a table to smoke a second cigarette. It would either be extremely easy to speak to Cardinal Alessandrini or impossible. Corvu would have found a way.

His deputy arrived at the office at seven thirty. He had told him a thousand times that on Sundays he could take it a little easier, but Corvu never listened. And with him came Giulia Piccolo, who immediately retreated into her cubicle.

Corvu's manner was more resolute than usual. "Sir, I've thought a lot about this and I have to say I'm not absolutely in agreement," he said, nodding to Piccolo in her cubicle.

"You're right," Balistreri replied. "Call her in. I hope she's gotten the message."

Corvu gave him a surprised look, smiled, and quickly went to get her.

Piccolo came in with her eyes lowered. "Captain, I'm sorry. Please accept my apologies."

"All right, Piccolo. Let's move on. I have to share some things with the two of you."

They leaned in closer with enthusiasm and listened attentively. They knew the Elisa Sordi case was still considered Homicide's worst botched job and that their boss was indirectly involved in the humiliation of its remaining unsolved. Piccolo was also told about how Belhrouz died. The only thing Balistreri kept to himself was the question over Colajacono's death. He needed to break his feeling of isolation, but not to that extent.

Corvu immediately called his trusted friend at the Vatican. After a few minutes, Balistreri was speaking to Cardinal Alessandrini's personal assistant.

"Via official channels, it would be impossible, as you well know, Captain. But the cardinal will see you informally. He'll be at the Pontifical Lateran University at ten thirty this morning, before the Angelus. After that, he leaves with His Holiness for Castelgandolfo."

Balistreri nodded. "Okay, while I'm out, you two start filling in some answers on this damned blackboard. And find Ornella Corona. I want to speak to her before I see Ajello."

"With your permission, I'd like to take some time off this afternoon so I can take Natalya out to lunch. She's leaving tomorrow to visit her family in Ukraine." Corvu appeared to be holding his breath as he waited for Balistreri's answer.

Balistreri said, "Why don't you go to Ukraine with her? You really should see a bit of the world beyond Sardinia."

Corvu said, "But we're in the middle of an important investigation."

"Ask Natalya if she wants you to come," Piccolo said. "If she does, I'll be able to handle the investigation on my own for a few days."

Balistreri left at nine thirty and began to walk slowly to St. Peter's Square. The citizens of Rome were still asleep, but dozens of tourists were converging on the Vatican by foot and by bus for the papal blessing.

He arrived early. The cardinal's personal assistant ushered him into a large lecture hall filled with young priests of every race and nationality. It reminded him of the day he'd first met Alessandrini in his penthouse. The cardinal was up on the stage, handing out diplomas.

As opposed to the count, Cardinal Alessandrini had never made him feel uneasy but he rather irritated him more than anything else. In 1982 he had been a newly appointed cardinal; now he occupied one of the Vatican's highest positions. Alessandrini had to be around eighty, almost the same age as the new Pope. His hair was white, but his face beamed with the same intelligence and energy. Alessandrini saw him and, without worrying about protocol, gave him a small sign of welcome.

At ten thirty the hall emptied rapidly, and the cardinal beckoned him to come forward. "They're rushing to snag the best seats for the papal audience," he explained when he saw Balistreri watching the young priests swarm out of the room.

The Cardinal had his usual air of a thinking man who preferred action, greeting him as if they had seen each other every day over the past twenty-four years.

"I'm glad to see you in good health. I heard they almost performed last rites over you."

"I'm fine, Your Eminence. I was lucky."

Alessandrini smiled. He hadn't forgotten his verbal duels with the younger Balistreri, when he had tried to persuade him that only divine justice had the blessing of infallibility.

They sat behind the professorial chair. "I've thought a great deal about Elisa Sordi over the years," the Cardinal said, "and even more this week after her mother's suicide."

"I've thought about it myself, Eminence, and I haven't found a solution to the crime nor an excuse for my sins back then."

A shadow passed across the cardinal's face. "God forgives all sins if the repentance is sincere."

"But there are sins for which there's no redemption, isn't that so?"

"No, there's forgiveness and possible expiation for every sin. If you confessed and were really penitent, then any priest would absolve you."

Balistreri decided to change the subject.

"In any case, I must thank you for seeing me, Eminence. The agreement between Italy and the Vatican doesn't permit me to bother you. Besides, I'm embarrassed to tell you, but—"

"I'm happy to help. And I know you aren't here about Elisa Sordi. Paul already told me about your visits to San Valente."

"You should be proud of Father Paul. He's doing amazing work, just as you hoped he would one day."

"Paul already possessed an extraordinary soul all those years ago, but he was confused. We helped him channel his positive energy. I'm pleased you noticed."

"Valerio Bona seems to be a different story, though."

"Each individual has his own way of behaving. Valerio has his demons, as we all do. He's more troubled because he's more fragile."

The cardinal paused. He seemed to be thinking about something. "Alina Hagi. That's what brought you back to San Valente, isn't it?"

"Yes, Marius Hagi's wife."

"Marius Hagi. Isn't he connected to the men who shot you?"

"I see you're well informed. Hagi was the employer of the men who shot me, but he hasn't been implicated in their activities in any way."

"Is the death of that young Romanian woman, Nadia, connected to all of this?"

"Yes, Your Eminence, it is. We're trying to determine whether Mr. Hagi was a mild-mannered, hard-working young man or a violent one."

"Is there some kind of link to Elisa Sordi's death?" the cardinal asked.

The unexpected question shook Balistreri. He couldn't understand the reasoning behind it. And yet the cardinal wasn't the type to make inconclusive deductions.

"There's no evident link among these crimes. But some of the same people are involved in them, and not just Hagi. Father Paul probably told you about Anna Rossi and Francesco Ajello: two people who were connected with San Valente and the residential complex on Via della Camilluccia."

"They are two very different and separate places, Captain Balistreri."

The atmosphere changed slightly. The cardinal looked as if something had suddenly occurred to him—something troubling.

"Separate but connected, Your Eminence. And at least three people involved in these current events had something to do with San Valente, directly or indirectly."

"How do Anna Rossi and Francesco Ajello fit into your current investigation?"

Balistreri stared straight into his eyes. The cardinal knew the official response. They were dealing with a confidential investigation. Not even a close confidant of the pope could be informed.

Balistreri, however, decided to tell almost the whole truth. "Francesco Ajello runs the nightclub where Nadia spent the evening before she was killed."

"And Anna Rossi, Samantha's mother? Are Nadia's and Samantha's cases connected?"

He couldn't tell him that. It would have put the lives of his squad at risk. He was already mourning a member of his team. The cardinal might seem like a saint, but he was still a mortal man with a mortal man's weaknesses and secrets.

"I can't tell you that, Eminence."

The cardinal seemed more worried than offended. His eyes wandered over to the balcony where the pope would stand in a little over one hour. With the young priests gone, the room was silent, which was in keeping with the somber surroundings. Balistreri realized he was asking a lot, maybe too much.

The cardinal pushed up the sleeves of his red vestment, as if it were a sweatshirt he'd thrown on.

"You have your work cut out for you, Balistreri. I shall try to be less of a hindrance to you this time."

"Do you think you hindered the investigation back then, Eminence?" Balistreri asked, surprised.

Again, the cardinal looked distracted by distant memories. "Perhaps," he said, but he didn't give any further explanation.

"We had two different opinions. Yours turned out to be the correct one," Balistreri admitted.

"Yes, I'm still convinced it was. However, you wish to know from me whether Hagi was a gentle man or a violent one. I honestly don't know. I saw him with Alina on no more than two or three occasions."

"Still, you must have had a personal opinion."

Alessandrini smiled at him. "I see you haven't changed much. I believe all those years ago we discussed how dangerous personal opinions can be in these situations."

Balistreri nodded. "That's right, but I'm convinced there's always a reason behind certain feelings. And the feeling I have about Marius Hagi—"

The Cardinal stopped him with a gesture. "I told you I would help you this time, and I'll tell you one thing about Marius Hagi. The man I knew as Alina's husband was an absolutist—you could read it in his eyes. For him there was only good and evil. He could take on four men single-handed, but he wasn't the kind to take pleasure in strangling a defenseless young girl. He would have seen that as too cowardly."

"What about Alina? And Anna Rossi?"

"Hagi revered Alina as if she were the Virgin Mary. I saw Anna Rossi very few times, and then I saw her again a year ago at her daughter's funeral."

"That leaves Francesco Ajello."

There was a slight pause, the usual slight irritation that Ajello's name evoked in many people.

"Francesco was a promising and ambitious young man; he handled some paperwork for me very skillfully. Then he broke up with his girlfriend and stayed away from the parish. But Paul can tell you more about him. He's taking the kids to the beach today, but he'll be at San Valente tomorrow."

It was eleven thirty. He could have gotten out of there with the excuse that the pope was waiting for him, but he didn't move to go.

"If I have to make a confession one day, would you give me absolution, Eminence?" Balistreri asked.

Alessandrini placed a hand on his shoulder. "Yes, but only if you are sincerely penitent."

. . . .

"Ornella Corona's at her beach house in Ostia. She's expecting you after dinner," Corvu announced at lunchtime.

"All right. I'm going to stay here and try to get some work done today while it's quiet."

"Angelo called from London. He says hello."

"From London?"

"Today's the Texas Hold 'Em world championship final, live on TV starting at four. Angelo's one of the finalists."

"Is Margherita with him?" he asked.

Corvu pointed to the open letter on her desk. "That's from Margherita. She's asking to extend her holiday for a week and to be transferred."

Balistreri raised his eyebrows. "All right, Corvu, enjoy your lunch with Natalya."

"Do you need me this afternoon?"

"Corvu, it's Sunday, and your girlfriend's leaving town tomorrow morning. Don't you have something better to do than sit in the office?"

"All right, thanks. But if you need me let me know."

"I need you to tell Natalya you're going with her to Ukraine tomorrow. That's an order."

Corvu started to protest, but then he looked at Balistreri's face and thought better of it.

Afternoon

For a while Balistreri did nothing but smoke and drink a beer as he looked out of his office window at the flow of overheated tourists walking below. He was now smoking nearly a pack a day. His stomach burned from the cigarettes, not to mention too much coffee and beer. He pushed the thought aside. Then he realized he'd forgotten to take his antidepressants. Despite feeling tired, he wasn't depressed. So many things had happened in just one week, starting with Italy's victory. Linda had left him. Or perhaps it was he who had left her. He thought about it constantly and wasn't sure what had happened. Something inside him was changing. His buried memories were rising up again, together with that anger he had managed to quell.

In that week, so many years before, he and his friend had continued to chat a great deal, almost always in the car parked on the pavement, and they had tacitly avoided going back to that terrible night. But from that July in 1982, Angelo Dioguardi had reacted by throwing off his previous existence and, with a great effort, had tried to live a little for himself and a lot more for others. Balistreri, on the other hand, had slowly started to disintegrate in his own remorse.

I've gone to sleep, leading a life that's not mine in a world I hate.

But now Giovanna Sordi had taken him back to that night. Angelo had disappeared and had finally called from London, sending his good wishes but no invitation to call back.

He went downstairs to buy a slice of pizza and another beer. Then he had another espresso and smoked another cigarette. He then went back up, closed the blinds, and turned on the air-conditioner. He looked at the blackboard. By now he had plenty of answers. Not all of them, but most. And now there were other questions and old acquaintances from 1982.

He switched on the television and found the right channel. The poker final hadn't started yet. He stretched out on the sofa; the quiet, the beer, and the darkness took effect.

. . . .

Pasquali's private cell phone rang immediately after lunch while he was playing a hand of *tressette* on the porch of his country house in Tesano, his hometown.

He excused himself and walked away to take the call. As usual, he pressed the button and said nothing.

It was the icy voice he knew all too well. "There are serious issues. Begin removal."

"Couldn't we—"

"No."

He attempted a feeble protest. "But in my view—"

"I'll send you a detailed message."

The call was broken off. Pasquali returned to the card game with his legs feeling like lead. With his head in a daze, he wasted a magnificent hand and lost the game.

. . . .

Balistreri awoke suddenly in the middle of the afternoon, sweaty and dazed. Angelo Dioguardi was staring at him from the television screen as he swept a large number of chips toward himself in a gesture that was familiar to Balistreri.

He followed the game easily. He knew Angelo's tactics by heart. Twenty minutes from the end, there were only two players left, and his friend was clearly in the lead. All he had to do was sit out each hand, until he got the cards that would allow him to eliminate his final opponent. Angelo Dioguardi had the Texas Hold 'Em world title in his hands. All he had to do was be cautious and wait for the right hand.

On the table there were four cards face up on the table: the three, six, and nine of clubs and the nine of diamonds. The camera that allowed viewers to see the cards the players held showed two clubs for the opponent, who therefore already had a flush before the fifth card. Dioguardi had the four of spades and the jack of diamonds and no possibility of winning that hand, no matter what the fifth card was.

His opponent made his call, high enough to dissuade Angelo from placing a bet on the last card if he held only a pair or three of a kind. It was a predictable situation. Balistreri waited to hear him pass.

Then Angelo Dioguardi turned and stared out at him from the screen. He immediately knew two things with absolute certainty: Angelo was looking at him personally, and he would do the same thing that he had done on the night he and Balistreri first met, which was to call and match his opponent.

Angelo Dioguardi was looking at him, Michele Balistreri. He was showing him his thoughts.

All in, playing for everything.

The viewers must have thought Dioguardi was crazy, risking a world title that was as good as his. The dealer dealt the fifth card, the nine of hearts. Dioguardi's opponent turned pale. He thought long and hard, wringing his hands. He could risk everything for an unlikely victory, or else he could keep the chips he had in front of him and try another hand. "Fold," he said, shaking his head.

Angelo's face wore the same disinterested and absent expression it had on that first night, when Balistreri had seen him bluff at the card table in Paola's apartment. His opponent looked at him one last time, then shook his head and put his cards down.

Angelo didn't even smile as he took the pot. The freeze-out came in the next hand. Angelo Dioguardi was world champion.

. . . .

When Balistreri came out of the office, the sun was beginning to set, but the air was barely any cooler. He walked home, sweating furiously. The sound of his cell phone shook him out of his thoughts.

"Corvu, you haven't gone back to the office, have you?"

"I'm running there now to get a car. Where are you, Captain?" Corvu wasn't the type to get excited easily, and Balistreri could hear him breathing heavily. Something serious had happened.

"I'm on my way home. I'll wait for you outside," he replied, without asking any questions.

Corvu arrived five minutes later.

"We're driving to L'Aquila. They found the body of a girl there this afternoon."

"Another prostitute?"

"No, a foreign student at the university. The last time her friends saw her was Sunday night during the World Cup celebrations, but they didn't report her missing because the day after she was supposed to come to Rome and fly home from here."

"I've got that, Corvu. But I don't understand what it has to do with us."

"The victim is Selina Belhrouz, the sister of the lawyer in Dubai."

Balistreri turned to stone.

It was my fault. I broke the pact. The truce is over.

Corvu sped down the highway, and in an hour they were there. The body had been found at the bottom of a well at an abandoned farmhouse near Tesano, Antonio Pasquali's hometown. Pasquali was at the scene. He was there for the weekend and had followed the police cars that drove past his villa.

He was dressed differently this time, wearing a jacket and an open shirt, and he looked very shaken. "What are you two doing here?" he asked Balistreri.

"If you don't mind, I'll tell you afterward in private. Right now I'd like to find out what's happened."

"Then hurry up. Forensics is finished, and they'll be taking the body away soon."

But Balistreri was already on his way to the well. The girl's body had been placed on a stretcher and was covered with a sheet. He introduced himself to the local police captain.

It looked just like Vasile's farmhouse. A clearing, a little wooded area, a tumbledown farmhouse, and a well. And only a few miles from the country home of Antonio Pasquali. There was nothing to see apart from the body under the sheet. Forensics would have taken care of the rest. The body had been down there for a while, and the smell was overpowering. Everyone else on the scene was wearing a mask, and Balistreri and Corvu followed suit.

The paramedics were waiting to load the body into the ambulance. L'Aquila's medical examiner was writing a few last notes.

"Has she been dead for long?" Balistreri asked him.

"I'll have a better idea after the autopsy. At least three days, maybe four."

"And the cause?"

"There are clear signs of strangulation at the base of the neck, besides the bruising, cuts, cigarette burns, and various fractures."

Just like Samantha, like Nadia, like . . .

In his anger, he dismissed the thought of the last name. But he couldn't drive away the feeling of dismay. It was there, fixed, immovable in a corner of his mind. He turned to the captain. "I'd like to see the body before they take it away."

"Please, be my guest. It's not a pleasant sight, but I imagine you're more used to it than I am."

Struggling for breath, the paramedics folded the sheet down to her feet. The body was badly decomposed, but the marks around the base of her neck were very clear.

"Can you turn her over?" he asked the paramedics, who reluctantly performed the task.

At the base of her spine Selina had a tattoo, one of those half-hidden ones that rose above the panty line. They were popular among young girls. This one depicted a sun surrounded by its rays and a half-inch V had been scored at its center.

Evening

Pasquali's villa was as sober-looking as its owner. His wife served them dinner and left them alone.

Corvu was clearly uncomfortable. "If you'd like me to leave I can."

Pasquali reassured him. "That's not necessary. Maybe this terrible event can be of some use to us."

His usually smooth and relaxed face was marked with deep lines. Pasquali waited until the end of the meal, then offered a stiff drink. He lit up a cigarillo and led them out onto the patio. "It's cooler out-side. It'll help us think."

Balistreri realized he could no longer skirt the issue. He told him what they'd seen in Dubai: the SUV, the death of Belhrouz, who hap-pened to be the brother of the girl found in the well. As usual, Pasquali showed he was an excellent listener. He also decided not to ask why this had never been mentioned to him before.

"So, you don't know whether it was an accident or a murder," he said.

"We weren't sure until this afternoon," Balistreri replied.

"It could be another coincidence," Pasquali offered, but it was clear that even he no longer believed that.

"Is it a coincidence that they tossed her down a well behind your house?" Balistreri asked sarcastically.

Pasquali let out a kind of resigned groan.

"There's more," Balistreri added.

Pasquali grew visibly nervous listening to the account of the events and people connected to San Valente. "You contacted Cardinal Alessandrini?" he murmured, incredulous. "And he actually met with you?"

"He's very friendly."

"He's one of the top five people at the Vatican. What did you ask him?"

"ENT's mixed up in something serious," Balistreri said.

"Even I have gathered that," Pasquali replied. "But that doesn't mean it's mixed up with these murders. And what's Cardinal Alessandrini got to do with it? To say nothing of Count dei Banchi di Aglieno."

"Do you know the count?"

"By reputation. Everyone does. We golf at the same club."

"May I say something?" Corvu cut in timidly.

"What is it?" Balistreri asked.

"It's just that there was an anonymous call."

"What?"

"He's right," Pasquali said. "The local police station received an anonymous call today about five reporting a terrible smell coming from the well. It must have been someone passing by who didn't want to get involved."

Corvu looked at Balistreri. "I'm sorry, Captain. I should have mentioned it."

"I'm not sure I follow. Does that change anything?" Pasquali asked.

Balistreri suppressed an evil thought. "It's the second anonymous call after the one made to Colajacono. And now we have the third letter, a V. Another coincidence?"

"All right. Next week you can question the three Roma who killed Samantha Rossi. But not a word to the press about the letters."

I should tell you how Colajacono died on that hill. But I can't, not yet.

. . . .

They said good-bye to Pasquali about eleven and got back on the highway. Balistreri was exhausted. His stomach burned. He smoked in silence in the dark, his eyes fixed on the taillights of the car in front of them.

They managed to distract themselves by chatting about Angelo Dioguardi and his big win. Corvu decided to call him at his London hotel. He dialed on speakerphone.

They heard the phone ringing, then someone at the hotel desk put them through to Angelo's room.

"Graziano." A television was playing in the background.

"Angelo, you were great. I'm in the car and Captain Balistreri's here with me."

Silence. Then Angelo said, "Hello, Michele."

Those two words and the way in which they were spoken made Balistreri feel—for the first time since he'd known Angelo—that there was an unbridgeable gap between them.

"Well done, Angelo. We need to talk about that bluff sometime." It was his way of telling Angelo that he'd gotten his message.

"Okay, sure, Michele." Angelo's tone didn't encourage further conversation.

They said good-bye then, still distant with each other.

Corvu and Balistreri began to talk about the afternoon's events.

"I don't like anonymous calls, Corvu, especially this one."

Balistreri suddenly remembered something. "Did you tell Ornella Corona that I wasn't coming this evening?"

"I didn't think it was necessary. She said she'd be home after dinner anyway and you could just come by. It wasn't a real appointment."

"Call her now."

"Sir, it's almost midnight. She's probably asleep."

"Call her."

Corvu punched the number and got a recording saying the phone was off.

"Call her landline," Balistreri said.

"I don't have her home number in Ostia."

"Never mind," Balistreri said. "Turn on the siren and step on it."

Ornella Corona had heard that voice on the phone, just like Selina Belhrouz.

They didn't exchange a word for the rest of the journey. It took less than an hour. Corvu only switched off the siren once they entered Ostia. Along the seafront there were crowds around the ice cream parlors that were still open. They entered the calm, silent residential area. Ornella Corona's two-story villa was completely dark, surrounded by a small garden.

They rang the bell on the gate. No reply. They rang again. Nothing.

"I'll climb over," Balistreri said.

"But, sir—"

"You stay here."

Corvu stiffened. "Let's call the local police station. Let's not risk—"

But Balistreri was already at the top of the gate. He didn't have his gun, but he knew he wouldn't need it. If the Invisible Man had paid a visit, he was already gone.

He landed in the yard. The only light came from the back of the house. He rang the front doorbell. Nothing. He decided to go around the back. As soon as he turned the corner, he saw a parked Golf. Its doors were closed, but a single light was glowing on the dashboard.

He stopped to inspect the car. Beside him was a small lamppost. He pressed a switch and the scene was illuminated.

He knew where to look. The light on the dashboard indicated the trunk was unlatched.

Ornella was inside, her eyes wide open and filled with fear. She was dressed, but her leggings were pulled down around her thighs. The letter I carved on her began at her belly button and ran down her pelvis.

THURSDAY, JULY 20, 2006

Morning

BALISTRERI PASSED THE ENSUING nights sitting in front of his television set and his window. His cigarette and whiskey consumption had spiraled out of control. He had full-blown insomnia, his head filled with unpleasant conjecture about the past, the present, and the future. The routine he'd shared with Linda Nardi for a few months now seemed like the last quiet moments in his life, a last failed attempt to forget who Michele Balistreri really was. He brushed her angrily from his thoughts, but she always came back.

Dawn found him worn out from thinking, smoking, and drinking. His eyes were red, his beard unshaven, his clothes even more disheveled. All caused by his twin obsessions: Linda Nardi and the Invisible Man.

A serial killer who carves letters on his victims, or a plot by my former colleagues in the secret intelligence service? Who am I chasing? Two shadowy figures, one on top of the other, which then split in two. Or was there only one?

From a good, sensible policeman, albeit one who was a little depressed, he was turning into someone disturbed; halfway between an alcoholic and a homeless vagrant. Corvu and Piccolo defended him strenuously against the cruel comments going around the special team office. The special team had never been accepted by the other divisions, and now its much talked-about boss, who was unpopular with both suspicious politicians and jealous colleagues, was on his knees.

Pasquali was also defending him strenuously, as was Floris, the chief of police. There had been three days of hellish media frenzy. Fortunately not a single journalist had a spark of illumination to link the discovery of Selina Belhrouz's body with Pasquali's house in the country. But Balistreri, who knew Pasquali well, was aware that he was eaten up by the possibility.

Information about the letters carved on the victims didn't reach the media. Even the "Deep Throats" on the force were keeping quiet on account of reprisals threatened by Floris and Pasquali.

In this way, no one saw any link between the two crimes. Selina Belhrouz's murder was likened to Nadia's because of the way in which the body was found, although no one questioned the guilt of Vasile, locked away in prison. The most strident criticisms were about Ornella Corona's death. A beautiful Italian woman killed like that in her seaside home, probably by an ordinary thief—surprised in the garden—who had also tried unsuccessfully to rape her. Moreover, some witnesses had seen and heard a man, probably a Romanian, speaking in an East European language into his cell phone, wandering around outside the villa after dinnertime.

The first reports from Forensics and the pathologist on the two cases were clear enough. In both cases there were no fingerprints, nor were there traces of any organic material. This already spoke volumes about the theory of the thief surprised by Ornella Corona. Whoever went into a house wearing surgical gloves and a ski mask so as not to let a hair fall had something far worse than a robbery in mind. There was no sign of sexual violence at all in either case, but there were significant differences.

Selina Belhrouz had been taken off to an isolated place and stripped, bound, and tortured. But she hadn't been raped. The bag with her personal effects and cell phone had disappeared. It didn't really look like a robbery. There were fractures, bruises, cigarette burns. An act of sadism or an interrogation? She had already fainted by the time she was strangled.

After coming back from the beach, Ornella Corona had engaged in seemingly consensual sex shortly before being killed. She had gone out into the yard, perhaps drawn there by a noise, and there she'd been attacked and strangled. The winking wristwatch had disappeared, but if it was a robbery it was an ineffective one. The leggings had probably been pulled down immediately after death in order to carve the letter I. The car was unlocked because it was parked inside the villa's gate. It was clear the murderer knew there was little time. The pathologist had calculated the time of death as falling between eleven and midnight.

Once again, the movement against Casilino 900 and the other camps exploded, this time more violently than ever, and the city council was again in a jam. The opposition had launched a vicious attack and the Catholic Church alone was trying to defend the Roma from generic and total condemnation. In the outlying suburbs patrols of young Italians began throwing Romanians out of bars, then chasing after and assaulting them. When the police tried to arrest one such juvenile for making mincemeat of his grandfather's Romanian nurse, after having accused her of theft, they found themselves facing the entire neighborhood opposing the arrest and praising the boy for having taken the law into his own hands. The police were drawn up in force to protect Casilino 900 and the other camps, but the idea of leaving it up to the crowd was beginning to circulate among them. In July's torrid heat the peace created by the World Cup win was swept away by the latest murders, and by now it needed little for the situation to become explosive, much to the joy of those who were expecting that very thing.

Balistreri hadn't seen Linda Nardi at the press conferences. She hadn't even published an article on the matter, until that morning.

Sitting in Pasquali's office at eight o'clock were Floris, Balistreri, and Pasquali.

"This is terrible," Floris moaned, looking at the newspaper.

The headline read, FOUR DOTS TO CONNECT? The official police versions of the murders of Samantha Rossi, Nadia, Selina Belhrouz, and Ornella Corona were offered. Linda Nardi made no comment in that part of the article; she simply repeated what official sources had stated.

But at the end there was a question: *If there is a common element among these four crimes and the investigators are aware of it, do they have the right to remain silent about it so as not to compromise their investigation, or should they tell us how things really stand?*

Pasquali was his usual cool self. "Linda Nardi is posing a question to us. We can either ignore her or reply. I say we should consider the pros and cons."

"If you want an investigative analysis rather than a political one, let's bring in Corvu and Piccolo."

Pasquali looked at the chief of police. "We need to make an investigative analysis to use as the basis for a political decision."

Corvu and Piccolo were summoned. Corvu was a little intimidated by the chief of police, but not Piccolo.

"Balistreri," said Floris, "would you guide us through this minefield?"

"Linda Nardi's asking if we have the right to keep quiet about a common thread among these four cases. I'd like to dispel any doubt about one thing. In the past, as Pasquali knows, I've used Linda Nardi as a channel for investigative purposes, but I never mentioned the letters in the first two crimes, nor have I seen her since July 11."

"All right," Pasquali said. "There are no doubts about Balistreri's discretion. Let's continue."

"We have four letters, probably carved using the same instrument: a scalpel or a sharp knife. An R, an E, a V, and an I. And they come in that order, assuming that the order and the letters mean something. This is the one common thread among the four murders," Balistreri said. "And we can no longer consider it a coincidence," he added, addressing Pasquali.

"There may be more letters to come," Piccolo said.

Balistreri saw the chief of police touch the wood of his chair in an automatic superstitious gesture.

"Agreed," Pasquali said. "So I propose we shelve the letters, for a moment only, and ask ourselves if there are any other common elements among the four cases."

Corvu raised his hand to speak. "Actually, there are five cases. There's Camarà as well, and that's leaving aside the deaths on the hillside. If we want to analyze the deaths of the four women, we have to remember that Nadia's death is linked to Camarà's."

"And the last two murders could be connected more closely to Camarà's death than to those of Nadia and Samantha," Balistreri said.

"Necessary killings," Pasquali observed.

"Exactly. The first two crimes were preceded by sexual attacks and concern two females chosen at random. But the last two victims are not random at all. They're two women linked in some way to the investigation into Nadia's death, and the motive could be the same as in Camarà's case: getting rid of an inconvenient witness. It could all be disguised as part of a sequence. The letters could simply be a cover-up."

Pasquali said, "So you're suggesting that we're not dealing with a sadistic serial killer who attacks, kills, and carves letters into his victims, but with a premeditated murder that in turn causes more murders by one or more other murderers?"

It's as if the Invisible Man had two personalities and two faces. But the same hand does the killing.

"If you'll permit me, sir," Corvu said, nodding toward Pasquali, "I'd like to pick up on your question about any other similarities among the four cases." Corvu looked at Balistreri as if to ask his permission, then said, "The Invisible Man comes into play here."

The chief of police stared vacantly at him. "What invisible man?" he asked, looking from Corvu to Balistreri to Pasquali.

"In the case of Samantha," Corvu continued, "the three Roma say there was a fourth man—who later disappeared—who got them drunk, gave them drugs, and was the first to attack the girl. In the case of Nadia, according to Vasile, there was a man who telephoned, and in exchange for the loan of the Giulia GT brought him Nadia and two bottles of whiskey."

"But there's nothing of the kind in the other two cases," Floris protested.

"If you'll permit me to speak, sir," Corvu replied obsequiously to the chief of police, "there was an anonymous phone call that led us to Selina Belhrouz's body in the well, and a suspicious individual who was speaking on his cell phone in Romanian near Ornella Corona's villa. Furthermore, there's a motorcyclist involved in Camarà's case."

And there's the phantom who announced Colajacono's death and killed him in cold blood.

"Help me to understand here," Pasquali said. "Let's suppose—for a moment only—that the murders were all committed by the same hand and that the perpetrator is this Invisible Man, as you call him. You're saying that the choice of the first two victims was random or in some way different from the last two, who were chosen by necessity. I can buy that Camarà was killed because he'd seen someone at the Bella Blu he wasn't supposed to see, but I don't understand where Selina Belhrouz and Ornella Corona come into all this. What did they see?"

"It's not what they saw but what they heard—a certain voice on the telephone," Balistreri blurted out.

They all stared at him. Pasquali in particular seemed to drill right through him with his eyes. Balistreri felt as if he were being X-rayed.

The fear I see in your eyes worries me more than anything else.

At last Pasquali heaved a sigh. "I'm telling you right now that if you have any more cards up your sleeve you'd better pull them out now. There isn't much time left. Tell us about this voice."

"One day Ornella Corona received a phone call at home. The person on the other end said that her husband's cell phone was off and asked her to find him and tell him he had to go to Monte Carlo that evening. When she protested that it was already five o'clock in the afternoon, the man told her in no uncertain terms that this was why they had a private plane. Then he hung up."

A long silence. The dark shadow of ENT was again falling across the murders.

"This ENT . . ." Floris began feebly.

"I beg your pardon, Chief," Pasquali said, interrupting him. "I'd like Balistreri to finish his explanation with regard to Selina Belhrouz as well."

"In Dubai, just before the accident in which Selina Belhrouz's brother lost his life, he told us that during one of her visits to Italy, his sister accidentally answered a call on his cell phone. According to him, this was a problem because Selina heard a voice she wasn't supposed to hear."

Pasquali had turned very pale. He made a single note in his diary. "All right," he said, taking charge of the meeting again, "let's leave ENT aside for now. We have two women chosen at random and killed, then Camarà and two other women eliminated because they were inconvenient witnesses, and the letters are only a red herring to put us off. Is that it more or less?"

"No," Piccolo said without requesting permission to speak. The others turned to her. "We can argue about Samantha, but Nadia wasn't chosen at random. They twisted the arms of Colajacono and Tatò and got them involved, and they went ahead with Nadia even after Camarà saw them, at the cost of killing him and getting Bella Blu and ENT involved. They could easily have dropped her and chosen another victim. But they wanted Nadia. For some reason, she had to be the victim."

"That doesn't make any sense to me," Floris said. "A poor young Romanian prostitute. Why her?"

"Maybe she'd discovered something she shouldn't have," Corvu suggested.

"But that's absurd," Pasquali said. "They would have shot her and thrown her down a well. End of story. Instead of this whole charade with the trip to Bella Blu, the motocross bike, the Giulia GT, Vasile."

Balistreri knew Pasquali was correct. But Piccolo was, too: Nadia hadn't been chosen at random, but for a particular reason. He just couldn't figure out what that was.

"And where does Elisa Sordi come into all this?" asked the chief of police, ever more confused and worried. "Pasquali told me you went to question Count Tommaso dei Banchi di Aglieno and Cardinal Alessandrini."

"Friendly chats, not interrogations. And neither of them was upset. They thought I was there to reopen the Elisa Sordi case after her mother's recent suicide, but I was actually there for another reason. Everything starts with Alina Hagi, who at that time was at San Valente. Her best friend was Samantha Rossi's mother, who was then dating Mr. Ajello, who today is an ENT shareholder and linked in some way to Ornella Corona."

"This is like a soap opera. These coincidences are unbelievable," the chief of police said.

Balistreri shook his head. "Exactly, unbelievable. *If* they were coincidences."

It was Pasquali, as ever, who drew the conclusion.

"Let's go back to the beginning, to Linda Nardi's question about the investigators having something to link the four murders. Yes, we do. Do we have reasons for not revealing it? Yes, we do. If we said there was a serial killer going around carving letters of the alphabet into his victims, panic would ensue. Can we keep this a secret indefinitely? I would say no. Certainly, a fifth murder with another letter would be totally unacceptable."

"Then what do you propose?" the chief of police asked.

Balistreri could see that Pasquali had made a decision. The news of the voice heard by Ornella Corona and Selina Belhrouz had had its intended effect.

"Balistreri, you now have forty-eight hours to arrest the murderer. Once the perpetrator's in prison, we can tell the press part of the truth and they'll forgive us for hiding it."

Pasquali's voice was cool, calm, and decisive. There was no room for any doubt or objection.

Floris stared at him incredulously. "I'm sorry, Captain Pasquali, but who would this perpetrator be that you're speaking about?"

Pasquali wasn't in the mood to mince words. "He wields enormous influence over the entire Romanian community. He never has an alibi. He speaks both Romanian and Italian. He could have used Adrian's bike to go up the hill to Vasile. Samantha's mother was his wife's friend in 1982. Nadia lived in an apartment he owned. The four men who killed three policemen and almost killed Balistreri were his henchmen."

"But we have no proof," Floris said.

Pasquali looked at Balistreri. "Find proof, Michele. Tomorrow morning you can see Vasile and the three Roma who murdered Samantha. By Friday I want you to nail Marius Hagi on a multiple murder charge."

Balistreri left the meeting with the uncomfortable feeling of having revealed too many things to Pasquali, and with regret for not having told him about the most dangerous thing he knew.

. . . .

"I imagine you have a very good reason for calling me." His voice was calm, but not encouraging.

"We have to meet," Pasquali whispered.

"I don't think so."

"You've gone too far, and on my own doorstep!" Pasquali was trying to keep the rage in his voice in check.

"Merely a fortuitous coincidence."

"We have to stop this, right now," Pasquali muttered in desperation.

"On that we're in agreement. I'll see to it. Prepare yourself for tomorrow."

Pasquali hung up. He turned to the crucifix and began to pray. "Our Father, who art in Heaven, hallowed be thy name."

He felt Christ's gaze on his head. He'd made a terrible mistake, and now the game was out of his control. Or perhaps it had never been in his control.

"Lead us not into temptation, but deliver us from evil. Amen."

. . . .

Balistreri was aware that speaking with ENT's sole known shareholder was a final act of defiance toward whomever had warned and advised him in every possible way to keep his distance.

But Giovanna Sordi's suicide had unleashed instincts in him that time and regret had gradually tamped down. His antidepressants were no longer any use, nor were his acid reflux pills. Cutting down on smoking and drinking had no effect, and getting into bed with a good book no longer did the trick for him. He could no longer put off the uncertain encounter with God, no use waiting for or fearing His judgment. The only thing that was any use at all was what he had sought ever since he was a boy, no matter what it cost—the truth. Without any compromises, with whatever force necessary, even at the risk of his own destruction.

Francesco Ajello appeared relaxed. Balistreri and Corvu caught up with him mid-morning at his golf club, where he had just finished playing a round with his son, Fabio. The four of them sat down at a table in the shade.

"It's so hot," Ajello complained, wiping away perspiration with a face towel while his son finished off a soda. "It's only 10:30 and it's already unbearable."

"Aren't you working today, sir?" Corvu asked.

Ajello brushed away the idea with an irritated gesture. "I work at night, as you know. But I was home yesterday, so this morning Fabio and I were playing the first hole by 7:00."

Balistreri kept stealing glances at the son, who appeared totally disinterested in the conversation and was fiddling with a brand new BlackBerry.

"To what do we owe this visit? Have you found the man on the bike?" Ajello asked, lighting a cigarette.

"Can you talk about this in front of your son?" Balistreri asked.

"No problem. Fabio's an adult and we have no secrets between us."

"All right. Let's talk about Ornella Corona."

Ajello shook his head; Fabio stopped playing with the device and looked at Balistreri for the first time with all the scorn his teenage eyes could muster. It was clear that Balistreri was far from his idea of a success: a nobody of a civil servant, unshaven and badly dressed.

"We live in a ridiculous country," Ajello said. "We allow young men to go around raping and killing."

"I'd like to know when you last saw Ornella Corona," Balistreri said flatly. Enough with the bullshit.

Ajello stopped smiling and examined the fresh manicure of his long sunburned hands as if he had spotted a small defect.

"How is this question relevant to your investigation?" he asked.

"We're attempting to determine Ornella Corona's movements on the night she was murdered. We know for certain that she was sunbathing at the beach resort until sunset. She left alone, and we presume she went directly home. We found a plate with the remains of a salad and a glass with a few drops of wine left in it. Then, toward midnight, before she was murdered—"

Ajello held up a hand to stop him. "Fabio," he said to his son, "could you pop into the pro shop and check whether the new golf bags are in?"

The young man stood and walked away.

"Please, do carry on," Ajello said, all politeness once his son was out of earshot.

"Before she was killed, she had what appears to have been consensual sex," Balistreri said.

"And you want to know if she had sex with me? I still don't see the relevance."

"If you were there, you might have seen or heard something."

"Or I might have killed her."

"That depends on your alibi."

"At the time I was in my car on my way to Bella Blu. I got there about midnight, I think."

"That's not much of an alibi, unless you went there straight from home, although as you know a spouse's testimony counts for little."

"I didn't go there from my house," Ajello said calmly. "I went there from Ostia, where I'd been with Ornella Corona."

Corvu and Balistreri exchanged glances. Ajello hastened to add, "Naturally, Ornella was alive when I left around eleven thirty."

"And did you see anyone around the villa on your way out?" Corvu asked.

"Absolutely not," Ajello replied quickly.

"Please think carefully," Balistreri insisted.

A small shadow crossed the lawyer's face. "I saw no one. But I drive a convertible and I had the hood down, and I did hear a voice—someone speaking loudly into a cell phone. In Romanian, I think."

"Would you recognize the voice of Marius Hagi?" Balistreri asked nonchalantly.

There was a lengthy pause. Ajello took his time lighting a cigarette. He gave Balistreri a sideways glance.

"I know that name," he said, "but I can't place it"

"He's the husband of Alina Hagi, Anna Rossi's best friend," Corvu said.

Balistreri thought that Ajello could have been a very good poker player, but not a world-class champion like Angelo Dioguardi. Something showed on his face. Fear? Anger? Guilt? It was difficult to say.

"Anna Rossi," he said with a smile, recovering his composure. "My God, how many years has it been? Alina Hagi I certainly remember, but not this husband of hers, Mario."

"Marius," Corvu corrected him.

"Marius Hagi. Yes, I must have met him once or twice. But I haven't seen him since then. Once I got my degree, I didn't hang out with the San Valente parish crowd. I was working for—"

"Count Tommaso dei Banchi di Aglieno," Corvu said.

"How did you know that?" Ajello asked.

"The count told us himself. We went to ask him about this Marius Hagi and your name came up."

Ajello nodded to acknowledge the coincidence, but he seemed to have decided to feign ignorance.

"Valerio Bona also mentioned you," Corvu added.

"Valerio Bona! My expert helmsman."

"Valerio Bona was working at San Valente with Father Paul for Cardinal Alessandrini."

Ajello absorbed this information in silence. He seemed neither surprised nor disturbed.

Balistreri decided it was time to get to the point. "There was a major crime back then, do you remember?"

Ajello met his gaze. "Elisa Sordi, poor thing," he said.

Balistreri was surprised. "Did you know her?"

Ajello shook his head. "Only by sight. I never went to Via della Camilluccia. But Valerio introduced me to her once and we went for a coffee together."

Balistreri saw that Fabio was coming back. He looked directly at Ajello. "Do you remember where you were the day Elisa Sordi died?"

"Well, if it had been any other day I wouldn't remember, but it was the World Cup final in Spain. I'm sure you watched it, too."

It was difficult to say if there was any irony in the question.

"Anyway, I'd been alone on the boat all afternoon, and at seven thirty I was in the sailing club with friends watching the game. And later, naturally, I was out near the Colosseum celebrating."

Ajello looked at him with amusement. "You must have celebrated yourself that evening, Balistreri, or maybe not."

This time the message was much clearer.

Afternoon

It was lunchtime. Summer storms always break out when the temperature is high. Thunder and lightning accompanied them back to the office, while hundreds of tourists in T-shirts and shorts sought refuge in the bars and Metro stations.

It began to rain heavily as Corvu parked the car. It was the first downpour since the beginning of July. Balistreri decided to take advantage of it for a restorative walk through the city center's now deserted streets. He sent Corvu up to the office and walked toward the Tiber in the pouring rain.

R.E.V.I. Was it a red herring or the key to something? Only the first letters of their names could directly link Samantha, Nadia, Selina and Ornella. But the Invisible Man wants us to find another link. He wants to enjoy our fear.

He felt the drops of rain trickling down his back through his open shirt collar. Absorbed in his thoughts, he suddenly found himself on the riverbank. Linda Nardi lived on the other side.

When did Alina die?

It was a ridiculous question. Linda Nardi could easily have found out when Marius Hagi's wife had died. What did it matter?

He and Angelo Dioguardi had spent the evening of July 11, 1982 watching Italy's World Cup victory. That same day, Elisa Sordi had been beaten, slashed, burned with cigarettes, and killed.

Balistreri's mind had resisted seeing the similarities from the moment that San Valente came back on the scene. But there were similarities: a young girl beaten and tortured, albeit not raped, then suffocated and thrown into the Tiber, but with no trace of a letter on her.

Was there one? Are you sure, Balistreri? Do you remember how distracted you were?

He leaned on the railing. The river's gray surface was running slowly, stippled by the rain. Elisa's body had been in the water for days. The effect of the water and the rats had been catastrophic. He remembered the autopsy photos with a grimace. Bruises, burns, bite marks, but nothing scoring her skin.

Really only one bite mark, and even that was uncertain. The medical examiner had noted a semicircular scar on what remained of her left breast. Possible cause: bite, cut, scratch. A cut.

He was soaking wet, alone, disturbed, exhausted. His eyes were burning, and he was ready to drop. He looked over toward St. Peter's and Linda Nardi's apartment and then, with an ugly premonition, turned his away from the Tiber.

. . . .

When he returned to the office, without having eaten, it was already three.

Corvu and Piccolo made no comment about the state he was in. His clothes were drenched, his stubble was thick, his shoes caked in mud. If they didn't know him, the policemen guarding the entrance would have rudely sent him packing, taking him for a homeless person.

"Big news," Piccolo said.

"Two pieces of big new," Corvu chimed in.

"Mastroianni's back in Romania. With the help of a friend, I got permission for him to see the secret archives opened up after Ceausescu's death. The two victims that Mircea and Greg were accused of murdering were retired employees of the ministry of the interior. They were secret police with serious résumés. Among other things, they were responsible for the disappearance of Marius Hagi's brother."

A man who never forgives. Alina must have found out as well.

"Excellent information," Balistreri said. "Not directly linked to the current investigation, however."

"The second piece of information is, though." Piccolo was beaming. So she had nailed Colajacono, or at least the memory of him.

"After today's meeting with Pasquali I asked Rudi if he could think of anything strange that Hagi did or said on the morning of December 29. That's when I went to the Torre Spaccata police station and spoke to Colajacono. Rudi remembered that Hagi was ending a phone call in the billiard room when he went in to bring him coffee. He only heard the last thing he said, but I think it's enough."

Piccolo paused.

Balistreri said, "All right, Piccolo, spit it out. What did Hagi say?"

"He said, 'Don't worry about them. They're just street sweepers in paradise.'"

. . . .

Balistreri shut himself in his office to think about Marius Hagi. What was he doing on his last day of freedom? The next day, Pasquali was going to have him arrested even if he had to fabricate additional proof beyond the evidence that was already taking shape. On an empty stomach, Balistreri drank two beers and a double whiskey and smoked four cigarettes.

He turned the air-conditioning up to maximum and closed the blinds against the sweltering afternoon. Finally, he switched on the reading lamp and took it over to the sofa along with three folders. The first contained all the interrogations of the three Roma youths who had brutally attacked Samantha and killed her. The second contained those of Vasile, Nadia's presumed rapist and murderer. It took over two hours to read through them all.

Then he grabbed a magnifying glass and opened the third folder, containing Elisa Sordi's autopsy report. After twenty-four years, he still remembered it. The photograph was number 43. Semicircular scab of recent scarring to left breast, broken sharply by the loss of a part of the breast. Possible causes: bite from the superior dental arch of a human being, cut or gouge from branches or piece of metal in the river.

Truly an amateur investigation: a real collection of doubts, superficialities and absurdities. A textbook example of what errors not to make.

There was no need for the magnifying glass to discount the idea that the cut or gouge mark was accidental. The line of the curve cut into what remained of the breast was continuous and regular, a quarter circle. Superior dental arch? It could match the central and lateral incisors and the canines. He used the magnifying glass to see it better. It was no line of an ellipse, it was definitely a circle. A piece of the letter O. Certainly, no pathologist would have sworn it was a cut. The letter O cut into the flesh.

But now we know many things we didn't in 1982. Four young women murdered: R.E.V.I. And perhaps an O. Perhaps the same hand for all of them—the Invisible Man's.

He worked until the evening, fighting off sleep and hunger. He called in Corvu and Piccolo. They read Elisa Sordi's file together three times. It was a job he should have done all those years ago. All the details, all the alibis. But now there were new names to add: Hagi, Ajello. And new facts.

Finally Corvu wrote on a sheet of paper: *Check alibis of the following people for all the crimes.*

Pasquali and Floris would have been appalled to see some of the names, and would have easily ruled out a number of them. But Balistreri had no intention of asking their permission.

Evening

At the end of the day, Corvu offered to give him a lift home.

"You're tired, sir, and it's late. Tomorrow's going to be a tough day between questioning the Roma and arresting Hagi."

"Take it easy, Corvu. I still need to walk on my own for a while and clear my head."

Rather than head toward home, he set off again toward the banks of the Tiber, which were crowded with noisy young people. He had no idea where he was going, not consciously. The heat and humidity were suffocating. He walked wearily, smoking one cigarette after another.

It was his thoughts that spurred his steps on over the bridge, where he should not have gone, and as far as the street where Linda Nardi lived. It was fate that decided it for him. A few seconds more or less would have changed everything. But destiny led him to turn the corner at the precise moment when Linda Nardi was opening the front door to the apartment building, accompanied by Angelo Dioguardi whose arm was draped around her shoulders.

. . . .

He decided to try sleeping in his office with its air-conditioning on, when he returned there at midnight. There were few policemen around and no one on his floor. The flower in the glass still on Margherita's desk was now completely dead, and he knew with certainty the flower had always been destined to wither.

Taking off his jacket and shoes he made himself comfortable, switching off all the lights and turning the air-conditioning on high. He poured a whiskey and lit a cigarette. Then he went into the bathroom and threw all his medicines into the toilet. First the gastroprotectors, then the antidepressants.

He felt better now that he had a few answers. Angelo and Linda: two adult children, insensitive as only children can be and clever at hiding themselves as only adults can be. And traitors, like those other two thirty-six years ago.

FRIDAY, JULY 21, 2006

Morning

HIS PRIVATE CELL PHONE rang at seven, while Pasquali was getting ready to go to Mass before heading to the office. That morning he had been less punctilious than usual. He had cut his chin and his part was crooked.

The familiar voice spoke. "Everything is set. We'll end it this morning."

Pasquali tried to sound confident. "I've arranged a meeting for him at ten o'clock, so he won't get in the way."

"Excellent. Take care of it yourself. No outside help."

"The subject must be armed. And he has to react in a certain way when arrested."

Pasquali had never thought of having to shoot at anyone, not even a serial killer. But if he shot at an armed serial killer it would be more than justified. He dared not look at the crucifix as he formulated the thought.

"You'll be a national hero." There was a mixture of irony and contempt in the voice.

"This thing has gotten way out of hand. We need to talk after it's over." It was a small act of rebellion, the most his fear would allow him to say.

"Of course. Our friend will be in suite twenty-seven. Be careful not to get your shoes dirty."

A last jab at his compromised respectability. He did not dare take Communion that day.

· · · ·

They arrived punctually at ten. He had chosen Piccolo to come with him so she'd definitely be under control, given she was prone to going over the top. They had brought the three Roma boys to Regina Coeli, the prison nearest to Trastevere.

They left their pistols and cell phones at the entrance and were accompanied to a room where the three Roma were waiting for them with an interpreter and a lawyer. They were between eighteen and twenty-one years of age, but they seemed much older than Balistreri remembered them.

Piccolo started at the beginning. When had they arrived in Italy? What were their casual jobs? Thefts. How had they met? The boys replied in monosyllables. They weren't particularly interested. When the evening of the murder came up, Piccolo's questions became more detailed. Which of them had been approached by the fourth man? His description? Medium height, black hair, long and straight, metal-rimmed glasses. Where was he while they were drinking his whiskey? In the bar, maybe. Maybe outside. Did he invite them to go outside? Yes. And the cocaine? Yes, it was his. Now, Samantha. Who suggested the idea? He did. Who hit her first? He did. Then they'd dragged her to the garbage dump. He had more cocaine and more whiskey. The story became much more muddled. Who had raped her first? Who had been last? And where was he duirng all this? There, somewhere around. They could hear him coughing as he smoked.

"Stop," Balistreri said. Piccolo nodded. She'd picked up on it, too. He asked each of them again in turn, "Where was he while you were raping the girl?" One of the three was a little more specific. "He was nearby. We couldn't see him, but we could hear him coughing."

Piccolo checked their earlier statements. "You never mentioned the coughing before."

The guy who had spoken shrugged and replied in Italian, "What the fuck does that have to do with anything?"

They were shown a recent photo of Hagi. They looked at it reluctantly. "No," said the first. "Don't know," said the second. "Could be, maybe," said the third.

Then they were shown a photograph of Hagi with long hair and glasses added to it by computer. "Yes, that's him," they all said.

"Which one of you was the last to speak to him?"

No one could remember. The man disappeared at a certain point, as if vanishing into thin air. They all confirmed the same story. Samantha was alive, she was moaning, when they left. This time Balistreri had no doubts: they were telling the truth. It was the Invisible Man who had finished her off.

. . . . .

Every time a cell phone disappeared that was connected in any way with a crime, the phone company was informed and told to take note and notify the police immediately of the eventual reactivation of the SIM card. The news came to Corvu in the office at exactly ten o'clock, at the precise moment when Balistreri and Piccolo were entering Regina Coeli. Selina Belhrouz's SIM card had been reactivated and the phone company was very precise in its information. The microchip had been pinned down to the very narrow area of Rome where Casilino 900 was located.

Not being able to communicate with Balistreri, and wanting to follow procedure, Corvu informed Pasquali.

"Let's go in with two men. No sirens—we don't want to give anyone time to get away," Pasquali said.

"But, sir, it could be dangerous with just two men," Corvu protested.

"We're going to make the arrest. You park a car at each exit, discreetly. Let's meet downstairs in five minutes," Pasquali said.

Corvu put on his bulletproof vest and his holster containing his Beretta. He got ahold of two plainclothes officers. It was the standard format for a simple arrest. But there was no telling that this would be a standard arrest. He tried the cell phones of Balistreri and Piccolo again. No answer. He left both of them a text message: *Call me ASAP*.

Pasquali did three things at great speed. He put on his bulletproof vest, readied his Beretta, and turned to the crucifix.

"Lord, forgive me for what I am about to do."

. . . .

Corvu and Pasquali sat behind the two plainclothes officers in the car.

"Good," said Pasquali. "The telephone company's circled an area containing a total of six broken-down trailers. We'll go in quietly, as if it were a normal patrol. They're used to seeing the police these days. After we've gone in, no one can leave without being searched and having their ID checked."

Corvu said, "With all due respect, sir, I think it would be better to search in groups."

"No. We'd only find the cell phone in a dumpster. I want to catch someone holding that phone in his hands."

"It could be dangerous," Corvu protested.

"That's precisely why we're here. And I want one thing clear. We've already lost three able policemen and Captain Balistreri only survived by some miracle. If you see even a hint that someone's going for a gun, open fire immediately. Don't wait for them to fire first."

The two plainclothes officers were clearly intimidated by Pasquali's authority. They looked at Corvu.

"But, sir, that's not proper procedure."

Pasquali gave him a withering look. "Deputy Corvu, I will not allow another criminal to shoot at a policeman. I take full responsibility. There certainly won't be any shortage of political support if you shoot an armed Roma in self-defense."

His face strained, Corvu leaned his head back, stifling his thoughts. "All right. How are we to proceed?"

"We'll start with the trailer closest to the entrance to the camp. One of you will knock. If they open up, we go in, check IDs, and continue to search until the Belhrouz woman's phone turns up."

"And if no one opens the door?"

"We go in and search anyway."

Corvu didn't like this at all, and he knew Balistreri would have been furious.

· · · ·

Vasile confirmed that the man who had called on December 23 spoke excellent Italian. "Did he have an accent?" Piccolo asked.

"I don't know. He sounded Italian to me."

"What else do you remember about the call?"

He repeated what he'd said in his statement.

"What was his voice like?"

"Raspy. He coughed a lot."

Balistreri and Piccolo exchanged glances. Perhaps this wouldn't be enough for the prosecutor's office. All they had was circumstantial evidence. Many people have a cough. Many people have friends with motocross bikes. The deaths in Romania weren't attributable to him. His wife Alina was running away from him when she had her accident on the moped, but so what? And he didn't have any alibi? Neither did millions of people.

Piccolo tightened her lips in rage. "But we know it was him."

Balistreri got up, troubled. Something wasn't right. He'd never liked coincidences, and here there really were a great many—too many.

I must tell Pasquali how Colajacono died. And as soon as I can.

· · · ·

They entered the camp under a blazing sun that had dried the mud left from the previous day's storm. There were a good many people around, mainly women, old men, and children jumping off a heap of old mattresses for fun. The garbage gave off a dreadful smell in the sun and mingled with the smell of urine from the port-o-potties. Groups of children swarmed happily around the policemen. Corvu shivered—this was sheer folly. Their holsters were open below their jackets and visible to the expert eye. He saw Pasquali, disoriented and sweating in his impeccable gray pinstripe suit, and looking around.

He made a last attempt to call Balistreri. Nothing. They were still in Regina Coeli.

They knocked on a trailer door. A toothless old woman holding a child in her arms opened the door; she could as well have been the mother as the grandmother.

They went in. The heat was suffocating, as was the smell. Water was boiling on the small camp stove. There was no one there besides the old woman and the child.

"You search the trailer, Corvu. I don't see any danger here. I'm going next door," Pasquali said.

Before Corvu could protest, Pasquali was out the door.

Corvu imagined that he wanted to make the arrest himself because he wanted to be the star of the show. He indicated to the two plain-clothes men to go with Pasquali.

"Do you have a cell phone in here?" he asked the old woman as he looked around. It was a stupid question, but he had to ask.

The woman didn't understand Italian. The child began to cry while the pungent smell of its feces spread through the caravan along with the stink of rubbish.

Corvu had a feeling he was going to vomit and went to a window to get some air. From where he was he saw one of the policemen knocking at the door of trailer twenty-seven. Pasquali and the other policeman were a yard behind him. A moment later the door opened. It was another old woman. Three small children ran out between the legs of Pasquali and the two policemen.

Corvu saw with surprise that there was a motocross bike parked behind the trailer. And he didn't notice the old man in a hat and dark glasses coming up behind the men and Pasquali. Then he heard the sound of a cough.

He swore in Sardinian and, turning sharply around, bumped into the old woman, knocking her to the ground along with the child, whose feces spattered across the floor. He lost a few seconds apologizing and helping her get up again, then he burst outside with the Beretta in his hand, shouting, ready to shoot.

Pasquali turned but did not raise the pistol in his hand quickly enough. He only managed to see Marius Hagi's malicious grin below the dark glasses as he squeezed the trigger. He had no time to ask God to forgive his sins before the bullet passed through his head. Hagi threw the pistol far away and raised his arms above his head in the sign of surrender. The plainclothes men pointed their weapons at him, trembling with fear and rage.

"Stop! Don't shoot!" Corvu shouted to the plainclothes men as he ran toward them, keeping his Beretta aimed at Hagi. Hagi looked at him with a mocking smile.

"Call an ambulance and block all the exits," Corvu shouted desperately.

"No accomplices. I acted alone," Hagi said. He was completely unruffled.

Corvu didn't dare look at Pasquali. He ordered the other policeman to handcuff Hagi, who offered no resistance. A huge crowd had gathered around them and many patrolmen were running toward them, weapons in hand.

Hagi watched the scene with seeming amusement. He smiled at Corvu. "Where's your boss, chief street sweeper in paradise?"

Afternoon

Balistreri refused to participate in the press conference arranged for the early afternoon. He watched it on the television in his office along with Corvu, Piccolo, and Mastroianni. First the minister of the interior spoke a few words of praise for the police and Captain Antonio Pasquali's heroic sacrifice to rid the Italian people of this source of evil. He promised that within a few days the government would take drastic measures to control all immigrants, using a decree with the force of law so as to avoid bureaucratic delays in Parliament's red tape.

To a question from a French journalist about possible protests from the UN, the Vatican, and humanitarian organizations, he replied with scant diplomacy: "We do not expect protests from anyone, and they will not be welcome."

He then handed the floor to the chief of police for a reconstruction of events. Floris was visibly shaken, but he maintained his composure. He gave a succinct precis of the deaths of the four young women, which were linked by the four incisions in their bodies. He spoke about the Invisible Man and, by way of illustration, the mountain of indirect evidence that converged on Marius Hagi on whom, incidentally, Selina Belhrouz's cell phone had been discovered. He recalled that four Romanians linked to Hagi had been killed in an exchange of fire in which three heroic policemen had lost their lives and the head of the special team, Michele Balistreri, had been gravely wounded.

He ended by saying he was certain that Marius Hagi's arrest had delivered the city from a nightmare and added that, together with the minister of the interior, he had summoned the mayor of Rome for urgent talks. He used the word *summoned,* as if calling for a servant.

Then all hell broke loose, the journalists unleashing a barrage of questions at the top of their voices, but there were no further statements.

Corvu was overcome. Television's merciless footage had shown his face drained of color as Pasquali's body was taken away from Casilino 900 and Hagi was loaded into the police van that would take him to jail. Balistreri had tried everything to get him to go home, but without success. He had explained in every way that he was not at fault; it was only Pasquali's rashness and desire to play a leading role that had led to this outcome.

"Corvu, you can't be in the room for Hagi's questioning. You're in shock. You've filed your report. Take a few days off and go see Natalya in Ukraine."

Corvu shook his head. "No, thank you," he said firmly.

But Balistreri had made up his mind. "I bought you a ticket. You're leaving tonight. Natalya's expecting you. In two hours, my brother, Alberto, is going to come by and give you a ride to the airport."

I have to protect you right now, Graziano, because this isn't over. Indeed, it's only just begun.

Corvu raised his head. He looked shaken. "Thank you, sir," he whispered, getting up. Then the ever duty-conscious Corvu said, "I checked the list of alibis you asked for and gave it to Mastroianni. If it still matters."

Piccolo and Mastroianni hugged Corvu. Balistreri put a congenial arm around his shoulders and walked him to the exit. He was trembling.

Out on the sidewalk, something occurred to Balistreri. He turned to Corvu and asked, "How much time did Pasquali have from the time he saw Hagi to when he tried to shoot?"

"Less than a second."

Less than a second. He already had his gun drawn.

. . . .

In the hot afternoon, Balistreri went to Regina Coeli for the second time that day. This time, he didn't bring Piccolo.

Attorney Massimo Morandi was waiting for Balistreri outside the interrogation room. "I'm sorry about Pasquali."

Balistreri looked at him.

You're only sorry about your own reputation, you son of a bitch.

"What happened was unfortunate, but it does clearly confirm what I told you last time."

"That I should have stayed in Dubai?"

"You now have the perpetrator. My client will confess to everything."

"Really? Will he tell me why he faked an argument in order to kill poor Camarà?"

Morandi turned pale despite his tanning-booth complexion.

"Be satisfied with what is obviously the truth," Morandi said icily.

Balistreri resisted the temptation to lay his hands on him or else they would have relieved him of the investigation; this time he wanted to get to the truth. He congratulated himself on his self-control. He turned his back and went into the room, Morandi following.

The public prosecutor was already there. He muttered a few words to the lawyer and then turned to Balistreri.

"Mr. Morandi has already told me that his client will plead guilty to all the murders, including the murder of Camarà. He'll give a full and detailed confession."

Hagi was brought in wearing handcuffs. His black eyes rested calmly on those of Balistreri. He had grown thinner since he had last seen him seven months earlier and was coughing much more. But his eyes now burned even fiercer above the huge dark bags beneath. The resemblance to a demon was now complete.

After the preliminaries, the public prosecutor let Balistreri take over the questioning.

"Let's start from the beginning, Mr. Hagi."

"Fine. Let's start with Samantha Rossi."

Balistreri shook his head. "No, Mr. Hagi. The beginning was in 1982."

Hagi nodded with a smile. "Elisa Sordi?" He said it as if it were the most obvious thing in the world.

The words surprised everyone: the public prosecutor, Morandi, the corrections officers. Only Balistreri failed to react.

Hagi said with obvious contempt, "You did quite the job on that case, didn't you, Captain Balistreri?"

"Please just answer the questions without making any extraneous comments, Mr. Hagi," the public prosecutor said.

Morandi raised a hand. "Hold on just a minute. I need to confer with my client. I don't know anything about the connection to the Elisa Sordi case."

"Don't worry about it," Hagi said placidly. "Your job is to ensure that these gentlemen don't distort what I say. I want everything to be extremely clear, and we've got some people in this room who always seem to make a mess of things and have been doing so since 1982."

"When did you meet Elisa Sordi?" Balistreri asked, ignoring Hagi's remark.

"I don't remember exactly—a little before the summer of 1982. I went to the residential complex on Via della Camilluccia, where Alina introduced me to a young man. Elisa was with that young man."

"What was the man's name?"

Hagi shrugged. "I don't remember. I didn't take much notice of him. I couldn't keep my eyes off of her, on the other hand."

He's trying to provoke you. Stay cool.

"Why did you go to Via della Camilluccia?" Balistreri asked.

"I'd gotten some work through Alina. I was hired to organize a trip to Auschwitz for a woman there."

"Do you remember her name?"

"She was from northern Europe. Her husband was an Italian nobleman with a very long last name."

"All right. We'll come back to that. You met Elisa Sordi. And then?"

"What would you like to know exactly?"

Balistreri saw the public prosecutor and Morandi shifting uncomfortably in their seats.

"What happened next?"

Hagi stared at him brazenly. "Did you not get that there was an O on her left breast? You were young then, but surely you've figured it out by now, haven't you?"

Morandi almost fell off his chair. The public prosecutor jumped to his feet and began pacing.

"Was that your first letter?" Balistreri asked impassively, as if they were talking about the weather.

"I took her body out into the middle of the river on a small boat. I was going to weigh it down with rocks. I figured even the rats would want a piece of her."

The public prosecutor and the prison officers looked ready to go off. Balistreri gestured to them to calm down. Hagi's game was clear: he wanted to drag everyone down to his level.

"And why did you hide such a work of art with so much care?" Balistreri asked.

"I couldn't be sure I hadn't left traces of organic material or fingerprints on the girl. So I let the river see to it."

Balistreri came to the most complicated point. "Alina found out everything, didn't she?"

Hagi had a coughing fit. Balistreri saw some blood on his handkerchief. Then the coughing subsided.

"I've already told you I have no intention of talking about my wife. I would never have hurt her."

"I find that hard to believe, Mr. Hagi. I know what you did to the two men who killed your brother in Romania."

Hagi shrugged. "I couldn't care less what you believe, Balistreri."

"How many women did you kill in the twenty-four years between the murders of Elisa and Samantha?"

"None," Hagi said. "And I have no reason to lie to you. Alina's death changed my life."

"Then why did you kill Samantha a year ago?"

"Because a year ago I was diagnosed with lung cancer."

The public prosecutor looked at Balistreri, who motioned to him to hold on and continued.

"We can verify that later. You found out you were ill, so you fell back into your bad habits? I don't believe that."

Hagi wiped a trickle of blood from the corner of his mouth. "If you want more answers, take these cuffs off me. I want a cigarette."

The public prosecutor looked at Balistreri, who nodded consent. A corrections officer removed the handcuffs. Balistreri offered Hagi a cigarette and lit it for him with the Bella Blu lighter. Then Hagi picked up his story again.

"Alina knew the truth. She was too smart for her own good. I beat her, because she was going to report me, and for a while she let it drop. Then Anna Rossi began to interfere. She saw Alina's bruises, and she suggested that Alina leave me and go and stay with her. That terrible evening I tried to convince her to stay, but Alina ran away on the moped to go stay with that bitch."

Another coughing fit, more blood on the handkerchief. Hagi's face was contorted with rage and hatred.

"I never forget a friend, but I also never forget anyone who crosses me. It gave me real pleasure to have her daughter killed by those three Roma. But what really pleases me is the thought of how Anna Rossi is going to feel when you inform her that she was responsible for her daughter's death."

Balistreri was extremely thankful he hadn't brought Giulia Piccolo with him. No one could have managed to hold her back from tearing Hagi apart. Hatred filled the room as if it were a layer of poisonous gas. Morandi held his head between his hands, incredulous, while the public prosecutor was no longer even taking notes, his face parchment white. The prison officers appeared ready to jump on Hagi and take him apart right there in the room.

"Why did you kill Nadia? What did she have to do with anything?"

"Nadia could have been Alina's identical twin. I wanted revenge on my wife, symbolically at least. She ruined my life by dying like that."

A well-rehearsed reply, far-fetched. Don't reply.

"Your wife ruined your life because she'd discovered you were a murderer, and she died running away from you. Whose fault was that, Mr. Hagi?"

"A wife must never betray her husband. She must remain with him come what may. It was the atmosphere at San Valente parish that turned her against me, her uncle the cardinal and the joke that is the Catholic religion."

"You took a big risk killing Nadia after Camarà had seen you together in the private lounge and she'd taken the lighter from there—the same one I just used to light your cigarette. Why not kill someone else?"

Hagi hesitated. "She was the spitting image of Alina. I wasn't going to find anyone who looked so much like her. Anyway, it was easy enough to cut up that fucking nigger."

"What about Selina Belhrouz and Ornella Corona? What did your vendetta have to do with them?"

Hagi coughed for a long time, spitting blood into his handkerchief. "You didn't like the V and the I?"

He was avoiding certain topics. Balistreri decided to try another tactic.

"We have five letters, Mr. Hagi, beginning in 1982: O, R, E, V, and I. Can you explain what those mean?"

"I'll give you a hint," Hagi said. "You have to take my wife, Alina, into account."

"What's her letter?"

"Her initial, A."

"O, A, R, E, V, I. What does it mean?"

Hagi stared at him with malevolent eyes. "I see nothing that I say surprises you, Balistreri. I'd like to give you something new to think about."

Balistreri understood beforehand what Hagi was about to say. In that brief moment he was certain he was facing not a simple serial killer but a merciless plot, and that they had no idea where it began and where it would end.

"You're going to like the next letter, Balistreri."

. . . .

Fiorella Romani, twenty-three, granddaughter of Gina Giansanti, the former concierge at Via della Camilluccia, newly graduated and recently employed by a bank, had left her home in the suburbs at seven thirty that morning, the same as every day, to take the Metro to the office. Except that she never got there. At six that evening, seeing that she wasn't home, her mother Franca called her cell phone repeatedly, but it was switched off. After calling all her daughter's friends, she decided to report her missing.

"Too many hours have gone by," Mastroianni said at the start of the meeting later in Balistreri's office. "Hagi probably kidnapped her at seven thirty, as soon as she left home, and killed her right away. Then he buried her in the woods or dumped her in the river or down a well. Then he went to Casilino 900 to kill Pasquali."

Balistreri listened in silence, smoking and leafing through Mastroianni's report on the search of Hagi's house. They had found the Invisible Man's disguises—wigs, sunglasses, hats.

"I've got Corvu's list, too," Mastroianni said. He handed over the list of alibis that Corvu had checked on Balistreri's request.

It was the check on the alibis he'd asked for.

In order to avoid any trouble they hadn't directly questioned the count, or his son, let alone Cardinal Alessandrini, on the murders of the previous year. Corvu had confined himself to checking the official record.

In the Nairobi newspapers were photographs of the opening of the new hospital wing, which had taken place on December 25 in the presence of Manfredi, Count Tommaso, Manfredi's colleagues, and the local authorities. Corvu had even checked that the only direct flight from Europe that could have taken Manfredi to Nairobi in the early morning left Zurich at midnight and that the last flight from Rome to Zurich on the evening of December 24 left at six, before Nadia was kidnapped. There was no sign of Manfredi in Rome either on the passenger lists or in passport control. So while Nadia was being killed, Manfredi was in Nairobi. On the other hand, for the murders of Samantha, Selina, and Ornella, neither the count nor Manfredi had a secure alibi.

Corvu had also noted Cardinal Alessandrini's movements in the Vatican for official events during the afternoon and evening of December 24, but it wasn't possible to check if he had been temporarily absent. On the day of Samantha Rossi's death he was in Madrid, but it wasn't known when he had come back. And on the evening of Ornella Corona's death he was at home alone.

Ajello, Paul, and Valerio had been questioned. They had seemed more worried and surprised than angered. Paul and Valerio were together in San Valente on the evening of December 24 for the orphans' Christmas Eve dinner; from at least eight o'clock onward their movements could be traced. Ajello was certainly at the opening of an ENT nightclub in Milan the night Samantha was killed, and there were many witnesses. There was a ridiculous coincidence in that, for different reasons, all three found themselves in Ostia on the night of Ornella Corona's death. Ajello had had sex with her, Paul had taken the orphans to the seaside and had slept over there with them, and Valerio had been out on a boat on his own and no one knew what time he'd returned. As for the case of Elisa Sordi, there was no one who could confirm Ajello's alibi after so many years. One result was clear: Hagi alone never had an alibi. And he was the one charged with having committed all the crimes.

Balistreri was exhausted. Around him he saw looks on his colleagues' faces that ranged from commiseration to contempt to derision.

Late in the day, he received a phone call from the chief of police.

"Balistreri, this is a disaster from start to finish, beginning with the victims and their loved ones all the way up to the media circus and the political consequences."

"Sir, if I may, we're dealing with something highly complex that was planned down to the last detail."

"So you don't think Marius Hagi could have done all this on his own?"

"I don't know. And this might be just the start."

"The start?" Floris shouted. "Five young women have been brutally murdered, the first twenty-four years ago, then Camarà, Colajacono, Tatò, Coppola, Pasquali—you were nearly killed yourself—and now Fiorella Romani. The start of what? World War III?"

There was no way Balistreri could reassure him. The fact that Pasquali already had his pistol in his hand while the plainclothes officer knocked at the trailer door was a real concern.

"I have to talk to Hagi again," Balistreri said.

"He has a plan. If we want to try to save Fiorella Romani we have to play along with him."

"What good will it do to play along with him?" Floris asked.

"Either Fiorella Romani is already dead or she will be soon. If Hagi's got her hidden away somewhere and we don't find her, she'll die of starvation. On the other hand, maybe he wants us to find her. Maybe Hagi's playing a game with us."

"What are you talking about?" the chief of police asked, exasperated.

"It's too complicated," Balistreri concluded.

Floris sighed, exhausted. He'd been a well-respected man, but now he was flailing. He was chained that was sinking into on quicksand.

Evening

It was already dark when Balistreri returned to Regina Coeli for the third time. The image of Angelo with Linda was tormenting him. He brushed it aside angrily and tried to concentrate on Hagi and Fiorella Romani. But that image took him back to his worst nightmare, back to Africa in the summer of 1970.

Corvu called from Kiev to ask how things were going. Balistreri told him Hagi had confessed to everything, including the killing of Elisa Sordi and the letter O. Then he told him about Fiorella Romani's disappearance.

"I'm coming back tomorrow. I can't stay away any longer."

"Okay, Corvu. In that case I'm going to ask the chief of police to transfer you to the beautiful and peaceful mountains of Sardinia immediately. You can count goats there. That should calm you down." And he snapped his cell phone shut.

Balistreri entered the room with the public prosecutor and Morandi, who felt it was his duty to mutter some more words that Balistreri ignored completely.

Hagi appeared to have rested for the last few hours. The corrections officers who were watching him said he had eaten a little and had slept. Medical reports confirmed he had late-stage lung cancer. The doctors said he had little time to live.

"You're tired, Balistreri. You've got terrible bags under your eyes. If you keep going like this you'll die of a heart attack before I die of cancer," Hagi said cheerfully.

"Don't worry about me. I'd like to talk about Fiorella Romani. Is she alive?"

Hagi appeared to consider the question carefully. "I think so. Naturally that depends on how strong she is."

The public prosecutor couldn't contain himself. "You should be thankful that in this civilized country, where no one can torture you like Ceausescu's hired killers tortured your brother. I only wish I were allowed to torture you."

Hagi looked at the public prosecutor pityingly. "You wouldn't have it in you to harm a hair on my head. You people are as spineless now as you were during the fall of the Roman Empire. The people you call barbarians are going to rape your women, steal your houses, and take over your country, while you sit and watch."

Morandi felt moved to intervene. "Mr. Hagi, I'm begging you to save Fiorella Romani's life. The court will take it into consideration."

Hagi laughed. "I'll die before I go before a judge. But I'm willing to save Fiorella Romani's life on certain conditions."

Balistreri bent toward Hagi. "What do you want in exchange?"

"The truth, Balistreri. It would be simple if you weren't so incompetent."

The public prosecutor and Morandi looked at him, disconcerted.

But Balistreri was ready for him; he knew what truth he meant.

The one I haven't found. The one I gave up finding all these years. The one I thought to atone for by giving up on life.

"He wants me to speak to Fiorella Romani's grandmother and reopen the investigation into Elisa Sordi's murder. In the meantime, Fiorella could be dead," Balistreri said. He might as well have been speaking Chinese for all the comprehension displayed by the public prosecutor and Morandi.

"We'll do our best to keep her alive a little longer. But be a little quicker this time, Balistreri. Fiorella won't live another twenty-four years."

The public prosecutor cut in. "I don't understand. You confessed to killing Elisa Sordi, Mr. Hagi. Are you retracting that statement?"

Hagi looked at them with scorn.

"I never said I killed her, just that I threw her body in the Tiber. You're as incompetent as Balistreri here, this street sweeper in paradise. I want the truth—only the truth can save Fiorella Romani."

The chief of police and the public prosecutor agreed to reopen the investigation immediately and contact eighty-four-year-old Gina Giansanti. Her daughter, Franca, Fiorella's mother, told them that Gina was ill and had been living in Puglia for more than twenty years in a residential neighborhood on the outskirts of Lecce, her birthplace. A military airplane would be provided to transport Balistreri and Fiorella's mother there the following morning.

. . . .

It was almost midnight when Balistreri left Regina Coeli. He had smoked at least thirty cigarettes and drunk a dozen cups of espresso. He was physically and psychologically destroyed. Keeping himself from reacting to Marius Hagi had been extremely tough. His nerves were in shreds, his thoughts roiling.

He's kissing her right now on her terrace, where I hesitated. Next he'll take her to bed.

. . . .

He took the walk home from Regina Coeli through Trastevere, where the chaos was greater because it was Friday night. There were cars everywhere tooting horns, music at top volume, ice cream, kids with bottles of beer walking in and out of the traffic. And yet he didn't hear a thing—he was walking down a tunnel that had only one possible exit.

And if he carves up another girl? This had been Linda Nardi's question the first time they had gone out to dinner on December 30, 2005. It was time to know where that idea had come from.

Don't confuse the investigation with your anger. Stop here, Michele, while you still have time.

But his footsteps led him toward her apartment. When he got to the main door it was a little after midnight. He looked up and saw a faint light in the windows. He still had the key she'd given him. Breathing heavily, he walked up the staircase.

Linda Nardi's door was the only one on that floor. The lock was gleaming, evidently new. He rang the bell. He heard steps coming to the door. He was tempted to run away but remained nailed to the spot in front of the door like a man condemned to death facing a firing squad.

"Who is it?" Linda asked from inside.

"It's me."

There was a brief silence, then Linda opened the door but left it chained.

She looked not surprised, but sad. "What do you want, Michele?"

"We have to talk. Right now."

He saw the vertical line furrowing her brow. She could have said no, never. Or not now, we can speak tomorrow. But that would not have been Linda Nardi.

She can leave you outside of her life, but not outside of her door.

When she took off the chain and opened the door, Angelo Dioguardi was standing in the middle of the small, softly lit living. His hair was more ruffled than usual, his eyes tired, the lines deep on his face.

"He has to leave," Balistreri said to Linda.

Angelo didn't wait for her reply and stepped toward toward the door. As they brushed past one another, Balistreri felt him hesitate a moment and halt as if he had something to say, a last attempt to clarify things. But it was only an exchange of silences and then Angelo left, pulling the door behind him.

Linda stared at him, arms folded. She wasn't angry. "I'm listening, Michele."

She was so beautiful. He had never seen her more attractive. Her blouse was buttoned almost to the neck and held the breasts he'd imagined so often but only now wanted to fondle and kiss. Her trousers, as usual, were baggy but were more intriguing precisely because of that, and he wanted to put his hands inside them, where perhaps a few minutes earlier Angelo's hands had been.

The desire he had repressed during the months they had spent together suddenly erupted with a violent force, making him almost reel. He felt his knees buckle. He should have taken her in his arms instead. He should have told her he did not understand her, but he trusted her. He should have promised her he would do everything for her, anything at all, even without understanding. He should have. But he didn't want to, not anymore. Linda Nardi was now only flesh and blood, a woman he desired, a woman who had sent him packing and thrown herself into the arms of his best friend.

Surprising himself, he said in a harsh voice "Who told you about the letter carved on Samantha Rossi?"

Her eyes were sad. Linda felt sorry for him, and he couldn't stand it. "You told me yourself, Michele, the way you reacted that night in the restaurant."

His desire added to his frustration and his frustration added to his anger, which was flowing through his veins with an effect so strong it might have been heroin.

"Bullshit! You knew. Someone told you."

"I had my suspicions, but your reaction that night made me certain," she said calmly.

"I don't believe you. About anything." He stopped himself before he cut all ties between them forever. He recognized the uncontrolled anger that the young Michele Balistreri had felt when things didn't go the way he wanted—the anger he'd tried to bury at the bottom of the Mediterranean in the summer of 1970.

She knew what he was going to say. "Angelo doesn't have anything to do with this."

"If someone lies about something, she's capable of lying about everything. Did you play nurse with me to be sure I'd get better and continue looking for the Invisible Man? Did you want the scoop when I found him?" His voice was growing louder and more threatening.

"Michele, get out of your prison cell now or you'll never get out of it."

"I should have fucked you like an ordinary whore. So much for all your bullshit about Saint Agnes."

She was looking at him with a different light in her eyes. She was looking at him with regret. She was saying good-bye.

"Yes, you should have. Maybe then you'd understand."

The words themselves, her calm tone, her eyes shining in the semi-darkness. He found himself as he had been thirty-six years earlier, in a place where there would never be enough remorse to find repentance.

His slap sent Linda reeling against the wall. He held her wrists together with one arm and grabbed her hair with the other, forcing her to look at him. He kissed her violently. He forced his tongue into her mouth. She didn't cry out or offer any resistance. She was lifeless, defenseless.

It was her passivity that was the last straw, the absence of any attempt to defend herself. He ripped off her blouse and bra and flung her on the sofa. Linda confined herself to covering her breasts, crossing her arms while he took off her sneakers and pants. Then he leaped on top of her, breathing heavily from desire and fury.

"Have you already had sex tonight?"

She turned her face away and he tore off her underwear. He would have done it; he was ready. But he had to stand up to unzip his pants, and when he did, their bodies separated in the dim light. In the silence broken only by his own heavy breathing, Balistreri saw the slim figure of a seminaked woman with her clothes torn, her breasts shielded by her arms, naked from the waist down. She could have been Elisa, Samantha, Nadia, Ornella, Alina, or Saint Agnes. She could have been another woman, too, one he'd never forgotten since that last night of August in 1970.

And, as Linda had predicted, he saw the first glimmer of truth. It was only a sensation, not a real and fleshed-out idea. Incredulous, horrified, he took a step back, staggering. He crashed into a table lamp, which fell and broke, and he left the apartment in total darkness. He took advantage of it to escape into the night.

SATURDAY, JULY 22, 2006

Morning

BALISTRERI ARRIVED AT THE airport after yet another sleepless night. His beard was unshaven, his clothes dirty and wrinkled. He smelled of alcohol and tobacco. He wasn't sure whether his excitement, wedded to his fatigue, was the result of going off of his antidepressants or was simply the result of how quickly things were happening now.

I don't care. I'm going to get to the bottom of this, wherever that may be.

The last time he saw Franca Giansanti was twenty-four years ago on that wretched day when Ulla had launched herself into the air and the concierge had come back from India with her part of the truth. She was somewhat bewildered to find him in a state of total disintegration, but acted as if nothing were amiss.

During the flight to Lecce, Franca spoke through tears about her daughter, Fiorella. She was thirteen when Franca's husband had died from cancer. Cardinal Alessandrini found a place for her in a boarding school, where they encouraged her studies. Then Fiorella went to

Milan, where she graduated from the Catholic university, and recently she had begun working for a bank in Rome.

Balistreri's thoughts wandered from Linda Nardi to Fiorella Romani—locked up without food and water in an isolated farmhouse where they would find her starved to death.

When they landed, a car with two policemen was waiting for them. They passed through Lecce's splendid Baroque center, which was already hot in the morning sun. On the bypass they encountered the Saturday summer traffic and Balistreri ordered them to switch on the siren.

"My mother has heart trouble. We haven't told her what happened to Fiorella."

He remembered Gina, the touchy old concierge, devoutly religious and taciturn. "We may have to inform her in order to get her to help us."

The car stopped outside a row of terraced houses on a quiet street in Lecce's outskirts. Franca rang the bell, and Gina came to the door. Her severe, tight-lipped face was now wrinkled with age. The dark shadows under her eyes, her trembling, and her swollen ankles all indicated that she wasn't in good health.

The house was full of crucifixes and photographs of Padre Pio, the pope, and Cardinal Alessandrini, as well as many photos of her daughter and her granddaughter, Fiorella: recollections of a life that was about to be shattered.

"I'm not surprised to see you, after Elisa's mother's suicide," Gina Giansanti said. "Are you here to arrest me?"

"I'm here to talk about Elisa Sordi, but not to arrest you, although I suspect that twenty-four years ago you forgot to tell us something."

"You're only getting suspicious now?" Gina said harshly.

Franca intervened. "Mamma, did you hear on TV about that Romanian who killed the policeman and all those women?"

"Of course. They said that animal confessed to killing Elisa Sordi."

"No, Mamma. He said he'd killed all of them except Elisa."

The lines on Gina's face deepened as she frowned. "What did the gypsy have to do with her then?"

"He was there at the time," Balistreri replied. "He was working for Count Tommaso dei Banchi di Aglieno."

"Oh, the count," Gina mumbled with a tone that spoke of resentment that had survived for decades. "Only a man like him would give work to an animal like that."

"It wasn't the count's fault—he didn't know what kind of a man Hagi was. But please try to remember. Was there something you didn't tell us at the time?"

"No," Gina Giansanti replied firmly. "There's absolutely nothing I didn't tell you."

Balistreri looked at Franca. She was biting her lip.

"Mamma, this is very important. I want you to swear on Fiorella's life that you're not keeping anything from Captain Balistreri."

With the kind of contempt and authority that only a Southern Italian mother could muster, Gina Giansanti said, "How dare you ask me to swear on Fiorella's life."

"If you lie, Fiorella will die," Franca replied.

Balistreri saw that threat transfigure Gina. There was no limit to the pain that Marius Hagi was able to inflict on his victims even from inside prison, using Balistreri as his blunt instrument.

"I don't understand, Franca," she said. All of a sudden she was an old trembling woman with a heart condition.

Franca burst into tears. "That man kidnapped Fiorella and is holding her somewhere, Mamma. And he says he'll let her die if you don't tell us the truth."

Gina Giansanti looked as if she might pass out. "Oh, my God. Lord have mercy upon me." She hugged her daughter and wept silently.

Balistreri watched the two women cry. Their bodies distorted with pain; their bony hands clutched each other's shoulders. He remembered them embracing like that on a rainy morning outside the Via della Camilluccia gate, while Cardinal Alessandrini held Gina Giansanti's hands in his.

He clearly remembered the sound of Teodori's cup as it shattered on the floor tiles, the end of Michele Balistreri's dreams of power, and the beginning of his farewell to life.

Elisa Sordi left while I was getting into the taxi to the airport, at eight that evening.

He cursed himself for having believed her, for having given up thinking and reacting, then and for the next twenty-four years, and for not having the courage to follow his instincts and his convictions, for not remembering Christ's words to the Jews, when he said that faith comes before morality for God's children, and also Cardinal Alessandrini's words about divine and earthly justice.

How many times since then had Gina Giansanti remembered that untruth and then cursed herself for telling it? What debt had she paid with that lie?

Balistreri knew he had little time. "Gina, you have to tell me when you really saw Elisa Sordi for the last time."

Gina Giansanti lifted her sorrowful face to him. "Elisa called me on the intercom just before five, before you and Angelo Dioguardi arrived. I went up to collect the paperwork from her to take to Cardinal Alessandrini. She was glad to be finished. That was the last time I saw her, poor child."

There was no time for Balistreri to ask any more questions.

"I have to leave immediately," he said.

The old woman embraced him, and for a moment she pressed her face against his chest. "I'm begging you, Captain, please save my granddaughter."

In the car, Balistreri looked at the marks that Gina Giansanti's tears had left on his jacket: damp rivulets right near his heart. They brought back ugly memories.

Twenty-four years earlier, in a residential complex that had seemed like paradise, a group of people above suspicion had deceived inexperienced and unconcerned police officers with lies and cover-ups.

Balistreri thought again of poor Teodori and the inglorious end to his career, and of all the deaths caused by that shameless lie. The truth that everyone was looking for had been buried under it for twenty-four years.

All of them, the investigators and those under investigation, had contributed to leaving a horrendous crime unsolved and had put in motion an infernal mechanism whose victims were still piling up.

Afternoon

He spent the return trip rereading the Elisa Sordi file. Gina Giansanti's false testimony had turned the case upside down, raising suspicions again against Manfredi and all the other possible guilty parties associated with the Via della Camilluccia residential complex. By saying that she had seen Elisa leave the office at eight o'clock, Gina Giansanti had given alibis to everyone. With the World Cup final beginning at eight thirty and the celebrations afterward, everyone had a friend ready to swear they were somewhere else.

Now they were coming back to the point of departure, to the time card Elisa had stamped at six thirty. Between six thirty and eight o'clock, no one had a solid alibi: certainly not Valerio, Manfredi, or Paul. The count had gone to see the minister of the interior, and it would be necessary to reconstruct the details of that visit. Cardinal Alessandrini had gone to the Vatican, which would be difficult to check. And there were other people to add to the list: Hagi, Colajacono, Ajello—and who knew where they had been on July 11, 1982, after such a long time had passed?

The airplane landed in Rome early on Saturday afternoon. Balistreri crossed the blazing hot city by taxi; it was empty of its residents, the streets full only of tourists. Anti-immigrant graffiti was everywhere. He saw that the Pakistanis, who had once raced up to cars stopped at intersections to offer to squeegee their windshields, now approached cautiously. Passing by the Termini train station, he noticed that the Africans selling counterfeit goods had disappeared. Not a single Romanian was out. They had vanished into thin air.

When he arrived at the office, Piccolo and Mastroianni were waiting for him. They said nothing about his appalling appearance. The air conditioning was on and the blinds were half-closed. Balistreri immediately noticed the changes on the blackboard, the latest questions and answers were written in capital letters.

. . . .

What does the letter R mean? And the E? Is that the right order? OR BEFORE? AFTER THE V AND THE I OR BEFORE THE O AND THE A.

Why did Colajacono want to take Marchese and Cutugno's shift? Because he knew Ramona might come in about Nadia.

And how did he know that? Mircea told him.

Why was Colajacono already tired on the morning of December 24? BECAUSE HE'D BEEN AT BELLA BLU ON THE NIGHT OF DECEMBER 23.

Why was Deputy Mayor Augusto De Rossi serviced by Ramona? In order to blackmail him and make him change his vote.

Who blackmailed him? Mircea and Colajacono. AND HAGI.

On behalf of whom and why? THE SAME PEOPLE AS IN DUBAI.

Is there an Invisible Man in the Samantha Rossi case? Who is he? There is, AND IT'S MARIUS HAGI.

Is he the same person who phoned Vasile to ask for the Giulia GT? YES.

When was the Giulia GT's headlight broken? IT DOESN'T MATTER.

Where was Hagi between six and seven on the evening of December 24 when Nadia was taken away? And then after nine? FIRST COLLECTING NADIA, THEN KILLING HER.

Same question for Colajacono and Ajello. WE DON'T KNOW, BUT IT DOESN'T MATTER.

Where was Hagi the night Coppola and the others died? WE STILL DON'T KNOW.

Same question for Ajello. WE DON'T KNOW, BUT IT DOESN'T MATTER.

Were Mircea and Greg guilty of murder in Romania? And who were the two victims? THE MEN WHO KILLED HAGI'S BROTHER.

How did Alina Hagi die in January 1983? SHE WAS RUNNING AWAY FROM MARIUS HAGI.

Why did Colajacono want Tatò with him, even though he knew he intended to spend time with his sister? HE WAS TOLD TO HAVE HIM THERE. IT WAS A TRAP SO THAT HE'D HAVE NO ALIBI.

Why did the Giulia GT slow down when the driver saw Natalya? HAGI TOOK HER FOR NADIA.

What was the relationship between Ornella Corona and Ajello and his son before her husband died? SHE ALREADY KNEW THEM.

Who suggested that she take out a life insurance policy on her husband? AJELLO.

How did Sandro Corona really die? IN AN ACCIDENT, PERHAPS LIKE THE ONE IN DUBAI.

Why did Camarà die? Because he'd seen Nadia with someone in the private lounge on December 23.

Who owns ENT? SAME PEOPLE IN DUBAI WHO WERE BLACKMAILING DE ROSSI.

WHERE WAS HAGI WHEN ORNELLA CORONA DIED? HE WAS THERE TO KILL HER.

WHERE WAS AJELLO WHEN ORNELLA CORONA DIED? HE WAS THERE JUST BEFORE.

WHAT DO THE LETTERS R, E, V, I, O, AND A MEAN?

WHAT WILL THE NEXT LETTER BE?

WHAT'S THE CONNECTION BETWEEN HAGI, BELLA BLU, DUBAI, DE ROSSI, ETC.?

IS FIORELLA ALIVE? WHERE IS SHE?

. . . .

The writing was Piccolo's, but Balistreri recognized Corvu's style. "Where did he call from?" he asked Piccolo brusquely.

"He's back but he stayed home. He says that if you don't want him in the office, he'll take some personal days and spend them in Rome."

Balistreri decided to ignore the tone of disapproval in Piccolo's voice. This series of calamities had forged an indissoluble bond of solidarity between these deputies who were otherwise very different.

"Tell him to come in immediately. There are some key questions missing."

Piccolo smiled and immediately sent a text message. Balistreri went up to the blackboard and added his latest questions.

WHY NADIA IN PARTICULAR?

WHOSE VOICE DID SELINA AND ORNELLA HEAR ON THE TELEPHONE?

DID HAGI DO EVERYTHING BY HIMSELF?

. . . .

Corvu arrived fifteen minutes later, looking contrite.

"What did Natalya say?" Balistreri asked him.

"That I should come back here, finish what I'd started, and then come back to Ukraine. If you don't send me off to count goats, that is."

"I wouldn't want to inflict you on the goats, Corvu."

He told him about the new details gleaned from his visit to Gina Giansanti. Corvu stared at the latest questions on the blackboard.

"So, there's definitely a link to Elisa Sordi?" Piccolo asked.

"Yes, it all starts there, with Alina Hagi and the church of San Valente. And Hagi wants to know the truth. Why?"

"To get his revenge on someone who injured him. We've seen how cruel and vengeful he is. He waited years to get even with his brother's killers."

"Hagi played a role in Elisa's death," Balistreri explained, "and Alina learned about it from Ulla, I think. That's where the problems between them started, and then she fled on her moped and died."

"And in his sick mind, Hagi blames everything on Elisa's murderer," observed Piccolo. "For him, it's as if the murderer killed Alina, too."

Balistreri said, "Correct, but if he knew for sure who it was he would have taken his revenge already—he's not lacking in means or imagination. But Marius Hagi knew that Gina Giansanti had lied. That's why her granddaughter, Fiorella, is his latest victim. But did he know back in 1982, or has he only recently come to know?"

"How could he have known?" Mastroianni asked.

Balistreri thought about Mastroianni's question. The answer was obvious.

Hagi knew that Elisa was already dead at eight o'clock that evening.

Corvu made a few calculations. "Now we know that Elisa did indeed leave at six thirty, as her time card showed. And no one has a rock-solid alibi. In the space of an hour and a half, someone she knew could have led her away to a secluded place, attacked her, tortured her, and killed her, then tied weights around her and thrown her in the Tiber and still gotten back in time for the game."

Balistreri listened.

Corvu went on. "Then there are the letters." The gears of his analytical mind were hard at work. "I've thought about it for the last few hours. Hagi was determined to let us know that we have to consider the letter A as well, the initial of his wife Alina. He wants her included among the victims. And that there's still a letter missing. Now, if we accept for a moment that this isn't a red herring—"

"Only for a moment," said Piccolo, not entirely convinced.

"That's fine, Corvu. We'll accept it for a moment. Let's say there's a message in those letters. What is it?" Balistreri asked.

"What's the most obvious meaning a series of letters could have?" Corvu asked.

Mastroianni said, "The name of the killer. That's what it would be in a detective novel."

Corvu wasn't laughing.

Piccolo voiced an objection. "I don't follow, Graziano. We already know who the killer is: it's Hagi."

"Except he didn't kill Elisa Sordi. He knows all the details of the case, but he says he didn't do it. And I don't see why he would lie; one extra murder isn't going to change anything. Besides, the man is dying."

"Keep going, Corvu," Balistreri said.

"Hagi says the last letter is missing, the one that will be carved on Fiorella Romani. I think it'll be an L."

Balistreri studied him.

Too simple. Or too complex.

"What do the letters mean?" Mastroianni asked. "

"Why on earth would Hagi go to all this trouble?" Balistreri asked.

"To suggest a solution for us. Because he knows who the perpetrator is, and he wants us to find the proof so we can nail him before he succumbs to cancer."

"But Corvu, if he knew who it was already, he'd have killed them," Mastroianni objected.

Piccolo the psychologist intervened. "Unless Hagi prefers to think of them locked in a cell for the rest of their lives—a worse revenge than a pistol shot. Hagi's suffered all his life for Alina's death. An eye for an eye."

Balistreri came to a decision. "Notify the prosecutor and the judge. Today's Saturday, so he'll be out on his boat at Ostia. Go and pick him up—we'll see if you're right. But before that I want you to arrange another meeting with Cardinal Alessandrini."

. . . .

Halfway through the afternoon he spoke to Floris, the chief of police, to bring him up to date.

"Cardinal Alessandrini will refuse to be questioned, Balistreri, and the treaty between Italy and the Vatican is clear: we can't force him."

"Leave it to me. It'll be an informal chat. I don't think he'll refuse."

"Do you really think the cardinal is connected to all of this?"

"Yes. It all started in 1982. Hagi thinks the person who killed Elisa caused his problems with Alina. Of course, he may simply be trying to frame an innocent person, but that's a risk we have to take."

"We'll never figure out what happened in 1982—it's too long ago," Floris objected.

"Agreed. My priority is not to find Elisa Sordi's killer but to save Fiorella Romani if she's alive. Elisa Sordi is just the key to making Hagi tell us where Fiorella is."

"Pasquali's funeral is Monday afternoon, forty-eight hours away, and the government and the city council are concerned that if we don't solve this case by then, the press will crucify us. That doesn't concern me, Balistreri, but I am anxious to save that young girl's life."

. . . .

Linda was looking at the dome of St. Peter's in the midafternoon light. There were so many things she could have told him, but in the end none of them would have changed reality. He wasn't the one she needed. He had been, at one time. But not anymore.

Now she needed someone who could play for everything, someone who could bet it all on one hand. A different kind of man.

. . . .

At five o'clock on that sweltering afternoon, Balistreri arrived in St. Peter's Square, which was packed with priests, nuns, and tourists. The assistant had said Cardinal Alessandrini would be waiting for him in his private study. Even Corvu's contacts probably wouldn't have gotten him back into the Vatican, but the kidnapping of Fiorella Romani had thrown the gates wide open.

He followed the assistant along the silence of the wide marble corridors, with their huge religious frescos. He found Alessandrini in gray pants, the sleeves of his white shirt rolled up, sitting at his desk buried under a mountain of paperwork. This time he greeted him without a smile and came to the point straight away.

"Captain Balistreri, I'm afraid you were right about Hagi. He seemed to me the type with a moral code that didn't entertain the deaths of young women. Evidently I was wrong."

Balistreri made no comment. He had no more time or patience for useless digressions. He had chosen a route toward the truth, impassable but necessary.

"I'm here for two reasons, Your Eminence, one professional and one private although closely connected. I'd like to begin with the private one."

Alessandrini was quick to catch on. "Why exactly do you want to confess to me, Captain Balistreri?"

"You're the best equipped to judge whether my penitence is enough. Besides, there's a second private reason, which I'd prefer to talk about during confession."

Alessandrini took his Cardinal's cassock from a coatrack nearby and put it on. "We can go into a private chapel."

Balistreri followed Alessandrini down a short corridor. The chapel was very small. It was dark and cool and smelled of incense. There were a few pews, an altar, a confessional. Alessandrini entered the booth and closed the door. Balistreri knelt and put his face to the grate. He could see the cardinal's profile.

"I'm listening. Please go ahead." In the darkness of the confessional, the cardinal's voice seemed different, both closer and farther away.

"I haven't made confession for more than forty years, since the priests wanted me to serve as an altar boy when I was in middle school."

"Don't worry; the Lord has no deadlines."

"In forty years, I've committed a great many sins. But some are worse than others."

"You don't have to tell me all of them. The ones that trouble you the most will do—the sins that have brought you here today."

Balistreri began to tell his untold story. He'd gone over it thousands of times in his own head, but he'd never spoken the words aloud before.

"I lived in Tripoli, Libya, as a child. I had a friend, a very good friend. And there was a girl I loved."

For the first time, he told someone else the story that had shaped his whole life and, in doing so, he moved slowly toward a different and deeper level of understanding. His guilt was serious, but even more serious was the way he had chosen to atone for it: a progressive renunciation of life, a self-inflicted penitence, the equivalent of millions of Our Fathers and Hail Marys.

Alessandrini listened to the story in absolute silence.

"Would you grant me absolution, Eminence?"

He knew the reply, even before he heard it. "Do you repent, my son?"

A strict Catholic education. An overbearing, obsessive father. An adolescent incapable of being what his father wanted and who, in order to run away from his lack of success, went in the exact opposite direction, mimicking the heroes of the films he'd loved as a child. Honor, courage, loyalty.

"Eminence, my continual repentance and the need for salvation and forgiveness haven't done anything for me except help me die a living death."

The cardinal's voice was a whisper. "My son, if you want God's forgiveness you must allow God to be your judge; you cannot be the judge of religion."

Fundamentally, that was what he had wanted to hear; that was where his adolescent rebellion had started. And he was coming back to it, to the one really great disagreement with his brother, Alberto, that had continued through the years. The only serious disagreement they'd ever had.

Nietzsche. Mamma. It's not that today's Christians believe in loving thy neighbor that stops them from turning on us. It's the impotence of loving thy neighbor that stops them.

Balistreri stood up from the kneeler.

"Eminence, if there's a penance I can pay, I'll pay it here on this earth, whatever its nature. But it'll be neither you nor God who decides."

Alessandrini sighed and stepped out of the confessional. They were standing facing each other. Now they were two adversaries and, finally, equally armed.

"There's one more thing, Your Eminence. The professional reason I'm here."

Alessandrini sighed.

"Do you want to talk to me about Elisa Sordi?"

"I do, Your Eminence. I want to talk about an evening in July 1982 when I wanted to watch a soccer game in peace."

"You were a young man, Balistreri. You wouldn't make those same mistakes today."

"All these years I thought it was impossible to find the killer among the crowd, so I tried to silence my conscience. I buried Elisa Sordi in a corner of my memory."

"And now that's no longer the case?"

"Eminence, as you know, before his arrest Marius Hagi kidnapped Fiorella Romani. This morning I went to Lecce and spoke to Gina Giansanti."

During the long silence that followed, Balistreri realized he was finally succeeding in controlling the anger he felt toward Alessandrini and turning it into positive energy. There was no doubt the Cardinal had performed good works for a great many people and a little evil for a few. Whatever reason he had in 1982 for asking Gina Giansanti to lie, it was unacceptable and had caused other deaths. No earthly justice would absolve him, and no God, either. But now what was needed was the truth. The truth that Hagi was demanding in order to free Fiorella Romani.

The cardinal kneeled in a pew. Balistreri let him pray undisturbed. He was a little light-headed from the smell of incense, on edge from tension and lack of sleep, shattered by Angelo and Linda's betrayal and by disgust for what he had done to her himself the night before. But it was pulling back from that deranged state that had brought him back to life to seek the truth.

Alessandrini finished and motioned to him to come over. Balistreri knelt beside him.

"Gina Giansanti is not to blame. I asked her to say she'd seen Elisa Sordi leave at eight o'clock that evening. I called her in India and told her what to say. She had no interest in protecting Manfredi, but I swore to her that he hadn't killed Elisa Sordi. I said the same to Ulla, poor soul. Unfortunately, Gina came back too late to save her."

"I knew that, Eminence. What I don't know is why."

Alessandrini was plainly suffering. "To save an innocent man, Balistreri. I wanted to correct the mistakes that earthly justice was about to make. Manfredi was innocent. I knew this, and I know it to this day with absolute certainty."

"Then you should have said so to the police. Here on earth we live in a secular and sovereign state. You should have given us the proof you had, rather than distorting the truth."

"I couldn't. I was bound by the confidentiality of the confessional. I couldn't share what I'd learned."

"The murder was committed in Italy, not the Vatican. I could have you arrested, Your Eminence."

They both knew he could not, not even if Alessandrini had confessed to having done away with Elisa and all the other women himself. But the prelate had a more valid reason to speak out than Balistreri's useless threats, and that was the life of Fiorella Romani.

"From six forty five to seven forty five on that day Manfredi wasn't at the gym, nor was he murdering Elisa Sordi. But I couldn't tell you that, and I decided to save him from those unjust accusations by means of Gina Giansanti's lie."

"Eminence, if you want to save Fiorella Romani, I have to know what really happened."

Alessandrini, too, had been haunted for twenty-four years. And now, as both a Christian and a man, he would be haunted for many more if Fiorella died.

He said, "Ulla was very religious, but that went against the count's principles. Unbeknownst to him, she came to me to confess almost every day."

"Even after Elisa's death?"

Alessandrini nodded. "The afternoon of the World Cup final, before the game started, something terrible happened while the count was out at his party meeting. After lunch, Ulla had gone to her room to sleep. She was very upset, so she took a sleeping pill and slept soundly. Around , she was awakened by loud noises from Manfredi's room. She could hear him in there, shrieking like an animal. She opened the door and found Manfredi covered in blood. There were cuts all over his body. The count came home right then and told Ulla to leave, but she stayed and listened from the other side of the door."

"What did she hear?"

Alessandrini ignored the question. "After twenty minutes, the count called her. He'd given Manfredi a sedative to calm him down and had tended to his cuts, which weren't deep. He ordered Ulla not to tell a soul what had happened, for the sake of Manfredi's future. Then they all left together. He went to see the minister, and Ulla went shopping. Manfredi left on his bike. The count had ordered him to go to the gym as usual."

Balistreri was trying to put his jumbled thoughts in order. "When did Ulla tell you these things?"

"That same evening, before the final. While the count was changing before he went to see the minister, Ulla managed to persuade Manfredi not to go to the gym and to come with her to the Vatican instead so that he could speak to me. Ulla called me while you were in my apartment and Angelo Dioguardi was on the terrace, checking Elisa's work."

Balistreri remembered the call. He remembered, too, that right after that the cardinal had left in a hurry. "Did Ulla and Manfredi come to see you in the Vatican?"

"Yes, they came to see me without the count's knowledge. He'd forbidden Ulla to involve Manfredi in anything that had to do with the Church. They arrived a little after six thirty on Manfredi's bike. I was waiting for them in a taxi outside a side entrance, and we went to my private study."

"What did you talk about?"

"Manfredi made confession for the first time in his life. The poor young man was shattered."

"Shattered by what, Eminence?"

"It was a confession, Captain Balistreri. Just as I would never reveal the confession you just made to anyone, I would never reveal his. But I am concerned for Fiorella Romani's life, so I will swear to you by the Virgin Mary that Manfredi was with me between six thirty and seven thirty and therefore could not have killed Elisa Sordi."

"That doesn't even make sense. Why didn't Ulla tell the truth to prove her son's innocence?" Balistreri said.

"You obviously don't know Count Tommaso dei Banchi di Aglieno very well. Ulla was afraid to tell him that she'd taken Manfredi to confession. The marriage would have been over, and the count would never have spoken to Manfredi again. She begged me to keep quiet, and then I asked Gina Giansanti to lie."

Balistreri realized that there was some sense to the explanation, but there were other consequences to the lie that Alessandrini could not pretend to ignore.

"Other people have benefited from Gina Giansanti's lie, Your Eminence."

"I know. I decided that saving an innocent man was more important than punishing the guilty. Honestly, I thought the police would find the real culprit—a face in the crowd."

"And you don't think it could have been someone on the inside, someone who received a cast-iron alibi from Gina Giansanti?"

"No," Alessandrini replied sharply. Then more softly, "I don't think so. Valerio Bona wouldn't have done anything like that. And Father Paul is out of the question—he was at San Valente the whole time."

"You could be mistaken, Eminence."

"I admit I was mistaken about Hagi, but not about Valerio Bona and Father Paul."

Balistreri decided to say nothing about Valerio Bona's forthcoming interrogation.

"There's also the count," he said instead.

"Of course," Alessandrini said, getting up. "And there's me, Captain Balistreri. Now, however, I must tend to the living."

The conversation was at an end. The cardinal rose, made the sign of the cross, and left.

. . . .

Balistreri went back to the office by bus, winding past sun-baked tourists in shorts and Romans out for a walk at that hour to avoid the worst of the heat.

When he arrived, Valerio Bona was waiting for him in the interrogation room. Balistreri wanted to see him under pressure. He was the former boyfriend, the one without an alibi. And the letters carved on the girls formed an anagram of his name.

He was accompanied by a young female lawyer who sailed with him. The public prosecutor had assumed responsibility for the Elisa Sordi investigation on the grounds that it was linked to the principal enquiry. Balistreri sat in front of Valerio, with Piccolo and Corvu at either side.

"I'd respectfully like to inquire why my client has been summoned here," Bona's lawyer said to the public prosecutor.

"We've reopened the investigation into Elisa Sordi's death based on new evidence that emerged. Captain Balistreri will question your client, then we'll decide whether to detain him."

Bona looked shocked. "You've decided to reopen the investigation? That's not what you said the other day."

"New evidence has emerged in the last few hours, some of which involves you directly. We have to reconstruct the events of the afternoon of July 11, 1982."

"What's the point?" Bona's lawyer protested. "Marius Hagi has already confessed."

Balistreri remembered Valerio Bona's insecurity and apprehension. At least back then, he'd given in to pressure easily.

"Hagi didn't kill Elisa Sordi," Balistreri said sharply.

Valerio turned pale and started fiddling with the gold crucifix around his neck.

"There's important new evidence," Balistreri continued. "Elisa Sordi could have been killed any time after six thirty. She left the office then, not at eight o'clock."

Valerio Bona's face displayed the incredulous look of someone called to account after twenty-four years. But he also showed a touch of relief. That surprised Balistreri.

Bona's lawyer cut in. "I assume there's no chance you'll share the basis for this new theory with us."

"You assume correctly," Balistreri replied. "Now, Mr. Bona, let's start at the end. Where were you after six thirty?"

"You already know; I told you at the time. I saw Elisa right after lunch, near the gate on Via della Camilluccia. Then I went to Villa Pamphili on my moped. I sat under a tree and studied for my exam. Around eight fifteen I went home to watch the game with my parents and some other people. Then I went to bed. My parents' friends testified to that effect back then."

"I'm well aware of that. Every other time Italy won, you went out and celebrated with your friends, but after the game of the decade, you went to bed."

"I was worried about the exam. I wanted to get some sleep."

"And because of an exam you didn't end up taking, you didn't go out to celebrate Italy's victory in the World Cup. I don't believe you. I saw the pictures of the 2006 champions on your boat. I think you were upset, Mr. Bona, about what had happened that afternoon."

Valerio Bona was shaking. "No. I didn't speak to her again that day, I swear to God."

A mix of emotions flitted across Bona's face: pain, shame, and remorse.

He shook his head. "I don't believe you. And, leaving God out of it, there are other reasons I don't believe you."

The lawyer lost her patience and turned to the public prosecutor. "I'd appreciate a little more transparency here."

The public prosecutor nodded to Balistreri, who then continued.

"We think there's an outside accomplice in the series of crimes attributed to Marius Hagi in the past year. You knew him back in 1982. And you have no alibi for these crimes. In fact, you were in Ostia on your boat the day Ornella Corona was killed."

Valerio Bona's eyes opened wide. "You've got to be kidding," he said.

"I'm deadly serious, and you should take this seriously, too, Mr. Bona. Tell me the truth about that day in 1982."

The lawyer asked for a break in order to speak to Bona alone. Balistreri took the opportunity to smoke a cigarette in his office.

"He's guilty," Corvu said.

"I'm not sure," Piccolo said.

"He's guilty of something, but I don't know what," Balistreri said.

When they went back into the room, Valerio Bona looked resigned and relieved, almost resolute. He was gripping his crucifix tightly.

"My client will make a voluntary statement about the events of the afternoon of July 11, 1982," his lawyer said. "He will respond to any questions on that matter. He will not respond to any questions about more recent events and states categorically that he has no connection with them."

"Okay, Mr. Bona, let's hear what you have to say," Balistreri said.

Valerio was now resolved, like a child who's been persuaded to take some very bitter medicine and wants to do so quickly, to get it over with.

"I couldn't concentrate in the park at Villa Pamphili. I was sure that Elisa was seeing someone, and I wanted her to tell me to my face. A little after five, I went to Via della Camilluccia to speak to her. I parked my moped around the corner and saw you, Captain Balistreri, with Count Tommaso, who had just arrived. It must have been around a quarter to six. You and the count spoke for less than a minute, and then he went to Building A and you went around the long way to the cardinal's."

Balistreri nodded. He remembered every instant well.

He wanted to go up to see her.

Valerio took a breath and continued. "I was hiding around the corner. I saw Father Paul hurrying out—you'd probably already spoken to him. He got into his Volkswagen with Gina Giansanti, who was going to Mass, and they drove off together."

While I was looking up at that window and couldn't make up my mind.

"The door to Building B was open. I went in. The elevator was in use—it was you going up, Captain Balistreri. I waited a minute, because I couldn't decide what to do. Then I made up my mind and went up to the third floor on foot."

Valerio Bona stopped. His face reflected the horror of that memory.

"I knew Elisa wouldn't let me in, and the door to the offices was closed, but not locked. I went in and immediately noticed that it was absolutely silent. I figured she'd gone out to buy cigarettes and left the door unlocked. I paused outside her office door."

Valerio stopped to take a breath, and in that moment, before he opened a door that had remained closed for twenty-four years, Balistreri knew that the mistake he'd made that day was far worse than he'd imagined all this time. Now the specter glimpsed while he was attacking Linda Nardi began to take shape.

"If I hadn't gone in, my whole life would have been different. I'd have stayed with IBM and gotten married. I'd have children today. But I wanted to speak to her. I was desperate, so I went in. Elisa's body was on the floor next to the wall. Her blouse and her bra were torn and there was blood on her breasts. She had a black eye, a cut lip, and a bruise on her cheek. I didn't go any closer. I stood and stared at her for a moment. Then I ran out and shut the door behind me. A minute later I was on my moped, and I got out of there as fast as I could."

The public prosecutor looked at Balistreri in disbelief, and Balistreri looked at Bona. He felt no sympathy at all for him. What he felt was fury. If only he had had eyes, ears, and a heart that day.

He shook himself out of his pointless, gloomy thoughts. He had to save Fiorella Romani. That was the only real, urgent, fundamental thing to be done. And the road was laid out—he only had to sweep aside whoever had put themselves in the way.

"There are two possibilities, Mr. Bona. The first is that you're lying and you killed Elisa Sordi outside the office between six thirty and eight. The second is that you're telling the truth, and if you'd told the truth at the time the perpetrator would now have been in prison for many years."

"I know, and I've tortured myself over that. I didn't say anything because I was so shocked, and later I was confused. The body was found in the Tiber. The concierge said that Elisa had left at eight that night. I thought I'd had some kind of hallucination."

Have you confessed to this? Has a priest given you absolution? How many Our Fathers and Hail Marys? Do you think you've earned a spot in heaven?

All his hatred for those who had deceived him was focused on Valerio Bona, as if by destroying him he could wipe out his past.

"I hope you're lying, Mr. Bona. I hope so for your sake, because if what you're saying is true, your silence caused the death of four young women, a young Senegalese man, and four policemen, as well as the suicides of Manfredi's mother and Elisa's mother."

Valerio looked petrified. His hands with their chewed fingernails searched desperately for the crucifix, but his eyes stared off into space.

His lawyer said, "At most, you can charge my client with making a false statement in the Elisa Sordi case. He's not involved with anything else."

There was no more caution, no balance, no remorse, only his carefully controlled anger and the thought of Fiorella Romani.

Balistreri said in an icy voice, "That's the legal position. But your client is a practicing Catholic, someone who believes in heaven and in hell."

He did what he should have done without a second thought twenty-four years earlier and had not done until Giovanna Sordi leaped from her balcony while Italy exploded over another victory.

He looked scornfully at Valerio Bona huddled on his chair. "You thought you could bury your guilt by giving up your cushy job at IBM and working with the orphans. Is that it, Mr. Bona? Would you like to see photographs of the corpses of these young women, all dead because of your cowardice?"

He caught Piccolo's disapproving look, the lawyer's contempt, the Prosecutor's and Corvu's embarrassment.

Marius Hagi. The grief you're dishing out is endless. And I happen to be the right instrument for your vendetta.

Valerio Bona lifted his tear-streaked face, the face of an old man. "You're right, Captain Balistreri, I can't wipe away my guilt. But the Lord will be my judge. All I can offer you is the truth, no matter how late."

"Tell me the whole truth then. You lost control of your boat when I asked you if Francesco Ajello had gotten Elisa into bed."

Valerio shut his eyes. "Once when Elisa came to watch one of my regattas he got a look at her, and he begged me to introduce him to her, but I refused."

"There's more to it than that," Balistreri said.

Bona nodded. "That afternoon, when I ran out of Elisa's office and went to get on my moped, Francesco Ajello's Porsche was parked around the corner."

A recent abortion, an unknown lover.

Balistreri spoke to the public prosecutor. There was insufficient evidence to hold Valerio Bona. They seized his passport and let him go. The public prosecutor would try to get a warrant for Ajello from the judge that evening.

Now they had to reconstruct the journey Elisa's body had made from her office on Via della Camilluccia to the bottom of the Tiber.

. . . .

On the telephone the count's personal secretary said he was out of the country, but that Manfredi was home and was willing to meet with him. Balistreri went to Via della Camilluccia alone at dinnertime. The area was deserted: all the wealthy residents were away for the weekend at their villas and on their boats, or dining outside in the center of town. The residential complex was silent and almost completely dark; only the lights of Building A's penthouse shone brightly.

The young secretary ushered him onto the terrace, where Manfredi joined him. He was silent; no smiles or pleasantries were exchanged. The atmosphere was very different than it had been a few days earlier. Balistreri decided to pick up where their last conversation had ended.

"Last Saturday you asked me to uncover the truth about Elisa Sordi. Since then many others have asked me to do the same."

Manfredi looked at him. He had Ulla's eyes, though they now contained his father's cold arrogance as well.

"Did you really need encouragement, Balistreri? Aren't you interested in the truth for its own sake?"

"You all lied in 1982."

Balistreri could hear the rage creeping into his voice and fought to control it.

Rage is not a shortcut to the truth.

"And so? You're the police, not us. And in 1982 you were consumed with your vices and prejudices. According to you, a disfigured young man, and a nobleman to boot, was the perfect suspect."

"Did you kill Elisa Sordi?"

Manfredi assumed his father's scornful tone.

"After everything that's happened, that's all you can think to ask?"

"Of course. Either we clarify this point definitively or we go nowhere. And this time you'd better be more convincing. Another young girl's life is in the balance. I've got no more time or patience for your lies."

For some ridiculous reason Manfredi gave a half smile, then nodded.

"Good. I see you're finally resolved, Balistreri. Will the truth about Elisa Sordi really help save this young woman?"

"Yes. Marius Hagi, the man we arrested, is demanding the truth before he'll help us."

I could ask if you know him, but I wouldn't know if you were telling the truth.

Manfredi absorbed that piece of information in silence. "All right, I'll tell you something I won't ever repeat to anyone under any circumstances."

"I'm listening."

"I was very attracted to Elisa Sordi. So were you, right?"

Balistreri said nothing.

"Of course you were attracted to her. Everybody was. But all you wanted to do was get her into bed, while I was in love with her."

Manfredi continued, "The afternoon of the World Cup final, Rome had come to a halt. It was deserted. Most people were resting up. It was as if every Italian was going to play in the final. But Elisa came to work. I saw her arrive mid-morning, then I saw her leave for lunch and come back again, followed by Valerio Bona. They were arguing. Then she left him outside the gate and went up to her office."

"Where were your parents?"

"My father was at the Hotel Camilluccia, near here, at a party meeting. My mother had taken a sleeping pill. The two buildings were completely deserted; the only two people awake were Elisa and myself. It was the ideal moment to have a quiet word with her. What would you have done in my position?"

Balistreri didn't reply. He was transported back to that afternoon. He was hot, half-drunk, and excited about that evening, when he wanted to be free to do whatever he wanted. He saw it all in slow motion, second by second.

I wanted to go up and see her.

Manfredi continued, "I hoped maybe she liked me at least a little. I knew she wasn't going out with Valerio, but I suspected she was seeing someone. I couldn't stop thinking about it. I was obsessed. I kept going from my room to the terrace and back. I took several showers. In the end I made up my mind."

The truth. The truth you confessed to Cardinal Alessandrini.

"I saw Gina Giansanti go up and then leave."

"What time was it?"

"I think it was a little after five. I went down, then crossed through the interconnecting basements so Gina Giansanti wouldn't see me from the gatehouse. Then I went up the stairs. The door was closed. I knocked and called out to Elisa. She let me in and said she was happy to see me. She asked me for some help with her new computer. I fixed the problem she was having."

Balistreri looked toward the window of Elisa Sordi's office. Behind the closed blinds he saw Linda Nardi's dark living room the previous evening. He could imagine what came next.

"Elisa kissed me on the cheek to thank me. I tried to kiss her on the mouth. She politely pushed me away. She was smiling. But then I glimpsed my own face in the mirror and thought she was laughing at me. I lost it."

Someone who fights monsters has to be careful not to turn into a monster himself. If you stare into the abyss long enough, the abyss starts to stare back at you.

"I shoved her and she flew against the wall. I held her wrists with one hand and tore at her blouse and bra with the other. She offered no resistance at all; she was paralyzed with fear."

Manfredi stopped. He didn't appear upset at the memory. He must have gone over it thousands of times with his psychiatrist in Kenya. He was just pausing to give Balistreri a chance to take it all in.

"When she didn't react, I turned into an animal. I punched her in the face. I think I broke her cheekbone. Her head hit the wall, hard, and she fell to the floor. I stood and watched her for a while. She was breathing softly. Eventually, I calmed down a little. I took a compact from her bag and held the mirror in front of her mouth to check whether it fogged up. She was breathing."

"So, Elisa was alive?"

"Absolutely. But I didn't know what to do. I was desperate. I could hear the elevator traveling to the floor above. I was shaking with fear. Then I heard Angelo Dioguardi ring the bell and say hello to Cardinal Alessandrini. So I took Elisa's keys, which were in the door, locked the office, and hurried back here through the basement. It took me less than five minutes."

"And you did nothing to the girl while she was passed out?"

"You want to know if I put out several cigarettes on her and suffocated her? Absolutely not."

Balistreri decided to press on further. He could have come back at another time to carve the letter O.

"And once you were home what did you do?"

Manfredi looked at him calmly. "What would you have done?"

"I would have called my father, especially if he was a powerful man."

"I called him immediately from the telephone by the balcony and told him everything. He ordered me to go to my room and not move from there. He said he would be home in a couple of minutes and would take care of everything. Before I went back to my room, I looked out with my binoculars and saw you, Balistreri. You were smoking a cigarette near the gatehouse, chatting with Gina Giansanti. Then I went straight to my room."

I looked up toward the balcony of Building A. A fleeting reflection, then nothing. Manfredi was acting shy that day.

"My father sent Ulla away and gave me a sedative to calm me down. He promised me that my life would change, that our relatives in Africa would help. He would talk to Elisa and apologize; he would give her a permanent job. In those few interminable moments my life was decided. For better or worse."

I stopped to look up at her window. It was the only one open, and this time there was a flower on the windowsill. She must have put it there when the sun was no longer as strong. I still didn't know what to do, so I stayed there for a couple of minutes, thinking about her. Then I got into the elevator. When the doors opened on the cardinal's landing, Angelo was standing there.

"I gave Elisa's office keys to my father. He told me to act normal and go to the gym until the guests arrived for the game. A person he trusted would talk to Elisa while he went to his appointment with the minister of the interior."

Balistreri remembered it clearly.

"I saw you leaving; he took the car with Ulla and you took your bike. But you didn't go to the gym."

Manfredi told him exactly the same version of events as the cardinal had. He was with Ulla at the cardinal's. The count didn't know about this part. He would rather have gone to prison than told him.

"What about the next day, when Elisa's body couldn't be found and the police arrived?"

Manfredi said, "My father never told me what happened. That night after the game, he told me to deny having seen Elisa Sordi that day."

"You didn't ask him for an explanation when they fished Elisa's body out of the Tiber?"

"I didn't have the courage. You don't know my father. He told me again that I should deny having seen Elisa Sordi that day. I asked him if he believed I'd left her alive. He told me it didn't matter. When things died down, he was going to send me to Kenya and I'd be happy there. Even as you were taking me away, he told me to hang tough and be patient and everything would be sorted out."

"And your mother? Didn't she suggest you use her as an alibi? You could have said you and she were together with Cardinal Alessandrini."

"She was too upset, and then the next day she killed herself."

"Manfredi, I need to speak to your father right away."

"I'm afraid you won't be able to do that until tomorrow evening. He went away three days ago. He's with his brother, Giuliano, and my cousin Rinaldo in Uganda; they're sailing down the White Nile in an area that even satellite phone can't reach. But tomorrow afternoon he'll be in Nairobi. From there he's flying to Frankfurt. We're meeting there Monday morning, then I'm going back to Africa and he's coming back to Rome. You can see him then."

"So you maintain that you don't know what your father did that day. And expect me to find out the truth? After twenty-four years?!" Balistreri asked, furious.

"We've never spoken about Elisa Sordi again. It's as if she never existed. He never asked me if I killed her and I never asked him how she came to be killed or what happened to her body. Someone killed Elisa Sordi after I attacked her. You accused me because it was the most obvious answer. Ulla killed herself because she saw no way out."

Balistreri looked him in the eye. "Don't you feel any remorse for what you did to Elisa Sordi?"

Manfredi turned to look at what had been Elisa's office window.

"I can look at that window today, Balistreri, better than you can. I still come back here, and I bet you've avoided walking down this street ever since. Remorse is useless. Look at what I've done for the poor in Africa, while you can't even sleep at night."

Manfredi stared at him with something worse than hate—something deeper and more painful.

"It's time you made yourself useful, Balistreri. You look like hell. Go home and get some sleep. Tomorrow morning, take a shower, shave, and eat a good breakfast. If your mind is in the same condition as your body, that missing girl doesn't stand a chance."

Balistreri got up. At the door Manfredi said good-bye without shaking his hand.

"At least try to save this girl, Balistreri, rather than your own soul."

Evening

Balistreri returned to the office at ten, exhausted. Ajello was nowhere to be found. Corvu had checked his home, but his wife said he had left on a business trip and she didn't know where he was. They had checked with border control, the ports, and the airports, but there was no trace of him.

Balistreri decided he needed to talk to Hagi again and tell him all that he'd done to save Fiorella Romani, if she was still alive. The Prosecutor was absolutely against sharing confidential information with Hagi, such as what had been learned from Valerio and Manfredi, but

Floris was in agreement with Balistreri. He called Avvocato Morandi on his cell phone and suggested an informal chat without lawyers, just Balistreri and Hagi alone in the prison courtyard. Morandi was helpful and said he would suggest it to Hagi right away. Ten minutes later Balistreri called Floris back to say that Hagi was agreeable.

Corvu and Piccolo went with Balistreri to Regina Coeli by car around eleven. They had to switch on the siren to get through the heavy Saturday night traffic. Trastevere's bars and restaurants were humming with sunburned crowds fresh from the beach—coated with moisturizing cream and now in need of drinks, amusement, and a cool breeze.

Balistreri was shattered at the end of an interminable day that had begun at dawn with the trip to Gina Giansanti in Lecce. But saving Fiorella Romani allowed no time to pause.

Hagi was ready and waiting, handcuffed, in the prison courtyard. Balistreri coud see that since he last saw him, Hagi's physical state had deteriorated; his cough was heavier, continuous. His body was quickly being eaten up, but his black soul was still thriving.

"I'm a dying man, but you look worse than I do. Take off my handcuffs and light me a cigarette."

Balistreri did as he asked. The yard was empty but floodlit. The air was cool, and the traffic and general racket of Trastevere were just discernible. They walked and smoked.

"I did what you asked, Mr. Hagi."

"Good. I'm listening."

"First you have to give me your word that Fiorella Romani is still alive."

Hagi's deep black eyes stared at him with curiosity. "You'll take my word for it?"

"In this case, yes."

"I can't be sure she's alive, but she was in the best of health when you arrested me and I have no reason to believe she's dead. Now tell me who killed Elisa Sordi."

Balistreri told him the information he'd gotten from Gina Giansanti, Cardinal Alessandrini, Valerio Bona, and Manfredi. Hagi nodded and listened.

"That's all?" he asked finally.

"I still have to question the count and Ajello; without them we're at a standstill."

"Why is that?" Hagi asked.

"Because we have to know what the count did with those keys and how he took care of Elisa. Did he send Ajello, or did he go himself? Was she dead or alive? Do you have anything you want to share?"

Hagi said, "This case is yours and has been for twenty-four years."

"But everyone lied," Balistreri protested.

"Exactly. Everyone lied, despite the fact that you Catholics have a commandment against it, if I'm not mistaken."

"Mr. Hagi, I'll do anything you ask me to do, but I want Fiorella Romani alive and back with her mother. We can't wait until the count comes back the day after tomorrow. It'll be too late."

"That's true, it will be too late," Hagi said. That sentence hung in the air with brutal force.

Hagi looked at him in silence. Balistreri felt fatigue coming over him in waves, together with the memory of his attack on Linda Nardi and the image of Fiorella Romani tied up in a cave. His body was giving in to sleep while his brain was fighting to stay awake, grasping at the hope of saving Fiorella. Suddenly another image made its way into the fog of his mind.

"You were on the hill the night they shot me," he said.

"Of course I was. I was the boss," Hagi admitted.

"And you killed Colajacono but decided to spare me?"

Hagi smiled. "We're getting off track, Balistreri. You're supposed to tell me who killed Elisa Sordi."

"Who carved the letters on the victims?"

Hagi started coughing. He spat blood onto the ground. "The same person who carved one on Elisa Sordi," he answered.

Balistreri knew he was telling the truth.

"You already know who it is."

"Balistreri, we're back at the beginning again. It's you who has to know. You've been going around in circles for years. Have you any idea how much damage you've caused with your fucking amateurism? If it wasn't for you . . ." Hagi's cough swallowed up the end of the sentence.

If it wasn't for my lack of professionalism Alina Hagi would still be alive. But we only have the future in our hands.

"The letters point to Valerio Bona," Balistreri said.

Hagi looked at him, laughing. "The letters? At the same time you're forgetting the suicides of two mothers—that's another two letters."

"Another two letters?" Balistreri repeated.

"What kind of killer would carve his own name? This isn't some nineteenth-century British crime novel. Have you gone and accused poor Valerio Bona?"

You know very well I have, you bastard, because you're the one who led me down that path.

Hagi looked at the prison wall, as if he could see through it.

"Are you worried yet, Balistreri? And has Cardinal Alessandrini repented for what he did? Will he think about it as he's reciting prayers with the pope?"

Balistreri had no more cards to play. Fiorella Romani was lost.

Just then Corvu and Piccolo burst into the yard.

"Valerio Bona hanged himself from the mast of his boat," Corvu announced.

Hagi's eyes showed a gleam of interest. A Mephistophelian grin appeared on his sick face.

"Finally, someone is repenting in earnest, Balistreri."

Balistreri reeled at the news. He turned to Hagi. "Valerio Bona didn't kill Elisa Sordi or any of the other victims. He just lied about what happened."

"Everybody lied. A very grave sin. But not everyone's paid the price like I have. Now it's their turn to pay. Only the judge is not your benevolent God, Balistreri. The judge happens to be me."

"Mr. Hagi, I'll pay any price if you'll spare Fiorella Romani."

Hagi leaned against the wall. "Give me another cigarette," he said, coughing.

Strangely, smoking seemed to calm his cough. Hagi spat a mouthful of blood onto the ground.

"I want an answer by tomorrow noon, Balistreri. If you give me the right answer, Fiorella Romani's life will be saved. Now pay close attention, I already know something here. If you try to trick me, Fiorella dies."

"What do I have to do?"

"There's another reason Cardinal Alessandrini forced Gina Giansanti to lie. Make him confess his sins in full. Show me that you know how to act like a policeman outside the gates of paradise as well as inside them."

. . . .

Balistreri sent Corvu and Piccolo back to the office, arranging to meet them again at eight the following morning. He left the prison by himself a little after midnight after that infinitely long day. The Saturday night partying around the Tiber was in full swing with rows of vehicles tooting horns, crowds with beers and ice cream cones, open-air restaurants jam-packed.

Only twenty-four hours had passed since he'd fled from Linda Nardi's and himself. He walked on, staggering with fatigue. He'd been deceived by everyone: Gina Giansanti, Cardinal Alessandrini, Manfredi, the count, Valerio Bona, Ajello, even by Angelo and Linda, up to the point where he now found himself in a labyrinth—and Marius Hagi was holding the thread.

He needed to sleep, to sort out the ideas that were scattered around like playing cards by the gust of his emotions. But he needed peace to find that sleep.

He hadn't dialed that number for over two years. Antonella answered at the first ring. She was at home, alone, and said she'd be waiting for him.

He found her in an old sweatsuit, her eyes puffy and underlined with dark shadows. Despite everything, Pasquali had been a courteous and properly behaved boss toward her—something rare for the time. Balistreri knew, however, that those tears were partly wasted. Pasquali had gone to Casilino 900 with a gun in his hand, intending to kill Marius Hagi and put a lid on the whole business, but someone smarter and more powerful had decided otherwise and had drawn him into a deadly trap. But there was no point in saying this to Antonella.

Seeing him in such a state, she made him lie on the sofa with his head resting on her knees, and lit one of those joints that, during the years of their relationship, he had always disdainfully refused.

"What was Pasquali like during his last few days?" Balistreri asked, exhaling slowly.

"Pretty much the way you are right now. Of course, for Pasquali if the knot in his tie was crooked or he had a hair out of place, he felt as miserable as you look right now."

Antonella stretched out an arm and picked up a small book from the table.

"I cleaned out Pasquali's office, Michele. This calendar was in a hidden drawer."

It was a small black calendar, the size of a deck of cards. It was for 2006. Balistreri was reminded of Coppola's calendar, handed over by his son, which had reopened the case. He leafed through Pasquali's calendar, but his eyes kept fluttering closed. There were no names and no numbers, no appointments. Several dates were circled and there were a few cryptic notes.

Antonella slowly ran her fingers through his hair and caressed his face. Those dates were familiar, but his fatigued brain didn't know why. At last, he closed his eyes and slept.

SUNDAY, JULY 23, 2006

Morning

HE WAS AWAKENED ON Antonella's sofa by a cell phone ringing. It was Corvu calling. It was already eight thirty, and they were waiting for him in the office. While he took an ice-cold shower, Antonella made him a double espresso and some toast. He smoked two cigarettes as he drank his coffee.

"You're back on caffeine and tobacco?" There was no reproach in her voice; actually, she appeared to approve.

"I flushed all my pills, too, together with some old ways of thinking."

Antonella smiled. "Now you just have to get back to having sex. Or have you already started?"

He gave her a light kiss on the lips and called a taxi.

Corvu, Piccolo, and Mastroianni had been in the office since six that morning, trying to reconstruct the case from the beginning.

"In light of the new information, I've checked out all the alibis for Elisa Sordi's death. I hope you don't mind, but I also checked up on Angelo Dioguardi," Corvu said apologetically.

"You did very well, Corvu. Go ahead, I'm listening."

"Okay. We know for certain that Elisa Sordi was alive at five o'clock when she spoke to her mother on the phone, because it shows up in the phone records. Immediately after, or immediately before, the concierge came up to her and took the work she'd finished to Cardinal Alessandrini. Then Manfredi paid Elisa a visit, or else he was already there when she received her mother's call. He stayed there for about twenty minutes, while Balistreri and Dioguardi arrived at the main gate and were talking to Gina Giansanti. Manfredi was still in Elisa's office when Angelo came in and went up in the elevator. He heard the cardinal open the door. Manfredi left Elisa beaten unconscious, if we believe him. He locked the door, went to his building, and called his father, who was at the Hotel Camilluccia, which is about five minutes away—we checked. Then he went out onto the terrace and saw Balistreri talking to the concierge through his binoculars. He went to his room, where he started cutting himself with a razor blade and moaning. That woke his mother. The count arrived after a few minutes, met Balistreri, exchanged a couple of words with him, and went up to the penthouse, while Gina Giansanti was getting ready to go to Mass. As Balistreri was walking over to Building B he met Father Paul coming out, then went up in the elevator to the top floor, where Angelo Dioguardi and the cardinal were waiting for him. Father Paul left the complex with Gina Giansanti. She went to Mass, and he went back to San Valente."

Corvu paused to consult his notes.

"Valerio Bona took advantage of the concierge's absence—she'd left with Father Paul—and, following Balistreri, entered Building B. He went to see Elisa and found her dead. That is, Valerio thought she was dead. Manfredi swears he left her unconscious. One of the two is lying or mistaken, or she died in the interim. The six people in the Via della Camilluccia complex all moved around at six o'clock. Balistreri, Dioguardi, and Cardinal Alessandrini came down and saw the count and Ulla leaving in their car and Manfredi on his bike. From that point on we know exactly where five of these people were. Balistreri and Dioguardi went to watch the game, while the cardinal, Ulla, and Manfredi were at the Vatican. And we know the count went to see the minister of the interior. At the time, the police checked the registers and found he went in at six fifty and left at seven thirty five."

"Corvu, I want you to get a complete copy of the ministry's logbooks."

Balistreri pointed to the blackboard where they'd put the letters in chronological order.

O (Elisa)

? (Ulla)

A (Alina)

R (Samantha)

E (Nadia)

? (Giovanna)

V (Selina)

I (Ornella)

? (Fiorella)

"For the three we don't know, we can use what Hagi said about his wife, Alina," Mastroianni said. "Where there's no letter carved, we should use the first letters of their first names."

"I have my doubts about the last letter being an F," Corvu said.

It depends on what they find carved there, he thought, but avoided saying it.

"So we have O U A R E G V I F. But it doesn't have to be in that order," Piccolo said.

"I've read up on similar cases. The order is part of the obsessive behavior and is always important."

Balistreri lost patience. "These letters tell me nothing." And yet in his mind a memory was stirring. It took shape, rose and fell, and disappeared. It was something he had seen somewhere.

Piccolo took the floor. "Valerio Bona's death was a suicide. After being questioned he went to Ostia—two witnesses saw him getting onto a boat by himself and going out to sea as it was getting dark. He anchored in a quiet cove. The boat was five hundred yards from the shore. A finance police patrol boat sighted it around ten. Valerio Bona had hanged himself from the mast."

Piccolo paused, then said, "He left a note. It's confirmed that it's in his handwriting"

She looked down at the piece of paper and began to read.

"We should have told the truth then, but we weren't brave enough. I leave my punishment in God's hands."

"Was it addressed to anyone?" Balistreri asked.

"Not the note, but there is something else," Piccolo said. "There was a single outgoing call from Valerio Bona's cell phone after he was questioned. The phone company checked the records: the call was to the Vatican switchboard."

. . . .

This time Cardinal Alessandrini's personal assistant was adamant. The cardinal was celebrating Mass, then he had to accompany the wife of a foreign head of state on a private visit to the Sistine Chapel, and then he had to go over the pope's sermon for the Angelus, which he would give at noon from Val D'Aosta where he was on vacation.

Balistreri knew he'd already overstepped his boundaries, but made up his mind to force the situation. A spat between the Italian state and the Vatican paled in comparison to the life of Fiorella Romani.

He called Floris at nine that morning, went to meet him, and spelled out his plan. The chief of police heard him out attentively, his reactions somewhere between incredulity and horror. Finally he smiled and shook Balistreri's hand.

Floris called the minister of the interior. The minister was strongly opposed to it, but Floris pointed out that Balistreri was a loose cannon and would certainly get in touch with Linda Nardi to call a press conference if things did not go his way.

The minister called the prime minister's undersecretary, a man famously close to Vatican circles. Only the explicit threat of a press conference, during the course of which Balistreri would attribute direct responsibility for Fiorella Romani's death to the cardinal, persuaded the undersecretary to call Alessandrini. He made his apologies, saying that Balistreri was out of control and would be replaced as soon as possible but suggested that the Church, already under accusation for its defense of Roma rights, might like to try to avoid any further trouble. The cardinal allowed Balistreri thirty minutes at ten sharp in the Sistine Chapel. Although he had lived in Rome for so many years, Balistreri had never been there.

Alessandrini's assistant was shocked and disgusted by Balistreri's scruffy appearance. The cardinal arrived punctually, dressed in his vestments. Coming dressed like this further underlined the light years' distance between them, a gap that Balistreri had only a few minutes to bridge.

The greeting was extremely cold. "I thought we had finished with our reciprocal confessions," Alessandrini said instantly. "Nevertheless, let's take a walk together—perhaps it will do your spirit good. I hope it's in a better state than your appearance."

They walked slowly, while Balistreri tried to gather all his strength. He was there for one reason only and could not allow himself to be distracted either by his contempt for the cardinal or by the wonderful ceiling that people from all over the world came to admire.

"You don't have much time, Eminence, and Fiorella Romani has even less."

"I told you everything I know yesterday."

"Marius Hagi says Fiorella Romani will die this afternoon unless you tell me—"

Alessandrini held up a hand to stop him and came to a halt before *The Last Judgment.* Christ presided over the scene, directing a severe gaze at those descending into the pits of hell; beside him sat the Virgin Mary, looking away, resigned.

"What do you see, Captain Balistreri?" Alessandrini asked.

"I see a God who strikes fear and beside him a woman who looks unhappy because she doesn't have the power to make decisions. I see miserable people looking horrified, no matter which side they fall on. There may be justice in this painting, but I see no mercy."

Alessandrini was lost in thought. "Evil is a part of the divine plan, Balistreri. Christians like Gina Giansanti know that and accept it as a test. They wait for the moment you see depicted here, when God metes out justice."

A lesson in theology. He doesn't want to help me. Or can't. It's part of the divine plan!

Balistreri took an envelope from his pocket and showed Alessandrini the photographs of Elisa, Samantha, Nadia, Selina, and Ornella. Burns, bruises, letters carved into their flesh.

Alessandrini wouldn't touch them. He moved sharply away and walked toward the exit. Balistreri looked desperately at his watch—his time was up. He saw the master of ceremonies with the wife of the head of state already waiting. The cardinal was some distance away when he turned back toward him.

"Pass on our conversation to Marius Hagi. Tell him to listen to the Angelus address."

. . . .

Balestreri called Floris on his cell phone to tell him about the conversation while he drove back once again with Corvu through the traffic in the morning heat to Regina Coeli prison.

"The prime minister and the minister of the interior are very concerned," the chief of police informed him.

"About relations with the Vatican, I imagine, not about Fiorella Romani."

"Balistreri, I'm not worried about my position. We already have too many deaths to mourn, and there's no point in useless debate. Offer Hagi anything you can."

"The man's dying, sir. We only have the truth to offer him."

"What are you thinking of doing?"

"I'm going to do what Cardinal Alessandrini said. I'll tell Hagi about our conversation."

"But he didn't tell you anything," Floris protested.

"Let's let Hagi be the judge of that."

The graffiti on the city's walls incited people to set fire to the camps. So-called civic organizations were having their say. Political posters proposed drastic solutions.

If Fiorella Romani dies, it'll start a riot. Hagi's always known that. It's part of his plan.

They got to the prison at eleven thirty. Hagi was waiting in an interrogation room that had been equipped with a television, as Balistreri had requested.

Balistreri told him everything—the alibis, Valerio Bona's suicide note, his conversation with Cardinal Alessandrini about *The Last Judgment.*

Hagi nodded, pleased with the news of Valerio Bona's phone call to the Vatican, but it was the conversation with Alessandrini that really piqued his interest. He asked for it to be repeated to him twice with barely concealed satisfaction.

Then he turned to Balistreri. "So? What's the answer to my question?"

"I'll tell you after the Angelus."

"Then let me have a cigarette." There was no smoking in the room. Balistreri lit one for Hagi and one for himself.

At noon, the television was going to start broadcasting live from Les Combes in Val D'Aosta, where the pope was spending his vacation.

"Dear brothers and sisters."

The pope was smiling and full of energy. He spoke about the Middle East, expressing solidarity with the unfortunates there. Then he changed the subject.

"Yesterday we celebrated the memorial of St. Mary Magdalene, Our Lord's disciple, who occupies a prominent place in the Gospels."

The pope went on with his sermon about Mary Magdalene, then came to the end. Hagi perked up and leaned toward the television set.

"Mary Magdalene's story teaches us a fundamental truth: a disciple of Christ is someone who, in the experience that is human weakness, has the humility to ask him for help, is healed by him, and follows him closely, thereby becoming a witness to the power of his merciful love, which is stronger than sin and death."

The pope ended with a reminder about the situation in the Middle East. Then he began to recite the Angelus.

"You can turn it off." Hagi was lost in thought. Then he came out of it and glanced at the clock on the wall. It was twelve forty.

"I'd like the answer to my question, Balistreri."

"The cardinal lied because he presumed he could distinguish between good and evil, and now he's humiliating himself like Mary Magdalene before God and asking for your help. He lied out of fear that we would accuse two young men, who he maintained were innocent, of a terrible crime. One was Manfredi."

Hagi was wracked by coughs. Balistreri could see the veins pulsating under his transparent temples and the bones sticking out over the ever-deeper hollows in his cheeks.

He's dying. And Fiorella Romani with him.

"And what will you do now, Balistreri?"

"I swear to you that Elisa Sordi's killer will be punished, whoever he is. But I beg you to save Fiorella Romani. She doesn't deserve this. She's not guilty of anything."

"Do you think my wife was guilty of something?"

Balistreri shook his head.

"No, Alina was guilty of nothing. But it was her fear of you and bad luck that killed her, not a murderer who tortures, strangles, and carves flesh."

Hagi said, "Wrong! It was your wretched Catholic religion that killed her! It was Anna Rossi, Valerio Bona, Cardinal Alessandrini, and that young priest with the red hair—"

"Father Paul."

Hagi was coughing and spitting blood. "Yes, Father Paul, who had lunch with Elisa that Sunday, the last day of her life. Alina told me. She saw them together near the parish. And she saw Valerio Bona there, too, spying on them."

That was why Valerio had called Alessandrini in the Vatican before he hanged himself—to remind him of the truth.

"Alina was terrified of you, Mr. Hagi, because of something you're holding back from us. And your wife wasn't one to scare easily."

"Well then, I'll spell it out clearly, Balistreri. Ulla had overheard a conversation of the count's. She told Anna Rossi, Samantha's mother, about it. And she passed it on to Alina that I'd thrown Elisa in the river. And my wife, poor innocent young girl that she was, was terrified by the damnation of hell into which your God threatens to send even those who remain silent in order to protect her own husband."

Balistreri was incredulous. "All these deaths twenty-four years later to punish someone who turned Alina against you? You could have thought about it before, couldn't you?"

"Believe me, I thought about it many times, but I didn't know who had killed Elisa Sordi. I threw her in the river, but when I carried her out of that office she was already dead."

"Do you know who did it now?"

"No, Balistreri. I still don't know. That's your fault." He pointed to his blood-spotted handkerchief. "But I can't wait any longer. You've got to find out who did it."

"What do you think you'll achieve by acting like this? The name of a killer? Or the massacre of Romanians in Italy? You're turning this country into a hellish pack of racists!"

Hagi looked at him mockingly. "Like that Coppola I shot between the shoulders that night—"

Enraged, Balistreri lost control and launched himself on him. He felt the blood pounding in his ears and bursting his eardrums and temples as he squeezed Hagi's neck. The prison officers rushed to stop him. Fortunately, one of them was built like an ox and pulled Balistreri off Hagi as if he were a leaf.

Hagi was spitting blood on the floor and coughing as he held his throat. But his mocking gaze never wavered while the prison officers were restraining Balistreri.

"Call a doctor," Corvu said.

"It's not serious," Hagi said, massaging his own neck. Then he turned to Balistreri. "You see how little it takes to kill? But you already know that, don't you?"

"That's enough for now," Corvu said. "You can take this animal back to his cell."

Hagi said, "But we're just getting to Fiorella Romani."

"Let me go. I've calmed down," Balistreri said to the officers, who loosened their grip on him but stood between the two men.

"You're not going anywhere, Hagi," Corvu said.

"Then say good-bye to Fiorella Romani and you add another death on your conscience, Balistreri. And what's it going to change anyway? One more, one less . . ."

He wants your rage. He wants to turn you into an animal like him.

The thought calmed him down. "I don't believe you, Hagi. You don't even know if she's alive."

Hagi glanced at the clock on the wall. It was a minute to one.

"Switch on your cell phone, Balistreri. Right now."

There's still one thing he wants to do, and that is to destroy you. It's his price for saving Fiorella.

As soon as the phone was on, it rang. "Hello?" Balistreri said.

He heard a terrified whisper. "This is Fiorella Romani. I'm begging you, come get me and bring Titti to me."

The call ended abruptly.

Balistreri called Fiorella's mother. "Does the name Titti mean anything to you?"

Franca Giansanti was surprised. "Titti? That's Fiorella's favorite stuffed animal. It was a present from her grandmother Gina. What's going on?"

"Just trust me, Franca. I'll let you know before this evening."

In order for Hagi to be allowed out of prison, even under escort and in handcuffs, the chief of police had to call the minister of the interior and the minister of justice.

"This is crazy, Balistreri. But it will all be worth it if we save her," Floris said.

"You're a decent man, sir."

"Thank you, Balistreri. So are you. Be careful."

Balistreri instinctively felt for the Beretta in his holster.

He came back into the room. "Where do we have to go, Mr. Hagi?"

"It's a beautiful sunny afternoon, or so they tell me. Let's go to the beach. I'll ride with you."

"We should go in a police van," Corvu said.

But Hagi didn't want to do that.

"No, let's go in a regular car. I want to enjoy the view. It's going to be the last trip I ever take. And besides, if I can't see the view I can't show you the path to her salvation."

Afternoon

They formed a line of five vehicles, the first and last two each containing four armed policemen. In the middle was the car with the four of them: Corvu at the wheel, Piccolo next to him, Balistreri in the back, and Hagi in handcuffs. They left at two thirty in the scorching-hot afternoon. The car's thermometer said the outside temperature was well over one hundred degrees.

"Take the Via Pontina toward the coast," Hagi ordered.

As they left the center of Rome, Hagi was silent, looking keenly at the pavements crowded with tourists, the Tiber, and the open-air restaurants. There was little traffic. In that heat everyone was at the beach or up in the hills. It took them only twenty minutes to get onto the Via Pontina, an minor highway leading south of Rome to the coast.

"Where are we going?" Corvu asked.

"Keep going straight. There's still time." Hagi seemed completely absorbed in the view.

Balistreri gathered this was not going to be a short trip.

"Take the handcuffs off and give me a cigarette, Balistreri," Hagi ordered.

"Not the handcuffs," Corvu said.

"Then you can turn the car around and go back. These are the last cigarettes I'll ever smoke and I want to smoke them with my hands free."

"Unlock his right hand and cuff the left to the seat," Balistreri told Piccolo. She leaned over and complied.

Then he gave Hagi a lit cigarette.

"Don't you have the Bella Blu lighter anymore?" Hagi asked him, inhaling.

So you want to talk? All right, let's talk.

"Who's waiting for us at the beach?" Balistreri asked.

Hagi gave a little laugh. "Don't be impatient; you'll see when we get there. But if you have other questions, I might answer some of them. I'm in a good mood today."

Balistreri caught Corvu's warning glance in the mirror, but he had no wish to be cautious. By now he thought he knew who had killed Elisa Sordi, but that wouldn't save Fiorella Romani. It was a mosaic that was still missing several tiles, one in particular.

"Let's start with Samantha Rossi. Why her?"

"I've already told you. It was Anna Rossi who told to Alina that I'd removed Elisa's body and then persuaded her to run away. It was as if she had killed her. I could have avenged myself on Anna right away, but I'd already learned the hard way that a greater pain is the death of someone you love. And so I chose her daughter. And please, I must insist, tell the lady that if she'd minded her own business, her daughter would still be alive today."

Balistreri heard a deep intake of breath from Giulia Piccolo and placed a warning hand on her shoulder. Hagi wanted to provoke them, but they had to remain calm and focused on one goal: saving Fiorella Romani.

"And why Nadia?"

"Oh, Christ, why all these questions I've already answered? Because she looked like Alina and Alina hurt me."

Balistreri wasn't convinced, not for a moment. "I just don't buy that answer, especially after Camarà saw you with Nadia in Bella Blu's private lounge."

Hagi shook his head. "It wasn't me. I could meet up with Nadia any time I wanted. Someone else wanted to meet her there."

Piccolo turned around. "Colajacono," she said.

Hagi had a fit of coughing mixed with laughter. "You are such a fool to be fixated on that man. Colajacono was invited that evening so that he'd be more deeply involved in what was about to happen. That idiot thought it was about blackmailing a politician and that Nadia was being used for that."

"But you called Vasile. You went to get the Giulia GT at the top of the hill with Adrian's bike. You left the bike there, picked up Nadia, took her to Vasile, and left on the bike." Piccolo came to a halt, confused.

Hagi laughed. "You're missing something, aren't you? Who killed Nadia?"

Corvu said. "You went up on the bike, took the car, and left the bike on the hill. Then you went to pick up Nadia in the car around six thirty. You slowed down when you saw Natalya, because you thought it was her. Then you were lucky enough to find Nadia by herself."

"I've never been lucky in my life. I've just had an excellent assistant," Hagi said placidly.

Balistreri had already reconstructed that part.

"It was the man who couldn't get it up with Ramona. That gave you time to make off with Nadia. You rode with him on the bike to collect the Giulia GT that would be used to pick up Nadia on Via di Torricola. Then you both came down from the hill separately, one on Adrian's bike and the other in the Giulia. At six o'clock you picked up Nadia while he kept Ramona busy. Then you handed Nadia and the car over to your assistant. He took her up the hill, while you went home, hid the bike, and then went to Casilino 900 to distribute presents to the children."

Corvu and Piccolo stared at him in the rearview mirror. Hagi clapped his hands. "Bravo, Balistreri. You're beginning to catch on after all these years."

Balistreri ignored the provocation and continued.

"Your assistant waited two hours while Vasile had sex with Nadia and then fell asleep because he'd had so much to drink. Then your assistant strangled her and carved the letter E on her. Alessandrini was right about you, Hagi—you're not the kind of man to rape, strangle, and carve letters into women."

Hagi nodded. "I prefer to torture the living. That's my specialty, Balistreri."

Balistreri made no comment and went back to his reconstruction of the events. "From Casilino 900, the others went to St. Peter's Square, but you went to pick up your assistant on the bike. You left the car up there and came back down together on the bike."

Hagi seemed genuinely pleased with Balistreri's progress, as if someone was finally going to admire his grand plan.

"That's right, Balistreri. He carved the letters into all of them, including Elisa Sordi. It was ugly. I wouldn't be able to do it, but that's how my assistant is. He enjoys that kind of thing."

"A collaboration that started twenty-four years ago," Balistreri said. "The count assumed Manfredi hadn't killed Elisa and wanted someone to go and talk to her, calm her down, maybe make a deal with her. The first thing he did was call Francesco Ajello."

Hagi made a slight bow. "Bravo, Balistreri. I see your brain is working today. Francesco was supposed to make a deal with her in exchange for her silence. But when he went into the office, he discovered she was already dead. He called me to help him out. We cleaned up the office, and then we put her body in the trunk of my car and took it away. Ajello went to watch the game with some friends, and I dumped the body in the river. That wasn't very pleasant, especially since I had to cut her and burn her with cigarettes to make it look as if she'd been tortured. I'm tired now, Balistreri. Give me another cigarette and leave me alone."

They didn't speak for a while. Hagi smoked in silence as the road signs went by one after another. Pratica di Mare. Pomezia. Anzio. Nettuno. It was nearly four thirty in the afternoon and Via Pontina was absolutely deserted under the blazing sun.

Balistreri was unsettled. Something wasn't quite right. That insistence on Nadia was ridiculous. Without her and the broken headlight on the Giulia GT, no suspicions would ever have been aroused.

"I want to talk about the letters of the alphabet," Corvu said all of a sudden.

"A childhood passion of my assistant, perfected over time," Hagi replied, as if they were talking about art or sports.

"I'd like to know if we have to use the initial of the first name for Ulla and Giovanna Sordi, as with your wife Alina."

Hagi was amused by the question.

"You're determined to solve the puzzle, aren't you, Corvu? I, on the other hand, find it childish, not to mention risky. But he's determined to finish it. U for Ulla is correct. But after her daughter's death, Elisa Sordi's mother wore an engraved charm on a bracelet."

"A golden heart with the letter E," Corvu recalled, thanks to his photographic memory.

"But there's already an E immediately before that, the one carved on Nadia," Balistreri protested.

"You're very quick today, Balistreri. It's true, there are two consecutive Es. My assistant is very particular, a little like Corvu here. He insisted that there be two. It might interest you to know that killing Giovanna Sordi was simple."

"Killing Giovanna Sordi?" Piccolo echoed.

Hagi coughed and spat blood into his handkerchief.

"A stroke of genius that your idiotic World Cup final made quite easy. My assistant met her that morning at Mass and told her that he was going to reveal the truth about her daughter's death, but in exchange she would have to join her daughter that same evening."

"I don't buy it," Corvu said. "Elisa's mother was ruined by grief, but she wasn't gullible enough to do that."

"You're wrong. He told her he knew the killer's name and offered it in exchange for her jumping off the balcony. She swore on the Virgin Mary that she'd do it. And besides, what better occasion than another World Cup final? If Italy hadn't won that shootout, she might not have jumped. But my assistant would just have killed her off anyway." Hagi was coughing and laughing.

Piccolo turned around, furious, and Balistreri shot her a warning glance.

"And how did your assistant convince her he knew who the killer was?" Corvu asked.

"He revealed a detail that only someone who had witnessed the attack on Elisa would have known. That was no problem for him."

Corvu said, "So, the sequence is OUAREEVI plus the last letter."

Hagi was clearly amused. "I see Corvu can't resist, so I'll give him a little help. The sequence is correct, but the first letter is missing."

The car skidded, and Corvu straightened it out, swearing in Sardinian. Piccolo turned and pointed her gun at Hagi's forehead. Balistreri put his hand between the gun and Hagi.

"Piccolo, put the gun away and put the cuffs back on him."

Balistreri tried to remain icily calm, but the restlessness he felt a little earlier was slowly becoming agitation. Something was not right. It was as if the shocks of a distant earthquake epicenter were approaching.

The truth is never a straight line. The truth is a circle. The first letter, before Elisa Sordi.

．．．．

The call came on Angelo Dioguardi's cell phone while he was out on Linda Nardi's terrace. It was nearly five thirty in the afternoon.

He went back into the apartment. She was sitting on the sofa bundled up in a heavy sweater, even though it was warm outside.

"That was Father Paul. He needs to talk to me about something important. I'm supposed to meet him at San Valente in an hour."

She nodded sadly. Perhaps the decisive moment had arrived. She smiled at him and caressed his hand tenderly. "Thanks, Angelo."

. . . .

The road signs announced that the Sabaudia exit was less than a mile away.

"We've nearly reached our destination, Corvu. Take the exit for Sabaudia," Hagi said. On her cell phone, Piccolo notified the officers in the cars in front and behind.

The five cars turned and took the long tree-lined avenue into Sabaudia's white central square with its bell tower and blocky Fascist-era buildings.

They drove toward the beach. The seafront was full of cars, parked among the sand dunes, and beautiful villas overlooking the sea. They proceeded under the still blinding sunshine opposite the sea crowded with swimmers, surrounded by families dressed in swimwear and carrying ice cream and rubber rafts. Hagi had chosen the most absurd setting: here death could slowly fill the space that life occupied in the way that a colorless and odorless—but lethal—gas could invade a beautiful living room full of people.

"The gate to the next villa is open. Park in front of it," Hagi said. He looked at Balistreri's watch. "Good, it's almost five thirty, so we're slightly ahead of schedule. Now I can tell you exactly what to do so as not to make this a wasted trip."

"And what do we have to do?" asked Balistreri patiently.

"My assistant is in the villa with the girl. Since five o'clock he's been holding a pistol pointed at her temple, so if you attempt to enter, Fiorella Romani will die. You'll have to let me go in alone and convince him you're going to find out who killed Elisa Sordi."

"No fucking way," Corvu blurted.

"As you wish," Hagi said calmly.

"Did your assistant know you'd be here at this time?" Balistreri asked.

"Of course. He knew he had to call your cell phone at one and he did so. If I don't arrive by five thirty, he'll kill her. As you can see, we leave nothing to chance," Hagi said looking pleased with himself.

He's enjoying himself; it's his big show. But he's got a surprise finale in store for us.

A five-year-old girl knocked on the car window, smiling and shaking an ice cream cone. Hagi waved at her. A man with few days to live, in handcuffs. And yet he was as happy and peaceful as a little kid on a field trip. Trouble was brewing. Balistreri had left Rome believing he had the situation under control: he knew who had killed Elisa Sordi, he knew who was waiting for them in Sabaudia. But now he wasn't so sure.

"Give me your word that Fiorella's still alive and will come out of there," Balistreri said.

"I'll need time to explain all the lies that were told in 1982 to my assistant and convince him that you're getting to the truth. But I swear on my wife's memory that Fiorella Romani will be returned alive to her family."

"I can't take off your handcuffs," Balistreri said, "and I'll stay outside and call out to you every so often. If you don't answer, we'll come in."

Hagi smiled. "Okay, but don't be concerned about my safety, Balistreri. My assistant would never harm me. And now I must go or it'll be too late."

They let him out. The thin little man in handcuffs was unsteady on his feet. He coughed and spat some blood onto the pavement under the brutal sun. Hagi paused a moment to contemplate the sea and the cheery scene around him. Looking at him in that moment, Balistreri felt certain that he, too, was suspended with Hagi in the no man's land between life and death.

Then Hagi went in.

. . . .

Hagi had been inside for a half-hour. Balistreri, Corvu, and Piccolo waited nervously under a tree in the yard, a few yards away from sunbathers on the beach. The police had the villa completely surrounded. Chief of Police Floris was in direct communication by cell phone. Every so often Balistreri called in to Hagi, who replied, "Everything's fine. We're still talking."

At five minutes past six, Hagi calmly came to the door. He addressed Balistreri.

"My assistant wants you to swear to him in person that you'll be able to catch Elisa's killer."

Corvu said, "Captain Balistreri's not coming in, and you're coming out of there right now."

Hagi looked at Balistreri. "I swore on the memory of my late wife that Fiorella Romani is inside here, alive. If you'll come in, I swear to you that Fiorella will go back to Rome, alive. Otherwise . . ."

Balistreri knew that only by going into that house would the girl be saved. He looked at the beach, bubbling over with life, then at the dark door of the villa. He was ready to pay his debt. Absurdly, Angelo Dioguardi's face on television and his senseless bluff came into his mind.

He was risking everything.

He turned to Corvu and Piccolo. "All right. If I don't come out with Fiorella Romani after twenty minutes, break the doors down and come in."

He saw Piccolo angrily wipe away a tear of frustration and heard Corvu swear in Sardinian. There were further discussions and objections, but Balistreri calmed down his deputy officers, then followed Hagi into the villa. It was six fifteen.

. . . .

At six twenty Angelo and Linda embraced on the landing.

"Are you sure?" she asked one more time. This was the point of no return.

"Yes," he said, stepping into the elevator. He was gathering the chips and sweeping them toward himself as the decisive hand of the game was dealt.

. . . .

The house was cool and shady with the shutters closed and the lights out. They went into the living room. Fiorella was blindfolded, gagged, handcuffed, and tied to a chair, but she was alive.

"I'm from the police, Fiorella. I'm going to get you out of here and take you home in a few minutes." She jerked mutely on the chair. Balistreri stroked her hair reassuringly.

Hagi was sitting in an armchair. The gun in his handcuffed hands was pointing directly at Balistreri.

"Sit down, Balistreri. We still have some things to say to each other before we say good-bye forever."

Balistreri sat down opposite Hagi. He was ready to look evil in the face.

Today your life has to end in order to save an innocent girl.

"I expect you to keep your promise, Mr. Hagi," Balistreri said, indicating Fiorella.

"I always keep my promises, Balistreri. But I always avenge the wrongs I've suffered. This is our last meeting."

He seemed like Lucifer in person. Dark shadows under his eyes, the thick eyebrows, his eyes a feverish red.

"Light me one last cigarette, Balistreri, and put it on that table without coming any closer."

Holding the gun in one hand, Hagi took the lit cigarette in the other cuffed hand and stuck it in his mouth. The sunlight filtered in from outside, along with the muffled sounds of the beachgoers. The barrier between life and death was a flimsy wooden shutter discolored by the sun and the salt air.

Hagi inhaled the smoke greedily, at ease in the armchair. He was enjoying every moment of his victory. He seemed to be in no hurry at all.

"Why have you done all this, Hagi? Plotting with a maniac killer for an accomplice and also with the secret intelligence service, then all those deaths among your Romanian friends, too."

"They were my troops, Balistreri, and they died in a war against your civilized people who are nothing more than deceiving bigots, whorish wives, and corrupt police, like those who plotted with Elisa Sordi and urged Alina to turn against me. But they will all pay for their guilt."

"I can understand the vendetta against Valerio Bona, Anna Rossi, and the cardinal. And I can understand the one against me, because I let Elisa's real killer go free. But what have the secret intelligence service, the Roma, ENT, and Dubai got to do with it?"

Hagi greedily took a few last drags on the cigarette.

"One year ago I was diagnosed with lung cancer. Incurable. I had to move quickly, and a war requires soldiers and allies, Balistreri."

"But you unleashed the hatred of the Italian people on the Roma, you and the part of the secret intelligence service that lets itself be used that way."

"The secret intelligence service used me and I used them, Balistreri. I wanted revenge, and they wanted to subvert once and for all the political bargain that's kept this rotten country going for the past sixty years. They counted on doing it by setting off a wave of general and uncontrollable violence against the Roma people. We gave each other a helping hand with great pleasure."

"That will never happen, however. The Italians have many defects; perhaps they are racist, hypocritical conformists and corrupt, but they're opposed to violence. There will never be an uprising against the Roma, much less against Romanians."

"You're mistaken, Balistreri. Mistaken once again. The next death will be a truly dreadful one. The victim will be a young Italian woman, and she'll be butchered to death. The Italians will certainly rise up." He gave a diabolical smile and a sneer. "And you, Balistreri, will be on the front line leading the slaughter."

You only deliver suffering to those who survive, not to the dead. Eternal suffering.

"You coughed on purpose while they were raping Samantha and while you were speaking to Vasile on the phone. You smashed the headlight on the Giulia GT on purpose to help the investigation along. And finally, you chose Nadia just because she was connected to you, to lead the police to you, so you'd be captured and brought here."

Hagi's ice-cold eyes stared at him in irony. The glow of his last drag on the cigarette lit up his face in the darkness. "Are you afraid at last, Balistreri?"

Hagi was only one half of the evil. The other half was the Invisible Man who had killed the girls and who had spared his life that night on the hill.

Balistreri felt the cold knife blade of fear pressing against him. He hadn't feared death since that moment thirty-six years earlier when he had stopped liking himself. But this fear was worse than fear of death he felt the fear of dying while still alive. A punishment demanded by the devil, not by God.

. . . .

The Invisible Man was feeling euphoric and a little depressed at the same time. In a little while his debt would be settled. By that evening all his enemies would be dead and his grand plan implemented. He thought about Balistreri at that moment miles away and allowed himself to smile.

Nothing compared with what he will suffer later. And later I will no longer have a mission to accomplish.

He had left Sabaudia at a quarter to three, when his informant confirmed the departure of five police cars from Regina Coeli, one carrying Marius Hagi. Before leaving he had had time to eat sea bass baked in salt with an excellent glass of white wine in a restaurant near the villa that looked out onto the sea.

He had arrived in Rome at five o'clock, in time for his first task, which he handled with great facility. Another debt paid, another enemy eliminated.

At a quarter past six he parked below the apartment. At twenty-five past he saw the man leaving in his car. The trick had worked. For an hour she would be alone while Hagi kept Balistreri busy in the Sabaudia villa. More than enough time to really enjoy himself and leave the traces of evidence collected by Hagi in Casilino 900 to implicate the Roma.

He decided to wait ten minutes, to make sure the other man didn't come back. It was now six thirty. Another five minutes.

. . . .

At six thirty Balistreri suddenly got up from his chair. Hagi did nothing to stop him, only followed him with the pistol in his hand. He had understood what was going on: Hagi wanted to keep him there as long as possible, but was not authorized to kill him. This was Hagi's pact with the Invisible Man.

He quickly crossed the hall and opened the door to the cellar. Immediately he smelled the sickening odor of death. He didn't even think of taking out his Beretta. While he went down the wooden steps he felt every step taking him closer to both evil and the truth.

He came down into a dark humid place, Hagi behind him with the pistol in his hand. Light was filtering in from a door at the end of the room. The smell of death was coming from it. He opened the door wide.

Francesco Ajello was stretched out on his back, naked, his wrists and ankles bound to the four corners of a bed, his castrated testicles and penis stuck in his mouth. His guts had been torn out from a huge gash in his abdomen and were spread over the sheet and the tiled floor.

Balistreri staggered and retched. Hagi gave him a push and made him fall into the vomit, guts, and blood. Then he pointed the gun at him. "Stay right where you are."

In a flash of understanding, Balistreri remembered that Hagi was only trying to stall for time and wouldn't shoot him.

In desperation, he forced himself to get to his feet. Hagi stepped back three paces and put the pistol in his handcuffed hands up to his temple. He stared at him one last time, his demonic eyes burning with a lifetime of hate.

"The first letter is a Y, and you're as good as dead, Balistreri."

Then Hagi pulled the trigger. It was six thirty five.

. . . .

At six thirty five the Invisible Man again meticulously checked the pistol he had used a little while ago, the scalpel used for the incisions still dark with Ajello's blood, and the skeleton keys he used to open the doors. He had forty-five minutes in which to simulate a break-in and a robbery. In a plastic bag he had hairs and fingernail fragments from two Roma in Casilino 900 that Hagi had given him.

He put on surgical gloves and a cap. They were probably unnecessary; no one would be looking for his DNA. Then he set off on his last mission. The front door opened for him easily. He went up on foot. Every step on those stairs took him away from his age-old unbearable pain and brought him closer back to life.

If things had gone differently that first time with her, maybe I wouldn't have killed the others. I often wondered about that in the beginning. After all these years I don't even know how many I've killed anymore, and I ask myself a different question: Would I be a better person if I had killed only her in that single moment of madness?

. . . .

While Corvu and the policemen searched the house and Piccolo tended to Fiorella Romani, Balistreri filled in the chief of police and asked him to send a helicopter for them. A few minutes later, at six forty five, he, Corvu, Piccolo, and Fiorella Romani were in the air.

Clouds were gathering in the sky and promised to deliver one of the intense storms he loved. But this summer rain also brought to mind that gray dawn when Ulla dei Banchi di Aglieno had jumped from her penthouse.

Unsettled, Balistreri put on his headset and looked out the window. Down below beachgoers were running for cover as the first drops of rain hit the beach.

The first letter is a Y. And the last one isn't for Fiorella Romani. YOUAREEVI_.

Suddenly, he remembered where he'd seen it before: YOU ARE EVIL.

It was where he'd felt he should look right from the beginning. Right back in 1982.

"Linda," he said aloud.

A living death. Eternal punishment.

. . . .

At six forty, the Invisible Man entered the apartment with no trouble and without making any noise. It was calm and quiet.

The setting sun was shining in from the French windows leading onto the terrace. She was sitting out there, her back to the living room, looking over to St. Peter's.

"Hello, Linda," the Invisible Man said. He had waited twenty-four years to say those two words again to his first victim, Y.

She turned slowly, her face calm. "Hello, Manfredi."

She had seen photos of him with his new face, handsome, smiling and official in his white coat, as he was opening the hospital wing in Nairobi on Christmas morning, only a few hours after he'd killed Nadia in Rome.

When they'd met at the Charlemagne School, they had much in common: both were young, intelligent, sensitive, and lonely. He suffered due to his deformity and his impossible father, while she had never known her own father. He was a tortured adolescent looking for love to make life was worth living.

Over the years, Linda had often reflected on this.

If, on that first occasion with him, things had gone differently, if I'd only considered how intelligent and sensitive he was and hadn't rejected him because of his deformity, perhaps Manfredi wouldn't have killed all the others.

But in the last twelve months she'd understood that, by now, whatever the change in Manfredi's face, nothing could change what that lonely adolescent had become: a benefactor of Africa's poorest and a killer of innocent women. The boy beast who wanted to become the handsome prince was now a handsome prince with a caged beast inside him that could never stop killing. A deliverer of pain and death to punish the world that had rejected him.

Manfredi came toward her. "I gave you notice I'd come."

"Yes, I got your card last year. Then the murders started. I knew you'd get here sooner or later. But I was surprised you'd be so careless."

This was true, he thought. That card had been a weakness, and careless of him. But the desire to terrorize her had been too strong in him. And then, after all, he was invincible.

"Good, Linda. Luckily we have some time for what I have in mind. Do you like my face a little better now?"

"I've already seen many photos of you, Manfredi, taken in Africa."

"Really? And who gave them to you?"

"Angelo Dioguardi. He went in search of you for me in Kenya ten days ago. And he discovered about all those young Kenyans killed and disfigured over these past twenty-four years."

Manfredi laughed. "That was my training for you, Linda. It wasn't so much fun with the natives, but I made up for it with Samantha, Nadia, Selina, and Ornella."

"If you kill me, Angelo Dioguardi will report you."

Manfredi looked at the gun in his hand and felt the scalpel in his pocket. This was going to be fun.

"Today I'm settling scores with my old enemies and untrustworthy accomplices. I disemboweled one before lunch, and then I paid a visit to Father Paul, Elisa's confidante. Before killing him, I forced him to call Angelo and ask him to come over. I wasn't planning to hurt Angelo, because he was the only one who didn't turn on me in 1982, but if I have to I will. Right now, though, I'm going to concentrate on you. I'll take care of him later."

Linda's cell phone rang. She looked at the screen and then at Manfredi. "It's Michele Balistreri."

Any one of them could have found himself in my place that first time. And it is to these men who have lived without remorse or honor that I intend to dedicate myself. And to one in particular.

It's too soon. There must have been some hitch with Hagi, Manfredi thought, mildly unsettled. Then he decided instead that it was a magnificent occasion. Indeed, an irresistible one.

He knew he was committing a small error, another act of arrogance like the card he'd sent a year ago to Linda. Two flaws in a genius plan. But they were justifiable risks. The thought of delivering terror to Linda Nardi and Michele Balistreri brought pure joy to his heart.

He took Linda's cell phone and hit the answer button.

"Hello? Linda!" Balistreri's voice was desperate as he shouted over the deafening roar of what sounded like helicopter blades.

"No," Manfredi said calmly.

"Is that you, Angelo?" Balistreri asked.

"No, Balistreri. We met that night on the hill. My name is death."

Manfredi hung up and pointed his gun at Linda. He was a little displeased because now he would have to hurry. He had been hoping to spend more time with her. But that conversation had made it all worth it. Balistreri would spend the rest of his life cursing himself.

"I'm sorry, Linda, unfortunately I have to hurry. In a little while Balistreri will be here to shed tears over your corpse."

She hesitated. She still felt a few pangs of sympathy for him, for all the suffering that being what he was had brought him. It was her rejection of him that had pushed him into violence and to his first criminal act. A very sweet adolescent who had really loved Linda. She had rejected him only because of his deformed face, and he had wiped her out and set off on his journey of death.

It's not a vendetta for what you did to me. It's for all those murdered girls. For all the ones you'd murder still. Because you are the deliverer of evil, Manfredi.

Linda closed her eyes. "Kill him," she said softly.

Manfredi felt the voice at his back before even hearing it.

"I'm here, Manfredi."

He recognized the voice and smiled. He certainly wasn't afraid of that big kid with no guts, he who had never been afraid of anyone. He turned round slowly, in no hurry, preparing to shoot.

But Angelo Dioguardi had been ready for this moment for a long time. His Beretta Combat Combo, 40 caliber, exploded five times in rapid succession.

· · · ·

Balistreri landed on the ministry roof at seven. While Piccolo took Fiorella Romani to their office, he and Corvu rushed over to Linda Nardi's apartment, sirens wailing. They arrived in less than ten minutes. "Wait for me downstairs, Corvu. Don't let anyone up."

Corvu protested, but Balistreri was already running up the stairs, gun in hand, his heart pounding.

Linda's dead. And so is my life.

The apartment door was ajar. He rushed in and came to a sudden stop. Linda was on the sofa. Angelo Dioguardi was sitting stiffly next to her, his eyes swollen with tears, his hands trembling, the Beretta Combat Combo at his feet. Manfredi's body was stretched face down on the tile floor in a pool of blood.

Tears stung Balistreri's eyes. His legs gave way from the release of tension and what felt like a lifetime of fatigue. He slowly sank onto his knees before them.

He wanted to hug them both but couldn't manage to lift his arms. He wanted to take part in their desperation and their joy but couldn't manage to open his mouth.

Now he knew. What had happened today was clear, but he also saw what pain had buried over time. He looked at his own hands, then at Angelo, then at Manfredi's corpse.

Any one of us could have found himself in his place that first time. We're all capable of killing. Me, Hagi, Manfredi, even Angelo.

Then Angelo, who was staring into space, spoke. "Michele, there's never been anything between Linda and me."

The words were pathetic, misplaced, pointless, and yet indispensable. That was Angelo Dioguardi. The likable big kid, good humored, a bit crazy and simple minded, who had become a poker player of international fame, and a man who would help anyone who needed it, exactly like Manfredi.

He had shared twenty-four years—nights of poker and talks till dawn in the car—with this man. And now Angelo had done for Linda what Balistreri had refused to do.

I only kill when forced to do so. But she wanted him dead, not in prison. And Angelo was the right man for the job.

"I know, Angelo. You were protecting her. But you should have told me. I should have been the one to do it."

"This was the right thing to do. I had to do it."

Balistreri bowed his head and squeezed Angelo's arm. Then he looked at Linda, but she would not return his gaze. She would never look at him again. She was holding Angelo's hand as if he were a small child who needed to be protected.

. . . .

Instead of calling the police, Balistreri told Corvu to come up. Then Linda and Angelo told them everything.

Linda was extremely calm. She held Angelo's hand and told her story without looking at Balistreri. "We were both students at the Charlemagne School. I was in middle school, and he was in high school. Manfredi was an intelligent, sensitive kid. He was so understanding."

Balistreri looked into her eyes, but there was nothing there for him.

"We were both in pain. I had no father, he had a domineering one. And that disfigured face."

Linda was quiet, as if she were searching for the right words.

"One day, at the beginning of spring in 1982, we were taking a walk in a distant corner of the Villa Borghese Park. Manfredi declared his love for me and tried to kiss me. I smiled to play down the rejection, but he felt I was mocking him and he slapped me, then he started lashing out at me."

She paused again, then continued.

"He tried to rape me, but he was impotent. Then he lost it. He started screaming about his face and said that all girls were teases. He took a razor out of his pocket and carved a Y between my breasts."

Her hand flew up to her breastbone. When Balistreri had attacked her, she'd crossed her arms over her chest, he recalled. "Finally he left me there. I went to the emergency room. I told the police I'd been beaten up by a group of drug addicts. Only my mother knew the truth."

"Why didn't you report him?"

"I was a mixed-up kid. I smoked a lot of pot, and I slept around. He was the only boy I ever rejected, and he was the only one who really loved me. But I wouldn't touch him because of his face."

"You had every right, Linda. It was up to you to choose."

Finally, she turned to look at him. "Oh, sure, it was up to me to choose. But I gave him no choice, neither then nor today."

"Didn't you worry that he might do the same thing to other girls?"

"Not at first. That's why I didn't report him. Then, when they reported on the news that he'd been arrested for Elisa Sordi's murder, I wanted to report him, but before I could come forward his mother committed suicide, and they said it'd all been a big mistake."

"And he never contacted you again in person?"

"No. Manfredi went to Africa and I started to live again, and with a lot of help from my mother I tried to forget. For years I thought of Manfredi not as a monster but as a victim. My victim."

By now he knew Linda Nardi. She had accepted the evil that Manfredi had done her with the tolerance of St. Agnes.

"Then he came back," said Balistreri.

Linda nodded. "A year ago, the day after Samantha Rossi's death, I found a card in the letterbox. It said: I'M BACK."

The Invisible Man's one mistake. His desire to terrorize Linda Nardi had been too strong to ignore.

"Why didn't you report the letter to the police?" Balistreri asked.

"At first I wasn't even sure it was from him. You wouldn't tell me whether a letter had been carved on Samantha. I had a private investigator make some inquiries, but Manfredi didn't seem to have been in Italy when Samantha and Nadia died."

"Then I told you that Ramona's client was impotent, and you knew it was him," Balistreri said.

"Yes. And you told me about Alina Hagi's death and I made the connection to Elisa Sordi. After Giovanna Sordi's suicide, I knew he had to be stopped. Forever."

Because your tolerance is equal to your decisiveness. I would have arrested him, and you wanted him dead.

She read his mind once again. "Thanks to his father they would have judged him to be mentally unstable and put him in the psychiatric ward instead of prison. Then he would have escaped to Africa and killed more women."

Balistreri looked at Angelo Dioguardi. "And you persuaded Angelo to help you."

"I couldn't do it on my own. I explained the situation to Angelo. The idea was mine alone; he bears no responsibility."

Angelo made a feeble protest, but she continued.

"He accepted, and we prepared. Angelo was with me always. We expected Manfredi to come forward in some way. Today, when Father Paul's call came, we knew it was him. Angelo went out to show himself to Manfredi, then he came back in via the garage before he came up and hid himself in the kitchen."

Balistreri shut his eyes. It was premeditated murder. Even with all the extenuating circumstances the sentence would be many years for both of them.

But Balistreri set it aside for a moment. Whatever different kind of justice Manfredi deserved, God would see to it, if he existed. And whatever injustice he'd suffered in his life, including that dished out by Balistreri, Linda Nardi, and Angelo Dioguardi, Manfredi had in any case lived twenty-four years too many, killing many people. Angelo Dioguardi and Linda Nardi had done what he should have done if he'd still had the stomach for it.

Balistreri and Corvu told them what they should and should not say to the police. Then they called Floris, and only after Balistreri and the chief of police had had a chance to talk did they call in the police.

No one asked Balistreri and Corvu what they had talked about with Angelo Dioguardi and Linda Nardi for a half-hour before calling the chief. There was no record of that half-hour in any report. Despite the clear conflict caused by Balistreri and Corvu knowing Nardi and Dioguardi personally, Floris and the public prosecutor allowed the two officers to take their statements. No one else questioned them; the public prosecutor simply recorded their replies.

The story Dioguardi told was very simple. He had been a member of a shooting range for years and had even been there that Sunday morning with his lover, Linda Nardi. There were witnesses. Then he'd been to lunch at Linda's and preferred not to leave the bag containing his earphones, gloves, and pistol in the car, which was parked on the street.

At six twenty he'd gone out to buy some cigarettes, but as soon as he drove off in the car he realized he'd left his wallet containing his driving license in the bag in Linda's kitchen. He'd gone back in through the rear entrance in the garage. Linda was out on the terrace, so he'd gone straight into the kitchen to look for the bag.

Then he heard Manfredi's voice, the threats to Linda, his confession about having killed all those women, and the phone call with Balistreri. He'd pulled his Beretta out of the bag and walked onto the terrace. Manfredi had his back to him. Angelo told him to drop his gun and put his hands in the air, but Manfredi turned with his own gun drawn instead. Angelo had no choice but to shoot him, which he did five times.

Evening

At a late evening meeting between the chief of police and the head of the team, no objections were raised about any of the incredible coincidences: that Dioguardi entered through the garage, was in possession of a loaded gun, and that he reacted so quickly to Manfredi. It was almost as if Dioguardi had been mentally prepared to shoot him dead.

There were no grounds for excessive use of self-defense or premeditation.

The reconstruction of Manfredi's movements was equally straight-forward. He'd left Via della Camilluccia on the Saturday evening after his meeting with Balistreri and joined Ajello at his villa in Sabaudia, where the lawyer had been entrusted with guarding Fiorella Romani. On Sunday morning, he'd given Ajello a sleeping pill and tied him up. When he woke up, Manfredi disemboweled him. One less inconve-nient witness, dispatched along with Colajacono and Pasquali.

Then he had eaten lunch in a Sabaudia restaurant—the receipt was in his wallet—and left town. Next, as the telephone company's records showed, he'd called Father Paul on his cell phone.

He arrived at San Valente parish church a little after five. Paul was alone; the children were all at the beach with the volunteers. He'd forced him to call Angelo Dioguardi and ask to see him. Then he'd taken him down to the basement, shot him, and left his body in the locked storeroom where the police would find it later. Finally, he had gone to Linda Nardi's apartment.

Ramona identified Manfredi in the photo sent via e-mail to Bucha-rest. He was the client who had wasted her time because he couldn't get it up. Hagi had handed Nadia over to him in the Giulia GT and had come back to pick him up with Adrian's bike at Vasile's farmhouse after Manfredi killed Nadia. Then they'd left the bike in Hagi's garage and taken the rental car Manfredi had used to pick up Ramona.

Hagi had taken him to Rome's Urbe airport, where they handed back the rental car and where the ENT aircraft was waiting for Man-fredi to take him to Zurich in time for the Nairobi flight. In this way, despite the two-hour difference in the time zone, he'd arrived in time to open the hospital. They still had to clarify why Man-fredi's name didn't appear on any passenger list, but Balistreri had his answer for that.

This was all purely investigative reconstruction; there wasn't even any proof of Manfredi's presence at the crime scenes, not even in the cases of Ajello and Paul. In regard to Giovanna Sordi, it was probable that he'd approached her on the Sunday morning after Mass. Man-fredi was with Elisa when her mother called, therefore he knew the subject of that conversation and so had persuaded her. But this was only more investigative speculation.

The only hard fact was the attack on Linda Nardi. During that long evening meeting on the evening of July 23, the government, the chief of police, the prosecutor's office. and the police all chose to keep the matter quiet. Manfredi's tragic end was minimized and set apart from the rest. An old Charlemagne School friend who was showering his attention on Linda Nardi. An argument with her actual lover, and then his tragic death. Nothing about a serial killer, nothing about scalpels, nothing at all.

The torture and deaths of the young women were all attributed to Hagi, who had been present the entire time—the perfect scapegoat. Hagi had been killed in an exchange of fire with the police during Fiorella Romani's dramatic rescue. Francesco Ajello had been his accomplice, and Hagi had killed him while he was alone in the villa. How he came to do this, given that he was handcuffed and unarmed, was never explained.

Count Manfredi dei Banchi di Aglieno was informed of the tragic accident in which his son lost his life by an apologetic chief of police, while he was in Nairobi and embarking on the night flight to Frankfurt.

Balistreri accepted everything without objection. He was able to make sure that the name of Linda Nardi's lover who accidentally killed Manfredi dei Banchi di Aglieno remained hidden away in the archives of the prosecutor's office. It was a feeble secret, but one that nevertheless would enable him to buy a little time.

SUNDAY NIGHT– MONDAY MORNING, JULY 23–24, 2006

BALISTRERI SHUT HIMSELF IN his office alone for the night. He thought again of Marius Hagi's words: *A lightning war requires soldiers and allies, Balistreri. They used me and I used them. We gave each other a helping hand.*

Somewhere along the line, Marius Hagi had met Manfredi, one of those allies. Had it been a chance meeting? Highly unlikely. Someone had brought them together. Someone who knew them both very well and knew their hatred and their desire for revenge. Hagi wanted revenge against the Catholic circles that had turned Alina against him. Manfredi hated the young women who had humiliated him.

First Linda, then Elisa: he had desecrated them, but he hadn't killed them.

So he and Hagi had chosen their first victim. A young woman, Samantha Rossi: perfect for Manfredi and even more meaningful for Hagi, as she was the daughter of Anna Rossi, who had alienated Alina from him. But that wasn't enough. There were other personal enemies: Linda Nardi, the source of all Manfredi's misery. Michele Balistreri, who had caused Manfredi's mother's suicide and let Elisa's real killer go free. Their destinies had been entwined from then on.

Corvu had been his usual efficient self. He had mobilized the right contacts and had a photocopy of the minister of the interior's appointments register for Sunday, July 11, 1982.

It showed that Count Tommaso dei Banchi di Aglieno had entered the ministry at six fifty and come out at seven thirty five, as Balistreri knew twenty-four years ago—nothing new there.

But it was another signature in that register that Balistreri wanted to check. The signature that countersigned the times—that of a young ministry assistant in 1982, Captain Antonio Pasquali.

He leafed through Pasquali's calendar, the one Antonella had given him containing the dates and a few cryptic notes in English.

The meaning of these notes was opaque, but of course Pasquali had made them for himself. He was marking down what the voice told him to do.

It was a perfect plan, one that only Manfredi's card to Linda had rendered null and void. But for Manfredi, the terrorizing of Linda Nardi and Balistreri's eternal remorse were indispensable, worth much more than the murdered and disfigured girls.

Nonetheless, Balistreri recognized something else in that plan, something grandiose, which had to do with a philosophy of life—an authentic personal signature.

Everything had been expertly planned, brought together, and carried out. Hagi's vendetta against the Catholic world that had taken Alina from him and Manfredi's against women had been ably inserted into a much wider plan to destabilize democracy in Italy. A plan that took advantage of the growing racism toward the Roma and Romanians, and of the Italians' fear of the barbarity coming from Eastern Europe. Young girls raped, tortured, and killed, as always by the Roma in the travelers' camps, up to the point where the people would turn and attack them. And then the police wouldn't have been enough—the army would have been needed. And, along with help from the friendly part of the secret intelligence service, a new strong political leader would emerge, who wasn't involved in the catastrophe and was incorruptible. A man of honor.

Everything had been corralled in the service of this plan.

ENT's nightclubs and arcades were used to launder money of dubious provenance; the purse of the secret inteeligence service's rogue element that financed the whole operation, and unfortunately became caught up in it thanks to the lighter Nadia took from Bella Blu; the accomplices who became superfluous or dangerous—Belhrouz, Colajacono, Pasquali, and Ajello—abused, and their guts torn out. Accusers from the beginning—like Giovanna Sordi, Valerio Bona, Father Paul—forced into suicide or silenced. And the necessary sacrificial victims—Samantha, Nadia, Selina, Ornella—slaughtered without mercy. Accidental obstacles, like Camarà, eliminated immediately.

The most atrocious part of the vendetta had been reserved for the two greatest enemies, Linda Nardi and Michele Balistreri, who had ruined Manfredi's life when he was still a teenager. And also the unscrupulous use of the Romanians, Hagi and the others, and the exploitation of the Roma and the travelers' camps; fodder that was indispensable for extending the plan beyond the limits of personal vendetta and developing it against the whole democratic political class, both government and opposition, and the Vatican, too.

The effects had been seen: crimes rightly or wrongly attributed to the Roma, camps like Casilino 900 roiling the emotions of Italians, hostile graffiti on the walls, the growing number of public statements that confused the Roma and the Romanians, the growing tension with the government in Bucharest, and the Vatican as the sole defender of the rights of people who were under siege.

Pasquali had been working to effect change in Rome's city council. But above him there was someone who was aiming higher, much higher: if a famous Italian journalist had been attacked, tortured, and killed in her own home near St. Peter's and the murder had been attributed to the Roma by means of the false evidence planted by Manfredi, the situation in Italy would have exploded. With the secret intelligence service's help, a witch-hunt would have been set in motion. There would have been calls for ethnic cleansing, a diplomatic crisis with Romania, and increased tension with the European Community that would call upon the Italian government to arrest and put on trial any Italians who attacked Roma and Romanians.

At that point, Italian democracy would have teetered on the edge of the abyss, and somebody wanted to push it. If Italy hadn't obeyed, it would have been kicked out of the European Community. If it had obeyed, Italians would have taken to the streets to topple the government. And the Vatican, marginalized, would have kept quiet.

In either scenario, the head of the special team was certain a solution had been waiting in the wings: a strong man with an impeccable image who would have arrived to put things right.

Balistreri recognized the absolute conviction of someone's rights and the wrongs they suffered, the use of the lives of others as if they were pawns in a game, the defense of one's honor as an absolute right. Balistreri recognized the style; in the end it was his own adolescent point of departure.

There remained one last aspect of Hagi and Manfredi's vendetta: Who really killed Elisa Sordi? In their absurd and twisted logic, this person was the true culprit of all their troubles and couldn't remain unpunished. Hagi and Manfredi had died without knowing the name that Balistreri had just barely glimpsed when he'd attacked Linda Nardi.

Now that everything was clear and he had all the answers, he wondered what the young Balistreri would have done.

A shot in the back of the skull. But then his accomplices would have taken revenge. They would have slaughtered Angelo, Linda, me, Alberto and his family, Corvu, Piccolo, Mastroianni.

He wondered what the adult Balistreri would do.

Charges and an arrest. A well-organized trial, a just sentence. Same outcome as above. Or rather, worse, because with the support the man had it would be difficult to have him found guilty.

He racked his brains the whole night. The count would have thought the same as he did, not like the cardinal. He wouldn't wait for divine justice. But where was the happy medium between the two?

MONDAY, JULY 24, 2006

Morning

AT DAWN, UNDER THE pretense of identifying Manfredi and taking advantage of the fact that the count was still traveling, Balistreri had the count's personal secretary, the domestic staff, and the residential complex's concierge brought into the station. They were taken to the mortuary. Before they entered the room, they were ordered to hand over all metal objects, including keys.

"Keep them busy filling out forms until I get back," Balistreri ordered Piccolo. He took a set of the penthouse keys.

Corvu and Mastroianni accompanied him. They arrived at seven thirty and entered the deserted apartment. They went immediately to Manfredi's room, where Balistreri and Teodori had questioned the boy back in 1982. It was unchanged, apart from the addition of a laptop computer and a new full-length mirror in the attached bathroom. The heavy curtains had been stripped from the windows.

The walls were still covered in heavy metal posters. The one Balistreri remembered was in the dark corner where Manfredi had taken shelter during his stormy exchange with himself and Teodori.

A man dressed as Satan and ten women, each one wearing a T-shirt with a letter painted in dripping blood. The ten letters made up the album title: YOU ARE EVIL.

He opened all the drawers, then rummaged under the sweaters piled in the wardrobe. It was all there: Elisa Sordi's missing earring, the blouse with the initials S.R., Nadia's sweater with holes at the elbows, the glasses worn by nearsighted Selina Belhrouz, Ornella Corona's winking watch.

They photographed it all.

Tucked below some underwear in a drawer, he found a crumpled sheet of paper. On it was a drawing in pencil. He recognized the view—it was from the terrace. The picture showed a window and a withered flower and beneath it were a few sentences in Manfredi's handwriting.

Afternoon

Pasquali's state funeral was held in the afternoon in a church in the historic center. The president of the republic, the prime minister and many other ministers, politicians, civil servants, and policemen were in attendance. Hundreds of ordinary citizens gathered outside in the churchyard and the square beside it. Television vans lined the street.

After the public ceremony, the coffin was taken to Verano. Pasquali's wife held a private mass for his closest colleagues, friends, and relatives from the small town in Abruzzo where Pasquali had been born and raised.

Balistreri was the last to arrive. He sat near the door, enjoying the smell of incense. The church was cool, while outside it was sweltering and humid. Corvu, Piccolo, and the others sat in the pews further down.

I confess to almighty God and to you, my brothers and sisters, that I have greatly sinned.

Balistreri was brought up short by the words. The ceremony went on.

Mea culpa, mea culpa, mea maxima culpa.

The words he'd rebelled against in 1970. The words that had slowly caught up with him like a nemesis, paralyzing the rest of his existence.

Count Tommaso dei Banchi di Aglieno materialized beside him. He was not in a penitent mood but had accepted the meeting Balistreri had asked for.

And here he was, the supreme evil, the single architect of the grand design, whose voice on the telephone terrorized Pasquali. The man who hadn't hesitated to exploit his son's private vendetta to aid his program of destabilization, the man who had littered his path with corpses not for money but for power, out of the total and blind conviction of his own ideas.

The man who for once should have given up, faced with the impossibility of knowing who had finished Elisa Sordi off after his son had beaten and disfigured her and left her unconscious in that room.

. . . .

They went outside into the open, without waiting for the Mass to end, and took a last stroll among the graves in the sunshine.

Balistreri was sweating heavily, while the count was his usual impeccable self. Not a drop of sweat stained his dark suit.

His first-class overnight flight from Africa hadn't tired him; the crow's feet around his eyes were only slightly deeper.

He's a father who just lost his son. His Achilles' heel. My life insurance policy.

"I only have a few minutes, Balistreri. I must pay my respects to the widow of my very dear friend Pasquali and see the minister of the interior, who wants to extend his condolences to me. Then, before I return to Africa, I have to see my legal team about transferring Manfredi's body to Kenya. I don't want him buried in Italy. Kenya was his real home."

Balistreri was ready to say what he had to say, but this man was something more than a mere enemy.

He is the supreme evil, not Hagi or Manfredi.

It was pointless to tell the count what had happened. He knew it all, and the little he didn't know he'd figure out in the next few days.

It was pointless as well to threaten him by talking about his calls to Pasquali recorded in a simple diary. There was no proof; the Count would have squashed him like a bug.

"I want to propose a pact," said Balistreri at last.

Walking in silence and showing little interest, the count listened to the description of the absolutely certain proof of Manfredi's guilt. He didn't appear to be surprised, let alone worried.

"I'll proceed in such a way that no one will know a thing. In everyone's memory, your son will remain a benefactor of the poor. In exchange, I want your word that you will not kill or have anyone killed anymore."

The count fixed him with his gaze. There was no anger, no threat, but only again that same subtle contempt of 1982.

"It's a pity you've turned out this way, Balistreri. I know your résumé. As a young man I shouldn't have disliked you—you had promise, you rebelled against the forces of obscurantism and corruption. A real pity. Quite a wasted life, yours."

"Don't you want your son to be remembered as a benefactor rather than a killer?"

The count stood among the graves.

"Manfredi was a murderer. He became a murderer because of the preconceptions of Western society and its bourgeois hedonism and Catholic hypocrisy. He was a kind, polite young man. Women rejected him because of his face. You accused him of a crime he didn't commit for the same reason. And then he was manipulated by me, his father. I introduced him to Marius Hagi."

"Manfredi didn't know that Hagi and Ajello had thrown Elisa Sordi's body into the Tiber?"

"He didn't know Hagi or Ajello. But my brother told me what Manfredi was doing in Africa—killing, disfiguring. I knew my son had an illness, and it wasn't his fault. Then a year ago, Hagi told me he had lung cancer and that he planned to kill Anna Rossi before he died. Manfredi was in Rome. We spoke on the terrace, the three of us. We were there all night. And we decided it would be better to kill Samantha Rossi. But everything has a beginning, Balistreri, and you were a fundamental part of that beginning."

The count stretched his arm and pointed to th
by side.

In the center was Elisa Sordi's grave, with thos
Giovanna on either side.

"There's only one thing that has always escaped
the name of Elisa's real killer. Can you disinter it? `
our pact."

The count stared at him for a moment, then turne
walked away.

Balistreri looked at the three graves. It was very hot
the flowers on all three were fresh.

MONDAY, JULY 31, 2006

THE ORDER OF THE day was *to let things settle*. Central government, city council, the opposition, the Vatican, the secret intelligence service, and the police all agreed: the dust should be allowed to settle on memory's antique furniture.

For a few days, Italy was in the international news. But the press never knew the full reality. It knew only what the politicians and the Vatican had agreed it should know. A deranged Romanian living in Italy, Marius Hagi, together with his gang and with the help of a nightclub owner, the Italian lawyer Francesco Ajello, had killed four young women and four courageous members of the forces of law and order: Coppola, Tatò, Colajacono, and Pasquali. The deaths of Father Paul and Manfredi had nothing to do with the above crimes. Elisa Sordi received no mention. Count Tommaso dei Banchi di Aglieno left for Kenya with the body of his son, Manfredi, the victim of a crime of passion after a disagreement over a woman.

By the end of July, the newspapers had turned to the more recent infighting in internal politics, the pope's vacation, and soccer team trades.

Chief of Police Andrea Floris ordered Balistreri, Corvu, and Piccolo to take the month of August off, something they hadn't done for years. Corvu and Piccolo set off by car for Albania and Ukraine with Rudi and Natalya as their guides. Balistreri accepted his brother's invitation to spend the month at his house in the Dolomites.

Before leaving Rome, Balistreri tried numerous times to contact Linda Nardi. Both her landline and her cell phone rang and rang, but there was never any answer.

On July 31, his last night in Rome, he had dinner with Antonella. They sat at one of the little wooden tables on one of Trastevere's many crowded sidewalks. Suntanned and relaxed in front of a pizza and a beer, Antonella looked very attractive to him. Her hair was cut in a new style that made her look younger. Her eyes were bright, her skin soft.

"You look terrific tonight."

"After Pasquali's funeral I spent five days at a spa. I haven't relaxed so much in fifteen years."

"Good, you let someone take care of you for a change."

"They really pampered me. Face masks, tanning beds, relaxing massages . . ." and she shot him a wicked smile, ". . . actually not very relaxing; the basic ingredient was missing."

Balistreri was feeling lighter in his soul, which he felt had been lost for years. He made a sudden decision. Fortunately the restaurant toilet was sufficiently large, clean, and private. It was something brief, a little uncomfortable, but very satisfying for both of them.

Afterward, they left the restaurant and walked to Antonella's apartment, where they made love again. They took their time. Then, stretched out on the bed, all the lights out and the windows open to the cool and the silence of the night, she lit a joint and began stroking his hair. He was drinking his third whiskey.

They were lying beside one another, worn out but alive, in a way that each of them hadn't felt—for different reasons—for a long time. Balistreri wasn't aware she was trying to hand him the joint. The glowing end was a small point in the semidarkness, following the movements of her hand.

He was lying on his back, staring at the old beams and panels overhead. Despite the semidarkness he could make out the plan perfectly.

He was rejected by women on account of his face and accused for the same reason. But he was innocent.

He could make out marks on the wood inflicted by time and damp.

A kid who was impotent. A love that was impossible. A recent abortion.

There were cracks in the wood at the points where the woodworm had been most at work.

A faded tulip on Elisa's desk. A fresh tulip on her grave.

Now seeming detached from his body, his eyes wandered toward the ceiling.

I should have fucked you like an ordinary whore. Yes, Michele, you should have. Perhaps then you'd have understood this business, at last.

While he was attacking Linda he had guessed the truth. Then he'd focused all his efforts on Fiorella Romani and he'd set that intuition aside. But after his pact with the count in front of those three graves, it had come back to him. His brain, however, was proving lazy and reluctant. It refused to connect the dots between the perpetrator, the motive, and the opportunity. Marijuana and whiskey were mingling in his body.

The beams on the ceiling were the features of a face, the cracks were its lines, the marks were its eyes and mouth. All of a sudden he saw it, the face that was desperate and upset: perpetrator, motive, opportunity.

EPILOGUE

ARRIVED IN THE DOLOMITES on August 1 and was welcomed by Alberto, his wife, and their two sons. I was put into the quiet and spacious guest room with a view of the mountain peaks.

Thus began my long summer idyll. I slept a great deal. I went on bicycle rides up and down the slopes. I played tennis with my nephews, went shopping with my sister-in-law, and chatted about everything with Alberto and his friends and neighbors.

Even the two house martins with shiny black heads that had made a nest under the portico guttering aroused my interest. One day, while they were off fluttering around, I climbed a ladder and saw the two eggs in the nest. At the end of the first week in August two chicks were born, and the father disappeared. My sister-in-law told me that at sea level baby birds were born in June, but that at a height of 4,500 feet the eggs hatched in August, and from that moment it was up to the mother alone to look after the chicks for about twenty days. Sitting in the sun, I watched the mother coming back with worms in her beak, welcomed by the chicks' insistent twittering. I found myself in an emotional state counting the days leading up to the first flight for the two house martins and, for me, the first autumn rain.

I gave no thought to work, to crimes, deaths, and perpetrators. Inevitably, from time to time, I thought about Linda and Angelo, losing myself in imaginary conversations with them, as if nothing had changed. Then I rapidly fled from those thoughts and retreated into nature and rest.

In the late afternoon I would sit out in the large garden, facing the green mountain slopes, looking down at the dots that were houses in the valley below. Every day I hoped for the rain that never came. I waited for sunset, feeling the days growing shorter and coolness overtaking the heat. Then, when dusk fell and the windows of the houses began to light up, I went into the house with the others.

The last Saturday in August a small house martin took flight from the nest and landed not far from me, where the lawn ended and the rock overhang began. As I was wondering how to help it, the little bird looked up at the nest where the mother and the other baby bird were watching it. Then it took flight, singing happily, toward the valley.

That evening Alberto told me that Angelo had called. He was coming by the next day. He came for lunch in his old beaten-up vehicle with presents for the boys and my sister-in-law. He looked different. He was surer of himself and at the same time more subdued.

We ate together out in the sunshine in the garden, talking of this and that: the vacation that was coming to an end, the school term that was about to start, and poker tournaments. After lunch, Alberto announced that he had to take his wife and the boys to an end-of-summer festival in another village. It was his excuse to leave us alone. Before leaving, Alberto took us both by the arm.

"When Angelo gets back from Australia, let's start our regular poker games with Graziano again." I was touched that my brother was trying so hard. Then they left for the festival.

The silence in the large garden was broken only by a desperate cry. The second house martin fledgling, much smaller than the one that had already flown away, was on the ground right below the nest. Its mother was hopping around it, concerned. The little bird had an injured wing; it must have fallen during its first attempt to fly.

We watched it, not sure what to do. We decided to let the mother take care of it and went to sit on the lawn. We looked out over the green valley and smoked cigarettes and drank whiskey. Years earlier, we would have talked about women, poker, and Paola Rossi. Now we smoked in silence, contemplating the mountains and the valley below. The twittering of the house martins was the only sound.

Two old friends with their memories, many of them good and a few very bad.

I came out with the question more to break the silence than anything else. "Do you know where she is?"

"She phoned me in mid-August; she was about to leave for Africa. She's organized a foundation in Manfredi's memory. She wants to build another new hospital there."

I wasn't surprised. I'd always known that Linda Nardi belonged to a different world.

"She's convinced that if she hadn't rejected Manfredi, he wouldn't have killed those other women," Angelo explained.

"But Manfredi wasn't the one who got Elisa pregnant, and Linda knew that," I said.

Angelo nodded. "Linda knows that Manfredi attacked Elisa, but she also knows that he didn't kill her."

I didn't ask how Linda could be certain. After all, I already knew the answer.

"You risked your lives, Angelo. A moment's hesitation and Manfredi would have shot you both."

He turned to look at me. "There are moments when I have no hesitation, Michele. You should know that by now."

All of a sudden, a dark cloud floated in front of the sun and a cold breeze swept across the lawn. Angelo Dioguardi was relaxed, observing the valley from a distance.

"I went by the cemetery before I left," I said. "There were fresh flowers on the three graves."

Angelo nodded. "Elisa loved tulips. She told me that a Turkish legend claims tulips are made of the drops of blood shed for the love of a young woman."

I had that flower before my eyes in 1982 and 2005, but I didn't want to see it.

"A tulip on Elisa's windowsill. A tulip on Manfredi's chest of drawers. A tulip on Margherita's desk. All of them faded, Angelo, except for the fresh one you placed on her grave."

Angelo Dioguardi gave me an apologetic smile, the same childlike smile he'd flashed that first day at Paola's between feigned bouts of retching in her bathroom. It seemed a lifetime ago, but the man was the same. The same man who always apologized for his highly successful bluffs in poker. Now he was apologizing for the bluff he'd used to risk life itself, winning and losing at the same time.

"Margherita's a little bit like her," Angelo said. "She's full of life, trusting, naive. The evening we met she even told me she loved tulips. For a while, I deluded myself into thinking I could go back to living again. Then Elisa's mother threw herself off the balcony and I was reminded of who I really am."

Who are you, Angelo Dioguardi? You crossed the line only once in your life for a beautiful young woman. And then you found out she was pregnant. Michele Balistreri would have resolved everything with a quick and brutal good-bye. But you tried to make it go away by lying to your girlfriend and her uncle, the cardinal. Then there was the abortion, Elisa's tears and remorse. She was about to confide in Father Paul. And for a moment, one single moment out of an entire lifetime, you gave in to desperation and rage.

It was cooling off. The sky was filling with dark clouds and thunder rumbled. There were flashes of lightning in the distance.

Angelo Dioguardi had reacted by facing up to life, trying to be kind and perform good deeds. But that wasn't enough. When Linda Nardi asked him for help with Manfredi, he told her the truth and agreed to kill Manfredi as a last act of atonement.

Angelo wanted to tell me what I already knew and had never wanted to hear.

"When I went up to Alessandrini, he was furious. He knew that Paul had had lunch with Elisa, and he ordered me to fire her. I was terrified, afraid that Elisa would tell Paul about the abortion, as they were talking to each other a lot in those days. Then Alessandrini and I called you from the terrace, and while you were coming over I told the cardinal I had to go to the bathroom."

"I know, Angelo. I called the cardinal yesterday. He remembered that you'd gone to the bathroom."

Angelo went on with his pointless explanation.

"I didn't go to the bathroom, I went down to see Elisa. I wanted to talk to her, calm her down, comfort her. Thirty seconds later I was on her floor. The office door was locked, which was odd. Now we know Manfredi locked it. I opened the door with my keys. Elisa was on the ground. Her face was swollen, and she was half-naked and bleeding from a cut on her breast. On the table, I saw a letter she was writing to Father Paul, telling him about her affair with me and the abortion. I put it in my pocket, and then I did it."

To Valerio she appeared to be dead. Manfredi swore he'd left her no more than injured. One of the two was lying, or they were both mistaken.

So Corvu had pronounced at the end of his detailed analysis of the alibis. But rather they had both spoken the truth. Manfredi had left her alive, and a few minutes later Valerio had found her dead.

"You were coming up, Michele. I had half a minute, a chance that wouldn't come again."

I should have understood right away, when I saw you on that landing and saw how upset you were that night. I should have understood when I saw that faded flower on Margherita's desk. You did everything you could to tell me, in your own way.

Angelo gave a last apologetic smile.

"There was a cushion she used to sit on. I used that. Thirty seconds later I was upstairs, waiting for you."

You can throw your whole life away in a moment of madness. A cushion pressed against the face of a young woman who was almost dead already. A boat in the middle of the African sea, and a boy wearing a wetsuit.

I knew he had thought about Elisa every day for all those years and that the suffering of her parents had tortured him every night. Unlike me, he had tried to make up for it. But I also knew his hands had held that cushion over her face.

The first drops of rain began to fall. I glanced at the mother that was jumping and twittering around the injured bird. The thunder exploded very near, almost shaking the mountainside, and the twittering suddenly stopped. The little house martin was lifeless by now. The mother looked at me uncertainly.

Any one of you could have found yourself in my place.

Manfredi dei Banchi di Aglieno had written those words—the evil man we had all been pursuing and then caught in a trap and, in the end, crushed. It had started like this, in a moment of madness.

It started to pour. We remained there in silence, while the pale light of day grew faint. The rain bathed our heads, faces, and bodies and soaked into our shoes. Then, one by one, the windows at the bottom of the valley began to twinkle in the dusk.

The mother looked one last time at the little lifeless bird. Then it hovered in the air and soared away alone, not happy, but it was singing.

ACKNOWLEDGMENTS

THANKS TO THE PUBLISHING team at Marsilio, especially to Marco Di Marco and Jacopo De Michelis, not only for the great professionalism they put into their work but also for their exceptional passion. Also to Filiberto Zovico and Chiara De Stefani for guiding me safely along roads not well known to me.

And thanks to my three readers who, during the course of my writing, were patient and full of good advice: my wife Milena and my two great friends Valeria and Fabrizio.